BEAUTIFUL
Savage

CAROLINE
PECKHAM

SUSANNE
VALENTI

Beautiful Savage
Dark Empire #2
Copyright © 2020 Caroline Peckham & Susanne Valenti

Interior Formatting & Design by Wild Elegance Formatting

Beautiful Savage/Caroline Peckham & Susanne Valenti – Special ed.
ISBN-13 - 978-1-914425-51-6

This book is dedicated to all the mountain men living alone in the woods. We know you're hot AF under all that hair, so come and whisk us away to your cabin anytime so we can get tangled up in your man bush.

Speaking of man bushes, if you love delving into dark places with your eyes closed, why not come and join a tribe of people whose souls are just as twisted as yours...

CHAPTER ONE

Light.

I cracked an eye open and dared to believe for one penetrating, all-consuming moment that this was really happening.

I'd lived within these four walls for a thousand days of hell. Maybe two. Brick walls, metal and blood were more familiar to me than my own voice.

I'd stopped speaking after a month in this cell. They beat and battered and burned me, so I stole away the single thing they wanted more than my screams, pushing it down, down, down deep into my belly. Silenced forever. My words, swallowed and locked away. I didn't have an answer to their question, the one they'd asked an impossible amount of times.

What is the code?

What is the code??

What is the code???

I only had one honest answer to give, because I had no idea who I was, let alone whatever code it was they wanted. But they thought it was an act. They thought I was a liar when I gave them the only answer I had: *I don't know. I don't know! I don't know!!*

Even *they* couldn't tear the truth out of me. So I'd stopped speaking altogether. I retreated into my own body like a snail coiling up in its shell. I reinforced my walls, built them high and made them impenetrable until I was so deeply buried that nothing which happened to my flesh could reach my soul. But now it might have been time to emerge at last.

The slit of light ran vertically down my body, making me squint. And hope. *God* was I hoping. I rose to my feet, the too big shirt I wore hanging over the ripped leggings which I'd picked holes into. There was nothing else to do in the silence and the dark. And if I wasn't doing something, then I started thinking. And when I started thinking, I started remembering. And I never wanted to do that. Because the only memories I had were of this room and the hell I'd endured here.

Don't let the demons haunt you in your mind as well as in the flesh.

I walked silent and bold, wondering if this was really happening or if the gift of death had finally come to steal me away from here. But I hoped it wasn't that. I'd dreamed of death, made friends with it, begged for it to take me countless times, but death always whispered in my ear, *deliver me to them first*. That was what I held onto. The image of the five of them bloody at my feet. I may have been small, delicate, but only on the outside. Inside, I was a raging inferno waiting to be unleashed. If only I were bigger, more powerful. If only I had a weapon strong enough to cleave them apart and make them bleed like I had bled, make them scream like I had screamed.

I pressed my palm to the rough wood of the door, every rivet memorised. There were fingernail marks and dents where I'd kicked and thrashed. I'd tried to get out so many times I'd lost count, but eventually I'd given up. And now, in a twist of fate, Jax had left the door open.

Jax: the big one with the greasy hair and lack of brain cells. The one who'd held my wrists while his brother punched me until bones shattered. The one who'd smiled while I'd screamed, the one who cheered on the others, but never had the gall to do anything more than hold me down.

I pushed the door wide and the familiar creak that always preceded the start of pain or marked the end of it sounded in my ears like a klaxon.

I stepped forward and my bare foot hit something soft. A breath fluttered past my lips and my heart thudded in time with it as I spotted Jax on the ground. His tongue lolled out of his mouth, swollen and blue and his eyes were bulging, his lungs labouring. His arm was twisted awkwardly where he'd fallen, his poorly-bandaged hand swollen and turning a nasty shade of purple. He'd turned up with the cut a few days ago and clearly hadn't thought a trip to the hospital was worthwhile. *Lucky for me.*

Sepsis. The word rang in my head from some past memory I couldn't grasp. From a time before they'd taken me, before my memories had been stolen away, my identity, my humanity. I was no one to me, but someone to them. And I didn't know who that someone was.

Jax groaned, trying to sound out the name he always called me. *Butterfly.*

But butterflies were fragile things with short lives and pretty wings. I'd survived unthinkable torture at the hands of him and the others. And he should have known better, because my heart could never be stopped by a single pin, no matter how sharp.

My lips twisted into a cruel smile as I dropped down beside him, reaching into his pocket. His arm flailed, but he was half dead, unable to stop me from taking his keys. I hesitated for a long moment, crawling close enough so I was all he could see as I stared into his eyes.

I wanted to speak my name so it was the last thing he could hear, but even if I had known what it was, my voice was buried so deep that I couldn't find a way to dig it out anymore. So my face would have to do.

One down, four to go, I mouthed instead and his widening eyes told me he'd understood.

I turned and ran, adrenaline flooding my veins which had nothing to do with pain for once as I raced up the wooden stairs. Freezing air hit my cheeks as I climbed higher and higher, reaching a hatch above my head. My fingers brushed a lock and I chose a key at random in the bunch, pushing it into the lock.

Click.

My heart soared. Luck was with me. Freedom had finally drawn my lot.

I'm not a butterfly, I'm a dragon with wings of iron and a heart of fire.

I shoved the heavy doors open with a grunt of effort and the blinding light above made me wince. The world was white, a bleached landscape that stretched in every direction. Snowflakes kissed my cheeks and my breath fogged before me as I climbed out of my underground prison and threw the doors shut behind me.

Fly. Fly away. Fly fast and hard and never stop.

With my eyes half closed, I took off into the endless expanse, aiming for a line of trees ahead of me as my pupils tried to adjust. My bare feet were frozen already, cold enough to ache.

I ran until my lungs burned and ice drove deeper and deeper into my blood. My crimson hair was sticky and lank, clinging to my cheeks and fluttering across my eyes. The smell of blood still hung in it from the cut on my temple Farley had given me last night.

I ran until the sun began to sink and heavier snow began to fall, wiping away my tracks.

I said their names with every footfall, over and over in my head. *Jax, Farley, Quentin, Orville, Duke.*

Farley: Jax's brother. He was just as big as Jax, but was built of muscle instead of fat. He trained his body so that when his ring-clad knuckles cracked against my slender frame, it left a welt for days. When Farley was in a foul mood, my flesh would face his wrath.

Quentin: the tall guy with the unruly blonde hair. He didn't care for beating me, but he found other ways to hurt me instead. Electricity, water boarding, sounds that screeched like knives against my eardrums for hours whilst I was held upside down by ropes. He spoke almost as little as me, but when he did, he whispered directly in my ear and sent a shiver of terror down my spine with his twisted fantasies of how he was going to hurt me next.

Orville: the one who tried to break the rules. He was skeletal with greying hair that he never seemed to wash. He wanted to touch me, bury himself in me and take away my final drops of dignity. Nothing lived behind his eyes except a demon pulling the strings. He always smelled like sweat and his voice was a purr that clawed under my skin. His hands had roamed more than once as he walked the line of what his boss deemed acceptable. He'd frightened me the most once until I realised that him staying his hand meant I was too important to defile. Though I had no idea why.

Duke: the one who set the rules, who held the other four in check. He had a horseshoe moustache and was always puffing on a cigarette. But despite his rules, he was the real one to fear. He liked me afraid. Liked to scrape a knife across the wall as he approached then run it down my skin. He liked me bleeding and had been the only one who'd had me begging for mercy back when I used my voice. He was the one who'd buried my voice for good. The night he put out cigarettes on my skin between wrapping a plastic bag over my face. Just long enough for me to think I was going to die. My voice had clogged in my throat and I'd found freedom in taking it away from him at last. He'd had plenty of screams from me since that day, but no more words.

My legs trembled beneath me as I started to slow, wading through the thick snow, my body so numb that I couldn't feel anything anymore except the pain in my bones.

My teeth chattered, causing an endless rattling in my skull. I hadn't eaten for two days. My vision was swimming and shadows flitted around in the dark, making me swing my head left and right. I expected them to descend, the monsters who held me, owned me. How could I escape them when they were all I knew? The broken memories of my past were a muddled jigsaw I couldn't piece together. Where would I go? Who would I run to?

I'd wondered a thousand times whether there were people waiting for me out here, longing for me, missing me. Or maybe I'd always been a girl with nothing and no one to belong to.

I found another inch of resilience in my soul and stretched it out, forcing myself to run once more.

I will not die when I have four deaths left to deliver!

An owl hooted somewhere above me in the trees and my heart lurched as I ran on, near-blind and entirely desperate. My dry tongue scraped the roof of my mouth as I gasped for water, my lungs heaving in ice-cold breaths and forcing them back out again. The cold was an enemy I wasn't prepared to face. If I'd thought it through, maybe I could have pulled Jax's coat from his body, but one more second in that place might have cost me my freedom. And I'd rather be battling the freezing wind and the biting ice than still be back there in that cell.

My knees sank into the snow before I realised I'd fallen. I clung to the bark of a pine tree, trying to haul myself upright, just about managing to drag myself to sit against it.

I was soaked through, my skin prickling with needles as the cold drove deeper. I shivered violently, dragging my knees to my chest and tilting my head to the sky. Clouds hung thickly above the trees and I swore on everything I was, I would live long enough to see the stars again and make a wish. Because I needed a little help if I was ever going to get revenge on the men who'd haunted me.

Four more deaths is all I need. Then I'll be someone. I'll be the last person they ever see.

Nicoli

CHAPTER TWO

"Tyson!"

Where is that damn dog now?

I swear I spent more time combing the woods for that mutt than chopping wood for the fire some days. He'd come back to the cabin on his own if I left him to his business, but no doubt he'd drag in some rotten old bone or roll in bear shit again if I allowed it. Not that he gave a fuck what I allowed most of the time, but I did try to rein in his more beastly qualities. Not least because he hated a bath and I wasn't going to let him sleep in the cabin reeking of bear shit.

"Tyson!" I called again, stalking up the snow-covered, rocky track through the trees.

The whole world was turning white as the blizzard tightened its hold on the forest and I grunted in frustration as I hunted the hillside for any sign of the damn dog.

My hands were growing numb and the memory of the fire I'd left blazing back in the cabin had me drawing to a halt. If the damn dog had gone walkabouts on his own in this weather then I wasn't sure it was worth the effort to find him. He'd make his way back sharp enough once he realised the snow wasn't letting up without me freezing my balls off in the attempt to find him.

I cursed him beneath my breath and turned back to head for the cabin and that fire. I'd get some food cooking and no doubt he'd come running once he caught a sniff of it on the wind.

I shouldered my rifle and started back down the hill, squinting through the snow storm to try and see the way on.

I took several steps then paused as the sound of barking called me to a halt.

I fell still, the oppressive silence of the snow-filled landscape the only thing I could hear for a moment before Tyson's barks came again.

I hesitated. Tyson may have been a half wild mutt, but he didn't make a fuss over nothing. If he was barking, there was good reason for it. Maybe we had company. Though it didn't seem likely the Cutters would be out in this weather and no one else ventured this far up the mountain and into the forest during winter. So maybe he'd found some other kind of trouble, pissed off a porcupine or made enemies out of a wolf pack…

"Tyson!" I bellowed one last time. If I could hear him then he could damn well hear me too, but the only response I got was more distant barking.

I gritted my teeth and turned off of the path as I took a guess at the direction his barks were coming from. There was an echo in this valley which played tricks on you if you didn't pay enough attention, but I was used to the ways of this forest and I was fairly confident in my route. Living up here for a year had made me adept in a lot of things which I hadn't been before. But these woods were devious and if you didn't keep your wits about you, you could find yourself falling prey to all manner of dangers. From the wild animals to pitfalls and sudden drops in the terrain.

There were old gold mines out here and the tunnels that had been carved into the earth by the men seeking their fortune were as likely to collapse beneath your feet as anything else if you passed too close to them. Not to mention the Cutters gang who occupied the north side of the mountain and the abandoned gold mines there for their cannabis crops. They'd built a community of savages who ruled their territory with an iron fist and held no laws to account. Not that I mixed it with them much. I'd come up here to escape from the world and the life which I thought I'd been destined to live.

When it turns out your entire life was a lie, there isn't much else you can do but turn your back on it and leave the past where it belongs. Perhaps one day I'd have to return to Sinners Bay and face the consequences of everything that had happened before I left, but today wasn't that day. And neither was tomorrow.

For now at least, solitude was my friend and Tyson my only companion, and that was the way I wanted it. That dog might have been a half wild beast, but since I'd found the stray mutt caught in a hunter's snare, he'd stuck by my side. And I had to admit that I was more than a little glad of his company. So if the mutt was barking with such urgency then the least I could do was take heed and see what had him so riled up.

The wind blew mercilessly and I was half blinded as the blizzard raged. It was so intense that my footsteps were disappearing behind me almost as soon as I stepped out of them. If I didn't know these trees so well, I'd be afraid about finding my way back to the cabin.

I rounded a rocky cliff and Tyson's barks grew louder as I squinted into the blizzard.

"Where are you, boy?" I called, the wind tearing my voice away the moment it left my lips.

A dark shape raced towards me through the snow and I tightened my grip on my rifle a moment before recognising Tyson's black and tan coat. He was at least some part German Shepherd and I half wondered if the rest of him was wolf at times due to the size of the beast. Though he was as soft as a boiled egg once you got him on side, he was a mean bastard if he didn't like the scent of you.

"There you are, boy. What are you up to now?" I asked him as he shoved a cold, wet nose into my palm. "Come on back to the cabin."

I turned to head home and he growled at me, catching the edge of my coat and tugging hard enough to make me stop.

That was some grade-A Lassie bullshit if ever I'd seen it. I just hoped he wasn't about to take me to see some kid stuck down a well because I didn't need the drama of that in my life right now.

I frowned down at him and scrubbed a hand over the soft fur of his head as I gave in and turned the way he wanted me to go.

Tyson yapped excitedly and bounded off through the snow. I followed him, carving a path through it as fast as I could to keep up.

He raced between trees and rounded a huge oak where he started barking again.

I moved as fast as I could, hurrying towards him as he barked anxiously and I stepped around the enormous trunk to get a look at what had him so worked up.

I'd expected the remains of a mountain lion kill or maybe a huge stick he'd been trying to drag home, but even in my wildest imaginings I wouldn't have expected to find a beautiful girl half dead in the snow.

She was leaning up against a tree, dark red hair falling lank around her pale face and her body curled in on herself as she shivered. She was unconscious and barely dressed, wearing only a thin shirt and torn leggings. The snow was settling on her and her breath didn't even fog as it escaped her parted lips.

"Shit." I dropped my rifle and ripped my coat off as I fell to my knees before her.

Her skin was icy to the touch as I reached out to cup her cheek, but the shivers which wracked her body let me know she was alive. I dragged her into my lap and wrapped the thick coat around her, zipping it up without even putting her arms through the sleeves. She was tiny, a fragile, skinny little thing, nowhere near dressed for this weather and way too close to death. I had no idea how the hell she'd ended up here, but I needed to get her out of this storm and back to my cabin before she lost the battle for her life.

I yanked the hat off of my head and shoved it onto hers as her head lolled against my chest.

Her feet were bare and half blue already. It would be a damn miracle if she kept all of her toes. I ripped my sweater off and pushed her feet into the thick material, wrapping it around them tightly and tying it in place.

As soon as it was done, I tossed my rifle over my shoulder and hoisted her into my arms.

A soft, pained groan escaped her and she leaned into my chest, seeking out the warmth of my flesh on instinct.

Tyson yipped excitedly before setting off through the trees, heading straight for the cabin we called home.

I moved after him quickly, as close to running as I could manage in the deep snow while carrying her in my arms. If I didn't get her back soon, she was going to die and I refused to let that happen. Whatever had led to her being out here in this storm, it couldn't be good. She needed my help and I wasn't going to let her down.

She was so light in my arms that it made my chest ache. What was this poor, fragile creature doing way out here? We were a hundred miles from the closest town. It didn't make any sense, but that wasn't what mattered now. I'd get her out of this storm and then figure out the rest later.

Tyson ran back and forth, urging me to move faster as I pounded through the snow as quickly as I could, grunting curses at myself for not going more swiftly.

The cabin finally appeared ahead of me, nothing more than a dark blur between the falling snow at first but quickly forming into the shape of the squat wooden building I'd made into my home this past year. My feet thumped up the stairs onto the porch and I yanked the door open.

The warmth of the fire washed over me the second we made it inside and Tyson raced forwards to dive onto my favourite armchair. I was too caught up in the girl to even bother reprimanding him for it as I kicked the door closed and made a beeline for the fire.

It had burned a little low while I was out so I gently placed the girl down on the thick rug before it and moved to toss some more logs on to feed the flames.

I kicked my snow-covered boots off and yanked my saturated shirt off too as I began to shiver. If *I* was this cold from being exposed out there for a few minutes then I could only imagine how she felt.

I crossed the cabin to the large bed at the back of the room, pulling the comforter and blankets from it and snatching a plaid shirt and thick socks from my closet before hurrying back to the frozen girl before the fire.

Her teeth were chattering and I growled in anger as I wondered again what the hell had happened to her to lead her out here in this storm.

"It's alright, baby doll," I murmured, reaching out to pull my jacket and sweater off of her. The thin shirt and leggings she wore were plastered to her skin by the thawed snow and I quickly yanked them off too.

I refused to let my gaze linger on her naked body as she shivered before me, but I noticed her ribs showing too keenly beneath her skin and a myriad of scars and bruises marking her flesh. She was the kind of skinny that wasn't healthy. The kind that spoke of a lack of food rather than some dietary choice.

I clenched my jaw as anger slipped through my veins, hot and potent at the thought of someone hurting this fragile creature.

"What happened to you?" I murmured before tugging my shirt around her body and buttoning it up. It swamped her, falling to her knees as I pulled it lower.

Her skin was icy cold and my gut twisted with concern as I wondered if I was already too late to save her. There was no way I could get her to a hospital, though that was undoubtably what she needed. We were a hundred miles from one and caught in this blizzard. I was the only chance she had at any kind of help, so all I could do was try.

I pulled the pair of thick socks over her feet then wrapped her in the blankets, stirring the fire again in hopes that it could thaw the ice in her veins.

She started to shiver more violently, but I held hope that that was a good thing. There wasn't much I could do aside from wait now.

So I took up a position in my armchair, turfing Tyson out as I sat watching her.

I'd done all I could. Only time would tell if it was enough.

CHAPTER THREE

Nightmares suffocated me. I was in a box of sand, sinking, unable to breathe. Then Orville's hands were snaking over my body, the scrape of a knife sounded against a wall as Duke approached. The scent of cigarettes, the whisper of Quentin's next threat, Jax's goading ringing in my ears as he egged them all on. Farley's fists pounding, pounding, pounding-

Fingers feathered over my arm and I lurched upright with a sharp inhale. Two liquid bronze eyes flecked with gold locked on mine and calloused hands pressed my shoulders down. He smelled like fresh snowfall and hazelnuts and despite my terror, it was the best thing I'd smelled in a long time.

Ragged breaths tore out of my lungs as the stranger leaned over me and I feared I'd run from one monsters' nest into another. He was huge, built with powerful, stacked muscles that made him look capable of snapping a man's spine in half with his bare hands.

"Shh, it's alright," he said, his deep voice as soft as if it had been dipped in butter. "I'm not going to hurt you, baby doll."

He released me, sitting back on his heels.

I pushed away the heavy blanket covering me, sweat coating my skin.

I wasn't used to a bed like this. I needed a hard floor and a cool breeze to find sleep. Not a soft rug and a warm fire. *What is this? Where am I?*

I was disoriented as I gazed around, half wondering if I'd lost my mind at last and was imagining this entire place. The cabin was large with a huge bed across the room and a small kitchenette to one side where coffee was dripping through a percolator.

My eyes locked on the stranger again and I rose to my feet, backing up as I searched for an exit. My gaze snagged on the front door, but a huge dog sat in front of it. The beast bounded towards me and I lurched backwards in alarm. Large hands braced me a second before the dog reared up and my heart shot into my throat.

"Down, Tyson!" the man barked and a scream ripped from my lungs half a second before a wet tongue rolled up the side of my face. "Hey look at that, he likes you."

I lurched out of the guy's grip, half falling over the dog as I raced toward the door.

"Wait – are you crazy?" he called just as I wrenched the door wide.

A blizzard was spinning wildly beyond it and a flurry of snow rushed over me, immediately making me back up. My heart pounded unevenly and I tried to figure out what to do as I stared at the storm barring my way forward. *Am I trapped between two deaths?*

I remembered falling in the snow, hunting for the stars above and my breathing slowed a little. This man must have found me out there, brought me here. I'd be dead if it wasn't for him.

I slowly pushed the door shut, turning and pressing my back to it as I assessed the beastly man and his wolf before me. His chest was bare, his towering muscles highlighted under the orange glow of the fire. He had a dark, scruffy beard and his hair was just as unruly. He had scars too. One on his shoulder and lighter ones marking his sides, his arms. Then one slim line running across his left cheek. But his eyes...they were kind, warm. Unlike any eyes I'd ever had look at me so far as I could remember. The eyes of the five men who'd imprisoned me always promised pain, they only shone brighter when I was screaming. But my fear had made this man look like *that* instead. Like he wanted to help.

"Don't be afraid," he said in that rich, velvety tone which sent goosebumps rushing down my spine. "What's your name?"

My voice remained in the locked box deep down in my chest, refusing to come out for anyone. Even someone with kind eyes.

"My name's Nicoli. You can talk to me," he urged and I released a breath of amusement. Because no I couldn't. Not even if I wanted to. My voice had been absent so long, sometimes I wondered if it would ever come back.

The dog, Tyson, jumped up onto the couch, curling up and placing his head down to go to sleep. I returned my eyes to the creature in the room who was more likely to be a monster. As far as I could remember, I'd never met a man whose heart wasn't black. And despite the fact that he'd clearly helped me and his aura invited me in, that didn't mean I could trust him. I'd be a fool to let my guard down. This could be a trick, his eyes luring like the devil's.

"Would you like some coffee?" He headed towards the kitchenette, turning his back on me and I eyed the deep scar on his right shoulder which matched the one on the front. A small flash of some half-memory pulled at my mind of a TV show with a bloody torso on the screen and the words *exit wound* resounded through my skull. This man before me had once been shot, and from the looks of his other scars, I guessed he was the sort of person who often got into trouble like that.

He poured two mugs of coffee and the scent made my nose wrinkle and my stomach twist. Duke had always smelled like it in the mornings when he first arrived. Before the pain started.

Nicoli turned to me, holding it out and I shook my head despite the fact that my mouth was parched. I eyed the sink beside him, pointing at the tap.

"Water?" he offered and I nodded eagerly.

He poured me a glass and my fingers itched for it as I stepped tentatively forward to take it. He closed the distance between us, placing it in my hand and I watched him out of the corner of my eye as I tipped it into my mouth and drained it. He took the glass from me as I ran my tongue over my chapped lips and the sound of my stomach grumbling filled the space between us.

Nicoli moved to the refrigerator, placing the glass down as he opened it, revealing so much food it made my heart beat out of rhythm. I'd never seen so much in one place. And memories stirred from my past as I recognised it all. I hurried forward on instinct and he stepped aside, gesturing for me to take my pick. I reached for a block of cheese, tearing it open and sinking my teeth into it. A moan left my lips at the delicious taste and I hurried away across the room before he could even think about taking it back. Quentin had loved to play that game. He'd place a whole plate of food in front of me, letting me take a few bites before snatching it away again, eating it himself while I watched. But Nicoli wasn't going to get the chance to take this from me.

I headed to the corner beside the fire, dropping down onto the hard wood and pressing my back to the wall as I ate my way through the block in savage bites.

Nicoli frowned at me across the room and I ignored him, eating like a feral animal as Tyson lifted his head and licked his lips at my cheese. I bared my teeth at him and the dog cocked his head like he didn't know what to make of me.

"Do you want some bread with that?" Nicoli half laughed and I scowled at him as he brought over a lump of fresh bread on a plate. There was a sharp knife beside it and as he placed it down before me, I snatched it up, pointing it at him, unable to believe he'd actually given me a weapon. It felt cool and heavy in my palm and gave me a drink of the power I'd thirsted for for so long. I may have been small, but that didn't matter when you were armed. When you were quick and hungry for blood.

"Woah, woah." He raised his hands in innocence. "It's just to cut the cheese with."

I eyed the block in my hand as Nicoli backed up and my shoulders relaxed. I sliced off a few pieces of the cheese, ripping off a hunk of bread and devouring them together.

Holy hell that's good.

I groaned in delight, continuing to eat and eat until there was no cheese or bread left and my stomach ached so much I was sure it was going to burst.

When Nicoli wasn't looking, I pushed the knife up the sleeve of the large check shirt he'd put me in, reassured by the cold lick of the blade against my skin. I'd stabbed Jax in the leg once. He'd dropped the knife he liked to flip in his hand like a cocky idiot and I'd jammed it right into his fat thigh. I'd been delivered to Farley's fists for it, but it had totally been worthwhile to hear that piggy scream. I could still smell his blood if I thought about it long enough. That memory had gotten me through a lot of tortures. It reminded me that I could make them bleed too, given the opportunity. I would one day get that chance again, and as soon as I did I'd cut deep and find arteries that would spill and spill and spill-

"Do you want any more?" Nicoli asked, perching on the edge of the couch beside his dog.

I shook my head. I couldn't possibly fit any more in.

"Will you tell me your name, baby doll?" he asked, a note of hope in his voice.

I placed a hand over my throat and shook my head to signal I couldn't speak. But telling him I had no name either was a little harder.

"Hm," he grunted. "Well, what will I call you?"

I twisted my lips in thought. My captors had called me plenty of things. Bitch, whore, slut, cunt. But I didn't really fancy any of those permanently funnily enough.

"Katie?" he guessed and I shook my head. I definitely wasn't a Katie. Katie sounded like she had her shit together. She probably wore nice dresses and went to the mall on Saturdays. No, that wasn't me at all.

"Nah, that seems too normal for you anyway," Nicoli murmured and my brows arched as he mirrored my thoughts.

"What do you like?" he asked and I rolled my eyes.

I can't answer, dumbass.

He chuckled at my expression and a smile hooked up one side of my lips. Shit, when had I last smiled? Oh yeah, when Jax had choked on his own tongue. Good times.

"Well, you clearly like cheese." He pointed at the empty wrapper beside me. "Maybe I'll call you cheddar."

Tyson barked enthusiastically and I pursed my lips, shaking my head furiously.

I didn't break out of hell to be called Cheddar, asshole.

Nicoli laughed again and I flipped him the finger, only making his eyes brighten further. Shit, if I gave any of The Five the finger, they'd have had me over a table for it and leave me with more scars to brighten my pale skin. They'd played tic tac toe on my back once, I'd passed out before I found out who won.

"Help me out here, baby doll," he pleaded. "Point at something you like."

I gave myself to the game as I gazed around the cabin; it was nice to be asked questions which weren't *what is the code, you piece of shit?*

I took in the soft blankets on Nicoli's huge bed then the fur rugs on the floor and the bare walls. My gaze strayed to the window where snow was piling up against the pane. I didn't know why, but I knew I liked snow. It had been the first thing I'd seen the second I'd stepped out of my prison and had looked like the fluffy clouds of heaven. Even if it had almost killed me...

I rose to my feet, keeping the knife concealed in my sleeve as I headed to the window and pointed at the dark, snowy landscape beyond.

"You like winter?" Nicoli asked.

Winter...it was dark, the end of everything, the death of the old in preparation for the new. It was perfect. It was me. It was my revenge.

I turned to him, finding he'd risen from his seat and I gazed up at his towering height, gripping the hilt of the knife in my palm. I nodded to him and a smile pulled at his mouth.

"Winter it is then," he decided and warmth filled my chest. I'd never had a name before. Well, I probably had. Maybe I was once called Judith and had lived in a convent with a bunch of nuns. Couldn't really picture me being so pious though. I'd thrown plenty of colourful curse words at The Five before I'd stopped speaking.

Nicoli's gaze scraped over my hair. "I'll run you a bath. Would you like that, Winter?"

The sound of my new name again made sunshine spill into my veins. Which was weird considering I wasn't called Summer. I nodded keenly, thinking of the hot water and the soap and being clean. It was almost enough to make me cry.

He headed away through a door beside the bed and the sound of running water set my pulse hammering. The closest I'd come to being clean with The Five was the weekly ice-cold bucket of water thrown over my head. Orville loved to be the one who threw it after he made me strip off my clothes. I shuddered, wrapping my arms around myself as his gruff voice echoed in my head. *"One day we'll get the truth from you and Duke won't care what happens next. He'll let me have my fill of you."*

That was a good enough reason on its own not to tell them the truth even if I *did* know what they wanted from me. But Orville had never seemed like the brightest button.

Nicoli returned from the bathroom after a while, leaving the door open behind him. "You can use any of my wash stuff. It's not much, baby doll, but it'll get you clean."

I nodded, moving forward, hoping he might back up a few steps from the door, but he remained in place as I approached.

He caught my arm suddenly and a gasp escaped me a second before he prised the knife from under my sleeve with deft fingers. "I don't want you hurting yourself."

It was you I was protecting myself from, mountain man.

27

"Or me," he said with a dark laugh that made my toes curl.

I didn't want to admit he was handsome. I mean, beneath the miles of hair on his face, I supposed he could be hideous, but I didn't think so. His powerful body only made me wary though. Farley had used his muscles against me and this guy had used them to take a weapon from my hands. So I wasn't about to let my guard fall. Especially as he twirled it between his fingers with a skill that said he knew exactly how to use it.

I slipped into the bathroom, pushing the door shut behind me and practically jumped for joy when I found a lock on the other side.

I slid it into place, then back out again before sliding it back in as I beamed. I mean sure, that bear out there could probably shoulder-ram his way in here if he really wanted to, but I'd never had even a chance of shutting the monsters out before.

I took in the wood-panelled bathroom and the giant cream tub that looked more like a jacuzzi than a bath. It was square and fitted into one corner of the room with a few steps that led into it. A couple of fluffy towels had been left beside it with a simple black wash bag.

I stripped out of my clothes and climbed up the steps, dipping my toe in the warm water and biting my lip in anticipation as I stepped in. Heat spread everywhere as I lowered into it, lost to the huge tub as I let myself sink right under the bubbles. My skin hummed with pleasure and a moan of utter happiness escaped me as I resurfaced. I'd never known water could feel so good. The forms I'd experienced it in were the brutal types, but this…this was its purest form. It was like a blanket wrapping around me and sinking deep into my tired body.

Blood and muck spread out around me and I set to work scrubbing the rest of it from my skin and hair, wincing as I occasionally split open new scabs. I opened the wash bag, finding shampoo, shower gel, a coarse brush, a small pair of scissors and a razor. I started with my hair, lathering the shampoo into it and sighing at how good it felt to get it clean at long last, even though my cuts stung. I scrubbed the dirt and blood out from under my nails then clipped them short. Next, I lathered up in Nicoli's shower gel, the masculine, nutty scent of it clinging to me as I washed every inch of my body.

I eyed the razor last, some deeply feminine part of my being calling to me from another life. So I took it into my grip and set to work shaving my body until I felt like a new girl. One with a name, one with hope, one with shiny ass smooth legs.

I finally pulled the plug out of the drain and everything physical from my old life was washed away. Everything but the scars. But I was happy to keep those, because each one was now a promise to destroy the men who'd laid them there.

I stepped out of the bath, wrapping my hair in one towel and my body in the other. A soft strumming of guitar strings reached me beyond the door and I stilled as Nicoli started singing a song I didn't know. It was mournful and beautiful and it sounded exactly like the way I felt.

I unlocked the door and pushed it open a crack, peeking at him on the couch where he played.

"In the belly of the raging storm, I'll keep you warm, I'll keep you warm," he sang, his voice sending shivers right through to my core.

I crept back into the room, but Tyson raised his head, alerting Nicoli and the music halted.

Don't stop. I wished I could speak in that moment more than I had in a long time.

"That better?" he asked and I nodded.

He headed to his closet across the room and pulled out a black and white check shirt for me to wear. I reached for it as he approached, dropping my towel to the floor and he stilled, his eyes falling down to my body and his throat bobbing.

I'd been naked in front of The Five so many times that I hadn't even paused to think how Nicoli might react. But I was as skinny as a rake and covered in bruises and scars. I wasn't exactly a sight to behold. Though maybe I should have been more careful around him all the same. I took the shirt from his outstretched hand and shrugged it on as he met my gaze, some dark and furious emotion pouring from his eyes. He looked like a creature of the night, but that wildness in him didn't scare me for some reason. Instead, it made my heart pound like it knew him. Like it wanted me to rise to his wildness and show him my own.

"Who did that to you, baby doll?" he asked in a dangerous voice that set the hairs on the back of my neck tingling.

I raised my hand, showing him all five fingers. I counted them off, saying their names in my mind. *Jax, Farley, Quentin, Orville, Duke.*

I saved my thumb for Duke. Because a hand couldn't function without a thumb. He was the glue that bound them all. The reason I was locked up and battered. Whatever they wanted from me, it all hinged around him.

"Five people?" Nicoli guessed and I nodded then pointed at him. "Five men," he corrected and I nodded again, my lips tight as I finished buttoning up the shirt.

I opened my hand again, showing him five fingers once more then putting down my little pinky. I ran my index finger across my throat.

"One of them is dead?" Nicoli asked.

I placed my hands together in a prayer and gave him an intent look. *I really fucking hope so.*

"When this storm stops, I'll take you off the mountain. You can talk to the police if you want?"

My heart jolted and I shook my head quickly, mouthing *no*.

Nicoli frowned, a line forming on his brow. "The police can help you, Winter."

I ground my jaw, shaking my head firmly and raising my hand once more. I put my fingers down one at a time, giving him a fierce look and telling him with my eyes, *not until they're all dead.*

His shoulders tensed and his eyes became shadowed. "You'd best get some sleep, you can have my bed." He gestured to it, pretending he hadn't understood me, but I had a feeling he had. If he thought he was going to drag me down the mountain tomorrow, he was sorely mistaken. I might have been a waif of a girl, but I had an unbreakable soul. And once I was strong enough physically, I'd find a way to bring those men to their knees. I just needed the right weapon to do it.

Nicoli tugged the covers back on his bed and I eyed the huge mattress with trepidation.

I slipped past him, snatching a blanket off the end of it and heading across the cabin to curl up on the floor beside the wall. I wouldn't be able to sleep in that giant marshmallow. As much as I hated to admit it, The Five had broken me in a few ways. And this was one of them. Sleep would only come on a hard floor. It was the only constant I knew.

"Take the bed, baby doll," Nicoli pressed, a note of concern wrapping around an edge of insistence.

I shook my head, tugging my single blanket over my shoulder as I rolled to face the wall. After a while, I heard him move back through the room and settle on the couch. He started playing his song again and the tension ran out of my body with every strum of the strings.

For once, I felt safe. And it was such a sweet feeling, I let myself drown and drown in it, hoping I could take it with me into my dreams.

CHAPTER FOUR

I shifted uncomfortably on the couch, tugging a cushion out from under me and tossing it onto the floor with a grunt. I moved up onto my elbows, glancing across the room to my bed which lay empty while Winter remained on the floor with only one thin blanket covering her.

I could have just moved back to my bed, but I wanted her to be able to claim it if she woke in the night, as uncomfortable as I was.

I groaned as I stretched my arms above my head, working a few kinks out of my spine as I pushed myself upright.

Tyson was lying before the door, his feet twitching as he dreamed of chasing rabbits, or maybe it was mountain lions knowing him.

I pushed myself up to stand and pulled on a pair of sweatpants as I moved to claim a glass of water from the sink but before I could get there, Tyson bolted upright and released a low growl.

I froze, turning to my faithful companion and frowning as he leapt up and placed his feet on the windowsill, ducking his head beneath the curtain and baring his teeth as he looked out into the blizzard.

I moved to his side, pulling the curtain back and straining my ears as I gazed out into the dark woods, the glow of the snow illuminating the landscape through the blizzard. I watched the trees with a prickle of anticipation rolling down my spine and the light from a flashlight suddenly caught my gaze.

Tyson growled again, his hackles rising and I pushed away from the window, striding towards Winter where she lay sleeping by the wall.

"Winter," I hissed, crouching down beside her and reaching out to shake her.

Before my hand could meet with her flesh, she whirled around, pointing a knife at me and baring her teeth. She must have gotten up and taken it from the kitchen while I slept and I had to admire her tenacity. She'd clearly been through hell but instead of letting it break her, she'd come out fighting on the other side.

"Someone's coming," I breathed in a low voice. "Would the people you escaped from be looking for you?"

A whimper of fear left her lips and she leapt to her feet, scrambling away from me as she darted for the door.

My heart stumbled in fear as she reached for the handle and I pounced on her before she could make it, slapping a hand over her mouth as a cry of panic escaped her.

She swung the knife at me but I caught her wrist with ease, fixing it in my grip as I dragged her back away from the door. I twisted my grip on her hand, taking the knife from her before she ended up stabbing one of us and I jammed it into the back of my waistband.

She clawed at my arm as she fought to get me off of her, but I kept my grip tight to stop her from running.

"You can't go out there," I growled, keeping my voice low as I moved her away from the windows. The cabin was dark but the glow of the fire might just give off enough light for us to be seen between the gaps in the curtains. "I have somewhere I can hide you."

Winter relaxed marginally, her grip on my arm loosening a fraction.

I released my hold on her, slipping my hand from her mouth as I turned her around to look at me.

"Can you trust me to hide you, baby doll?" I asked, looking into her bright green eyes and finding a river of fear there. But amongst the panic, I sensed her judging that question as she tried to figure out her answer.

After the longest pause, she nodded and I released a breath as I tugged her towards my bed.

Tyson growled again, running from one window to the next and nudging his nose beneath the curtains to get a good look out at whoever was coming.

I could hear them now too, their voices raised as they called out between each other in their hunt.

I released my hold on Winter and dragged the bed aside until I could lift the hatch that was hidden there. It was meant to be a bit of additional storage beneath the cabin, but I'd never made much use of it and the space sat empty.

Winter's eyes widened with panic as she looked into the dark alcove. I hurried to grab the blankets she'd been sleeping with and the clothes she'd been wearing when she'd arrived here before tossing them in.

"I'll be right out here," I promised her, cupping her cheek in my hand and holding her eye. "I give you my word, you'll be okay. And I've never broken my word in all my life."

Her lips twitched with panic as she looked down into the dark space again, but at the sound of men drawing closer outside, she suddenly dropped down into it.

I knelt down beside her and offered her the knife. "If anything happens to me, don't come out. Stay there until they leave. There's cash and a cellphone with charge in the kitchen drawer, but you'll have to get to the bottom of the mountain before you can get any signal to call for help. If you don't want to call the cops then you can message a man called Rocco. Tell him you know me and he'll help you."

At least I hoped he would. I didn't have anyone else that I could call on anymore though, so he was the best I could offer her.

I moved to close the hatch and Winter reached out to catch my hand, her eyes brimming with concern. I offered her an easy smile in an attempt to reassure her and leaned down to press a kiss to her red hair.

She stilled at the gesture and as I pulled back, she stared at me like she didn't know what to make of me at all. Like the concept of someone caring, or giving her anything other than pain was alien to her and the thought of that sent anger spilling through me in a molten wave.

"You'll be alright. I promise."

I gritted my teeth and swung the hatch closed, pulling the bed back over it as I straightened and moved to grab my rifle from beside the door.

I cast a sweeping look over the cabin to make sure I hadn't left out anything else that might give away her presence then wrenched the door open and stepped out onto the porch. I tossed it closed behind me to keep Tyson inside, much to his disgust, and he started barking frantically as he leapt up at the window to get a look at our unwelcome guests.

Duke Polinsky and his band of merry assholes were striding towards me through the snow and I cocked my rifle over my arm as I looked at them with a scowl on my face. These were the assholes who ran the cannabis farm over on the north side of the mountain and I usually made it my mission to avoid them as much as humanly possible. They were a bunch of power hungry motherfuckers and the best thing they'd ever done for society was to remove themselves from it.

"What are you doing out here in the middle of the night, Duke?" I demanded. "You woke my damn dog up and got me out of bed."

"You seen a girl out here, mountain man?" Duke called in a friendly tone as he strode up the steps of my porch looking like he owned the goddamn world. Snow had settled in on the wide brimmed hat he wore over his slicked-back black hair and his cold eyes swept over me for a moment before he turned his attention to my cabin. He eyed the window where Tyson was looking out, lifting a hand to smooth down his horseshoe moustache.

"The only ones mad enough to come out here in this blizzard are you assholes," I muttered.

Duke licked his lips as he came to stand before me, casually drawing a long hunting knife from his belt. "Remember that time I asked you if you'd seen a buck I was hunting when I met you up in the forest last summer?" he asked slowly. "And you told me it had run on down to the river."

I grunted in vague recollection of the memory.

"But then the darn thing appeared right behind you, in the complete opposite direction to what you'd just said."

"I'm not grasping the point of this tale and it's freezing out," I growled.

Goosebumps covered my bare chest and my breath rose in a fog before me so my statement was true enough.

"Point is…" Duke leaned in close to me so that I could smell the tang of cheap whiskey on his breath. I was taller than him and it seemed like he was standing up straighter than usual to try and match my height. "I don't *trust* you, mountain man. I think you've got a soft spot for a victim. But just like that buck, this girl's life is *mine*. And unlike that buck, I won't be so forgiving if you try to keep her from me."

"I like being alone," I growled, rolling my shoulders back. "I don't invite people into my home. Not missing girls or assholes who show up unannounced in the middle of the night. But if I see her, I'll be sure to tell her what direction to run from you."

Duke snarled at me, raising his knife and I raised my rifle in reply.

"You shouldn't bring a knife to a gun fight, Duke," I warned, my finger kissing the trigger.

The sound of all of his men cocking their own guns at me came as expected, but I kept my gaze fixed on the asshole in charge.

"Be a good boy and let us come in and check your story, mountain man," Duke purred. "It would be a shame to fill you with holes if it turns out you ain't lying this time…"

My lip curled back and I gave him a hard look before pulling my door wide to let them in. "Make it quick."

I whistled to call Tyson to my side and the dog shot to my heels, snarling as he eyed Duke with a look that said he wanted to rip his throat out. It was damn tempting to let him.

I lowered my rifle and placed a hand on Tyson's head, tussling his fur to calm him. Duke tipped his hat to me mockingly and stomped into my home without another word.

Four of his men trailed in behind him and I followed them with a scowl on my face, moving to stand by the doorway as they tore through the cabin.

Snow fell from their boots as they pounded over the wooden floorboards, shoving furniture aside and looking in cupboards.

One of them dropped down to hunt beneath the bed and my heart stilled as I forced my eyes away from him and released a sigh of irritation. It was seriously fucking tempting to gut each and every one of them right here and now. If they'd been keeping Winter captive and causing her harm then they'd more than earned that fate. But even I couldn't overcome these odds. Five men in my home, another ten outside, most of them armed with rifles of their own. But I'd marked them alright. Because their fate was sealed. If they'd laid their hands on that girl then they were as good as dead already. Hell, even the ones who were simply helping in the hunt had bought their fate.

Ever since I'd left home for this mountain to live alone and try to figure out who the fuck I was, I'd been circling around the few true and honest things I knew about myself that couldn't be shaken by finding out my entire upbringing was a lie. I'd been honed into a monster by the man who'd raised me. And I still had a taste for spilling blood. Just so long as those I hurt were deserving of their fate. These fuckers were the most deserving I'd come across in a long time. And I was already planning out the ways I'd make them suffer the next time I saw them.

"Are you done wrecking my home yet?" I demanded as Duke pursed his lips, frowning at the empty space.

"Seems that you were trustworthy this time, mountain man," he said, disappointment lining his cruel features. "Sorry to have imposed."

He whistled and his men gave up the hunt, traipsing from the cabin without a word to me.

"Feel free to leave it longer before your next visit," I remarked as Duke lingered by the doorway.

"If you do see a girl running around out here, you bring her to me, you hear?" he hissed, his gaze scraping over my home one last time.

"Sure thing, I'll add it to my to-do list," I mocked.

He tipped his hat at me and strode from the cabin behind his men as they headed off to continue their hunt in the forest.

I tossed the door shut behind them and bolted it for good measure as Tyson took up a position watching through the window, baring his teeth at the retreating assholes.

I could still hear them close by, shouting to each other as they tried to figure out where to head to next, so I left Winter where she was and started tidying up the mess they'd made with their search.

I didn't know what the hell that madman wanted with my frozen girl, but I wouldn't be letting him have her, no matter what it took to keep her safe from them.

And just as soon as I could be sure she was far enough away from them, I was going to come calling for the blood debt they owed her.

CHAPTER FIVE

My heart thrashed wildly as I stared up at the cracks in the floorboards above me. Farley's weathered face had passed over them just moments ago as he stuck his head under the bed. I imagined his strong hands ripping me from this hole and dragging me out of here, taking me back to my nightmare. A world where there was only them and me. The predators and their prey.

I couldn't focus, even when I was sure I heard the door bang shut. The confined space was pulling the strings of my memory, reminding me of the times they'd left me in a wooden crate hunched over on my knees. Hours and hours in the dark and freezing cold, where my body cramped up until I was in pure agony. My screams had gone unanswered. It had almost brought my voice back until I'd remembered that that was what they wanted. So I'd pushed it even deeper until not even I could reach it. *Gone, gone, gone. I'm lost in a river of darkness and all the pieces of me have floated away.*

I clamped my hands over my eyes, terror binding me, making my body stiff as I became a prisoner once more. A captive to the pain they'd inflicted on me which still echoed through my body like a drum beating at the centre of my being.

It was never going to leave until they were dead.

They had die. It had to be over. I had to do it now.

The hatch wrenched open and firm hands latched hold of me. I screamed as my captor dragged me out of the hole then his palm slammed over my mouth half a second later, stifling the noise and making me flail like mad.

I kicked and punched and fought for my life as he pushed me down on the bed, laying his whole body over mine so I couldn't move an inch. His weight was solid, unmovable. His powerful muscles rippled against my small frame as I thrashed as hard as I could.

I was trapped again, never to be free-

"Look at me, baby doll," he commanded and his deep voice rang through my skull, forcing me to take notice.

I blinked heavily, my breathing slowing as I found myself staring into Nicoli's warm bronze eyes. A breath of utter relief escaped me as the fears holding me hostage slid away into the recesses of my mind. I wanted to crawl into those eyes and live in the safety that resided there. Everything about him was so sturdy; he was a wall that could resist the fiercest tide. Indestructible. And he had stood between me and The Five. He'd kept me hidden, he'd sent them away.

I relaxed beneath his weight, reaching up with shaking hands to run my fingers over his brow, his cheeks, the faint scar running up in a straight line toward his ear. His lips parted and he suddenly drew away from me, scraping a hand through his hair as he stood above me. The absence of his weight on me left a hole in my chest. Something about being held down by him wasn't like it had been with my torturers. He'd done it to protect me. And though I could withstand the full wrath of The Five if I had to, I couldn't remember ever being protected from anything. It was strange, wholly alien to me. I was meat left for the crows to pick at. I wasn't to be looked at like that. Like I meant something, was something, *am* something.

I pushed myself up to sit on the bed as he strode across the room to the largest window, twitching the curtain aside for a second before dropping it again.

"The Cutters had you?" he questioned in a severe tone even though he already knew the answer to that.

He turned sharply as I hugged my knees to my chest, his calm eyes suddenly alight with hellfire. I had the feeling this safety I felt around him wasn't what other people usually felt in his presence. He was the sort of man people ran from in the street. The sort that could even unsettle men like The Five.

"Why? What did they want from you, baby doll? Did they…?" His eyes trailed to my bare legs and his eyes darkened to deadliest nightshade before he turned away again.

My throat burned with the need to answer, but I couldn't force anything out. I couldn't decipher what he was thinking as he started to pace the room and I watched him move back and forth in front of the fire for what felt like a thousand turns.

I sensed his rage like a scent in the air and I slipped out of bed, unsure what to do, but I was going to follow my instincts and see where they led me.

I moved behind Nicoli as he paced toward the window again and pressed my hand to his back. He stilled under my touch and I slowly wound my arms around him, pressing my cheek to his bare skin and closing my eyes as his hazelnut scent washed over me. He was so warm as if the fire I'd seen blazing in his eyes lived beneath his flesh too. I was frozen in comparison, my skin cool against his. I wondered if that was because I was just a shell of the girl who had once lived within this skin and bones. Her echo sometimes called to me faintly from afar. But this body had no past, no future. Up until now, it recognised nothing but pain.

He rested his hands over mine on his stomach and a weighted sigh heaved through his chest. "I wish you could talk to me."

I frowned, pulling my hands free of him as I thought of a way I could do so. I lifted my finger and slowly painted words on his back. *I can.*

He inhaled slowly. "You can," he echoed what I'd written and a small smile pulled at my mouth.

I lifted my hand again and wrote out *ask me again* across his broad shoulders.

"Okay," he breathed like he was wary of hearing my answer. "Why did those men have you, Winter?"

I painted the answer on his flesh, digging my teeth into my lower lip. *I don't know.*

"But you must know something?" he pressed, a note of anger in his voice. But not at me, at them.

I don't remember, I wrote.

"How can you not remember?" he asked in a strained tone, his hands dropping and curling into fists at his sides.

I think I hit my head a long time ago. When they took me.

"Oh," he whispered. "So did they…hurt you?" he asked in a tight voice.

Yes.

His muscles bunched. "Rape you?" he questioned in a gravelly tone that set my pulse racing.

No.

His shoulders dropped dramatically. "Well that's something, I guess," he muttered, but he still sounded angry as hell.

He turned around, his expression taut as he surveyed me. "Do you have any questions for me? I know it must be hard to trust me. I realise I'm not exactly a shining prince, baby doll."

I let my eyes run down to his chest, roaming over the scars which branded his muscles, the little imperfections that almost matched the ones on my body. I wondered if the people who'd placed them on him were lying in cold graves just like I wanted my attackers to be.

I brushed my fingers over the gunshot scar on his right shoulder then painted the word *how?* beside it.

"That's a long story," he said with darkness seeping into his gaze. "The short version is that I lost someone important to me once…when I tried to find her, some assholes did this to me." He pointed at a few more scars, including the one on his cheek and I nodded, painting another question on his skin.

Did you find her?

"Yes," he said thickly, clearly not wanting to offer me more than that.

I lowered my hand to his stomach as a sweeping chill took over my body. I didn't know why it bothered me so much, but the idea that this man was someone else's saviour made me feel kind of lonely. He had a life. One with tangible memories that made him a whole person. Not some half-creature who didn't even know her own name.

I dropped my hand but he caught it before it fell at my side, placing it back on his flesh with an intense look that made my heart pound.

"Ask me," he growled. "I can see the questions in your eyes."

I tentatively painted circles on his stomach as I hesitated and goosebumps raised on his flesh. He caught my wrist with a low noise in his throat and I lifted my gaze to his, my lashes framing my vision as I took in his beastly expression.

Who is she? I wrote the words slowly, knowing I didn't really have a right to the answer. But he'd said I could ask.

"She's…a friend," he said, his words carefully chosen.

I nodded, slipping away, my walls rising. I didn't even have a right to this man's safe haven, I certainly didn't have a right to know details about his personal life. Maybe a part of me was jealous. Because he could leave this mountain tomorrow if he wanted and nothing would be left behind. But beyond this mountain, I was nothing but a ghost. My reality existed here and nowhere else. And so did my destiny. To end The Five. If I managed that – no, *when* I managed that – I didn't know what would become of me. Maybe I'd be cast to the wind.

"You should get some rest," Nicoli said gently, pointing to the bed.

I nodded, heading towards it and taking a blanket from the end.

"Sleep in it, Winter," he demanded, but I ignored him, heading to the floor across the room and dropping down beside the wall.

I pulled the blanket over me, taking slow breaths as I gazed down at the grain in the wood. The Five weren't going to stop looking for me. And the longer I stayed here, the more danger I put Nicoli in. But I still didn't have a weapon or a plan or even shoes to go hunting them in.

Nicoli dropped down onto the couch and I glanced over at him before my gaze shifted to the rifle resting against the wall beside fireplace. If The Five came back, he'd know what to do. He'd wake me. He'd make sure I was hidden. And Tyson would bark if there was a noise beyond the cabin.

I fell into my latest nightmare, returning me to that cell deep underground where the sun never shone and the world forgot to be my friend.

My knees pressed against rough stone, chaffed and bleeding. My back was arched, my hands pressed to the concrete as blood spilled from the ripped flesh of my back. Duke was smoking in the corner, the low light of the single bulb hanging above me in my cell making my shadow seem like it was trying to hide beneath me. And I wouldn't be surprised. When Duke was around, even the mice tucked their tails and ran in case he cast a glance their way. But there was only one creature he ever wanted. Me.

"Gotta admire you sometimes, red, you take a whipping like a man," he laughed, sucking on his cigarette again as my shoulders shuddered with the lasting tremors of the torture. "It's not every day I meet a woman who I can say that about. Shame you're a scrawny little runt."

I reached for the old T-shirt they'd given me to wear, but before I could pull it on to cover my naked body, Duke spoke.

"Leave that. Stand up."

I swallowed the rising lump in my throat, digging deep for my grit and getting to my feet in nothing but the ugly, flesh-coloured panties they gave me to wear. Quentin sometimes gave me fresh ones, he didn't like seeing me naked. It disturbed him, or so he liked to whisper in my ear.

I winced as pain spread across my spine, getting to my feet on shaking legs and turning to Duke. Blood ran hot and thick along my spine, spilling over my ass and down the backs of my legs. It was the closest thing to warm

I'd been in a long time.

"Yeah," he tutted as he surveyed me. "Flat chested, that's your problem." He pointed at me with the cigarette. "Nothing for a man to grab onto. I like my women with more meat."

Any woman who catches your eye is an unfortunate fucking soul. *Of course, I didn't actually say that. Saying that meant I could say other things. And if he knew my tongue could give him the words he needed, he wouldn't be done with me today.*

Smoke snaked around me in the air and Duke smoothed his moustache down as he pushed out of the tattered wicker chair, his immense height sending a flicker of fear through me as he approached. But I kept my chin high, staring up at him. He hated that. He always wanted me bowing, didn't like when I looked at him too much while he hurt me. So I made a point of doing so as much as possible.

He blew a cloud of smoke into my face and I fought the urge to cough. "I'll have Orville come patch you up, hm?"

I shuddered, biting down on my tongue.

"Or you can say the word no and I'll do it myself, how about that?" he offered. "Just one little word, red." He leaned closer, his bushy brows arching as he stared at me, waiting for me to crack. "Say it."

The word was on my tongue, burning with the need to be said. Orville was the last person of all The Five who I wanted to tend my wounds. Even Farley who would be the roughest. They had to do it in case my cuts and lashes got infected. A dead hostage couldn't give them the information they wanted. But sometimes I wished they wouldn't fix me up so well, let an inch of rot get into me and steal me away from them for good. The world wasn't that kind though.

"Alright then," *he purred, grabbing my hand, turning it over and stubbing his cigarette out in my palm. I gritted my teeth and suppressed the scream in my throat as the burning cherry ate into my flesh. He tossed the stub on the ground with a hmph like he was disappointed then strode to the door,*

47

knocking twice and it wrenched open a second later.

I hooked up the T-shirt from the floor, a gasp of agony escaping me at the wounds on my back. I clutched it to my chest then climbed onto the table at the side of the room, lying face down on it like I knew I'd be ordered to. I didn't realise I was crying until I tasted the tears on my lips.

The door shut as another pair of footsteps entered the room. A ripple of disgust ran through to my core as Orville rested his hand at the base of my spine. His fingers were soft, like he never put them to hard work. He wasn't a man for heavy tools. He liked little knives and pins and anything delicate enough to be held in his girlish hands.

"Hey, little bird," he chuckled. "He cut you up real good today, huh? Don't worry, Orville's here to look after you." His fingers trailed over my flesh in that way that said he wanted to possess me, but Duke would hang him if he crossed that line. That was their one, golden rule. Nothing sexual. And I couldn't understand it. Though I was endlessly glad for it. But what possible reason did they have to protect me from that while subjecting me to everything else their vindictive little minds could come up with?

I scented alcohol in the air and a moment later Orville pressed a soaked cloth to my back. I bit my tongue, clamped my eyes shut as my flesh seared with the fires of hell and waited for it to be over.

CHAPTER SIX

This couch was not designed to be slept on. Especially not by a man of my size.

I grunted a curse as I shuffled about, trying to make the lumpy cushions squish into something vaguely comfortable while trying to ignore the crick in my neck from having my head awkwardly perched on the arm of the damn thing for half the night. The half where I'd managed to get some sleep. Though it had been fitful at best.

At least with Tyson on guard by the door I wasn't worried about Duke and his band of merry fuckers creeping up on the cabin again while we slept. That dog was worth his weight in gold for that reason alone. The fact that he was my one true and loyal friend only made him more valuable to me.

I cracked my eyes open and took in the sliver of pale blue light creeping beneath the curtains. It was probably still earlier than I would have usually gotten up, but there was no way I was going to be able to get comfortable enough to doze off again in my current position. I pushed myself upright with a groan, stretching my arms above my head and trying to force some of the ache from my muscles as my spine realigned itself.

I shoved my fingers through my overgrown, black hair and ran a palm down my face as I tried to think over my options.

Winter was still curled on the floor by the wall, the blanket she'd taken from the bed wrapped around her thin frame.

I crossed the room towards her silently, years of practice running jobs for the Calabresis helping keep my movements silent as I padded towards her on bare feet. There were more times than I could count where I'd needed to sneak up on someone and kill them quietly without making a scene. Though I'd had plenty of practice in making men scream too. The reason why I'd been the best was knowing which kind of death suited which mark. Of course, now I was questioning all of those deaths at my hands. I'd been sent to kill those men by a liar. A man I'd trusted and who had turned out to have the blackest heart of all…

I scrubbed a hand over my face to banish those thoughts and focused on Winter laying on the floor.

She looked so small as I stood over her. Almost childlike in her fragility, though I'd seen that unbreakable spirit shining fiercely in her eyes, so I knew well enough that she wasn't actually weak. To have survived what she had there was no way she could have been. In fact, I was starting to suspect she was one of the strongest people I'd ever met. And that just made my hunger to spill blood on her behalf even stronger.

I knew now who had done this to her. And better than that, I knew where they lived.

Duke and his men commandeered the huge gold mines, filled with heat lamps and fuck knows what else they needed to grow as much of the drug as their superiors wanted and more. The Cutters gang who lived over there to work the farm were a bunch of thugs and miscreants. I'd had run-ins with them from time to time, particularly when I'd first arrived here. They assumed I was an easy target as I was alone. But they were wrong in that respect. In fact, being alone only made me more deadly. Because I didn't have a single thing left in the world that I could lose.

My gut twisted uncomfortably at that thought as my mind rested on the three brothers I'd never known I had. They'd said they wanted to know me. But too much had happened, too much had been lost to me. I didn't even know myself anymore, so how could I expect them to get to know me? For my whole life I'd believed they were my sworn enemies. The Romeros- scum of the earth. But now...

I gave myself an internal slap for letting my mind turn to that. I had more pressing issues at hand.

There was a girl in my home who needed my help. And that definition encompassed several things. Firstly, she needed shelter, food, water – all things I could easily provide. But she also needed security, protection, safeguarding against those filthy motherfuckers who'd hurt her. And I was willing to offer her that too. Though maybe not in the way she expected. I meant to pay those men back in blood for what they'd done to her.

I wanted to memorise every scar on her flesh and deliver it back to them tenfold. I wanted to carve them limb from limb with a butcher's blade and bathe my fury in their blood. I wanted to make them beg and plead and scream for mercy just as she no doubt had done. And then I wanted to make them just as silent as her. More so. Permanently.

But I couldn't easily do that right now. Not while she was still here. I couldn't hike around the mountain with murderous intentions and leave her here unprotected. What if they split their numbers and some of them came here while I was gone? What if I died while trying to destroy them? They'd figure out why I'd come and they'd be back here for her in a heartbeat. And it would all be worth nothing if they ever got their hands on her again.

I was staring. I knew it. But it was hard to stop. Looking at Winter felt like looking at a wild creature who was preparing to bolt. Even in sleep, her brow was pinched and her hands tightened into fists.

I hated seeing her on the floor like that. Curled in on herself protectively as she tried to escape her demons and hide in the solace granted by sleep.

Her hair was deepest red and shone like wet blood where it pooled around her. With those big, green eyes of hers, she looked like something straight out of a fairy tale. Though I guessed her story wasn't all princes and happily ever afters. I doubted she'd ever fully heal from the scars those men had placed on her. And I didn't mean the physical kind.

My gaze slid to my rifle which was still propped by the door and I was flooded with the desire to pick it up and go hunting. But my quarry wouldn't be wild animals with innocence in their souls. No, I'd be hunting barbaric men with evil in their hearts and I'd soon be painting the snow red with their blood.

A soft whimper drew my attention back to the girl at my feet and I watched as she shivered, tugging the blanket closer to her.

It was always chilly in here in the mornings. The fire had burned low and I hadn't had the chance to stir it yet and add some new logs. The freezing winter air liked to creep into the place as it fought to reclaim it.

She shivered again and I huffed out a breath. It was ridiculous. The bed was right there, covered in blankets and far more comfortable than the goddamn floor.

I crouched down beside her and gently reached out, meaning to pull her into my arms and transfer her to the bed.

The moment my hand brushed against her spine, her eyes snapped open and she whirled on me. The flash of silver warned me about the knife just in time for me to smack her hand aside and send it skittering away across the floor.

But I was a fool to think she was done there.

She lunged at me, teeth bared, hands curled into claws as her wild eyes took me in, looming over her where she slept.

She collided with my chest and my position balanced on my toes as I crouched down meant that she managed to take me out.

My ass hit the floor and I was sure my back would have too if she'd weighed more than a hundred pounds. As it was, I found a wildcat in my lap and her teeth sinking into my shoulder as she punched me.

"It's just me!" I grunted as I was forced to try and wrestle her off of me.

Her fists collided with my ribs before her fingernails tore across my chest as I scrambled to contain her.

I cursed as she continued to attack me and somehow managed to catch her wrists in my grasp. But I'd been a fucking idiot to believe that would be enough to stop her. Her knee rammed into my balls and I really did swear as I lunged to my feet, dragging her upright in my arms, kicking and thrashing before tossing her down on the bed.

"It's me!" I yelled, holding up a hand to ward her off as she got up onto her knees, those wide eyes filled with terror as she looked up at me, standing over her on my bed, like she thought I meant to follow her onto it.

She scrambled backwards until her ass hit the headboard and then yanked on the hem of the shirt she was wearing like she wanted it to cover more of her body, hide her bare legs away from me.

"Fuck," I hissed, realising what a goddamn idiot I'd been to approach her while she was sleeping like that. She was staring up at me like I was some fucking monster come to hurt her and the way she was tugging that shirt down made me feel sick. "I'm sorry," I said thickly, backing away from her to prove that I really didn't mean her any harm. "You were shivering on the floor, I thought if I moved you to the bed you'd be warmer, be able sleep better. That's all. I wasn't trying to hurt you. You have my word that I'll *never* hurt you."

Winter chewed on her bottom lip, her green eyes falling to my bare chest and I looked down too, taking in the rows of fingernail marks and the bloody imprint of her teeth on my shoulder.

I sighed heavily and skirted the bed, picking up the knife as I crossed the room and tossing it down on the coffee table as I fought off the urge to massage my battered balls. I was willing to bet that if I started cupping my junk I'd just be giving her even more reasons to freak out.

Tyson was dancing from foot to foot, wagging his tail excitedly as he circled me like he thought that was one of the best things he'd ever seen.

"What happened to protecting your master, traitor?" I murmured to him as I unbolted the door and let him outside to relieve himself. Snow was still falling steadily from the sky, but it wasn't quite as heavy as last night.

He shot out quickly, cocking his leg against a tree ahead and painting the snow yellow before charging right back inside again. I arched an eyebrow at him as he tracked snowy footprints into the cabin, wondering why he hadn't gone for his morning mooch around the woods. The big dog ignored me entirely, shooting past me and leaping up onto the bed.

Winter squealed in surprise as he ran a wet tongue right up the centre of her face before promptly turning in a circle and curling up right beside her.

I watched them for a long moment, waiting as Winter's posture relaxed slowly and her hand fell down to caress the soft fur around Tyson's ears and his tail thumped against the mattress.

I bit my tongue on telling him to get his furry ass out of my bed and kicked my boots on before heading out into the cold to grab some more logs for the fire.

The sky was palest blue overhead and my breath rose in a cloud of fog before me as the frozen air instantly wrapped itself around my skin tighter than any blanket could ever manage. I piled some chopped logs into my arms from the store I kept cut and stacked in the woodshed around the side of the cabin and hurried back inside before I ended up with frostbite on my damn nipples.

I could feel her eyes on me as I kicked my boots off again and headed over to the fire, dropping the logs before it. I spent a little longer than necessary stirring up the embers and stacking the fresh logs on it to get the fire blazing again, giving Winter the chance to get over the shock of being woken by a fucking idiot and scared shitless for good measure.

Once it was done, I padded over to the kitchenette and set the coffee pot up before slicing some bread to make toast and whipping up a batch of scrambled eggs.

I was pretty sure Winter's eyes never left me but I kept my focus on the food, letting her find her own way back to trusting me. At least a little.

When the food was ready, I placed it all on the small table to the side of the room, clearing a stack of books off of the second chair so that she could sit too before taking my own seat.

"C'mon, baby doll, you've gotta be hungry," I said casually, pointing to the seat opposite me.

She leapt up and raced across the room, her eyes on the plate of food with a ravenous set to her gaze. A moment before she tried to snatch the plate away, I realised what she was going to do and grabbed the other side of it.

Her eyes widened with hurt and betrayal, like she thought this was some trick and I didn't mean to let her eat it at all. A knot of rage tightened in my gut at the thought of that.

"It's all yours," I promised her. "I was just hoping you'd sit with me to eat it." I pointed at the chair again and her gaze dropped to it like the idea of that was a totally foreign concept.

I released my hold on the plate and she lifted it into her arms, clutching it close to her chest and eyeing me cautiously. I decided to leave it at that and picked up my knife and fork, cutting into my own toast and filling my mouth with a low sigh of pleasure as I started chewing. I kept my gaze on my food and had to suppress a smirk as she slowly lowered herself into the chair like I'd asked.

She placed her plate down so close to her that it hung over the edge of the table and I glanced up at her just as she grabbed a handful of creamy eggs and stuffed it into her mouth.

After that first mouthful, she gave up any pretence of being civilised and stuffed food into her mouth fist after fist, demolishing her meal as I fought the urge to laugh. Although if I really thought about it, it wasn't fucking funny. This girl had been too hungry for too fucking long. She ate with wild abandon in a way that said she wasn't used to regular meals and feared when she'd get another.

I'd only made it half way through my own meal when she finished, licking the actual plate to chase down any last crumbs.

I chuckled beneath my breath and she shot me a death glare over the plate she was licking.

"No need to try and kill me with your eyes, baby doll. Do you want some more?" I pushed my plate towards her and she actually gasped.

I gave her an encouraging nod, leaning back in my chair to watch as she fell on that too. It was totally fucked up. But there was also something wildly captivating about my little savage girl which had my gaze fixed on her irrevocably.

I ran a hand over my beard, wondering exactly how long it had been since I'd seen a woman. And Winter wasn't just any woman, even with that hollowness to her cheeks and the cutting sharp lines of her bones pressing through her skin, her beauty shone bright enough to light up the whole fucking forest.

She would have been impossible to miss in a crowded room, but here, in the middle of nowhere, she was like a motherfucking siren luring me in.

I cleared my throat as I got to my feet, trying to banish the thoughts from my mind before they took hold. Winter had just escaped from a bunch of assholes, the last thing she needed was a piece of shit like me staring at her like some horny teenager who'd never seen a beautiful girl before.

I pulled the fridge open and grabbed a shiny green apple from it before placing it on the table for her to have once she'd finished inhaling my breakfast. When I'd seen that the winter storms were coming last week, I'd headed down the mountain to the nearest town and made sure my cupboards were well stocked with plenty of food to get me through at least another month up here, though at the rate she was eating, I might have to go again sooner than I'd thought. Not that I had any complaints about that. That girl needed to eat and I planned on letting her gorge herself to her heart's content. Assuming she wanted to stay here.

I started washing up but fell still as Winter released a moan of satisfaction which had a shiver running down my spine. I glanced her way and found her chewing into the apple with more moans of pleasure as the juice slid down her chin.

I bit my tongue and dragged my gaze away, ignoring my body's reactions to those noises as much as I could and focusing on cleaning up.

By the time I turned back to look at her, she was devouring the core, pips and all and I didn't have the heart to tell her to leave that bit, because the look in her eyes said she was in heaven.

"You can help yourself to food anytime you want it, baby doll," I murmured, my heart twisting at the idea of her being hungry for so long. She seriously needed to gain back some weight and I wanted her to feel welcome to eat whenever she was hungry.

Her eyes widened like she didn't know how seriously to take that offer and I smiled at her as I waved at the fridge vaguely.

It took her three whole seconds before her restraint snapped and she leapt to her feet, hurrying towards the fridge and grabbing another apple from its depths.

"I'm going to go out and check the perimeter," I said slowly as she leaned back against the fridge door and started eating with her eyes closed in pleasure. "You can just make yourself at home while I'm out. Tyson will stay to keep you company and I won't be far away. If anything happens, I'll hear him barking and come running. Okay?"

She just gave me the wide eyes and I offered her a smile which was probably hidden within the depths of my beard before making a move to go and grab some clothes from the closet. But before I could pass her, she reached out and caught my hand, laying her half eaten apple down on the work surface as I fell still.

Her gaze slid to the bloody marks she'd left on my chest and a deep frown furrowed her brow as she reached out to touch my stomach. I watched her as she painted a word on my flesh, trying to ignore the way my skin heated at her touch as she spelled out the word *sorry*.

"Not your fault, baby doll," I assured her. "I'm the one who should be sorry for trying to touch you while you slept. I have enough knowledge of what you've been through to understand that I shouldn't have done that."

She stared up at me in surprise, like me apologising was some alien concept to her and I tried to pull away but her fingers tightened around mine as she painted more words on my flesh. I had to concentrate to grasp what she was saying but as she touched me, every fibre of my being seemed to be focused on that point of contact and it was probably easier than it should have been to decipher her words.

Don't leave me here alone.

"You want to come with me?"

She looked up at me and nodded, those green eyes guarded as she bit into her lip, like she expected me to start laying out commands and tell her she had to stay here. But I was willing to bet she'd had way too many of those in her life and I wanted her to make her own choices.

"Alright…" I looked her over slowly, standing there in my shirt and socks with her pale legs bare. "But it's cold out there. I can lend you clothes…"

She nodded eagerly and I snorted a laugh as I led her over to my closet. After a few moments of staring at the options, it was pretty clear that there wasn't going to be anything that came even close to fitting her so I pulled out a pair of jeans and offered them to her.

She didn't seem to have an issue with how big they were and pulled them on, but I couldn't help but laugh as a foot of material trailed beyond her feet and the waistband gaped so wide that it was clear they had zero chance of staying up.

I reached into the closet again and retrieved a leather belt for her, trying to ignore the way she flinched at the sight of it and pressing it into her hands. She bit down on her lip and started trying to thread it through the loops in the jeans, but her fingers were trembling too much to get it through.

"Did they use a belt to hurt you?" I murmured as I laid my hands over hers to still them and she flinched again as she looked up at me, nodding just enough to confirm it.

"When I get my hands on them, I'll tie them down and whip them bloody for you," I growled. "I won't stop until all the flesh is stripped from their backs and they're lying in a puddle of their own blood and then I'll cut their fucking heads off and hand them to you in a goddamn gift basket."

She inhaled sharply and for a moment I thought I'd frightened her, but that wasn't what was blazing in her green eyes. No, what I found there was a pure and unending thirst for vengeance. She was excited by my words, and something about that made my heart pound.

I took over with the belt, winding my arms around her as I slid it through the loops, sharing breath with her as the action drew us close together and my fingertips skimmed along her flesh in a feather light touch. Her back arched in response, a shaky breath escaping her parted lips as I slid the belt through the buckle and cinched it tight.

Her hands landed on my biceps as I tugged a little too hard and knocked her off balance and she left them there as I forced a new hole through the belt to secure the jeans.

Her gaze took me captive as we hesitated in that space and I slowly sank to my knees before her, reaching down to roll the ankles of the jeans up for her while she just watched me like she didn't know what to expect. I hated that simple kindness confused her, that suspicion still swirled within her eyes no matter how often I proved that she had nothing to fear from me.

Once her jeans were turned up, I gave her two more thick pairs of socks to help hold the boots on her feet then gave her a sweater which swamped her, a thick, waterproof jacket, a hat and a pair of warm gloves.

By the time she had it all on, she was totally submerged in the layers of fabric and I couldn't help but chuckle at her all bundled up like that, but at least I knew she'd be warm.

I tossed my own clothes on next and we were soon heading out into the snowy forest.

Tyson bounded off into the trees the moment we descended the wooden steps and Winter kept close to my side as I led the way to the perimeter I liked to walk to see if anyone had come close to my home while I slept.

There was a clear trail in the snow which had been left by Duke and his men and I kept my rifle over my shoulder, ready in case we happened to see them again. But everything was so silent out here that there wasn't much chance of that happening without us realising they were coming. Tyson would give me plenty of warning and if they were unlucky enough to come across me out here in the trees, I was confident in my ability with my rifle to know I could take them all down before they got anywhere near us.

We started walking the wide circle around the cabin and every now and then I'd stop and check tracks left by animals in the snow, making sure there was no signs of anyone else being up in this forest aside from Duke and his men.

As we got close to completing our circuit, Winter caught my elbow and tugged so that I could look at her. She pointed all around us, then at me and then tugged off one of her gloves followed by one of mine so that she could paint a word onto the palm of my hand.

Why?

"Because there could be people looking for me," I replied, realising she wanted to know what I was doing out here.

Who?

"They're…" I didn't even know how to begin to explain who the Romeros were to me. Enemies. Friends. Brothers… "People from my life before this. I found out a lot of things I used to believe were lies and I just… needed to get away. To clear my head."

Bad?

"I used to think they were the worst men in the whole world," I said, knowing what she meant. "But now…I don't even know what to think of them."

Winter nodded slowly like that made sense even though I'd hardly told her anything, her gaze scanning the forest as Tyson raced between the trees before tracing another word on my palm.

Alone. She punctuated that by pointing at me and I gave her a sad smile.

"Yeah, baby doll. I'm all alone."

A soft smile touched her lips and she traced more letters on my palm.

Me too.

"Not anymore, Winter," I said, meaning to reassure her and realising that I was talking about myself too. "We have each other now."

Not that I had any idea how long that would be true for. But these storms weren't going away for at least another week and there wasn't much point thinking beyond then. One day at a time. That was all I ever worked with now.

The look she gave me in response to that was hard to decipher but as I turned to head back towards the cabin, she didn't return my glove to me. Instead she wrapped her small fingers between mine and kept hold of my hand as we walked. And as I watched her from the corner of my eyes, I had to wonder exactly what was going through her mind. Because if I'd even considered letting someone else come and stay with me in my cabin before she'd shown up, the idea would have repulsed me. But now that she was here, I had absolutely no desire for her to leave. She needed time to recover from what had happened to her and the one thing I had in abundance out here was time. So if she wanted to spend some of it with me then I was happy to let her. And who knew, maybe I'd be glad of the company too.

Frankie

CHAPTER SEVEN

I leaned back in my chair suppressing a yawn as I waited for Rocco's maid to finish laying out coffee for all of us and looked around the big room we were in. The wooden furniture was dark and decedent, the walls painted a forest green colour and the carpets patterned with some floral arrangement. They'd only moved in here a month ago but it just didn't really feel like their place yet.

"When are you getting this place decorated?" I asked casually. "I feel like some old business man in a smoking parlour sitting in here."

"That's because it is a fucking smoking parlour, stronzo," Rocco replied, rolling his eyes. "And we've had some more pressing shit to do recently than worry about colour schemes."

"You mean Sloan hasn't decided on what she wants yet," Enzo taunted. "So you haven't been able to get the decorators in."

"Happy wife, happy life." Rocco shrugged, pushing a hand through his curling black hair so that it was swept out of his eyes.

"Never thought I'd see the day when the great Rocco Romero got so pussy whipped," Enzo replied with a smirk, casually scratching at some new ink he'd gotten on his neck. The two sparrows circled each other in a way that seemed aggressive to me but which he claimed was them playing together. Then again, Enzo's games always ended in violence so I guessed the two things were the same to him.

"I'm not whipped, stronzo, I've just got more important things to do with my time aside from worrying about decorating the new house. If it bothers you that much then you can get fucked."

"I intend to," Enzo replied. "There's this hot new bartender down at Paulo's and I'm planning on spending the weekend breaking her in."

"I heard she's tied to Lucien," I said casually, inspecting my nails even though they were spotless. "So you'll have a fight on your hands if you want her." Lucien was a big bastardo with a mean temper and a possessive nature. Enzo could take him, but he might lose a few teeth in his efforts.

"That's half the fun," Enzo replied with a smirk. He seriously liked to think of himself as the most twisted Romero brother, but maybe he should have taken a closer look at me before he went awarding himself any trophies.

The maid set down a large plate of cupcakes in the centre of the table before bowing her head and hurrying from the room. The brightly coloured icing seemed like an odd choice for a bunch of gangsters to discuss our latest business dealings over, but as Roccos's wife Sloan was the one who made them, none of us were going to complain. That girl had a way with food which had my mouth watering at the mere sight of anything she created.

Rocco reached out and grabbed a cherry cupcake from the plate, smirking at it like it held some secret before taking a big bite.

I snared a strawberry one for myself and took a long sip of my coffee as I looked at the empty chair at our table for four. That was why we were here after all. Sure, we had other business to discuss, but the reason all three of us attended these meetings so diligently was because we were desperately trying to figure out where the hell our brother Angelo had run off to. Which was easier said than done because he'd basically disappeared into thin air the moment he'd checked himself out of hospital almost an entire year ago.

"Any progress?" Rocco asked with little hope to his tone. He knew if there had been, I'd have called before this meeting to update him.

"The guy is like a fucking ghost," I growled. And I really was pissed about it. I was the one who got called when a problem needed fixing, when a witness needed dealing with or an informant tried to run. I was damn good at flushing people out of hiding. I'd never taken this long to find someone. But I guessed I'd never gone up against a Romero before either. And even if Nicoli didn't want to face his real identity, he was going to have to at some point. He was our brother. There was no escaping that truth.

Rocco swiped a palm over his face with a growl of frustration. "I have some guys over in-"

His cellphone started ringing loudly and I arched an eyebrow at him as he lifted it from his pocket. He didn't even bother to apologise as he answered the call and I exchanged a look with Enzo. If either of us had done that he'd be losing his shit. He was such a fucking hypocrite sometimes.

"Principessa, I told you, I have to-" Rocco leaned back in his chair as he listened to whatever Sloan had to say. Enzo mimed striking a whip and I smirked into my coffee. "Right. But I-" He pushed a hand through his hair and started nodding as he shoved his chair back and got to his feet. "Yeah, I'll come and try. But I'm really not sure if…yeah, yeah, okay." He held a single finger up to us as he headed for the door and didn't even bother to offer any further explanation before leaving the room.

"Merda, if I ever get soft over a woman like that, I want you to swear to beat the shit out of me until I forget all about her," Enzo said, snorting a laugh as he started on his third cupcake. He'd shrugged out of his leather jacket and his shirt sleeves were pushed back to reveal the sleeves of ink which coated his skin. That coupled with the topknot he'd tied his hair in and the stubble lining his jaw made it hard to see the resemblance between us most of the time, but if you looked closely, it was there. All of us had Papa's strong features and dark hair. I just preferred to be more clean cut than he did in my appearance.

"Not much chance of that," I agreed. "For you to fall in love with a woman, it would require you having a heart. And I've never seen any evidence of that."

Enzo grinned like that was the biggest compliment he'd ever gotten and I turned the conversation to some business dealings we had with the Devil Hearts MC club. It was nothing major, but those MC stronzos liked to try and push the boundaries of our power from time to time. It seemed to be way too easy for them to forget who ran Sinners Bay. And if they starting disrespecting the Romeros again, we might have to get a bit creative in sending them a message or two written in body parts. We were all for different factions of criminals to thrive in our city, but they had to remember who their kings were. And if that took a bit of friendly bloodshed to keep them in line from time to time then so be it.

The door finally reopened and Rocco strolled in again. I barked a laugh and Enzo straight up started howling with amusement and he strode into the room shirtless but with a swathe of baby pink material wrapped all around him.

"What the fuck is that?" I demanded and Rocco offered up his most murderous look which looked utterly fucking ridiculous when coupled with all of that pink fabric crisscrossing his body.

"It's a baby sling, stronzo," he snapped, pointing at the lump in the centre of his chest just as a little murmur came from within it.

I was on my feet in seconds, grinning as I moved to peer in at my niece where she was nestled against his chest, her little eyes peering back at me as she snuggled close to her papa.

"I still have no fucking idea how an ugly stronzo like you created something so perfect," I said, reaching out to snag a tiny hand with my finger. River took hold of it and squeezed, my smile widening as I looked at her.

"She clearly takes after her mamma," Enzo said, his shoulder butting up against mine as he reached out to brush his fingertips over the soft, dark hair which coated her tiny head.

River just blinked at us, making one of those cute baby noises as she pressed her cheek to Rocco's bare chest, looking so fucking happy it made me grin.

"Let's hope so," Rocco agreed. "But I'm supposed to be getting her asleep, so the two of you can back off now."

"What's the matter, will Sloan have your balls if you don't stick to the sleep schedule?" Enzo teased.

"Where is Sloan anyway?" I asked.

"Trying to get some rest," Rocco said. "And River wasn't playing ball so I tagged in. Shall we get back to our discussion? What did I miss?"

"We were just discussing the possibility of sending the Devil Hearts a message," I explained as I retrieved my finger and took my seat again.

"I think we should take someone important and chop him up into pieces then deliver them all back to them in gift boxes," Enzo added with a dark smile as the others sat back down too.

Rocco clapped his hands over River's ears and narrowed his eyes. "No murder talk in front of the bambina."

"Don't bring her to our weekly murder chats then," Enzo replied, rolling his eyes.

"I'm good with the gift box plan," I said, ignoring the way Rocco continued to shield River's ears as if a three month old had any idea what we were saying. "It's clear and to the point."

"Fine," Rocco agreed. "Just run the target by me before going ahead. I've got a couple of informants in their ranks and don't want you butchering one by accident."

"Okay," Enzo agreed, his eyes lighting with the idea of carrying out that task. Sometimes I had to worry about him. I mean, sure, we were all technically murderers with a shit ton of blood on our hands, but that was just the profession we were in. But with Enzo, I got the impression he enjoyed it a little *too* much sometimes. Though he only ever killed nasty motherfuckers so I guessed it didn't matter.

"So, back to Angelo," I said. "I'm running out of leads to follow. Is there any chance Sloan came up with any new nuggets of info that might give me a fresh one?" I was hoping that as she was the only one in our family who had any history with him and actually knew him, she might have been able to come up with some angle I hadn't thought of yet.

"Nothing," Rocco said, his hands sliding from River's ears and circling his palm against her back instead as we moved onto a safer topic of conversation.

"He clearly doesn't want to be found," Enzo huffed. "But he's gotta come back eventually. Maybe we should just wait him out."

"No," Rocco snapped. "This famiglia has been broken for too long. It's time he came home and joined his brothers again."

"Then my only other idea is to capture a Calabresi and see if I can make them talk. Maybe he's been using his connections to them to help him disappear. I don't know where else to look," I said, though I had serious doubts that Nicoli would have gone to them after everything that had happened, but it wasn't like he had any other contacts.

"I'm always down for carving up a Calabresi," Enzo grinned and Rocco placed his hands back over River's ears with a scowl.

"Fine. Follow those leads you've still got and if they come up blank then take a Calabresi. I'll ask Sloan who he was close to and let you know who's a good bet," Rocco agreed.

Our conversation turned away from our lost brother as we went over various other business dealings which needed to be taken care of. Enzo was buying a new club to set up as a front for a gambling ring and I'd been working on securing a hotel chain for us to launder our dirty money through. Rocco had been more focused on his family recently and neither I nor Enzo had any desire to pull him away from them any more than necessary. Even Papa had been totally won over by River's arrival in our lives and it was really something to see the mean old bastardo melt over his granddaughter the way he did. He'd even gotten over Sloan's Calabresi heritage for the sake of her and that was something I'd been pretty sure would never happen.

Eventually, after River had fallen asleep against Rocco's chest and our conversation trailed to things aside from business, we finished up our meeting and Enzo and I prepared to leave.

"Can I take one of these with me?" I asked, snagging one of the cupcakes which were still left on the table. "I've got a girl chained to my bed who's probably going to need the sugar rush if I want her to be able to keep up with me while I fuck her. I didn't realise I'd be out this long."

Enzo laughed loudly and Rocco shook his head like I was the funniest fucker he knew before calling out for a maid to bag a few of the cupcakes up for me.

I got the feeling they didn't believe me, but then they never did. I was the sweet brother, the pretty boy, the nice one. Or at least I was outside of the bedroom, I guessed.

But I liked my girls just like I liked my liquor. Full of fire and really fucking expensive. I was pretty sure the girl had told me her name was Cherry or some bullshit like that. But whatever. The point was that she'd managed to take everything I had to give her last night and had been more than keen to take my money for round two today. And if she managed to impress me when I got back then I was pretty sure I'd keep her for the rest of the week. I'd never kept one longer than that. At that point they usually started asking questions about me. And if I wanted a girl to talk to as well as fuck then I wouldn't be paying out for high end hookers, I'd just get myself a girlfriend. So one week of raw, dirty sex was where I drew the line. And I was pretty sure Cherry would last until Sunday if her stamina from last night was anything to go by. So I had five more days of fun with her waiting for me while I tried to figure out this shit with Angelo. If I was still pulling up blanks after that, I guessed it would be time for Calabresi heads to roll. Not that I'd ever had much problem with that.

CHAPTER EIGHT

I raided the refrigerator while Nicoli slept in the early hours of the morning, as quiet as a mouse. He gave me whatever I wanted, but food had been so scarce for me that I'd taken to hiding the odd bits around the place in case he ever refused me it. A few granola bars under the bed and some pretzels in the bathroom cupboard made me feel more certain I wasn't going to go hungry any time soon.

I nibbled on a carrot while intermittently taking bites out of a slice of montery jack cheese. When my belly was satisfied, I closed the fridge and moved around, checking the kitchen knives were still where I'd left them. One under the mattress, one under the cushion of an armchair and one behind the toilet. Satisfied, I moved to the curtain and Tyson lifted his head, watching me as I peeked outside. The sun was just cresting the mountain and my lips parted as colours splashed through the sky. Yellow, amber, gold, the most beautiful mix of light I'd ever seen. The snow glinted like starlight and I watched in awe as the frozen world came to life.

Nicoli grunted in his sleep and I dropped the curtain, turning to him and biting on my thumb as I surveyed his face. I wished I could see beneath that beard. I wondered if his jaw was square or round. I wondered if his features would look as fearsome as they did like this. I wondered if there were more scars lurking beneath it all.

His brow was creased with lines and I sensed his sleep wasn't restful as his fingers twitched and balled. I wouldn't wake him though. It wasn't my business to disturb him from his nightmares. But I couldn't help but wonder what haunted this wild man.

I started moving around the room, checking his drawers and hunting for clues about my saviour's life beyond this place. What had brought him up this mountain in the first place? Why did he want to be so alone? Was he searching for something out here, or escaping something? Or did he just like the solitude and I was intruding on every inch of it?

As I pulled open a drawer in the cabinet near the fireplace, I found a stack of old newspaper articles inside. I frowned as I took them out and read the headlines.

Sloan Calabresi kidnapped from her wedding in suspected Romero gang attack.

Guiseppe Calabresi's body washed up in Sinner's Bay.

Calabresi/Romero child born between feuding families.

Was Nicoli involved with these people? I tried to rack my brain for any of this sounding familiar, but only came up with the usual hollow echo where my memories should have been. That echo gave me the awful, gut-crushing feeling of knowing I'd been someone once, and yet the entirety of that person had been carved out of me like seeds from a pumpkin. Now I was just a jar full of hate and vengeance waiting for redemption.

"What the fuck are you doing?" Nicoli's voice made me lurch around in alarm and the articles dropped from my hand, scattering across the floor. He was standing, his blanket pooled at his feet, his chest bare and his expression furious.

He took a step forward and my heart lurched with panic. I dove for the armchair, shoving my hand under the cushion and snatching the knife into my grip. Strong hands pulled me upright and a shriek of fright escaped me as I tried to whirl around, the blade angled to slice into flesh. He caught my wrist with his free hand, squeezing as he snarled in my ear and I gasped as his fingers hit a pressure point and the knife dropped from my hand, my grip going slack.

I mouthed a curse as I thrashed against him and he twisted me around in his hold, pushing me down into the seat and placing his hands down on the arms of the chair to cage me in.

My lip quivered as he loomed over me and I screwed up my eyes as I waited for his hand to strike me or his fingers to slide around my throat. His heavy breaths made my hair flutter and I cracked an eye when he didn't punish me, wondering why he was hesitating.

"You think I'd hit you?" he asked, a note of disgust in his tone.

I nodded. Obviously I thought that. It was what men did when they were angry.

"*Winter*," he growled the name he'd christened me with and my toes scrunched up in a way I was somehow sure I hadn't experienced before. "I would never and *will never* lay a hand on you, do you understand?"

I frowned, shaking my head. Because I didn't understand. I'd made him mad, therefore I would be punished. That was the only world I knew. There was a twisted sort of security in that. But he was standing there refusing me one of the few things that made sense in my small, dark existence. It was like standing in a lightless tunnel between two expanses of fog, the way forward as unclear as the way back.

Nicoli reached out and brushed the rough pad of his thumb across my cheek. "Don't fear me, baby doll. My wrath is for the sons of bitches who hurt you. Not you. Never you."

Heat invaded my body and my breath caught as I stared up at this animal of a man. I nodded, my heart rate beginning to settle as I accepted his words. I could see the sincerity of them blazing in his eyes and it set a fire burning in my soul.

He moved away, gathering up the articles and placing them back in the drawer, pushing it shut.

"You can read, I assume?" he tossed at me and I considered lying, but couldn't see the point in it. He already knew that I could write.

I nodded and he sighed, pushing his hand into his hair then grabbing the neck of his guitar where it stood beside the fireplace and heading to the front door. He pulled on a coat, kicked on his boots then unlocked the door and walked outside. It shut with a bang and I jolted in my seat. He was angry, fuming. And I wasn't sure what to do about it if he wasn't going to sate his rage on my flesh. Not that I wanted him to. I understood the concept of a good person, I just had no memory of one. So I guessed this was my first taste. And yet I sensed this side of him was something rare. Because if the The Five turned on Nicoli, I imagined they would soon regret it. I knew monsters, and Nicoli was one. Just a different breed.

Tyson got up from his bed, padding over to me and resting his chin on my knee. I reached out and tentatively brushed my fingers over his head and his eyes drooped like he liked that. His fur was silky soft and the longer I stroked him, the more he looked like a goofy cartoon character, his eyes half rolling back into his head.

You're not so scary.

When I stopped petting him he whined gently, looking to the door and I sighed as I pushed myself out of my seat.

I don't know if it'll work, wolf, but I'll try.

I padded across the floor and picked up a pen and paper which was laying on the coffee table, scribbling a note on it before walking to the front door. I paused as the sound of Nicoli's guitar carried to me and I rested my shoulder to the wood, closing my eyes as I listened. He hummed along with the dark tune, his voice a gravelly rumble that sent a shiver right through me. His song was raw and full of pain and it spoke to me in ways I'd never experienced.

"Drag me down, but my soul won't rest. Oh baby, the devil won't let me be blessed."

I pushed the door open, hoping he'd go on, but his fingers paused on the strings and he looked up at me like he was about to tell me off when his gaze fell on the note as I held it up for him to see. *Sorry.*

The air was freezing, immediately pinching my bare legs and making goosebumps rush across my skin. But its kiss was sweeter than the pain I'd endured below ground. I'd take this wild, winter world anytime over that.

Nicoli stood, his brow creasing deeply as he stared at me across the porch. "I'm sorry too. I didn't mean to frighten you."

I glanced down at the paper, wanting to write out another answer for him and he moved toward me, taking my hand and pulling me inside.

"Come on, you'll freeze out here." He shut the door and placed his guitar against the wall.

I guided his hand up in front of me, using my finger to paint words on his palm.

Sing more.

"You like my music?" he half laughed. "I'm a shitty musician at best. I sound like a man with a cut throat drowning in his own blood."

I tugged his hand, making him look at me and I pursed my lips sternly.

His brows arched in surprise as I lifted his hand again and wrote, *wrong.*

I wanted to say more than that, but there wasn't enough space on his skin and he seemed to realise that as he guided me over to the little table and chairs by the window and pointed to the notepad and pen I'd left there.

He pulled out a seat, releasing my hand and I moved to sit in the other one.

"I pulled it out for you," he said and my lips popped open in surprise.

I grabbed the pen and paper, writing out a reply. *Why?*

"Because that's what gentleman do," he replied, dropping into the seat and looking kind of pissed as he took his coat off.

You don't look like a gentleman.

He laughed low in the back of his throat. "I was once, if you believe that."

I don't.

He laughed again and a smile pulled at my mouth, drawing his gaze there.

He carved his hand through his long hair, holding it back from his face. "Can you see him clearer now, baby doll?"

A laugh tumbled from my throat, genuine and pure and something that hadn't left my body in such a long time.

"Oh fuck," he growled, releasing his grip on his hair so it fell around his face again. "Now I'm gonna want you to make that sound again, Winter."

Heat rose in my cheeks and I realised I was blushing. This was new. And I liked it a lot.

I wrote out a reply to him. *You'd better show me more of the gentleman beneath all of that hair then.*

He released a breath of laughter, sitting back in his seat. "I would, baby doll, but I'm about as good at doing my own hair as a fucking wildebeest. I'm used to professional barbers in another life, if you believe that. I wish to fuck I could do it myself, trust me."

My gaze roamed over his face and my fingers itched. *I could do it?*

He read my note with intrigue then shrugged. "It would be nice to get rid of this fucking mane." He pushed out of his seat, heading into the bathroom and returned a moment later with a roll-up barber kit with clippers, scissors and a comb inside.

Are you sure you trust me with those? I wrote, a smirk pulling at my mouth.

He released a throaty laugh. "I'm sure you can do a better job than me or Tyson would. Besides, I'm hardly trying to impress anyone up here barring the odd sexy as fuck snowflake." His eyes slid onto me, moving to my lips before he quickly looked away again.

I laughed, my whole chest lifting with the feeling and he growled in a way that made fire blossom up my spine. Not the hot poker kind for once. This type felt like a sweet form of torture.

He dropped into his seat and my gaze moved to his bare chest and the scars I desperately wanted to trace my fingers over. That was a language I understood better than English. Pain left marks on the heart, fractures along the soul. It moulded and shaped a person for better or for worse. It either built a fortress around your heart, or left you bloody and broken. Nicoli looked like he'd been forged by his pain. But there were always pieces which shattered along the way, and I could see those pieces as sharp as knives staring back at me from his eyes. I didn't have to be able to speak to share that I felt it too. When he looked at me, I sensed he recognised it in me as well.

I plugged the clippers in and laid them down beside him on the table. So far as I knew, I'd never done this before, yet the movements were familiar as my thumb grazed over the on switch and I sensed I could do it. I picked up the comb and scissors as I laid the clippers beside him on the table, wondering what he'd do if I ended up making him look like a yeti who'd been dragged under a lawn mower. It was weird that I knew what those things were and yet I had no idea of specific memories which could pinpoint their origin. It was like all my knowledge of the world had been injected into my head without context. In my cell, it had been intolerable. In this cabin, with Nicoli, it made me ache to be more than just a shell. I wanted to have something real beyond my time in captivity. Something that allowed cracks of sunlight to break through the dark and spill into the centre of my being. At least I was making new memories every day, ones that held no pain, no torture. And I found myself stashing each of them away for later. Because if I ended up back in my cell then at least I'd have something to think back on that wasn't bitter.

I ran the comb through his hair and his head tilted back a little as I continued to work out the snags. My fingers moved through the black curls, the lick of something so soft drawing me into a hypnosis as I worked. A low noise left him somewhere between a sigh and a groan and my heart pattered wildly at the sound. I dropped my hand, grazing my fingers over the hardened muscles of his shoulder and writing out a question. *You like it?*

He cleared his throat and I noticed his skin was pebbling with goosebumps where my hand laid on him. "It's just been a while since anyone's..." He shifted in his seat, clearly feeling awkward about the direction of that sentence.

I skated my thumb over his shoulder, admiring the way his tanned flesh was left with a white mark as I pressed down. No blood was drawn, no marks left. This was the way people were supposed to be touched. And he hadn't had anyone's hands on him in who knew how long. In the pit of my stomach, a knot tightened at the thought of that. I would have given anything to keep my body to myself back in my prison. I'd dreamed about a cage I could crawl into, built of iron, one that no one could ever get into. But Nicoli had built that cage in real life and it didn't look so good from the inside.

I started cutting his hair short ready for the clippers and I sensed we were both enjoying this small, but intoxicating contact. Maybe we weren't supposed to live life in cages of any kind...

"I didn't mean to get angry with you earlier, Winter," Nicoli spoke after a while and I frowned. "What you saw...those articles, it's just a part of my life that I'm trying to escape. I guess you can understand that better than most."

I remained quiet, but still curious. I didn't have any right to this man's nightmares. Quentin's words crept into my mind, and I shuddered at the memory of him whispering them against my ear. *What happens in the dark, stays in the dark.*

"I imagine you're pretty curious about me, baby doll. And I suppose it's better the devil you know than the one you don't..."

I brushed some cut hair from his shoulders, his neck visible now and damn he had a nice neck. All tanned skin, muscle and a freckle just behind his left ear which I wanted to trace my thumb over. I didn't think I'd ever appreciated a neck before. Except for the time I clawed at Farley's so badly while he held me down that he had four long gouges on it for days. But this

80

wasn't a neck I wanted to tear into, this was one I wanted to caress, kiss…

"Do the names Romero or Calabresi mean anything to you?" Nicoli asked.

I wrote *no* on the back of his perfect neck.

"Well, it's a long fucking story so I'll give you the abridged version. The Romeros and Calabresis are sworn enemies, two powerful lineages who fight to take control of Sinners Bay. Their families have been feuding for centuries and if you can believe it, I was once a Calabresi heir trained my whole life to take over as the head of the family."

My brows arched with interest as I picked up the clippers and started to run them up the back of his head, shortening his hair to tidy it up.

"I was…engaged," he revealed, his voice thick and my heart jerked at the word. I kept my hand steady on his hair though, ignoring the strange tugging in my chest. "Her name was – *is* – Sloan. But a Romero showed up on our wedding day and kidnapped her."

I halted the clippers, gripping his shoulder in surprise and he turned his head to look at me, giving me an expression that said he wasn't joking. *Woah.*

Is she okay? I wrote on his arm.

"Yeah, she is now," he said, a gravelly edge to his tone. His eyes darkened and he turned away again and my heart started twisting up like wire.

Nicoli continued on. "I hunted for her for a long time. Made it my life's mission. I'd worked my whole life to be a strong enough man enough to protect her, take over her family when her father stepped down and be the leader everyone so desperately wanted me to be. I tried to be that man, I tried to be the one who could fill the role. I gave every ounce of myself to it, even convinced myself I was in love with my wife-to-be because…well because if I wasn't in love then maybe I had to admit that our arranged marriage was just a big fucking farce that we were both partaking in to please everyone but ourselves. I mean, I didn't *not* love her, I just wasn't…"

In love? I offered.

"Yeah," he grunted. Silence fell and I finished cutting his hair, shaving it in shorter at the sides than at the top.

Then I moved around the table, setting the clippers down and climbing up to sit cross-legged in front of him to do his beard. I was pretty sure he smirked at me, but it was hard to tell beneath all that hair. Unfortunately for him, I was about to take away his mask so he could no longer hide.

I started trimming, my gaze fixing on my work as he went on with his story.

"I got her back eventually. But everything had changed. She'd fallen in love with a Romero," he half laughed at the ridiculousness of it and I looked up at him in surprise. "I guess she had her own desires, her own secrets. Just like I did."

I wet my lips then reached out, tracing a word across his chest. *Secrets?*

His eyes glinted darkly as he nodded and he lowered his voice as he spoke even though it was just us two and Tyson for miles around. "I never wanted that life, baby doll. Deep down, there was always something missing. My mask was welded onto my skin so tight that even I forgot that for a while."

What happened next? I wrote, grabbing the clippers and starting to shave in his beard.

"That was about the time when things went from shit to fucking catastrophic. Sloan's father found out about her affair with a Romero and he decided she was better off dead than in the arms of his enemy. So he tried to kill her – almost fucking did – but we got there in time."

We? I asked.

"Me and Rocco Romero, her kidnapper, lover. Now her fucking husband. But I didn't hang around to witness much of that. After I found out the truth, I left."

What truth?

"That my whole life had been a dirty fucking lie," he snarled so furiously that I sat back for a moment.

He reached out, resting a hand on my knee like he didn't want me to run, but I wasn't going to. Not this time. That anger in him was as sharp as my own. It stared back at me in his eyes like the barrel of a high calibre gun. And I wanted to see what happened when someone pulled the trigger.

"Sloan's father took me in as a boy, spun me some bullshit story about me being an orphan kid he'd taken mercy on. But fuck him. It turned out, I wasn't just any child. I was Angelo Romero. Rocco's brother, Frankie's, Enzo's. I'd been pitted against my own flesh and blood my whole life. The man I'd seen as a father figure, respected, loved, had murdered the Romeros' mother -*my* mother- in cold blood, stolen me away and raised me as his own in some twisted revenge plot against my real father. Martello Romero." His shoulders were shaking and I captured his chin as I placed the clippers down, forcing him to look up at me. His gaze bled into my own and I felt all the torture he'd been through. It was an entirely different kind to mine, but was still just as pure and as real as the type that drew blood.

He sighed, breaking my gaze. "So that's what I'm doing up here, baby doll. I'm trying to leave all that behind. Trying to stop the Romero brothers from finding me."

Why? I painted on his chest, the word almost coming to my lips with how much I wanted to ask it. He had a family hunting for him, didn't he want to be a part of that? If I knew I had a family looking for me, I would have dived into them with open arms. I'd wondered too many times what my mother and father looked like, if I had any siblings…if they missed me.

"They've been my enemies since before I can remember. I've killed members of their family, Winter. I've spilled the blood of my own people. I was Giuseppe Calabresi's weapon and knowing the truth can't take any of that back. All it means is that I know exactly what I've done. And now I have to live with that."

My heart broke for him.

You didn't know.

"Doesn't matter, Winter. There's no life for me in Sinners Bay anymore. I don't know who I am. I'm not a Calabresi and I can never be a Romero. And it doesn't matter if my true brothers would welcome me into their arms, because I could never look them in the eye without knowing the pain I'd delivered into their hearts. I didn't come up this mountain to hide, I came here to be lost. Because that's what I am, baby doll, in every sense of the word. And I don't plan on being found."

I found you, I wrote, a smile twitching at the corner of my mouth.

A low laugh escaped him. "Pretty sure my mutt sniffed *you* out."

I shook my head innocently, leaning back as I finished using the clippers on his beard so he had a layer of neat stubble and all of his beautiful face was revealed. He was even more handsome like this, the angles of his face hard and fierce. His mouth was a line of discontent, but as I surveyed him, it pulled up at both sides until his smile formed two crescent moons either side of it. Handsome didn't cut it, he was the sort of attractive you saw in movies. Hollywood would have taken him from me in a heartbeat if they found their way up this mountainside.

I grinned at him as I lowered my hand to write on his chest once more, my stomach flipping and flopping as he stared at me with an intensity that made me blush. *No, I found you under a mile of hair, mountain man. You're not lost anymore.*

CHAPTER NINE

Two weeks was a hell of a long time to spend cooped up in a small cabin with one person and as the days drew on, I found my attention fixed on my savage girl more often than it should have been. But it was almost impossible for me to tear my attention away from her when she was flourishing before my eyes. Three solid meals a day plus as many snacks as she wanted had done a lot to help take the edge off of that starved look she'd had. Her bones no longer pressed through her skin, and her wide eyes didn't look so sunken. I'd thought she was stunning before, but now that her cheeks had rounded out and I could no longer count her individual ribs when her shirt was off, I found myself addicted to studying her.

I'd managed to convince her to stop dropping her clothes in front of me without a thought and for the most part she kept herself covered now, but I was still helping tend to a few of the worse wounds she had. There was a particularly nasty gash on her back which kept opening up again whenever it seemed to get close to healing. Luckily I had some first aid supplies and I'd been applying cream as well as bandaging it for her and after she'd gotten over the initial fear of letting me tend to it, we were definitely making progress towards healing it for good.

Winter sat in front of me on the other chair from the dining table which she'd flipped around to straddle backwards while I worked. Goosebumps peppered her skin as I applied the antiseptic cream to her wound and carefully re-dressed it for her but as I finished, my fingers trailed across another scar beneath it. It was faint and almost white with age, but to the right of her spine, I could make out the outline of a grid with circles and crosses filling the spaces on it.

I released a long breath, an animalistic growl rumbling through my chest as I closed my eyes against that image, imagining the pain she must have been in as those fucking monsters did that to her.

"We need to get you out of here, Winter," I said in a low voice, my fingers still caressing that scar like it was the only thing keeping me from storming out of here right now and gutting every single one of them for what they'd done to her.

She stilled beneath my touch and I could sense the panic in her, the confusion, the fear.

"It's for your own good," I continued. "The storms are finally lessening and we'll be able to head down the mountain again soon. You need to get back to civilisation, people who really know how to help you deal with what happened to you."

I felt her hair brushing over my fingers where they were still pressed to her spine and I opened my eyes again to find her shaking her head, though she hadn't turned to face me.

"I know you're afraid, baby doll," I said, trying to rein in the anger in my voice before I ended up frightening her more. "But there's a whole world out there. You must have people looking for you. Family, parents, friends-"

She spun in the chair, knocking my hand from her flesh and tugging her shirt back down as her legs tangled with mine and she looked into my eyes with a fierce expression, first pointing at me and then back at herself.

"I don't understand," I murmured, though we both knew I did.

Her frown deepened and she jabbed her finger against my chest before pointing at herself again. My jaw hardened. I knew she was afraid, that she wanted to stay here with me in the cocoon of safety I'd built her. But it wasn't really safe here at all. We were only a few miles away from the men who'd held and tortured her. We were half way up a fucking mountain in the depths of winter and I was only one man. Though I hoped to prove that I'd still be more than enough to match those motherfuckers when the time came. Which it couldn't with her still here. I couldn't risk leaving her alone and I certainly wouldn't risk taking her with me when I went after them. And I needed to go after them soon. Every day that I put off the need in me to strike at them on Winter's behalf just added more rage and hatred to that which was filling my soul. The more I grew to care about Winter, the more I needed to see them punished for what they'd done to her. I dreamed of it, plotted it out, ached for the retribution which I was going to rain down on them. But not until I was sure she was safe.

"Winter," I said, my brow furrowing as I tried to fill my words with conviction. Because despite what I might have wanted in my fantasy version of some kind of life for the two of us here, it wasn't right for me to keep her like this. She still couldn't even talk so how the hell was she supposed to work through the shit she'd survived? She needed real help. From someone qualified. "I need you to be safe. I need to know that you're okay and being looked after. I need that so that I can go after those men who did this to you. I need to be able to hunt them down and butcher them for the things they've done without worrying that you're vulnerable while I'm doing it."

Her green eyes flared with emotion and I could see how much she hungered for their deaths in her gaze.

Winter reached out and caught my shirt, tugging on it so that it rode up over my chest, making my heart pound as I tried to figure out what she was doing.

Her palm landed flat against my flesh, right over my thundering heart and she stared at me like she was challenging me to deny it. But that wasn't going to make me change my mind. The way I felt about her was exactly why

I knew I needed to get her the fuck away from here.

She frowned like she could see that wasn't convincing me and caught my hand in her free one, pushing it between the open buttons at her neck until my hand was laying on her chest too, the thrashing rhythm of her heart calling to me like the sweetest of songs.

"It's not about that, baby doll," I said, knowing this was hurting her but saying it anyway. I understood that she felt safe with me and I wanted to protect her more fiercely than anything I think I'd ever wanted. But that was the point. She wasn't safe up here in the woods with me. She wasn't safe while those fucking animals who'd done this to her still drew breath. "It's about me making sure they never get near you again. It's about what's best for you in the long run."

She started shaking her head in fierce denial and a few tears slipped down her cheeks too.

I caught her face between my hands, drawing my palm away from her heart while she still kept hers pressed against mine.

"Don't cry," I breathed, hating that I was hurting her. I didn't want her to hurt any more than she was. I didn't want her feeling any kind of pain at my hand.

I swiped her tears away with my thumbs and she just looked at me like she was begging me not to send her away.

"It's for the best," I insisted and she jerked her head out of my grasp, anger flashing through her gaze as she reached out and drew a word across my chest with savage strokes of her finger which were damn near bruising.

LIAR.

She leapt out of the chair before me and ran across the room before diving into the bathroom and throwing the door shut behind her. The sound of the lock clicking into place echoed through my skull and I groaned as I leaned back in my chair, tilting my head back until I was looking up at the wooden panels of the ceiling.

I clawed my fingers through my hair and wondered if there was any other way for me to do right by her. But I knew in my heart that trying to keep her here was selfish. She'd had a life before she was kidnapped. She had a family out there somewhere desperate to find out that she was safe. And once she was with them, once she started to get her memories back, I was sure she'd realise that I'd been right to insist she go back too.

The next morning when we woke, we ate in tense silence as Winter refused to so much as look at me, but I wasn't going to be swayed. I understood her desire to stay here. Hell, I couldn't think of many worse things than waking up tomorrow morning and finding this damn cabin empty, of knowing that I was back to being alone in this world. Even after weeks of sleeping on the fucking couch and getting my spine all kinds of fucked up while she just stayed on the floor, I knew I'd prefer that over the comfort of reclaiming my bed.

But this wasn't about what I preferred. Or what I *wanted.* It was about doing the right thing. She needed to see doctors. She needed to find out if she had people missing her, have a chance to discover who she was before all of this. And most of all, she needed to be safe, away from the motherfuckers who had done this to her so that they never had a chance of getting close to her again.

And once she was gone and I knew for sure that she was safe, I'd have plenty to keep me occupied. Because these weeks spent with her had awoken more rage and bloodlust in me than I'd even realised I was capable of anymore. Even the thought of the vengeance I was planning to rain down on those sons of bitches had my heart pounding with exhilaration. They wouldn't know what hit them when I came for them. They wouldn't even see their death coming until it was too late. Not that I'd let them die quick. No, they'd earned themselves as much pain and suffering as I could inflict. In fact, maybe I'd set them in competition with each other. See which one of them could hold out the longest before the torture got too much and they escaped into death.

I took our empty plates and tossed them in the sink for later, trying not to go soft over the fact that it was the last time I'd be seeing two plates in there together like that for a while.

It was fucking ridiculous, to be this stuck on a girl who didn't even remember herself, who I'd had to name, who had no voice. Maybe I'd just been alone too damn long. Or maybe she really was something special and I was a fool for letting her go. But I was also well aware that I wasn't able to offer her much of anything stuck up here on this godforsaken mountain.

"Come on," I said, my voice breaking the silence as I moved to pull on a coat and my boots.

Winter did as I urged, wrapping up as well and tightening the too-large clothes around her slender frame.

"At least you'll be able to get hold of some clothes in your size once I get you back to civilisation," I teased, trying to cut the tension in the air.

Her gaze finally snapped up to meet mine, but the only thing I found there was hurt and betrayal.

The smile slid from my face like I'd been doused in ice cold water and I nodded as if I was agreeing with something she'd said. But I guessed all I was agreeing to was the fact that I was an asshole and confirming I wasn't going to change my mind on this.

I told Tyson to stay put as he lifted his head in excitement at the idea of heading out, but he couldn't come with us for this. I couldn't bring him all the way to town.

Winter reached out to pet his head and I turned away from the miserable expression on her face as she said goodbye to him in her own way.

It's for the best.

We headed out into the snow and I looked up at the blue sky for the first time in weeks. It had been pretty intense while it lasted, blizzard after blizzard causing the snow to pile up so much that I'd climbed up to knock it off of the roof of the cabin more than once. I'd once had a dream that the whole thing might cave in in the night and I'd be suffocated beneath it all and since then I'd had to make sure it didn't pile up too high. I'd been through too much shit in my life to die like that. I deserved to either live to a hundred and ten and go in my sleep or go out in spray of blood and a blaze of glory. So long as it wasn't some tragic accident then I was okay with whatever way my cards fell.

I missed the warmth of Winter's hand in mine as she failed to take it. Usually when we braved the weather to check around the cabin for signs of Duke and his men or the Romeros closing in on us, she'd do that. In fact, she seemed to be quite tactile naturally, seeking comfort in soft touches, leaning close to me whenever she could. I guessed after all she'd survived it made sense. She hadn't known anything gentle or caring in all the time she could remember. Though sometimes I wondered if there was more to it than that. But of course that was probably just my dick talking. The red haired beauty I'd found in the snow was the only woman I'd spent any real time with in a year. A whole fucking year with nothing, no looks, certainly no touches. And then suddenly this beauty was living in my space, sleeping beneath my roof, sharing my food. Of course I was going to have some pretty epic fantasies about what that might turn into. But I wasn't ever going to push anything like that with her. Not after what she'd been through. And now that she was leaving, those fantasies would definitely remain confined to my mind.

"I keep a snowmobile further down the mountain," I explained as we began our walk downhill. I preferred to keep it hidden away from the cabin so that I had an escape route ready at all times. Who knew when things might go to shit and blow up in my face. And knowing my luck, it was only a matter of time until they did.

The silence hung so thickly that I knew she wouldn't have been talking to me even if she had use of her voice.

We continued on for two more miles, carving a path through the thickest part of the forest to avoid the deepest snow as we descended. I hated that she was so angry with me. I hated that I was going to have to say goodbye to her

93

knowing that we were parting on bad terms.

"I know you hate me now," I began, wondering where I was even going with this. "But I really do believe that this is for the best. That this is the safest you can be and that in the long run you'll be glad, I-"

She punched me squarely in the bicep and I grunted as I turned to frown at her, but instead of anger at my words or more betrayal shining in her eyes, I found fear instead. She had a finger pressed to her lips and she cupped a hand to her ear, causing me to fall still and listen too.

At first there was nothing and then I caught it. The faintest buzz of snowmobiles chasing down the mountain from somewhere above us.

"Shit," I cursed as the sound of them drew closer.

We may have been in the forest here, but the trees were big enough that their trunks were spread apart. Couple that with the fact that I was wearing a royal blue jacket and Winter was wearing red and it was pretty clear that we were sitting ducks.

I looked around, hunting for somewhere to hide her as my heart pounded to a warning beat. There was only one group of people who lived up on this mountain aside from me. The same group who had been holding my girl captive.

I spotted a tree with thick leaves and branches just low enough for me to reach and grabbed Winter's hand as I heaved her towards it.

I reached the trunk and whirled her around to face me, looking into her green eyes which were wide with questions I didn't have time to decipher let alone answer.

"Stay hidden, baby doll," I murmured, catching her waist between my hands and lifting her off of her feet so that she could reach the branches above my head.

She did as directed and scrambled up, placing a boot on my shoulder to give her an extra boost before clambering onto the branch above us.

"Climb," I urged as I backed up, looking around as the sound of the snowmobiles drew ever closer.

She started moving up the tree, reaching for a higher branch and then another, but before she could get any higher, the snowmobiles appeared, speeding through the trees straight towards me. There were six of them in all, each ridden by a single asshole and stacked up with packages tied to the back of them.

I gazed between them as I pressed my back to one of the towering trunks, praying they'd just keep on going without taking much notice of me, but of course luck wasn't on my side.

Just as the lead rider drew level with me, he yelled out a greeting like we were old friends and whipped his machine around in a circle. The others followed his lead, churning up the snow all around us and thankfully managing to destroy the trail we'd left in the snow which would have led them to Winter's tree.

I shot a glance her way and could just see her there, gripping the trunk as she hid in the shadows, her eyes wide with fear as she looked back at me. I quickly looked away again, not wanting them to notice my attention fixing in her direction.

After a couple of minutes of them gunning their engines and kicking up snow all around me while I folded my arms and waited them out, the leader pulled up before me and cut his engine.

I slowly slipped my gloves off, wanting my hands free if I needed them to be.

The others halted their snowmobiles too and the silence that fell after the roar of the engines was thick with the promise of violence.

"Well, if it isn't our resident mountain man," he said in a voice low and rough, only just loud enough to be heard over the wind. The look in his steel grey eyes said he was used to people listening when he talked though. So I was guessing his low tones hadn't caused him too much trouble in the past.

"I didn't realise I was famous," I drawled, my gaze slowly sweeping over the assembled group.

They were all carrying rifles but they'd strapped them down among the

95

packages which were tied to the backs of their machines. It was hard to tell what other weapons they might be concealing beneath their winter coats, but the guy talking to me had a thigh holster with a hunting knife in it.

"There are all kinds of tales about the great mountain man over at our camp," the guy confirmed, pushing shaggy blonde hair out of his eyes as he assessed me. "They say you once killed a brown bear by choking him out-"

"I didn't kill him, just choked him long enough to put him to sleep, then got my ass out of there before he came back around," I deadpanned and a couple of the guys laughed while a couple looked wildly impressed. "I didn't catch your name," I added, my gaze firmly on the leader while I ignore the backup. Those five were easy pickings. There was always something about a man's eyes which told me whether or not I needed to watch out for them. And this guy looked like his soul was painted in blood and he enjoyed feasting on the hearts of virgins.

"Quentin," he said simply, his eyes narrowing like it pissed him off that I didn't know that already.

But I didn't make a habit out of learning the names of irrelevant pawns. Duke was the undisputed leader of his people so no one beneath him had ever drawn my attention. Until now.

I knew that name. My girl had written it down for me upon request. He was one of the ones who'd abused her. One of the ones whose death I'd already marked. I fought the urge to go for his throat as my heart began to pump with the desperate need for his demise.

"Where are you off to so early in the morning, mountain man?" Quentin asked, his gaze slipping around the trees like he was looking for something.

"Just going to get some more supplies in town while I can take advantage of the break in the weather," I replied, indicating the empty rucksack on my back. I slid it from my shoulders and dropped it to the ground casually, wanting to be able to move fast when I needed to.

"Is that so?" Quentin asked curiously, kicking his leg over the snowmobile and getting off of it as he stalked towards me.

"Yeah," I replied, offering him a scowl which promised him that I wasn't intimidated.

He was a big guy, built with broad shoulders and the kind of height which probably topped most men. But not me. I was six foot four. There weren't many fuckers who could meet my eye on a level, I generally ended up looking down on everyone. Quentin included.

"So then, why were there *two* sets of tracks leading into this clearing?" He smiled like he had me, his gaze sliding away from me and across the trees which surrounded us.

Something dark and hungry writhed beneath my skin as his grey eyes found the tree where I'd hidden my savage girl, a cruel smile twisting his lips as he spotted her hiding amongst the branches.

"Hello, poppet," he murmured, eyes ravenous as his tongue darted out to wet his lips.

My blood pounded and rage tore through me at that casual greeting as the thirst for vengeance in me grew to a roaring demand. I didn't care that I was outnumbered or that I was about to start a war of real proportions, his death called to me like the sweetest song and I wasn't going to leave here without giving in to that desire.

Before another word could escape him, I lunged forward, throwing a punch into his face that made my knuckles ring and a scream of agony tear from his lips. My other hand closed around the hilt of his knife before he could even stagger away from me. I ripped it from the sheath before swinging it across his gut as hard as I could, tearing through the thick material of his coat and driving it deep into his flesh as he howled with pain.

He dropped before me, screaming in agony, blood staining the snow a vivid crimson as he scrambled to place his hands on the wound and hold back the death he could feel coming for him.

The other men were shouting, leaping from their snowmobiles and scrambling to get their guns free of their bindings, but I doubted any of them would be fast enough to manage that.

These assholes had dismissed me as some lost soul living in a cabin in the woods and ignored me as much as possible. Maybe they should have looked a little closer and they might have realised they had a monster in their midst. But they'd let their arrogance and superiority complexes lull them into a sense of security which they really had no right to feel.

I may have been a sleeping beast for the time they'd known me up until now. But they'd woken me up with what they'd done to Winter. And I was starving for the taste of their blood.

So with Quentin's screams of agony colouring the world around us, I charged towards my next target with the knife in my fist and his death already written. I just hoped that at least one of them might put up more of a challenge before I was done.

CHAPTER TEN

The snow was coloured red. As red as poppies and cherries and the darkest of sunsets in hell which promised pain and bloodshed. Nicoli moved between Quentin's men like a demon, slashing and cutting and slicing. Their screams rang in my ears like the most beautiful orchestra, every crescendo meeting a dramatic, violent end as hearts ceased to beat.

I watched it all with my own heart leaping and my breaths crashing from my lungs. My nails were digging deep into the trunk of the tree as I crouched on a branch, bracing myself so I didn't fall. Nicoli was showing me the most monstrous part of his soul as he stabbed and punched and fought and bones shattered beneath his powerful blows. It was the most beautiful thing I'd ever seen.

Quentin was crawling towards his snowmobile, carving a path in the snow and leaving a trail of blood behind him. My upper lip peeled back and darkness seeped through my body, every muscle and fibre filled with hatred for this vile creature. I had one task in this world and one only: to kill The Five. And while Quentin's heart still beat, I wouldn't be satisfied.

I climbed down from the tree, dropping from branch to branch until I was low enough to jump into the snow. Then I stalked toward him, pulling the hat off that Nicoli had given me to wear so my crimson hair tumbled around me in the wind as I stuffed it in my pocket. Quentin looked up as I made it in front him, his mouth stained red and his eyes alight with fear. I crouched down, life flooding my veins and filling me with euphoria.

"Now, poppet," he whispered and I cocked my head to one side as he reached for my shoe, clinging onto it with shaking fingers. "Help out your old friend, Quentin. I'll look after you. It won't be like before."

Nicoli's heavy boot suddenly stamped down on his wrist and made him wail, forcing his hand off of my foot. His shadow fell over us, encasing me and Quentin. It seemed ten times wider and larger than Nicoli's body, like darkness was seeping from his flesh, unable to remain contained within it. His face and hands were splattered with blood and there was a fierceness in his eyes that drew me to him like a magnet.

He twisted the blade around between his fingers, holding out the hilt to me with an offering in his eyes. "You don't have to, baby doll. But if you want it, he's all yours."

I smiled, a grim and twisted piece of me needing this more than I needed air in my lungs. I took the blade, finding it heavy and warm in my palm. I peered down at Quentin as he stared up at me, pale faced and full of hate as he realised I wasn't going to be swayed to help him. He scrambled backwards, clutching his gut as he tried to stand, but Nicoli booted him in the side, sending him crashing back into the snow.

I crawled after him like a hungry tiger as he tried to get away, but he was slow and I was fast. I was the one with the knife now, I was the predator hunting her prey. I was free of my cage and my captors had better run, run, run for their lives or me and my wild man were going to flay and gut and sever until a river of blood painted this whole mountain red.

Quentin started whimpering and the sound made me smile harder before I leapt forward and straddled his back.

"Please, poppet!" he screamed and I grinned like the devil. I'd made the whisperer scream. And I was going to hear it a thousand times more before I finished this. I may have been small, but the power of hate was as strong as Thor's hammer. And it took no effort at all to slam the blade into his shoulder. His screams echoed across the mountain as I fell into a frenzy, losing myself to the bloodlust, the need to rip this man to pieces for what he'd done to me as I drove the blade into him over and over.

He started flailing and I sensed Nicoli drawing closer, ready to step in if Quentin got free. But he wouldn't, I had him at my mercy like he'd had me at his so many times. I thought of the knives he'd sliced into my skin, the time he'd pressed an iron to the backs of each of my thighs, or when he'd pumped some noxious gas into my cell until I'd nearly choked.

I grabbed a fistful of his unruly blonde hair and yanked hard to force his head backwards.

"*Please*," he rasped. "I'm sorry for hurting you, it was my job. I can't be blam-"

I slashed the hunting knife across his throat and blood splashed out into the snow. He thrashed for a minute longer and I watched and waited and yearned for his death.

He thought his crimes would stay hidden in shadow, he'd been wrong. And now he was finding that out in his final, painful moment on earth.

He jerked and fell still and I released his hair, letting him slump forward in the snow. I rose to my feet, my body trembling with adrenaline and I turned to Nicoli behind me, his eyes lit with awe.

Snow was falling, though I hadn't noticed when it had begun, the flurry growing and thickening as it twisted around him in the air. He looked like a reaper amongst the fluffy white flakes, a bringer of death upon my demons.

As I stared at him, I felt my voice loosening for a moment, the box in my chest starting to crack open. A fire built at the base of my throat, because I didn't want to hide my voice from him right now. And I shut my eyes, focusing as I dragged up the words from my belly that I needed to give him so deeply.

"Thank you," I said on a heavy breath, opening my eyes and finding Nicoli with a stunned look on his features.

"Your voice," he growled. "Fuck, say something else."

I parted my lips again, but my voice betrayed me once more, burying itself and refusing to come out. My heart twisted with pain at knowing I couldn't give Nicoli more than that. He deserved *so* much more. He'd killed with wild abandon just for me. He'd offered me Quentin on a plate. I growled in frustration and he reached forward to tuck a lock of hair behind my ear.

"It's okay." His eyes moved to the snowmobiles as he gave up on me saying another word. "We'd better make this seem like a raid on those packages, baby doll."

A heavy breath left me as I gave up too, looking to whatever these men had been transporting with a frown.

"It's cannabis," Nicoli answered my questioning look and I couldn't say I was surprised.

He started untethering a package from the back of the closest machine and I hurried to untie one of the others. We soon had all the packages unloaded and Nicoli led the way to an old abandoned mine shaft hidden in the trees close by that he said Tyson had chased a rabbit down once.

We tossed them down into the dark, one by one where they tumbled out of sight.

By the time we were done, my hands were frozen to the bone and my sleeves were soaked.

I looked to Nicoli as we arrived back at the snowmobiles and the bodies of the men he'd killed, his face pinched in thought. He was coated in the blood of my enemies, had bathed in it for me, had made them his enemies too. No one had ever done so much for me. It was overwhelming and with my head still spinning in the aftermath of my kill, I strode toward him with a reckless need driving me forward. It was a base desire, one I had to act on or I'd regret it forever. It burned up through my core and set a fire blazing along my flesh.

A blush was spreading everywhere, adrenaline licked the insides of my veins like liquid nitrogen. I was ablaze, hungry, *free*. But before I made it to him with the wild intentions my mind had conjured, he moved towards the nearest snowmobile and swung his leg over it.

"We need to lay a false trail and cover those tracks to the mine," he said firmly. "If you'd rather, I can take you back to the cabin first so you can-"

I strode towards him fiercely and his words fell dead on his lips as I climbed onto the back of the snowmobile and wrapped my arms around his waist. No way was I leaving him. I was with him in this no matter what.

He started the engine, taking off down the mountain at high speed. The snow eased as we headed lower and lower and eventually I could see where it disappeared altogether. Beyond the muddy ground ahead was a track that wound down through the trees towards a road in the distance. I gripped Nicoli tighter, the idea of leaving this mountain making me uncomfortable.

Not until they're all dead. And even then…what's really out there for me anymore?

Nicoli turned the snowmobile sharply and we started climbing the mountain again, towards the bodies. When we reached them, he circled back around, churning up the snow and covering our footsteps which led to the mine shaft then he drove down the hill once more as he continued to lay the tracks like several snowmobiles had come this way. By the time he'd circled the site three more times and we were approaching the bodies once more, my fingers were growing numb against his coat. I balled them up and flexed them as he drove into the trees beyond the bloody site which was now half covered in snow, trying to bring life back into them.

Nicoli stopped the snowmobile under the cover of the trees, taking my hands and pushing them up the bottom of his jacket where the heat of his body reached me.

He looked over his shoulder as my teeth started chattering, a frown knitting his brows together. "We'd better get back to the cabin. We can't get off the mountain today. Not covered in blood and frozen to the bone. I'll get you heated up soon, baby doll. Just hang in there."

I hugged him tight in answer and he chuckled low in his throat.

Before he started the engine again, a shout went up somewhere behind us in the trees.

My blood turned as icily cold as the wind around me and Nicoli stilled. He slid off of the snowmobile, pressing a finger to his lips as he glanced at me then strode back the way we'd come, pulling a hunting knife from his belt.

I shivered as I waited, cold, hard dread running deep into my veins.

I gazed after him through the trees and a moment later he came jogging back, gesturing for me to get off the snowmobile.

I obeyed quickly and he pushed it into the shadow between two tall trees, grabbing a fallen pine branch and using it to cover the tracks that led up to it.

Then he snatched my hand, pulling me into a run. "There's too many of them and they're armed to the teeth," he whispered to me and I was too terrified to give him any kind of response as we fled.

He led me to a rocky ledge and gave me a boot up before hauling himself up behind me. The snow had slipped from the sheer ridge of rock and we carefully picked our way along it, circling back towards his cabin without leaving any tracks in the snow that could be used to trace us.

Despite his larger strides, I kept pace, the fear of what lay behind us driving me on.

"I will fucking find you!" Farley's voice roared so loud that birds took off in the trees all around us. My heart juddered and terror snared me, dragging me down, taking away that sense of freedom I'd dared to feel just a moment ago.

I remembered his fists pounding into my body, the way his large hands had wrapped around my throat, the way his breath had tasted on my mouth as he watched up close. Ash and death and all things bad.

No, he's coming for me, he's going to take me back. He'll make me bleed and break. He won't stop this time. He won't stop!

I pulled my hand free of Nicoli's, scrambling over the rocks and dropping to the ground behind a tree, burying my face in my hands, clawing at my hair as I drowned in the knowledge that he was coming.

He's close, too close. It's too late.

"*Winter,*" Nicoli hissed, his hands closing over mine where they were locked in my hair. "Look at me, baby doll. I'm right here. Just look at me."

My breaths were becoming ragged and a vice was closing around my heart. I couldn't look up, I couldn't do anything. I was going to die. My heart was beating too fast, Farley was too near. And if he was near, that meant the others were too.

"They can't be far, the blood's still fresh," Farley barked and it was in the same furious tone he'd used against me. Every strike punctuated with a word that was intended to hurt deeper than his fists ever could. *Worthless. Empty. Voiceless. Nothing.*

A gunshot split the air apart and I curled tighter in on myself just as Nicoli threw himself over me protectively.

I rested my hands on his chest, hunting for bare skin and soon found his throat, painting a frantic word against it. *Run.*

I couldn't let him be found here with me, they'd kill him. And they'd do it slow and excruciatingly. I couldn't allow it. Couldn't *bear* it.

"You run with me or I'm carrying you. So which will it be, Winter?" he growled as he captured my chin, pulling so I was forced to look up. I met his eyes and a breath snagged in my throat as I found strength there in the depths of them. I didn't have to die. Not with him at my side. And I wasn't going to slow him down by making him carry me.

I nodded, the shaking of my limbs beginning to ease.

He pulled me up and suddenly we were running again, racing into the shadows between the thickest patch of trees where the snowmobiles wouldn't be able to follow even if they found a way around the rocks we'd climbed. The dark was my friend for once, surrounding us and giving us cover.

"The snowmobile tracks lead down the mountain!" a man cried and Farley roared a command to follow the trail we'd laid.

The growl of their snowmobiles moved away and the claws around my heart began to ease. I hated how much power The Five held over me, even though another one was dead. There were only three of them left, but I knew I'd never truly be free until they had all paid with their lives. I was starving for more blood, I wanted to wet my hands in the heat of it and watch as my demons left this world.

We sped up the hill, keeping to the trees and finally reached the edge of them, spilling out and tearing towards the waiting cabin. It looked like a haven and the moment we made it inside, I felt my shackles cracking and my heart hit a rhythm I didn't know. It felt like relief, but more than that. I was happy. Elated. We'd made it. They would be hunting for the culprits for weeks, but they'd never find them. And Quentin was dead. *Dead dead dead!*

A laugh left me as I pulled off the large jacket I wore, my skin burning hot. There was more life coursing through me now than there had been during my entire time with The Five. It was ecstasy in its purest form.

Nicoli shed his own coat, shaking his head at me with a playful expression. "You sure know how to make a guy worry."

I smiled guiltily, biting down on my thumb as I gave him an innocent look, but his features turned serious.

"They'll all meet their end, baby doll. Mark my words. You don't have to fear going back to them. I won't allow it." His jaw pulsed with his hate for those men and heat spread between my thighs as I took in the speckles of blood on his cheeks and wondered why this angel had been sent to me. Maybe someone had answered my prayers at last. He was the exact kind of dark creature I needed to defeat them, the weapon I'd longed for.

I pulled Nicoli's check shirt off and tossed it on the floor, leaving me in the tank top that was too long and the jeans that were too large. From the way Nicoli was looking at me though, I could have been in a ball gown fit for a queen.

His eyes roamed over my face and the wayward strands of my hair. "There is beauty in the snowfall, in the way the light breaks through the trees at dawn…there's even beauty in death, in the end of the world, the brevity of everything we will ever experience, the passing into nothing. But I've never seen beauty like you." He took a step closer and my lips parted as his words settled over my heart and made it squeeze and ache. "It's not even the way you look that captivates me most, it's the way you embody all those kinds of beauty. You are snowfall, and light at dawn, you are death and brevity and life and eternity. It bewitches me." He reached out as if to touch my cheek, then dropped his arm, seeming to think better of it. "I'll be your warrior, Winter. Because you need vengeance and I need redemption. But it's more than that. I'm under some spell when it comes to you. And I am perfectly okay with that."

He moved to turn away and my heart twisted, not wanting him to leave. I lunged forward and caught his hand, placing it on my cheek where he'd intended to put it and his eyes widened in surprise. I turned my face into his palm, placing a kiss against it, the gesture more powerful than words could ever be even if I'd had them to give.

His throat bobbed and he remained still, his thumb grazing my cheek as a low noise rumbled through his chest.

I pushed his hand aside and moved into the arc of his body, reaching up to wrap my arms around his neck and tracing the edges of his hairline. He didn't push me away and I smiled wolfishly as I tip-toed up and followed my instincts as I touched my mouth to his. He stilled, letting me take the lead as I pressed my body flush to his, his powerful muscles flexing beneath his shirt. My fingers roamed into his hair and my heart begged for more. So I traced that very word on the back of his neck. *More.*

His arms closed around me and I opened my lips in an invitation as my eyes fluttered shut. He clutched me tighter and a growl escaped him as his tongue met mine and my entire body arched against him. I lost myself to the movements of his mouth, kissing him back as hungrily as he kissed me. My pulse pounded everywhere in my body. I was in utopia, being held by a man who'd pledged himself as my warrior. He was the only person in the entire world who'd offered me kindness, but it was more than that, as his teeth grazed my bottom lip and a deep, unknown shiver ran down the length of my spine, I knew he was all I could ever have dreamed of for myself. Maybe I was still back in my cell, my mind conjuring the sweetest of fantasies, offering me my heart's greatest desire to escape the hell of my real world.

Whether that was true or not, I wanted all he had to give and I wanted to give all I had in return. But even as I thought it, I stepped back and broke the electric contact between us.

I was breathing too heavily as my heart began to sink and I turned my gaze to my feet. This was real. And as wonderful a reality as it was, that didn't mean it was going to last. I had nothing to offer him. I was just a shell. A girl with no name, a girl with secrets even she didn't know. I was never going to be enough for Nicoli. Because my body was a desert. And it was far too barren a place for love to grow.

Frankie

CHAPTER ELEVEN

I took the long route through the bay, chasing the water's edge and enjoying the view from the comfort of my Maserati GranTurismo while knowing that Aunt Clarissa was going to be pissed by the time I made it to her estate. I just found it hard to care a whole lot. I knew that I was drawing the short straw by being put on whatever job she had going on. Papa was pissed at me over the whole Devil Hearts escapade, but really, I blamed Enzo for that shit show. The mark I'd selected was perfectly good. And if I'd just been allowed to kill him cleanly like I wanted to, then none of this would have been an issue. But of course Enzo wanted his screams heard across the docks before he died. He wanted every biker in Sinners Bay to know what happened when you stepped out of line. And in true Enzo fashion, he hadn't considered the fact that those assholes only had six brain cells between all five hundred of them so a few of them had taken it upon themselves to launch a damn rescue mission. Which effectively equated to partially starting a war right down by the water over some lowlife stronzo who I would have just executed and forgotten.

Twelve of them had turned up, guns blazing, threats flying. It had taken us by surprise and the two of us had come damn close to being overwhelmed at one point. Of course, we never did things the dumb way and I'd had more than enough men close by to pen them in from behind. Couple that with the assault rifle I'd brought in case of emergencies and we'd found ourselves with not one, but twelve dead MC stronzos. And to top it all off, our original mark had fucking run off and escaped while the fight went down.

Papa had lost his damn mind, claiming we were going to have to eliminate the whole Devil Hearts club before a real war broke out, but luckily their Pres had seen the light. He at least had a bit of sense about him and had realised that the Romeros would fucking obliterate them if we had to. He'd offered up his apologies, sworn he had nothing to do with the botched rescue attempt, had stripped the dead men of their patches so that they'd be shamed in death and had even offered us up our original mark already dead with his head in a box. As far as apologies went, it was pretty convincing. He'd assured us that he knew full well who ran Sinners Bay, and we'd brokered peace once more. All in all, a pretty satisfactory ending to the whole mess, but of course, Papa was still pissed. And of course, both Enzo and I would have to pay a punishment for it. I wasn't sure what his was yet, but sending me to fucking Clarissa for a job was definitely mine.

Eventually, I turned away from the sea, taking the mountain road up and away from the coast where the houses were bigger, the security tighter. Clarissa's house was down a private road and had a guy positioned by the front gate.

I slowed the car and looked out at him, offering a level stare without bothering to lower my window and let the freezing winter air inside.

He murmured some kind of greeting, ducking his head respectfully and entering the code to open the gate. It swung wide and I drove in, aiming for the heavy doors which fronted the house and parking up right before the steps leading up to them.

I released a weighted sigh, painting on a smile like I was glad to see my aunt before throwing the door open and hurrying up the steps.

My breath fogged around me and I shivered a little in my tailored suit, but it seemed a bit pointless to pull on a jacket for the thirty second walk to the house.

The bell echoed inside the building as I waited and after a few moments, a serving girl opened the door for me.

She looked me in the eye and pulled the door wide to admit me, offering a formal greeting as I not so subtly checked her out. She was new or I definitely hadn't given her a proper look before if she wasn't because the girl was hot. I offered her a flirtatious smile and I could have sworn she rolled her eyes as she turned away from me, directing me to follow her as I stepped into the warm embrace of the central heating. *Interesting.*

My designer shoes clacked across the hardwood floors as I trailed the girl, dipping my hands into my pants pockets as I glanced around at the opulently decorated space. There were more than a few photographs of Clarissa's dead son Guido hanging in frames on the walls and I tried to ignore the repulsion I felt at seeing his smarmy face. The day that stronzo had been killed was a damn good day. Of course, Clarissa had no idea that I'd been involved in his death. Or that Rocco's wife had been the one to do it before he helped her burn the body. No, she believed the idiota had fallen down the stairs and broken his neck. And if that gave her comfort then that was fine by me, so long as she wasn't harbouring any great plans for revenge, she could think whatever she liked and mourn the memory of that monster to her heart's content.

The girl led me to the conservatory at the back of the house where the view looked out over the frozen gardens and Clarissa sat drinking a cup of coffee. Her dark hair was pulled up into a severe bun and her features were pinched with irritation as she cut a glance my way.

"Nice of you to join me, Frankie," she said, her tone hard as her gaze moved to the grandfather clock to my right.

I cut it a glance too, smirking as I realised I was almost an hour late. "Sorry, dear aunt," I said teasingly. "I got a bit caught up this morning. You know how it is."

Her gaze narrowed further, sensing the lie in my tone and she was right.

I'd woken late, worked out for longer than usual and stopped for breakfast in my favourite restaurant before taking the long route to get here. I was late because I didn't care to respect her schedule and that was really just a nod at the family politics which always hung between us.

My father was the undisputed head of the family and Rocco was his second as far and me and Enzo were concerned, though our oldest brother always stayed firm with us so that really meant the three of us were on a level. He didn't pull rank often and he always listened to what we had to say. So the whole hierarchy was pretty clear to me. But as Papa's only sibling, Clarissa seemed to think she at least matched if not out-ranked Rocco and she definitely believed she was above me in the pecking order. The fact that I didn't agree caused more than a little tension between us and I had no doubt she was crowing with fucking delight at the thought of setting me some task today. Hence my late arrival. It wouldn't do for her to believe she actually held power over me.

Sometimes I wished Papa would just set her straight, but I think he enjoyed watching us all battle it out for dominance beneath him.

I pulled out the chair opposite her, tossing a request for my own coffee at the serving girl before she could scurry away. She looked like she wanted to refuse my casual demand and I arched an eyebrow at her in surprise as she glanced at my aunt for confirmation and Clarissa gave a firm, slightly pissed off, nod to confirm my command.

"So, to what do I owe the pleasure of this invitation?" I asked, giving her my winning smile as I reclined in my chair like I owned the fucking world, spreading my knees wide and slinging an arm over the back of it.

"I have an issue that I need help with," she said calmly, brushing at her skirt as if there were crumbs on it. "A consignment of product has been stolen from me and my dealers will be low on stock until I can recover it."

I released a long whistle, failing to hide my smirk at that news. "How did that fuck up happen?"

"I have my own men dealing with the situation, I don't need your assistance with that. I'm asking for you to broker a deal with the Santiago Cartel to make up the slack," she said irritably, not answering my question.

"Fine," I replied. I had contacts in the cartel and even though I didn't really like the way they ran their businesses, I could easily make those arrangements. "They won't be cheap though," I added.

"I'm aware. But it's worth it to ensure the buyers don't go looking elsewhere while we fix this situation."

"What happened then? How did someone manage to steal from you?" I asked, my amusement clear in my tone which only served to piss her off more. But this was fucking brilliant. Papa would be pissed as all hell with her over this and if I helped fix the problem then it was only for the better.

Clarissa bristled, but she had no good reason to hide the information from me so she pulled her iPad across the table and opened up a series of images on it before handing them to me.

I took it and perused them carefully. There were seven men lying dead in the snow, blood all around them and their faces marked with agony. There was something about the wounds I could see that had my eyebrow raising. Though with their winter coats it was hard to inspect everything clearly, there was definitely something about them that seemed…professional.

"How many men ambushed them?" I asked as I continued to cycle through the photographs, eyeing the snowmobiles with blood splattered over the paintwork.

Clarissa huffed in irritation. "We think…*one,*" she admitted like that knowledge was painful. And I guessed it was pretty embarrassing to admit one man had defeated seven of hers so easily. "Some attempts had been made to cover up the evidence, but it's hard to do that thoroughly in the snow. And there were boot prints, though the storms had blown in to cover a lot of them."

"Well, colour me impressed," I murmured, continuing to scroll through the images. "Sounds like the kind of man we want on our payroll."

"He'll be dead by dawn," she hissed. "There's a mountain man living up there and we're pretty sure it was him."

"A mountain man?" I laughed as I looked up at her. "Like a yeti?"

"No," she snapped. "Like a crazed man who lives alone up in the mountains. He hasn't caused us any issues before now but if it really was him who did this then he wrote his own fate. Even if it wasn't, I'd prefer that mountain to be clear of anyone but *my* people. Men I can trust.

"Well, it is pretty embarrassing if a single man managed to steal a whole consignment from you," I said, smirking down at the images as I flicked onto the final one. "*Merda...*" The last guy hadn't just been executed, he'd been mutilated. Stabbed so many times I couldn't count the wounds. There was so much blood all around his corpse that I couldn't even see the snow beneath him. "Are you sure it was about the drugs? Because this shit looks personal."

I handed the iPad back to Clarissa and she clucked her tongue as she looked down at the photograph. "It looks *amateur* to me," she said dismissively and she was right about that, which didn't marry up to the other corpses at all.

I didn't think she had one killer here. She had two. And whoever had done that had felt every single swing of that blade with a hatred so pure that it had been cutting them open too. That was the real reason for this hit. Not stealing drugs. Which meant the pro had helped orchestrate the whole thing purely to give this killer the chance to take out this guy.

"Who was he?" I asked, pointing at the corpse.

"Quentin Renny. One of my most trusted men up there. His death won't go unpunished. Anyway, that's not your concern. How quickly can you arrange for the cartel to make up this shortfall?" Clarissa asked, locking her iPad and clearly moving on from the part of the conversation which interested me most.

"I'll have it sorted today," I assured her, my mind fixing on those photographs. There was something about them which just didn't add up to me. And I wanted to look into it myself.

If my instincts were right then I might just be onto something here. So it looked like I had a mountain man to investigate.

CHAPTER TWELVE

I lay on the couch with my arm behind my head and my heavy lidded gaze resting on Winter's small form where she was curled on the floor by the wall. I couldn't sleep. My lips still tasted of her and my body was still humming from that kiss. But now I had to lay here and look across the room at her where she was sleeping on the floor instead of holding her in my arms. It was infuriating, but I understood. Whatever had possessed her to kiss me had been short lived. The blazing flame of a freshly struck match which burned out almost as quickly as it was lit. I wasn't surprised when she'd remembered herself, remembered *me*, and pulled away again. But now I couldn't tear my gaze from her, wondering if my decision to send her back down the mountain and away from this place really was for the best. Or maybe I was just being selfish. Maybe now that I'd had a brief glimpse of something more than this lonely existence, I just didn't want to settle back into it. Maybe I was looking for someone to save me too.

I sighed as I pushed myself to sit up, scrubbing a hand down my face as, for the first time since I'd come up here to this hidden shelter in the mountains, I considered leaving. This cabin was no place for anyone to have a life, but maybe, if I had some reason to *want* a life again, I'd be able to leave. Though

I knew the moment I did, the Romeros would find me.

I didn't turn my cellphone on often, but whenever I did, there were always messages from Rocco. Messages that made my gut twist and my heart pound and the taste of bile fill my mouth as I fought to mesh the two people I was supposed to be into one. But it felt like an impossible task. How could I have been the Calabresi heir and the Romeros' lost boy all at once?

I sighed, giving up on sleep for tonight and pushing myself out of my spot on the couch. My brain was too active to shut down and my fingers ached for the release of strumming them on my guitar.

I slipped across the room to the kitchen and set the coffee pot up, trying to make as little noise as possible to avoid waking my sleeping savage girl.

I leaned back against the worktop and looked over at her where she slept. There had been something about the look in her eyes when we'd returned here that had been almost more powerful than the kiss she'd given me. It was fire and fury and the most beautiful kind of joy. She'd taken revenge on one of the men who'd tortured her, sated her fury for countless abuses and made him pay the price for his crimes. And I was pretty sure she'd needed that. I'd long since been made immune to spilling blood and taking lives, but I knew well the feeling of destroying someone who had wronged you so deeply. When Giuseppe's death had been confirmed in the press, my entire soul had felt lighter. Of course, that had left me with a whole plethora of unresolved emotions about the man I'd spent the majority of my life idolising. But the rose tinted glasses had well and truly shattered and I knew now exactly the depths he'd gone to to destroy my life. And the lives of the family I'd never had the chance to have.

I guessed I still hadn't really come to terms with all of it, but a year alone, hiding from the world in the wilderness was enough to let me make peace with it. I wasn't the man he'd tried to turn me into. I wasn't the man the Romeros wanted me to be either. But I was getting to a place where I might have been ready to start discovering who I was aside from all of that.

When the coffee was ready, I poured myself a steaming mug then slipped on a shirt and coat, kicked my boots onto my feet and headed out onto the porch with my guitar in one hand and the coffee in the other.

Winter stirred as I opened the door, a soft murmur escaping her lips which was so close to speech that I stilled. But as she rolled over and a throaty moan escaped her next, a shiver darted down my spine which had nothing to do with the cold and everything to do with *her*. My flesh tingled with the desire to be closer to hers and as she moaned softly again, I couldn't help but want to swallow that sound with a kiss and bring more of them to her lips.

My dick hardened in my pants at the mere thought of it and I swallowed thickly, wishing she hadn't broken that kiss, that she'd let me worship her for longer. I ached to show her all of the ways that human touch could bring pleasure to her flesh instead of pain, to kiss each and every one of her scars and make her flesh taste something so much sweeter than agony.

I blew out a breath and turned my gaze from the temptress on my floor, heading out onto the porch, tugging the door closed behind me as I moved to sit on the swing seat there.

I set my guitar aside and looked out into the dark forest as the snow continued to tumble from the sky in fat, lazy clumps which drifted down to cover all of the world in white.

An owl hooted somewhere in the trees and in the distance I was almost certain I heard a wolf howl. But I wasn't much afraid of wolves. I'd gone up against meaner, more bloodthirsty bastards than any wolf and lived to tell the tale.

I drank my coffee slowly, enjoying the heat of it as it rolled down my throat and filled my stomach, warming me from the inside out as it pooled in my gut.

I blew out a breath which swirled away as a thick fog before me and pulled my guitar up onto my lap. I wouldn't have called myself a musician in any real way, but the elite school that Giuseppe had organised for me to attend required a musical talent, so I was practiced enough to pass. And being up here alone for so long had made me crave the music more than once, if for no other reason than to hear my own voice. To remind myself that I existed in a real, tangible way rather than just being some ghost of two men and the entirety of neither.

This was *mine,* my music was something which hadn't been touched by anyone aside from me. The things I liked to listen to, the songs I liked to play and sing, they were a part of me that hadn't been tainted. And I liked to focus on the simple things like that whenever I needed reminding that I was more than just all of the things I'd been destined to become. That I was my own man. And of course Giuseppe and the Romeros and even Sloan had shaped me in some ways. But deep down at my core, I owned my own fate. The girl I'd promised to marry had never been meant for me and though it had taken a little while for me to come to terms with that, I'd realised that I was relieved by that fact. I'd known that I was destined to be hers for so long that I'd never even let myself consider the fact that I could be someone else's. Someone *I* chose, who suited me better. Who might even love me. Though of course, I really needed to figure out who *I* was before I could have any real hope of that coming to pass.

I grabbed my guitar and laid it over my lap, slowly strumming the strings as I let a song come together. At first I just let the guitar speak and then I found myself humming along in places, the murmured words of the song falling from my lips not long after. My voice was all grit and rough edges, but I'd only ever played for myself so I wasn't too concerned about expanding my range. I sang from the base of my soul, releasing the broken pieces of me that festered there and hunting down the lost fragments of my being which I'd never really known.

I wasn't sure how much time passed as my voice trailed from song to song, my fingers growing cold as I played while I ignored the bite of the frost and carried on. When the door cracked open and Winter slipped out, I paused for a moment, offering her a soft smile before I continued.

She'd wrapped a comforter around her like a cape, pulling it up over her head so that her red hair was covered as if she were wearing a hood.

She padded towards me on bare feet which pressed into the dusting of snow that had blown beneath the roof covering the porch, leaving footprints as she closed in on me.

I couldn't help but watch her as she moved to sit beside me, curling herself up on the swinging bench and tightening the comforter around her shoulders as she listened to me play.

I'd never had an audience before her, but something about the soft smile on Winter's lips made me push to keep strumming music from the guitar for her as my voice rolled over the notes of the song I was playing.

"Down by the river, I met a girl, whose soul was twisted moonlight and whose name I didn't know. She told me one day, I'd find my way and maybe I could meet her when the moon was high again..."

Winter shifted closer to me, her small frame leaning against mine as she rested her head on my shoulder and I continued to play.

When the song finished, I placed the guitar down and leaned back in my seat, placing my arm along the back of the chair and trying not to smirk like a fucking idiot when she shifted into the curve of my body.

"You know," I began slowly, the utter quiet of the snowy night making my voice sound loud even though it was little more than a murmur. "It's alright if killing him made you feel things aside from relief. It's okay if you're freaking out, or-"

Winter placed her palm flat against my chest and pushed back so that she could look at me, the comforter slipping off of her head and her red hair spilling loose around her shoulders. *Fuck*, she really was something to look at.

She shook her head firmly and I smiled a little.

"I'm just saying, the first time you kill someone can be-"

She released a frustrated huff and rolled her eyes at me.

"What *do* you feel then?" I asked, my gaze sliding to her lips before I could stop myself and then snapping back to those forest green eyes of hers.

She cocked her head as she considered it, looking like this fragile little bird or something. Then she glanced down at my clothes, shifting so that she

125

was sitting with her legs curled beneath her, facing me as best she could on the seat and reached out to unzip my coat.

My throat bobbed as she pushed it open before reaching out to unbutton my shirt at my neck, unfastening the buttons half way down and then touching a finger to my chest so that she could paint out the words she wanted to.

My gaze was fixed on her as her fingertips painted lines on my flesh and I was so caught up in the feeling of her skin on mine that I didn't even register the words.

"Sorry," I murmured as she looked at me expectantly, clearing my throat as I resisted the urge to touch her. "I didn't catch that."

She huffed in frustration, pushing up onto her knees and sliding a leg over mine as she moved to straddle me and my heart leapt in surprise. She gave me a stern look then started spelling out the words again, slower this time to make sure I caught them, not seeming to realise that her touching me this way while she perched in my lap made concentrating damn near impossible. But somehow, I forced myself to manage it.

I feel like one of the bars on my cage has just broken free.

My smile widened at that and she grinned too, this genuine flash of happiness that stole across her face and tore my breath away. In that moment I could see the girl she could be, or perhaps the girl she had been. And it made my heart ache to think of how much pain and suffering she had endured to only feel that joy in death.

"We'll break them all, baby doll," I promised her. "Once I know you're safe, I'll head over to their fucking stronghold and tear them all limb from limb. I'll bring you pieces of them wrapped in ribbons and take joy in every moment of agony I rip from their flesh."

She bit her bottom lip at my words, her eyes lighting hungrily and I knew what she was going to say even before her fingers moved across my skin.

I want to see it.

"It's not safe," I murmured and she frowned at me, shaking her head fiercely.

I need to.

I sighed softly and the wind whipped up around us, blowing strands of crimson hair across her face.

I reached out to catch them, tucking them behind her ear and letting my fingers linger against her skin when she didn't flinch away from my touch.

"I understand that, baby doll," I said slowly. "But…I just don't think I could bear putting you that close to danger. What if something went wrong? I'll be outnumbered, they have guns…if I die, I need to know that you're away from there, that there's no chance of them catching you again, or-"

Her lips pressed to mine so softly that all I could do was freeze, locked in the impossibility of that touch as the warmth of her body called to me on a primal level.

I groaned hungrily as I kissed her back, my lips caressing hers, worshiping them in a gentle dance as I had to force myself not to tighten my grip on her jaw, not to move my other arm from the back of the swinging chair.

I was fighting to be gentle with her even as she deepened the kiss, her tongue sliding between my lips and breaking down every defence I had in place as I met her kiss with my own.

I fucking *ached* for this girl, my heart pounding so fast that it felt like I was having an adrenaline rush. She slid down my thighs, shifting closer to me until she was pressed against the thick length of my cock and I growled with desire.

Winter gasped, breaking our kiss for a moment as she looked into my eyes, that vivid green showing up even in the darkness out here. She shifted in my lap again and a throaty moan left her lips which said she liked the way that felt.

"Shit," I breathed as I tried to find an inch of self control, but I was pretty sure I was fresh out of it and as she rolled her hips against me, grinding herself over my dick, I snapped.

I tugged on her jaw and pulled her in for another kiss, devouring the taste of her as I stopped holding back and pushed my tongue into her mouth. My other hand landed on her hip and I gripped her through the comforter as I rocked her against me again, flexing my own hips as the feeling of her grinding against me like that practically had me panting.

It had been so fucking long since I'd even been touched by another person that I felt like I was starving for this. Like I needed it more than I ever could have imagined.

My boots were planted on the wooden floor but the seat still rocked beneath us, urged into movement by our flexing bodies.

Her cold hands slid inside my shirt and she moaned into my mouth as she explored the plains of my chest, caressing my scars as she found them and sending shivers of pleasure racing through me.

The stubble coating my jaw scratched at her soft skin as I inhaled her, devoured her, consumed her. And the way she was kissing me said she felt the same. That she couldn't get enough of this, that she needed it just like I did.

As she continued to writhe in my lap, I felt my restraint snapping, my desire for her pushing through all of the perfectly sane reasons I had to stop this. But every rock of her hips, brush of her tongue, taste of her soul, had me wanting to forget them all.

I stood suddenly, gripping her ass through the comforter with both hands as I took her with me.

"You need to tell me to stop if this is going too far, baby doll," I growled against her mouth as I carried her towards the door. "Push me back, shake your head, punch me, whatever way you want to say it-"

She shut me up by kissing me again and I wrenched the door open as I carried her into the cabin.

My heart was thrashing painfully against my ribcage and I kicked the door closed behind us before whirling her around and pressing her up against it.

I almost asked if she was alright but she tightened her legs around my waist, dragging me closer as she rocked her hips again, moaning at the feeling of my cock between her thighs even with our clothes dividing us.

"You're like a fucking dream brought to life," I growled as I dropped my mouth to her neck, trailing kisses down her flesh and drowning in the gasp of pleasure which escaped her.

She pushed my jacket off of my shoulders and I managed to shrug it all the way off, tugging the comforter away too.

My hand slid over her body, searching out her breast beneath my plaid shirt and growling as I found her pebbled nipple straining against the fabric.

She moaned even louder as I teased it, hungry for this feeling, shivering at the whispers of my skin against hers.

I'd never wanted a girl like I wanted her in that moment. I'd never ached to satisfy and please someone the way I did with her. She'd had so much hurt, so much darkness in her life, she deserved pleasure. Countless pleasure, a whole fucking ocean of it to bathe in forevermore.

Tyson got up from his bed by the wall and started whimpering softly in a plea to head out, nudging against my legs as I tried my hardest to ignore him.

But the big fucker wouldn't give up, nudging me harder and barking in a demand.

I grunted a platitude at him, needing him to fucking wait a minute as he began to pace like he might just burst if he didn't pee soon.

I gave my focus back to Winter's mouth as I kissed her again and suddenly, two big dog paws slammed into my back as he leapt at me.

Winter laughed, breaking our kiss and I cursed as I scowled at the offending dog.

"Why now?" I snarled at him, but he only barked again, clearly refusing to wait for us to finish what we'd started.

I set Winter down with a groan of frustration and she backed away with a blush lining her cheeks so that I could let him out.

Tyson shoved his wet nose into my hand and I scruffed his fur between my fingers as I tussled his ears before unbolting the door to set him loose.

But instead of relieving himself quickly, he raced straight out into the

129

trees and disappeared into the dark forest.

I cursed as I whistled for him to return, wedging the door closed around my body in an attempt to shield Winter from the cold air which was trying to force its way inside.

"Tyson!" I bellowed as his barks echoed away through the trees.

I was seriously tempted to just leave him to it and get back to precisely what I'd just been doing, but there was a sudden shriek of pain from the forest and Tyson's pained howl cut the air in two.

"Shit," I cursed, yanking the door wide to bellow his name again.

Winter hurried to my side, taking my hand and starting to paint something against my flesh, but I wasn't concentrating enough to catch it.

"You need to hide," I commanded, catching her fingers between mine and tugging her back in as Tyson's cries of pain continued to echo all around us. "It's probably just another animal, but I can't go out there unless I'm sure you're safe."

I yanked the bed aside and Winter grabbed the comforter before dropping down into the space beneath the hatch, her wide eyes peering up at me fearfully.

"It'll be okay," I promised as adrenaline thundered through my limbs and my hard on sank with a seriously disappointing sense of finality.

I grabbed a knife from the kitchen and handed it to her before dropping the hatch closed again and concealing it beneath the bed.

I snatched my jacket from the floor and threw it on before grabbing my rifle and running out into the snow.

"Tyson!" I bellowed as I used the tracks he'd left to lead me to him and his howls of pain made me run even faster.

I didn't have many things in this world that I gave a shit about, but that dog was like family to me. If something happened to him, I wasn't sure how the fuck I'd cope. So I ran like the fires of hell were up my ass and raced into the trees to rescue my only friend.

CHAPTER THIRTEEN

I waited in the dark, my breaths coming shallow then hard, shallow then hard. I was warring with myself to stay calm, but the quiet was beginning to drill into my ears and the tight space seemed to be getting even tighter.

Despite my fear, my skin was still humming with the pleasure Nicoli had given me. No touch had ever felt so good. His hands on me had sent static sparking and twisting over my flesh. I'd wanted him closer, I'd felt the animal in him rising to meet the animal in me. But that moment had been severed by a sharpened knife. Reality had crashed down and reminded us that The Five would always come for their blood debt. And maybe they were here for it now. Even the cool blade in my grip wasn't enough to ease my terror about that possibility.

Everything's going to be okay.

Nicoli will come back.

But what if he doesn't? What if they've come for him? What if they bring an army to destroy him?

I shut my eyes and immediately fell into the darkest memories inside me. They were always waiting, lurking. Only the demons who still lived remained to haunt me. Jax and Quentin didn't plague my thoughts anymore.

They were gone. On a soul-deep level, I knew that. My body knew it. And my subconscious didn't taunt me with their cruelty any longer. But there were still three more and plenty of torture between them to make fear snake around my heart and hold me hostage. It wasn't just a fear for me anymore. It was a fear for Nicoli. For Tyson too. I didn't want my being here to bring any harm on them. I wouldn't be able to live with myself if it did.

I battled the memories for as long as I could, but whenever I was alone for long enough, they always won out.

"You've really done it this time, Farley, you fucking idiot," Duke snapped, his voice making my pulse jump out of rhythm. I lay on the floor, the heat of my own blood the only thing keeping me warm.

Farley hadn't held back today. He'd been angry about something, comparing me to some 'godforsaken woman' he had down the mountain, saying we were all the same, all sluts who couldn't keep their legs closed. I'd seen a monster behind his eyes which even Duke wouldn't have been able to hold back. I'd fought with all I had, but he'd had the upper hand before he'd even stepped into the room. He was twice the size of me and built of pure muscle. My body could only take so much when subjected to his wrath.

Now, in the aftermath of his beating, I was torn between wanting to die and the instinct to survive. This agony was unbearable. And I could feel the caress of death urging me to stop fighting. I'd wished for it to come to me so many times before, but now it was actually here, did I really want to go?

"Get her on the table, I need to see the damage. If she dies, you will pay for it," Duke snarled at Farley.

"She won't die. She's a fucking cockroach," Farley muttered then he scooped me up and placed me on the table. I screamed as fire raced across my ribs and around into my spine. Something was broken. Maybe several somethings.

"Hush, red," Duke commanded, pushing my hair away from my face to look at me. I gazed up at him through a glaze of tears in my eyes and found concern there. Though not for me. If I died, this whole interrogation would be

134

ruined. But didn't they understand that it had been pointless from the moment I'd arrived here? "If it's a break, she needs medical attention," he told Farley matter-of-factly. "If it's a fracture, she'll manage."

"So what do we do, boss?" Farley asked anxiously, shooting a glower at me like I was the root of all his problems.

"We keep her alive as best we can. Ain't no doctor coming up here though," Duke growled, turning to face me again. He stuffed a hand into his pocket, taking out a rolled joint and pushing it between my lips. "This will take the edge off, red."

I spat it from my mouth, not wanting any mercy from Duke. I'd rather suffer through this. I'd rather speak with death and decide if I wanted to give up at last. He was better company than them.

"Suit yourself," Duke laughed coldly, tucking the joint in the corner of his mouth and heading to the door. "Come on, Farley, leave the little wretch to suffer. She'll beg for my medicine soon enough."

I won't. Not ever.

Farley leaned down in my face with his upper lip peeling back. "Don't you die or I'll follow you into hell and drag you back here myself, you little shit."

Too late, I'm already in hell.

He followed Duke out of the room and I pulled my knees to my chest as I rolled onto my uninjured side. I winced from the bruises and cuts, every part of my body tender and screaming. I tongued a welt on the inside of my cheek and tried to remember what it felt like to be okay. For my body not to ache anywhere at all.

Maybe this would never end. Maybe I'd fooled myself into believing that when they realised I was never going to give them the answer they wanted, they'd give up and let me go. But of course that wasn't going to happen. If they gave up, they'd kill me. Why keep me alive? It was a miracle they'd kept me alive this long at all, even though it was clear I was their only hope at working out whatever code they were after. Eventually they'd give up though. They had to. And then what? Was I going to spend the rest of my life facing their torture until one of them put a bullet between my eyes and buried me somewhere I'd never be found? Was my future already decided? And if it was, why fight it? I could give into death's embrace and let it take me somewhere peaceful, somewhere quiet and dark and eternal.

But there was something holding me here, like a voice in the back of my mind that promised better days. They promised sunshine on my cheeks and the type of touches that didn't hurt. And maybe I could wait a little longer for that...

Thump.

My heart lurched at the sound which made my senses sharpen like a razor.

Thump – thump -thump -*crash.*

I clutched the knife tighter as the sound of the door caving in reached me and heavy footfalls pounded into the cabin. I knew it was them without needing to see. Who else would come here, who else would break in?

"Check the bathroom," Duke ordered and my heart turned to a frozen lump of ice.

"Yes, boss," Farley said, marching that way, his boots passing by the bed.

Furniture was overturned and the metal hilt of the knife bit into my palm as I tried to steel myself for a fight.

"We know you're here, red," Duke snarled. "If you come out, I'll go easy on you. Keep me waiting and you will be in for a world of pain."

Fear slithered up my spine and tears burned my eyes as I tried to keep my thoughts clear.

I had to be ready if they found me.

"Come on, little bird," Orville said and a floorboard creaked close by. "Come to me."

I could almost feel his hands on me again, the way he'd brushed his fingers over the curve of my hips or the swell of my breasts. He'd always been a predator waiting to pounce and I needed him ripped apart like Quentin had been. I pictured him beneath me bloodied and screaming and the memory leant me the strength I craved.

I forced my eyes open, staring at the tiny sliver of light leaking in through the crack in the floorboards above me.

I won't let them scare me.

Someone shoved the bed aside and my hand trembled against the knife as I clenched my teeth and awaited my fate. I'd be ready if I had to be. I would spill as much blood as possible.

Tension gripped my limbs as more light fell down on me and I worried the thundering beat of my heart was loud enough to be heard by these monsters.

A shadow blotted out the light and I froze, as still as flint and iron and steel. And I wanted to embody each of those things, to become a fearless entity which held firm in the face of anything.

A face appeared above me, pressing to the wood and one blue eye peered between the cracks, wheeling a flashlight down the gap. Orville saw me, and I saw him. He lifted his head long enough to smile in victory and I drew my legs to my chest with determination in my soul, kicking the hatch hard and forcing it up to smack him in the jaw. He reared backwards with a roar of pain and I leapt from my hiding place with a yell of defiance, my heart in my throat but my survival instincts taking over.

I slashed at Orville's face, but he brought up his arm at the last second and the knife sliced through his coat and found skin beneath. He came at me with a snarl, catching hold of my oversized shirt and dragging me closer. But that was his mistake as he struggled to get hold of my hand which gripped the knife and I lunged for his heart with all the power of my fury behind me.

Strong hands closed around me, dragging me back before I could land the blow, my weapon slashing uselessly through the air.

I kicked and screamed, trying to reach back and gut my captor with the blade, but he caught my wrist and squeezed until I yelped and it clattered to the floor with a brutal finality. Farley's scent of ash and death hung around

137

me and I cringed as he clutched me tighter. No matter how hard I thrashed, I couldn't get free. I was a wildcat in the arms of a titan, my claws and teeth useless against this beast.

Orville scrambled to his feet, pushing a hand into his greasy grey hair as he sneered down at me. "You'll pay for that, whore." He strode toward me and Farley held me still as Orville smacked me hard enough to bust my lip open. My head spun as my eyes focused on Duke across the room, his rifle cocked in a warning.

"You thought you could run from us, did ya, red?" he growled, his eyes darkening with a threat that terrified me. "And wield the mountain man against our people?" He tutted, pointing to the door. "Take her. I'm done playing nice. We'll have the code outta her this very night. No more rules. No more protection."

"No rules at all, boss?" Orville asked with the look of a salivating dog and my stomach churned with nausea as Farley hauled me across the room.

"None at all," Duke confirmed darkly, giving me twisted smile as he smoothed down his moustache. "By sunrise, she either squeals like a pig or we gut her like one."

Nicoli

CHAPTER FOURTEEN

I raced through the snow, following Tyson's tracks and the howls he was making as I closed in on him, calling out to reassure him I was coming and hopefully frighten off whatever the hell had attacked him.

I half skidded in the snow as I raced downhill, falling to one knee and righting myself again just as fast as my blood pumped through my veins with a wild savagery.

Every instinct in my body told me that something was wrong here. Seriously, fucking *wrong*.

I'd walked into traps before and I had that same sinking feeling in my gut.

I ran into a clearing and stumbled to a halt as I spotted Tyson, tangled in a net hanging from a tree ahead of me, a steady drip, drip, drip of blood colouring the snow beneath him.

He barked excitedly as he spotted me but I drew my rifle, aiming at the trees as I waited for the ambush to come. Because it had to come. He hadn't just been left hanging up there like that so I could cut him down and take him home easily. And that was no basic hunter's snare which had been accidentally tripped either.

I ducked back behind the tree and circled the clearing, trying to ignore the twisting in my gut as Tyson whimpered in panic. He wasn't bleeding much. But one wrong move on my part could easily equal death for us both right now.

I ducked between the shadows beneath the trees, hunting the snowy ground for signs of footprints, something to show me where the assholes who'd done this had come from or run off to.

When I made it almost the whole way around the clearing, I found the tree where the trap was tied alongside boot prints and snowmobile tracks. All the clues that pointed to whoever had done this without any sign of them anywhere.

That sense of unease only multiplied as I looked at the evidence of their departure, the snowmobile tracks heading off into the trees, wondering if it was just another trick. Maybe they weren't far away, lying in wait in the trees for when I stepped out of cover.

I pulled my hunting knife from my belt and reached up to grip the rope with my other hand so that when I broke it, Tyson wouldn't just drop like a sack of shit into the snow. With one forceful cut, I severed the rope and looked around once more before lowering Tyson to the ground.

He scrambled to get himself out of the net before I could reach him and I called out to calm him as I ducked low and raced to his side.

I yanked the net aside and quickly inspected the slash to his rear leg. The wound was long but not deep; he didn't want to press any weight down on the leg all the same, holding it off of the ground and whimpering pathetically as he slathered my hands in wet kisses with his tongue.

"Come here, you big beast," I murmured, grabbing hold of his two front paws in my left hand then the back paws in the right before slinging him over my shoulders and hurrying out of the clearing again.

He leaned around to lick the side of my face as I paused in the shade of an enormous pine.

Still no attack came, no gunfire, no shouts…nothing.

My heart stilled. It looked like whoever had set this up had already gone. Which meant that this wasn't a trap to catch me. It was a lure to pull me away from the real target.

I cursed beneath my breath and started running as fast as I could back towards the cabin with Tyson bouncing on my shoulders in time with my steps.

Panic reared its ugly head within me as my mind began to conjure all kinds of twisted fates that could have befallen my savage girl.

I shouldn't have left her behind. What the fuck was I thinking leaving her alone?

I ached to scream her name at the top of my lungs, promise her that I was on my way. That I wouldn't let anything happen to her. That I'd pay in blood for her safety, but I couldn't risk giving myself away.

When I reached the cabin, my worst fears were confirmed. The front door was busted open and the firelight revealed a whole heap of nothing and nobody within the wooden walls.

Gone. She's gone.

My heart felt like it might burst as sweat trickled down my spine and I charged up the steps, not slowing until I found myself looking down into the empty hiding place beneath the bed just like I knew I would.

"No," I breathed, like denying it might make it not so.

I pulled Tyson from my back, laying him on the bed as I took in all the signs of a struggle, the destruction that had taken place during their hunt and the utter lack of my beautiful survivor anywhere. They had her again. Every promise I'd made her had been a lie. A fucking useless lie told by a man whose word meant less than shit now.

But I wasn't going to leave it at that.

I'm coming for you, baby doll.

I whirled around, crossing the room in three long strides and ripped open the drawer at the base of the coffee table where I kept all of my spare rounds for my rifle. I started grabbing them out, box by box, stuffing them into my pockets with a growl of rage leaving my lips.

A long time ago, I'd left the man I used to be at the bottom of this mountain, but I was about to reclaim him. I'd been a mindless, brutal, killer of the worst kind. And tonight I'd be him again.

I turned for the door and stilled as I spotted a note pinned to it using the very knife Winter had been holding the last time I'd seen her. Blood coated the silver blade and had dripped down onto the page, but it hadn't done anything to hide the message scrawled there.

When we're done with her, we'll come for you.

"As if I'd wait that long," I snarled, tearing the page from the door and throwing it into the fire.

I cast a glance at Tyson, but now that he was curled up on my bed he'd stopped howling and the wound had already stopped bleeding so I didn't need to worry about him.

"I'm going for our girl," I told him and he lifted his chin like he actually understood that before I yanked the broken door back over.

It didn't shut right but I guessed that might be for the best. If I didn't make it back then Tyson needed to be able to get out.

But I had no intention of dying today. My savage girl wasn't going to be left in the care of those monsters. When I made it to their camp they were going to realise exactly how big of a mistake they'd made in underestimating me.

I didn't come up the mountain because I was afraid to live. I came up here because I was afraid of who I was and what I was capable of. I'd meant to leave that man in my past, but they'd dragged him up here to join them. And now they'd pay the price for that mistake in blood.

CHAPTER FIFTEEN

I hung over Farley's shoulder, pounding my fists into his back and fighting to break free, but if he noticed at all, he didn't show it. The sound of men laughing reached me beyond the dark trees and terror consumed me as Farley stepped out into a clearing and threw me to the ground.

Pain splintered across my spine as I hit compacted snow and I looked over my shoulder, taking in the camp I'd been brought to. There were men everywhere, guns and knives at their hips. Some of them sat around a large fire while others roamed in out of the trailers parked up at the edge of the woods. Around them were dark mine shafts that led down into the mountain and floodlights stood beside them, spilling light over the area. The moon hung directly above it all, staring down at me from the clear sky. I could see the stars for once and my breath caught as I looked to them, wishing on every single one that this was a nightmare which I was about to wake up from.

"We've got a guest, boys!" Duke called, grabbing a fistful of my hair and dragging me toward the fire. "This little waif says she's happy to suck every cock here, didn't ya red? Just say the word no if not." He leered down at me, tossing me before the fire where the snow had melted and the earth was dry. Several of the men cheered and a few even rolled down their zippers, getting to their feet. Duke chuckled as he smoothed down his moustache, taking out a cigarette and slipping it into the corner of his mouth as he lit it.

I snarled, pushing myself upright, trying not to shake as I stood and glared at the men who dared look at me that way. Half of them were drunk, sipping cheap beer and reeking of bad deeds. There was the general smell of unwashed men in the air too that made bile rise in my throat.

A hand brushed my back and I lurched around, raising my hands in two fists to warn off whoever it was.

Orville stood there with a dark and hungry look on his face. He was so lean, his clothes seemed to hang off of him and his greying hair looked like it hadn't been washed in weeks. "Did you kill our friend, Quentin, little bird?" he asked and I lifted my chin, my jaw tight as I nodded.

"*Bitch*," Farley spat, drawing nearer and I backed up, though that meant I was only getting closer to the drunken men behind me. "You kill my brother, now Quentin...you're gonna pay."

"She had help," Duke growled to my right and I glanced towards the fire, wondering if it was safer to move nearer to the flames than the men. "Isn't that right, red? You and the mountain man."

"She's been shacking up with that yeti?" someone called from behind me.

"Yeah," Orville purred. "Did you get on your knees for him, little bird? Did you take that big mountain cock all the way in?"

I raised my fists higher as laughter rang around the clearing. I knew it was useless, but I wasn't going to cower and beg for mercy. I'd fight until they won. I'd fight until I couldn't fight anymore.

Someone threw a beer bottle into the fire right behind me and I jumped at the noise, glancing over my shoulder and finding several of the men lurking closer.

"Get her on her knees," Duke commanded Farley. "I think red has an apology she wants to make to Orville for cutting him."

My heart lurched as Farley strode towards me, fear snaring me and

148

making my skin prickle all over. He came at me fast but I stood my ground, diving at him with an animalistic shriek as I clawed and tore at him. His fist slammed into my gut and I wheezed as I hit the ground, clutching my stomach and groaning as I scrambled to get up. Before I could, he moved around me, kicking me hard so I fell before Orville then yanking my hair so I was forced to look up at him. I bit back on a scream as pain flared through my scalp and tears of agony seared my eyes.

Orville stepped closer, rubbing a hand over his crotch as he patted the knife at his hip in warning. "You play nice or I'll take a few fingers from you, pretty thing," he purred, unbuckling his pants.

I sneered at him, my breaths coming frantically as he stepped closer so I was eye level with his groin. Farley's grip tightened in my hair and I winced as he forced my head closer to Orville's dick. Shadows moved in my periphery as more men moved to watch and my heart hit a wild beat as I was held at their mercy.

Orville rubbed himself through his pants and I glared up at him the whole time, my eyes pinned on his, making him struggle to concentrate. I wouldn't let him escape my hate, my disgust.

"Hurry up, Orville, there's a queue forming here," a guy called out and laughter hit my ears again, making my insides twist and writhe. If they thought I was going to stay here on my knees and open my mouth obediently, they were going to be sorely disappointed. I knew the alternative meant death. But better that than have my soul torn to pieces by these retched dogs.

"Stop looking at me like that," Orville demanded, but I didn't. I glared up at him unblinking, my upper lip peeled back. "I said stop!" His hand crashed into my cheek and my hair yanked tight in Farley's grip as my head wheeled sideways. The welt on my lip split open again and the taste of blood in my mouth made me starve to spill theirs. I could feel the animal in me rising, an ache for violence dripping through my core. If I had to die, I was sure as hell going out of this world with their blood painted on my flesh.

I twisted towards Orville as he removed his hand from his crotch, lurching forward and sinking my teeth into his pants, biting down until I met his hard on and sinking my teeth in deeper and deeper. Orville screamed and Farley yanked my head back, but my jaw was locked tight, only making Orville scream even higher.

"Get her off!" Orville begged and Farley released my hair, grabbing my jaw instead and forcing my mouth to open. I lurched backwards, throwing my head back as hard as possible and smacking it right between Farley's legs. He roared, stumbling away and I was up on my feet in the next heartbeat, my gaze on the trees as I ran as hard and as fast as I could towards them.

"Get her!" Duke boomed and the sound of several footfalls reached me from behind, drawing closer and closer.

Panic snared my heart as I made it to the tree line. They were gaining on me and before I could make it into the shadows of the woods, a hand caught hold of my shoulder and I was twisted around and thrown to the ground. I sank into the snow, but wasn't left there long as two men picked me up between them and started carrying me back to the fire as I fought them with everything I had.

I punched and kicked and scratched, but it did no good as they tossed me down then started pulling at my clothes. I was on my back, throwing my legs out in frantic kicks as they tore at my shirt and more men surrounded me like wolves fighting for pieces of a fresh kill. Farley was amongst them, watching and laughing as they fought to get their hands on me first. His broad form couldn't be missed, his meaty head with thick black hair sprouting from it standing half a foot above them all. Orville started cursing my name somewhere close by, but I couldn't feel any satisfaction towards that because someone was squeezing my breasts and breathing heavily in my ear. Another was trying to pin my ankles down and several were trying to tear Nicoli's plaid shirt from my body. My thoughts muddled and panic made me scream.

As a man with grisly blonde hair leaned over me, I lunged for the knife at his hip in desperation, drawing it with a growl of rage. I didn't hesitate as I slammed it into his gut and his eyes widened in delayed shock as hot blood spilled over my hand then he reared back with a bellow of pain and I started slashing at everyone surrounding me like a wild woman. The group backed up and I made it to my feet again, swinging the blade left and right as I tried to keep them back.

"That fucking slut!" someone barked.

"Get her!" another roared.

Farley came at me like a freight train and Duke's laughter reached me as I wielded the blade, ready to maim and gut and *kill*.

Farley lunged for my hand which held the knife and I managed to slice his arm before he caught it, snatching the blade away from me and tucking it into his belt.

"I'll make it stop if you give me the code," Duke called as Farley turned me towards him. "What'll it be, red?"

I shuddered in Farley's grip. I didn't have the code Duke wanted, like I'd told him a thousand times before I buried my voice. So I'd known this moment was coming for too long. I was always going to end up here. I doubted I'd see another sunrise, but I let my eyes fall closed and pictured those I'd seen from Nicoli's window. I recalled the kisses we'd shared and the way his touches had soothed the deep ache in my soul. No one could take those moments from me, not even these monsters. At least I could say that in my short and painful existence, I had experienced something good and sweet and worth living for. It broke my heart that I wouldn't get any more than the brief window of light I'd been gifted. But maybe after tonight, I'd at least be at peace.

"She needs to learn her place," Farley spoke to the surrounding camp then latched his hand around my throat until I choked, shaking me so I opened my eyes and fell into the infernal hell waiting for me in his. "Let's see how much fight you have left after I break every bone in your body, whore."

CHAPTER SIXTEEN

My chest heaved with deep breaths in and out, causing a fog to billow from my mouth on each exhale and a burn of ice to fill my chest as I inhaled the freezing air again and ran on. I didn't even need to follow the snowmobile tracks – I knew where their fucking camp was, but keeping in the smooth tracks helped me keep my sanity. She'd followed this same path just minutes ago. She'd been here before me and waited ahead of me. It wasn't good enough, but it was something.

Sweat stuck my thick clothes to my flesh and my muscles burned with the relentless pace as I ran on and on. With the machines to help them, they'd gotten ahead of me, but it was only six miles from my cabin to their camp. Without the snow I could have run it in no time, with it I was labouring uphill in two feet of the white stuff and fuck knew how much time that was adding to my run. But that didn't matter, I wouldn't slow. And as I finally drew close enough to see firelight through the trees ahead of me, a surge of relief spilled through me which couldn't be contained.

I forced myself to slow down, calming my hammering heart and steadying my breath so that I could hear every sound between the trees.

They were dumb as fuck, the lowest kinds of scumbags, sent out here to work where no one higher up in their gang or cartel or whatever had to deal with them, but no way had they overestimated themselves enough to go without lookouts.

I slipped off of the track created by the snowmobiles and headed into the thickest patch of forest I could see to the right of me.

Snow crunched softly beneath my boots but there was a commotion taking place at the campsite, men yelling and cheering, screaming encouragement for some game I couldn't let myself focus on right now.

I pulled my knife from my belt, leaving my rifle slung over my back for now. This first move needed to be silent. They couldn't know I was coming until I was in position to take them all out. After that, I was about to paint the world in red.

The lookouts gave themselves away as they spoke to each other ahead of me, one complaining about missing out on the fun as the other took a long swig from his bottle of beer and grunted his agreement.

I crept closer to the lookouts, using the shadows to hide me as I circled around them and came at them from behind.

I waited until their attention was back on the trees ahead of me then made my move. I caught the first guy from behind, slapping a hand over his mouth as I yanked his back to my chest and drove my blade straight into the heart of his friend. The guy I was restraining started to struggle, but I'd already ripped the knife free and I slit his throat before he could do more than slam a badly aimed elbow back into my gut.

I left the two of them bleeding out in the snow and jogged away, forcing myself to keep my pace measured as raucous laughter sang to me between the trees.

It didn't take long for me to reach the wide clearing with bonfires blazing and men drinking everywhere in sight. There were a bunch of cars half buried in snow which they must have driven up here before winter came and several huge fallen trees had been cut up to use as benches. Beyond that was a sprawling collection of trailers where the men who worked the cannabis farm lived. They looked like pretty crappy places to live, run down and uncared for, dirty – kinda like the men they housed.

My vantage point was to the north of the clearing, right alongside the main entrance to the old gold mine they used to grow their marijuana which offered employment to this bunch of merry miscreants.

I skirted the rocky opening, clambering up on top of it and using the light of the fires to my advantage as I stayed hidden in the shadows.

Some idiot had hung a floodlight above the mouth of the mine entrance and I smirked to myself as I positioned myself right above it, using it to my advantage as it would blind anyone looking my way.

I laid down, taking my rifle from my back and lining it up as I set a box of ammo down ready beside me.

My heart was thrashing with the desperate need to start spilling blood, but I had to figure out where she was first. My savage girl. The one with the unbreakable spirit and the soul forged in the depths of hell yet still so full of light.

I looked out over the crowd of assholes, trying to figure out the layout of this fucking shithole. I never came up this way usually, happy enough to leave the drug dealers to their industry so long as they left me alone too. But I was regretting that now. Regretting not knowing more about this place. Regretting the fact that Winter had been up here all this time and I'd never had a clue. I wondered if she'd been here before I'd arrived. Or if they'd brought her here since. Either way, that act had been their deaths in the making. And I was more than happy to take the job from the Grim Reaper.

My gaze skimmed across the drunken assholes then suddenly caught on movement on the far side of the largest fire. A flicker of scarlet hair. As my gaze zeroed in on that spot, my skin prickled and rage licked down my spine.

Winter was there, her lip busted open and her clothes half missing. She only wore the plaid shirt I'd given her, now full of rips and tears that showed bloodied flesh.

Several assholes surrounded her, shoving her between them like she was nothing but a toy and they were determined to play with her.

A man grabbed her, big with thick, dark hair that hung down his back and a laugh so loud that I could hear it over the noise of the crowd separating us.

My upper lip peeled back as he caught her by her hair and yanked her towards him, pawing at her breasts through the shirt. She swung a fist at him but he deflected it, then she drove a knee into his balls.

He bellowed in pain, throwing her away from him so forcefully that she fell to the ground and I pulled the trigger the moment she was clear.

The bullet caught him right between the eyes and my heart leapt and pounded with a raging need to finish every single one of these motherfuckers.

Chaos broke out at the gunfire, the men yelling and screaming, drawing their own weapons as they tried to figure out where the shot had come from and I started firing into the crowd to the left of Winter's position with abandon.

Some of them tried to fire back, their shots going wide even when they aimed my way. More of them tried to run and I cut them down too. They'd all been there, taking part in that torture or watching it, or ignoring it. I took each crime as equal. She was just a girl who'd done nothing to any of them and not one man here had been interested in helping her. So why should I have mercy on them?

The men closest to Winter managed to get hold of her again and I growled in frustration as they dragged her away. I spotted Duke with her, swinging a rifle around as he ran but I couldn't risk taking the shot while she was so close to him.

More bullets were fired my way as the men began to narrow down my position above the main mine entrance, but I didn't flinch. I was practically impossible to hit laying down like this and with the floodlight blinding them, they couldn't get a good aim on me anyway.

I fired again and again, pausing to reload when I had to, my lip pulling back grimly as the survivors began to flee instead of trying to fight back. It was like a turning tide. First one ran, then two, three. All of a sudden they were all running for their lives and leaving their friends bleeding out in the snow. I let them run, there were more important things for me to do than hunt down cowards. My girl needed me.

I rolled over and slid off of the ridge, skidding back down to solid ground where the snow crunched beneath my boots. The silence was filled by the groans of dying men and the crackle of the bonfires, but there was nothing else to be heard.

I darted between the trees, my ears ringing from the gunfire and my pulse pounding with adrenaline and fear as I headed in the direction I'd seen them take Winter.

A few guys were laying in wait behind a parked car, but they didn't see me slip by in the trees and by the time I opened fire, they didn't have time to return it.

This was bloody, brutal work, but I wore death like a mask and was happy to do its bidding. These men stood by while my girl was abused before their eyes. They'd been here through her torture and they'd done nothing to stop it. They were all guilty as far as I was concerned.

I was happy to be the judge of that, jury too and most importantly of all, executioner.

My feet tracked bloody boot prints through the snow as I ran on, darting between trees for cover and hunting for some sign of my lost girl.

A cry of pain which I recognised as hers set my hackles rising and a snarl of rage escaped my lips as I turned towards the source of the sound, spotting another mine entrance to my right. The cave was narrow, wooden props holding it up and lanterns bolted to the roof to light the way.

Winter cried out again and a prickle ran down my spine. This felt just like the last trap they'd set me, with Tyson howling in the woods. They were using her to lure me closer, hoping anger would blind me to their games and lead me to my death. But I'd been playing more dangerous games than this for much longer than they could imagine.

I looked around carefully and spotted another mine a few hundred feet to my left. There were no lights illuminating that cave, but I was willing to bet the shafts linked up somewhere.

I cast another look towards the lit up mine then decided to follow my gut, darting to the other one and heading down into the dark.

The ripe, pungent scent of the cannabis plants which they grew down here swept over me as I moved beneath the earth and the biting winter air was cut off.

The mine shaft descended into darkness, robbing me of my sight while my shoulders brushed against the walls and the temperature steadily rose.

I caught the distant murmur of male voices and paused as I tried to decipher the words, but they were lost to the shadows. Regardless, I was pretty sure that meant I'd guessed right about these shafts being connected.

The walls widened out and I paused, waiting for some new sound to guide me on, only moving again once I heard their voices, followed by a muffled cry of pain from Winter.

My heart lurched and stumbled in my chest before picking up a furious rhythm which pounded to the beat of violence.

I'm going to rip those motherfuckers apart.

I headed right, keeping my hand to the wall as the marijuana scent grew thicker, more cloying and suddenly I spotted light up ahead.

It was just a sliver of yellow in the dark at first but as I found another passage to turn into, the light grew. I hurried on, careful to remain silent as I crept across the stone floor in my heavy boots. The further I went, the hotter it got, sweat trickling between my shoulder blades and across my brow.

Each twist and turn of the mine shaft revealed more and more light until I was almost blinded by it.

I squinted against the glare and found myself at the entrance to a huge cavern set up for growing their illegal crops. The plants were growing in long rows beneath the high powered heat lamps, the overpowering scent of them billowing across the space.

At the far end of the cavern stood three men who surrounded a small girl in a ripped shirt.

"Hit her again, Farley," Duke commanded, his tone emotionless, his rifle aimed at the narrow passageway ahead of him.

The biggest fucker among them laughed darkly before swinging his fist straight into Winter's gut, sending her flying back with a cry of pain.

The last guy caught her before she could fall, his hands sliding over her body as she fought to get out of his grip, her features written with disgust.

I gritted my teeth against the desire to dive into the room, roaring her name as I opened fire on them, forcing myself to remain calm instead, stick to the best course of action that I could to get her out of here alive.

I ducked behind the closest row of plants, raising my rifle and cursing internally as I failed to line up a clear shot.

They were shoving Winter back and forth and she stumbled between them, too close for me to risk sending a bullet their way in case I hit her instead.

I slung the rifle over my back, pulled the knife from my belt and began to creep closer.

A bullet was too good for these motherfuckers anyway.

I wanted them to die slowly, painfully, to know exactly what had happened to them and why.

"I don't think he can hear her," the grey-haired guy said, grabbing Winter and dragging her against him as he pawed at her torn shirt.

"So what do you suggest, Orville?" Duke snarled, his upper lip curling over his horseshoe moustache, never once lowering his weapon as he kept it aimed at the shaft where he expected me to appear.

"I say I really make her scream," Orville replied, yanking on her shirt and ripping it off of one shoulder so that her breast was exposed.

Winter shrieked in disgust, thrashing and flailing so violently that she managed to break free of him.

She ran for the exit, yanking her shirt back up to cover herself as she sprinted away and I made it to the end of the aisle I'd been stalking along.

Duke fired a warning shot over her head which echoed so fucking loudly in the confined space that it felt like my eardrums might start bleeding. A low rumble sounded through the mines in response to the sound and a shiver ran through my veins as I half expected the roof to cave in.

Winter ducked with her hands over her head and Orville collided with her a moment later, taking her to the ground.

I leapt out of my cover as Duke lowered his gun, slamming into him from behind and driving my knife straight into his kidney.

He screamed like a stuck pig, blood splattering the cave walls as I ripped the blade free and swung at him again. But he was fast, throwing an elbow into my ribs and driving his foot down on my instep even as he bellowed in agony.

He knocked my aim aside and whirled around, raising his gun towards me.

I tackled him with a cry of hatred, knocking him to the ground just as he fired, deafening us all again as the shot went wide over my head.

Stone crumbled from the cave roof above us and a deep rumble trembled through the mine like the whole thing might fucking collapse on us at any minute. These abandoned gold mines were old and I wouldn't have been surprised if that did happen. I'd known more than one of them to cave in lower down the mountain during my time living up here.

"Why the fuck are you messing in our affairs, mountain man?" Duke yelled as he fought to get the gun between us, managing to avoid the swing of my blade.

I dropped my knife and grabbed Duke's rifle between my hands as I tried to wrestle it away from him. He fought wildly, cursing me as he scrambled to pull the trigger again, but I ripped it out of his arms before he could and slammed it down on his temple hard enough to knock him out.

I swung around at the sound of movement behind me, finding Farley levelling a pistol at me and making my heart leap with panic.

He fired the shot as I tried to dive away, the bullet grazing my thigh and sending pain splintering through my flesh.

I swung Duke's rifle up between us and pulled the trigger before he could fire again, catching him in the side and sending him crashing back into the wall behind him.

I snatched my hunting knife back into my grip as that terrifying rumble sounded through the mines once more, afraid that if I kept firing with the rifle I'd bring the whole thing down on top of us.

Winter screamed as she fought against Orville who had her pinned beneath him on the rocky ground.

I scrambled to my feet, racing towards them and kicking him in the side hard enough to break ribs.

He fell off of her with a curse and I was on him in a moment, stabbing him straight in the dick before I took aim for anything more life threatening. No motherfucker was going to get away with trying to assault my girl like that.

Orville screamed as I pinned him beneath me and drove the blade into his chest, putting him out of his misery far too fucking easily for my liking, but having little choice while the fight still raged.

A solid weight collided with me and I hit the ground hard, rolling over beneath the huge body and losing my knife in the process.

I slammed down onto my back and cursed as Farley wrapped his hands around my throat, tightening his grip as he tried to choke me out.

I threw my fist into his side and then the other again and again as darkness drew in around my vision and he continued to squeeze with all of his strength, even as his ribs cracked beneath my blows.

Winter shrieked at him in fury and she suddenly appeared behind him, my hunting knife gripped in her hands as she drove it straight at his back. He twisted aside as he saw her coming and the blade sank into his shoulder before being ripped out of her grasp as he lurched away.

He tore it free but I was already rocking up to meet him, throwing my fist into his face so hard that I felt bones break beneath my knuckles and the knife fell from his hand. It clattered onto the stony floor somewhere but I didn't even bother to look for it. That asshole had taken his fists to my girl.

And I knew this hadn't been the first time.

He was going to find out what it was like to have the shit kicked out of him by someone bigger and badder than he was before he died.

Farley roared a challenge, lunging towards me and I swung my forehead straight into the bridge of his nose to meet the attack.

Blood poured and he fell back, giving me the advantage I needed to take him. I dove on top of him and threw my fists into his face, his chest, his gut, everywhere and anywhere that I could to deliver as much pain to him as I could manage in retaliation for what he'd done.

I saw red, the blood, my fury, her pain, all of it etched into my flesh and burning with this desperate need to destroy the men who'd tried to destroy her. But they'd failed. They couldn't have her and I was ready to lay out their corpses at the feet of my hungry goddess.

I didn't even realise he'd fallen still until Winter's hand landed on my shoulder.

I looked up at her with a feral snarl on my lips, but instead of fear or horror, I found wonder and desire written into her beautiful features.

My breaths were laboured and my heart rate unrelenting as I sat before her, straddling her enemy, bathed in his blood and all I wanted in that moment was to drag her into my arms and kiss her until I took all of her pain away for good.

The knife was in her hand again and she offered it to me, her intentions clear. Farley was dead beneath me, I could tell, but she didn't want any what-ifs haunting her. I drove the blade into his heart with one swift blow to seal his fate without question.

I stood again, panting as I looked around, expecting the fight to continue but finding it over instead.

"Shit," I cursed as I looked over to where Duke had been sprawled out on the ground and seeing nothing more than a puddle of blood where he'd been. A trail of it led away from us, between the rows of cannabis plants towards the darkened mine shaft I'd used to get here.

My gaze moved to Farley and I realised he'd escaped this world too easily too. My fists and fury sweeping him away before he'd had a real chance to suffer. *Fuckers got off easy.*

"Are you okay, baby doll?" I growled, turning to her instead, the only one here who truly mattered anyway.

She was staring at me with her lips parted, those green eyes wide with an emotion I couldn't quite place.

I moved towards her, reaching out before realising my hands were stained with blood and lowering my arm again.

But she closed the space between us anyway, launching herself at me and leaping into my arms.

I wrapped my own arms around her in return, crushing her against my chest and inhaling the sweet scent of her hair as I swore to myself that I'd never let her go again. It hurt to hold her like that, to know I'd come so fucking close to losing her for good, to letting her down in the worst of ways. We lingered there in each other's arms, gripping one another so tightly that it seemed as though we might fuse ourselves into one being if we didn't stop soon.

"You're safe now," I promised her. "I've got you."

She squeezed me so hard that I could feel it right down to my soul, the salty tracks of her tears slipping down my skin where she'd buried her face against my neck. I let myself feel the relief of holding her again, of knowing she was safe in my arms and that I hadn't completely failed her.

With a grunt of determination, I pressed her back and inspected her with a critical eye, hating myself for every cut and bruise I saw marking her pale flesh. *This is my fucking fault, every mark on her skin may as well be my name branded there in accusation.*

I pulled my rifle off of my back and shed my jacket, wrapping her in it and zipping it up to her chin to keep her warm. I doubted she wanted pants from either of the dead men, so I left it at that for now.

"Stay by my side," I commanded as I bobbed my chin towards the exit. "I'm not letting you out of my sight again."

163

She nodded firmly, seeming to demand the same of me with one firm look in her emerald eyes. And if she truly wanted that then she could have it. Have me. Whatever I might be worth. I'd stand by her no matter what. I'd be her knight, her shield, her demon. Whatever she needed, I was hers.

I led the way out of the mine, taking the brightly lit passage around twisting turns all the way back to the surface. I paused at the exit until I was sure it was clear and then drew her out behind me with my rifle in my arms.

I glanced over at the other mine entrance and spotted fresh prints in the snow and a line of blood leading towards the trailers.

"Duke," I hissed, pointing out the tracks and glancing at Winter. I wasn't sure what to do. I wanted to chase him down, but I didn't want to put her in danger again.

Before I could make the call, Winter pointed firmly at the tracks then tugged my sleeve to make me follow them. She was right. We needed to finish this.

"Yes, my queen," I teased. "One more corpse, coming right up."

It was more than just vengeance for her. I could see it in her eyes. She needed him dead. Needed it over. It was the only way she'd ever be able to move on from what they'd done to her.

We followed the tracks as quickly as I dared and I was pleased with the amount of blood I saw splattered between the boot prints. He'd be lucky to survive that wound whatever happened, but I wanted him bleeding out at my feet all the same.

But as we reached the end of the trail he'd left, my gut plummeted. Fresh snowmobile tracks took over from the boot prints and the fact that I couldn't even hear the machine told me how far ahead he'd managed to get.

"Fuck," I cursed, looking around for another snowmobile so that we could chase him.

As I hunted, Winter suddenly caught my hand and shook her head, pointing at the bloody gunshot wound on my thigh with a terrified look in her eyes.

"It's fine," I said, dismissively. I'd been trained in the art of pain and torture and I could compartmentalise the throbbing heat of the wound while I focused on the hunt. It was bleeding a fair bit, but it was a flesh wound and I wasn't too concerned.

I tried to tug my hand away again but she frowned, keeping hold of me and tracing words against my palm.

It's not.

I sighed heavily, looking down at her in my jacket as she shivered, her bottom lip bleeding and blood staining her scarlet hair an even darker shade of red in places. I didn't care about some wound on my thigh, but as I looked at her I knew I couldn't drag her around out here. She was freezing, terrified, in shock. She needed to get somewhere safe and warm.

"I'll find him for you," I promised her as I reluctantly gave up on the idea of chasing Duke down right here and now. "I'll hunt him down once I can know you're truly safe somewhere."

She nodded like she really did believe that and I sighed as I pulled her against my chest once more, savouring that feeling of her in my arms.

"I'm so sorry, Winter," I breathed, the weight of responsibility I held for them capturing her again hanging over me like the weight of the world.

She shook her head in denial but I didn't let her pull away. She was shaking, her limbs trembling from the cold or shock or…

"You don't need to be afraid anymore," I swore to her, pushing her back just enough so that I could look into her eyes.

She glanced about and the fear there was impossible to miss. It wasn't just what had happened to her or the men we'd killed or Duke escaping. This *place* was the root of her fear too. It was where she'd spent her entire existence as far as she could remember. And it had been hell on Earth.

"You wanna see it burn?" I asked her, looking around at the mixture of mine shafts, trailers, cars and cabins that made up this ramshackle place.

Winter's eyes widened like the idea of that excited her and I smiled darkly as I moved towards the trailers, taking two huge tanks of propane which had been hooked up to heat them and dragging them back towards the mine shaft.

Next, I found a snowmobile and got it started, riding it over so that it sat idling beside the shaft, ready to ride just as soon as I was done.

Winter climbed on at my command and I gave her a dark smile as I grabbed the propane tanks again.

I found a heavy rock and used it to smash the valves off, the hiss of the gas escaping letting me know it had worked before I rolled the leaking canisters down into the dark. I pulled an old matchbook from my pocket and leapt up onto the snowmobile behind Winter.

I struck the match and tossed it into the shaft, ripping back the throttle in the same moment so that we sped away from the mine just as an explosion tore through it.

The ground quaked and trembled as the fireball erupted from the mouth of the cave and we shot away downhill at high speed as the networks of mines began to collapse like a tower of dominoes, destroying the cannabis farm with them.

Winter leaned into me as we raced away and I held her tight, smiling as a laugh filled with pure light escaped her as she craned her neck to look back at the burning campsite behind us.

"I'll destroy anyone and anything that ever hurts you, baby doll," I swore as I held her tight. "You only have to point me at them."

CHAPTER SEVENTEEN

N icoli's body surrounded me as the scent of blood and smoke tangled in the air mixed with the heady scent of *him*. His muscular arms built a cage around me as I sat between his thighs on the snowmobile, my body so small that I fit perfectly within the walls he made around me. It was the first cage I'd been in which didn't steel my freedom away at all. This one made me safe, and I knew I could escape it at any moment if I wanted. I just had to ask. And that meant more to me than words could ever convey.

We bumped over the snowy ground, sailing across the sheen of white as the stars glittered overhead and I stared up at them in awe. The sky was a huge and endless expanse. Nothing could keep me in this world if I chose to leave it, but right now I had more reason to stay than I'd ever had before. I was in the arms of a man who had come for me in my darkest moment. Who had stormed into an army, ripped through them like cannon fire and raced to my aid. But he was no valiant knight on a white horse, he was a violent attack dog sent from the very depths of hell. And he was exactly what I needed. A creature whose soul was as twisted up as mine.

I'd bled too many times to fear blood, and Nicoli had drawn it too many times to resist doing so again. And again. He was merciless and beautiful, and in the depths of my soul I wanted to keep him, even though I knew this time was fleeting.

He drove up to the cabin, parking the snowmobile and climbing off, a chill finding me the moment the warmth of his body left me. He picked me up before I could complain, cradling me in his arms and hugging me to his chest, his face a stony mask. My limbs were battered and bruised and there were enough fresh cuts on me that they stung in the freezing air. But I felt none of it like I felt the adrenaline sliding through my veins or the happiness caressing my heart at knowing two more of my monsters had been brutally ripped from this world. Orville and Farley would never haunt me again. Nicoli had made sure of that. And I was in awe of him for becoming my fists tonight, my armour.

He pushed though the broken door that The Five had kicked down and Tyson jumped down from the bed, his back leg lifting a little as he walked. My heart lurched at the sight of the wound on it and a noise of pain escaped me.

"He's alright," Nicoli growled, his breath against my ear making goosebumps rush across my skin. "It's nothing serious and he's tough." Tyson nuzzled his master's legs before heading to the broken doorway and sitting there like he was ready to guard us against anything bad that came this way again. But he didn't need to. The only man who would come for me now was Duke, but he was probably bleeding his guts out somewhere halfway down the mountain. Unless he received medical care soon, he wouldn't make it. I hoped he fell from his snowmobile before dawn and the crows picked him clean when he couldn't get up. At least that would serve him with the justice I'd intended for him. It was a gruesome enough death that even the image of it gave me some satisfaction.

Nicoli placed me on my feet, moving to prop up the broken door and wedge it in the doorway with a chair to hold it closed before stoking the fire to get the flames rising. Then he took my hand and strode into the bathroom, shutting the door behind us. The silence in the room made a sigh of relief escape me. We were safe. *Home.*

My eyes fell closed and I leaned in to Nicoli as I just appreciated the fact I was free. I hadn't met my end this night. And it seemed as though maybe, there was a real chance I didn't have to die up on this mountain. Perhaps there really was a life waiting for me at the bottom of it. But tonight, all I wanted was to be here with my warrior and wash the blood of my enemies from our flesh.

He lifted a hand, his thumb skimming my jaw as he checked me over. He growled angrily as I apparently didn't pass the assessment and I wasn't really surprised. I must have looked a fright, but as his dark gaze raked over me, I smiled. It didn't matter how hurt I was, I was only standing here at all because of him.

His eyes were drawn to my lips and a frown tightened his brow.

"I'm not sure I've ever been so afraid in my life as I was for you tonight," he admitted and my skin tingled from his words. Where did this saviour come from? Why did he look at me like that? Like I was far more than nothing, like I was *everything*.

He turned away from me, starting to draw a bath in the large square tub and I moved to the mirror, gently pulling off my clothes. I didn't want to remain in the items that had been half ripped from my body. I wanted to shed them like a second skin and release the horrors of this night through the action. When I stood naked in front of the bathroom mirror, I assessed my injuries. I rarely looked at myself in here. It wasn't something I was used to and had never really understood the benefit of. But now I could see it. The blood speckling my flesh like freckles brought life to my face. I could see the parts of my body that had filled out during my time with Nicoli, what being well nourished had done for me. I was...pretty. Even with the bruises and the scars. And especially with the blood of my demons coating me in warrior paint. There was no fear in my eyes like I often felt, just life and hope and maybe something deeper that I couldn't quite put into words, even if I'd had access to my voice.

"I would say you steal my breath away, Winter, but that's not quite right. You steal my entire lungs and my heart along with them."

I turned to Nicoli with my stomach flipping, his eyes on mine and a fierceness in his gaze that filled me up with strength and made my smile widen. He didn't ask me to cover up like he often did. Maybe he knew how important it was right now for me to be free of clothes, of chains, of everything.

"Come here, climb in." He held out his hand to me as steam swirled up from the tub and I moved towards him, sliding my palm into his.

I winced as I climbed into the heated water, but the pain was strangely like a balm too. Tonight was branded on me in every way possible, and I wanted to find more ways to keep it alive.

Nicoli released my hand, but I caught his again, tugging in a demand for him to follow me.

He looked to me with his frown deepening and I pointed to the wound on his thigh then to the water. He knew what I meant, even though his face didn't give it away.

"Baby doll..." he murmured in warning. "I should go."

I shook my head in refusal, tugging on his hand again as I slid deeper under the water so my breasts were covered and my hair fanned out around me in a sea of red.

He watched me like a hawk in the sky, but I wasn't some innocent creature waiting to be taken into his claws, I was a predator in my own right. One who hungered for blood like he did, who would follow him into a hunt at any opportunity. And he would follow me in turn. The look on his face said he knew that as well as I did.

He released my hand and tugged off his shirt, revealing the sculpted muscles of his body and the scars left on him from his past. The sight of his naked flesh made my stomach clench and my tongue feel heavy. He reached for his belt, unbuckling it slowly like he was hesitant, but his eyes remained on mine, waiting for me to tell him to stop. But I didn't.

"Are you going to sit there watching me, savage girl?" he asked with a smirk dancing around his mouth.

I nodded easily and a rumbling laugh escaped him that sent a shiver through my body.

"Suit yourself," he muttered as he undid his jeans and pushed them down. His boxers came off next and he didn't try to shield himself from me.

I bit into my lip as I took in the hardened length of him, proving his desire for me. My heartbeat quickened as he got into the tub and lowered down into it opposite me. The water was coloured red as the blood washed from our flesh and we bathed in it together like two soldiers home from battle.

I moved towards him on instinct, realising the welt on my lip had split again since I'd bitten it and the tang of iron filled my mouth as I swiped my tongue over the cut.

Nicoli's chest heaved as I moved toward him and I took a sponge from the side of the tub, soaking it in the water. I brought it to his face, washing away the blood then moving to his shoulders next before sliding it further down his chest. He caught my hand, his eyes darkening a shade as he pulled the sponge from my fingers and jerked his chin in a gesture for me to sit back.

My heart stammered and disappointment filled me as I moved to sit on the far side of the tub again, sucking on my lip as I stemmed the bleeding. My breath snagged in my throat as Nicoli followed me across the water and took my chin into his grip, his touch so achingly gentle that it felt like feathers against my flesh.

"You tend to no one tonight," he insisted, his fingers skating up to my ear where he tucked a lock of hair behind it. "I'll be looking after you, do you understand me?" His deep and commanding voice set my veins alight and I nodded easily, wanting that. I'd never been cared for like Nicoli cared for me and I wanted to be his ward tonight, and him my protector. Even if it couldn't stay that way forever.

He brought the sponge to my face, washing away the blood with impossibly gentle strokes, cleaning me inch by inch, his eyes fixed to my skin. I could feel his gaze on me like it was an elixir spreading across my flesh, everywhere he worked feeling as though it was melting like butter, soothing away the pain.

He cleaned my hair before moving to my shoulders and all the while I sucked on my lip, my own blood swirling over my tongue. He took my hand in his as he inspected every bruise and cut on my arm, his brows stitched together and a look of abhorrence in his eyes. I wanted to tell him that it was okay and ease that ache I saw in him for the sake of me. But my words didn't seem necessary tonight, even if I could have reached them. I just wanted his hands on me and that was enough to fill up my heart and make it beat with the kind of passion I had never known the taste of.

When my arms were clean, his gaze moved back to meet mine, the intensity of his expression making the air seem too thick to breathe. His eyes fell to my lip which I was sucking like he needed to tend to that too and I released it from the grip of my teeth so he could. He didn't lift the sponge as I expected, he pinched my chin with his finger and thumb, squeezing so my bottom lip pulled lower then he leaned forward and sucked it into his mouth. I shivered as pain and pleasure danced through my flesh and he leaned forward, bracing one hand on the tub's edge behind me and releasing my lip from his mouth, his breaths coming heavily as he stared me dead in the eye.

"I'm yours, Winter. In all senses. You can have my tainted soul to keep or to destroy, I don't care which. You've given me purpose when I thought I had none left in this world. I can't thank you enough for that." He leaned in closer and my heart fluttered and pounded. I reached out to his chest, painting two words on his skin in slow and fluid movements, a blush rising in my cheeks as I did so.

Kiss me.

A low growl sounded in his throat and his muscles flexed. "If I kiss you, I'll want to kiss more of you. I'll want to seek out each of your wounds and scars and brand them with something sweeter. If I kiss you now, I'll never stop kissing you until the world ends."

I smiled, my fingers still laying against his chest as I wrote out my reply.

So kiss me until the world ends.

His throat bobbed, then his restraint gave way at my offer and his lips met mine. I gasped into his mouth as his tongue pushed between my lips and I fell into the purest kind of heaven. Our kiss deepened, yet I still wasn't touching nearly enough of his flesh. I wanted to feel the heat of him against me and I arched my back in a demand for more, but he took my hips and pushed me down into my seat. His tongue moved more urgently against mine until a breathy moan left me. I painted one word on his skin everywhere I could reach, his arms, his shoulders, his back. *More, more, more.*

His hands trailed down my body beneath the water and he cupped my breast in his palm, his thumb grazing my nipple and making my back arch at the incredible sensation. He was like a jar of the sun spilling into my veins and making everywhere tingle with heat. It was addictive and made my thoughts tumble away before I could manage to grasp them.

"This," he said against my mouth, skimming his thumb over my nipple again so I gasped. "Is perfection. *You* are perfection."

Another moan left me and his kiss grew more fervent like he enjoyed that sound, his thumb circling my sensitive flesh to draw it from me again. His other hand rested on my thigh and my legs parted as he slid it higher up my leg. He didn't taunt me, but his movements were slow and measured like he was afraid of how fragile I was. It was frustrating as hell.

I drew words along his collar bone as I broke our kiss, meeting his gaze and making him pay attention.

I am not made of glass.

"Winter," he warned, rubbing the tip of his nose against mine. "I don't want to hurt you."

I wrote three words in response that made him stop looking at me like I was a china doll and instead lit that hungry fire in his eyes which I craved.

I trust you.

His hand shifted between my thighs and he watched me as his fingers brushed over my clit and I gasped, my head dropping back against the edge of the bath as he started rubbing and teasing me. I may not have remembered having sex before, but my body did and I followed my instincts as he drove me wild.

His other hand squeezed my breast and his thumb started up a tormenting rhythm against my nipple in perfect time with the strokes of his fingers between my thighs.

I moaned as pleasure skittered through me and I forgot everything, all the darkness in the world drifting away until there was just us and the rush of light blazing through my body. His fingers moved lower between my legs and he hummed his appreciation as he found my hot centre ready and desperate for him. He pushed two fingers inside me and I gasped, my back arching again so my body bucked out of the water. He started pumping them in and out and my muscles tightened around him as he laid claim to me. His forehead pressed to mine as he leaned over me and the brush of his hard length against my thigh had me aching for more.

He panted as hard as I did as he brought my flesh to life with every movement of his hand. I was suddenly burning hot as I clutched his shoulders and my hips rose to meet every movement he made. He curled his fingers inside me and I cried out as he rubbed the perfect spot, making me writhe and gasp as he brought me to the edge of oblivion. And this was the kind which I'd happily throw myself into, it wasn't a place to hide or crawl into, it was a place where I could ascend, a place to be seen and known and desired. Every touch told me how much he wanted that, how much he thought I was worth. And no one in my brief and painful awareness of my existence had cared enough to see me as a girl with something to offer outside of codes and screams and blood.

He lowered his hands from my breast and when his fingers met my clit and pinched, every part of me fell to ruin. I was crying out, moaning and clutching onto him as I rode out wave after wave of ecstasy, my eyes practically rolling into the back of my skull as he continued to pump his hand inside me. When it finished, I was no longer made of anything solid, my muscles weak and my body limp. I was still full of light, full to the brim, full for once in my life. I'd never even known I could feel pleasure like that, all I could remember was pain. Every touch in my memory was cruel and spiteful except from Nicoli. He was the only good thing I knew, and the only one I wanted to know.

He grinned darkly at me, kissing the corner of my mouth and I leaned into it, taking more and more. I slid my arms around him and the freedom I felt there was something I wanted to bottle and keep. But I wasn't done. I needed more than just his hands. I wanted to experience all of him.

I pushed him back and he moved away immediately, dropping down on the other side of the tub with his jaw tight. I could see his desire for me burning from the depths of his eyes and if he thought I wanted space between us, he was seriously deluded.

I moved forward, climbing over him and resting my knees either side of him, feeling his hardened length butting between my thighs. He stared up at me and I gave him a look that told him exactly what I wanted, then I reached between us, taking his solid shaft into my grip and gliding my hand up and down the smooth length of it. He hissed between his teeth, his hands falling to my hips and gripping firmly as I tightened my grip around him. Then I lifted my body and guided him to my entrance, a quiver running through me as I held his gaze, drinking in the longing in his expression.

"You beautiful, perfect thing," he growled then pushed me down onto him and I cried out as he drove himself deeper and deeper inside me. Inch by glorious inch, he filled me up and I braced my hands on his shoulders as I adjusted to the incredible feeling of him possessing me.

I started rocking my hips and he swore as I rode him, a primal part of me awakening and taking over as I dug my nails into his flesh and increased the pace. He wrapped his arms around me, letting me set the rhythm as I moved on top of him, drawing him in and out as he dipped his head to kiss my neck. His teeth grazed my skin and I shuddered with pleasure, moving faster still as I felt that urgent heat building in me once more, desperate to be unleashed. He reached up to fist a hand in my hair as he carved a line of fire along my collar bone with his mouth.

I could feel him swelling inside me as he continued to curse between breaths, his grip on me unyielding as I moved faster again. My world was spinning once more and the noises leaving me were purely animal as my body tightened around him and it felt a thousand times better than his fingers. He was thick and throbbing inside me and I could sense him holding back as his grip tightened in my hair, just hard enough to tug a little and I gasped as that kind of pain felt impossibly good.

I was already coming apart again and this time it was an explosion somewhere deep inside me as he hit the exact place I needed him to over and over. My body squeezed his and he lowered his mouth to my breast, sucking my nipple as the orgasm washed through me, his hips rising to meet mine as I moved frantically to prolong the force of nature crashing through my being.

"*Nicoli*," the word tumbled from my lungs and he groaned long and hard.

He pushed me down onto him with a fierce thrust of his hips and held me still, finishing with a dark growl that made me dig my nails deeper into his skin. He rested his forehead to my chest, panting heavily as he held me close and we both bathed in the bliss we'd delivered each other.

He was mine in that moment and I was his. And I never wanted that to change, no matter what fate had in store for us.

CHAPTER EIGHTEEN

I lay in my bed with Winter wrapped in my arms, our naked flesh hot against each other even while it remained freezing cold outside. Her head was on my chest and her fingers trailed over my skin, searching out my scars and caressing them with this fervent kind of attention like they meant something important to her.

After we'd gotten out of the bath and dried off we'd just ended up here like this, quietly resting in each other's arms and fighting against the need to get moving even as the sun rose beyond the windows. We hadn't slept. Just laid here together, peaceful in our own company as I kept hearing the way she'd moaned my name and the memory brought a smile to my lips every damn time I thought of it.

"What is it?" I murmured, sensing that something was on her mind.

I was fighting against the desire to stay here like this, prolonging the moment a little so that I could just bathe in this fucking perfect feeling.

I knew we needed to leave. Duke could be out there still and his bosses weren't going to just forget the fact that I'd killed half of their men and destroyed their whole operation. We couldn't stay. In fact, we should already be gone. But it was hard to leave. Hard to say goodbye to this place and the people we were here. There were identities waiting for me beyond these walls. Names I wasn't sure I wanted. Nicoli Vitoli…Angelo Romero…I was both of those men and neither of them. And who knew who Winter was aside from my savage girl. Someone must have been missing her, someone must have loved her before she was taken to this particular slice of hell. We were just two fucked up creatures with too many names and identities between us and I felt like the only place we both knew exactly who we were was right here. Together. What we were to each other was pure and simple, untainted by anyone or anything else. Just us. Alone. And I wished it could stay that way.

She began tracing words on my skin and my cock stirred against her thigh which she'd draped over me. I couldn't help it. I wanted this girl more than oxygen, I couldn't get enough, I didn't think I'd ever be sated. And the sex between us hadn't just been sex. It was like the joining of our souls, a place where unspoken words came to light and promises were made that didn't need voicing. I didn't care if it was insane or made no sense to anyone aside from us. We belonged together. I could feel it in every ounce of my being. It wasn't about instant love or the undeniable heat that burned between us. It was about all of the broken pieces of us feeling a little less jagged when we were together. Some days I felt like a puzzle with bits missing, stopping me from ever feeling complete, but with her, those holes didn't matter. She made new pieces which didn't fit the same as the old ones had, but which burned with beauty and colour and made everything seem brighter and more worthwhile.

I forced myself to concentrate on the words she was painting on my flesh, but she stopped before I got more than a few letters.

"We're the same, you and me," she breathed and the sound of her voice made a shiver run right through my body, hardening my cock even more and making me ache for her in a desperate kind of way.

"Yeah," I agreed, because there was no denying it. "But you deserve to be better."

An irritated growl rumbled through her body and her hand shifted down my chest, making my skin bristle with goosebumps before she took my cock in her hand. I groaned with desire as I traced my fingers up her spine, loving the way she arched into me as she continued to tease me with soft and confident strokes of her fingers.

"You're making it seriously hard for me to get out of this bed, baby doll," I groaned and her laughter called to me like rain on a hot summer's day.

I rolled onto my side and captured her lips with mine, kissing her slowly, teasing her lips apart with my tongue and massaging hers in a deeply sensual way that had her moaning into my mouth.

I rolled her onto her back slowly, my weight pressing her down into the crisp sheets as I continued to kiss her, waiting to see if she'd tense up or freak out at the feeling of me taking charge of this. I didn't want to do anything that might trigger the trauma of the things she'd been through, but it was so hard for me to hold back with her now that I'd started letting go.

Winter pumped my cock a little harder, as I ran my hands down her body, moaning again as I toyed with her breasts, rolling her nipples between my fingers and loving the way she arched into that, like she wanted more. Like she couldn't get enough.

"Are you sure you don't remember doing this before, baby doll?" I asked as I slid my lips from hers and started working down her neck, kissing, licking, biting a little before I remembered to go soft with her.

But she didn't flinch at the brush of my teeth on her flesh, she gasped, her thumb rolling over the head of my dick and making me groan in a desperate kind of way.

I dropped my mouth lower, tasting her flesh, kissing her scars, her bruises, her soul and marking all of it as mine. I wanted to worship every blemish on her flesh and let her know how much I adored them. They weren't reminders of pain and suffering or marks left by men who'd tried to destroy her. They were badges of honour. The marks of a survivor, the symbols of her strength and tenacity and never ending desire and determination to live through all of the worst things that life could throw at her.

I moved lower and she let out a frustrated breath as my dick was tugged from her hand, making me smile against her skin just before I took her nipple into my mouth. Winter moaned loudly, her hands moving to caress my shoulders before she caught my free hand in hers and threaded our fingers together.

I kept our fingers entwined in my left hand as I released her nipple with one final tug of it between my lips, bathing in the sounds she made in response to my touch. Even without the seductive purr of her voice, this girl could communicate to me on a level that was deep enough to reach me without words. She writhed beneath me as I moved lower, a murmur which was almost a protest leaving her lips, like she wasn't used to pleasure like this, like it was too much for her body to take and she didn't know how to handle it. But I was going to teach her how, I was going to train her flesh to crave softness and caresses which would ease away the memory of pain and fear. I was going to dedicate myself to giving her only the best of things in this world, letting her touch, taste, see and feel everything on a visceral level until the echoes of her torture faded away.

I knew they'd always be with her on some level, there was no way to stamp out the things she'd been through. But she could harness all of that pain into strength. I'd seen it myself. And I only wanted to stoke those flames in her.

My mouth trailed over her hipbone as I pushed her thighs further apart to accommodate my shoulders and she suddenly fisted her free hand in my hair, halting my progress with a gasp as she realised where I was heading.

Her green eyes were wide with hesitation, maybe a little fear too, like she didn't know if she wanted me to do this or not.

"It's just a kiss, baby doll," I purred tightening my grip on her hand as I pressed it down into the sheets. "Don't you like it when I kiss you?"

Her lips parted like they were caught between encouragement and objection and I smirked at her as my gaze dipped down to her pussy and I licked my lips slowly, loving the feeling of her eyes on me.

"How about you keep hold of my hair like that?" I asked her. "If you don't like it, you can pull me away. And if you do, you can press me down harder and fuck my mouth until you come around my tongue."

My gaze made it back to hers and my dick hardened at the sight of her dilated pupils and her ragged breaths. This was all so new to her, yet her body craved it, I could tell. She'd been too long in the dark, she was owed a thousand years of pleasure and I wanted to give her every second of it.

Slowly, without another word passing her lips, she used her grip on my hair to push my head down between her thighs.

"Fuck, baby doll, I'm gonna make you scream in all the right ways."

A soft moan urged me on and I dropped my mouth to her inner thigh a moment later, loving the way her grip on my hand and hair tightened simultaneously. I worked my way up to her core as slowly as I could manage, making her pant for me, stealing her hesitation away with desire instead even though I was starving for a taste of her.

When my mouth finally made it to the centre of her, I groaned as I lapped my tongue over the wetness I found waiting for me there. My poor, savage girl had been starving for this, for care and adoration and desire to fill her flesh.

Winter gasped as I ran my tongue around her opening, devouring her slowly, tasting, exploring, licking her delicately before I started in on my feast.

I took another slow lap of her pussy, loving the taste of her on my tongue and the way her hips shifted into the movement, demanding more.

I laughed against her flesh, letting the vibrations of my chuckle dance through my lips and into her body before licking around her again and again. When I finally ran my tongue up to her clit, she cried out, fisting her hand in my hair so tightly it hurt.

My grip on her other hand tightened and I tugged her thigh over my shoulder as I made my movements deeper, harder, loving the moment when she circled her other leg around my back too and clamped her thighs around my head.

She drove my head down with her hand in my hair and ground her hips against my mouth, fucking my tongue just like I'd promised she would. She was moaning so loudly that I couldn't help but wrap my free hand around my cock, relieving some of the desperate ache in it as I stroked myself.

Winter was moaning and panting, her movements urgent and her grip on me tightening everywhere she held me as I pushed her towards the cliff. It felt like she was fighting it, working against her own orgasm like the pleasure of it terrified her, but there was no way I was stopping until she fell into it.

I circled my tongue over her clit in a figure eight, releasing my grip on my cock and slipping two fingers into her wet heat.

I pumped them in and out a few times and suddenly she was coming, bucking against me, riding my fingers, ripping my hair out at the roots, heels driving into my spine.

It was so fucking hot that I almost came myself as I lapped at her wetness, prolonging the pleasure until her muscles fell lax again and she lay there panting as she tried to recover from what I'd done.

I laughed darkly, moving up the bed while trailing kisses up her flesh and loving the way goosebumps chased the course of my mouth.

I leaned over her, kissing her slowly again, wanting her to taste herself on my tongue, letting her know how good her desire felt.

She pressed her palms to my chest to move me back an inch, looking me right in the eye as she took my cock in her hand again.

I closed my eyes for a moment as she began stroking me, only opening them when she let go.

"Do you want to stop?" I breathed, still unsure about how far I should be pushing her like this. But she didn't seem to want me to stop and I certainly didn't want to.

She gave me a wicked smile and I watched as she dipped her fingers between her own thighs, slipping them inside herself and coating them with the evidence of her own desire before reaching out to take my cock again.

"I want to watch you fall apart for me like that," she said, almost shyly, but unapologetically and I could only curse as she used the lubrication from her own body to aid the journey of her hand around my thick shaft.

"Fuck, Winter," I groaned, my dick hard and throbbing in her palm.

She bit her lip as she watched me break for her, my arms trembling as I held myself up over her.

She seemed to realise the issue I was having and used her other hand to push my shoulder, urging me to roll onto my back before climbing up to straddle me.

I gazed at the perfect imperfections of her naked flesh as she pumped my cock harder, her thumb caressing the head in a way that made my balls ache and all of a sudden, I was growling her name and coming for her hard.

A trail of white cum spilled over my chest and she smiled like a fucking seductress as she appreciated the way she'd just brought me to ruin.

She leaned down slowly, her red hair spilling all around us as she lapped the cum from my flesh, moaning like she enjoyed the taste of me just as much as I had her.

Her mouth made it to my lips and the salty taste of my own desire danced against my tongue as she kissed me. This girl had me at her mercy and she knew it. I was hers. All in. Mind, body and soul, she could do what she wanted with me and I'd never regret a single second of it.

"Are you finally finished?" a voice came from outside the cabin and Winter shrieked as I bolted upright, swinging her off of my lap onto the bed beside me and grabbing my rifle from its position resting against the nightstand.

Tyson suddenly started barking in the bathroom and I cursed myself for shutting him away. But I just didn't want his doggy eyes pinned to me and Winter when we were naked together. It gave me the creeps.

"Who the fuck is there?" I snarled because there had been something familiar in that voice and we weren't dead yet, so I had just enough reason not to start firing right away.

"It's Frankie Romero, don't you recognise your own brother's voice, Angelo? I have to say I'm surprised - I came here to find some murderous mountain man and end up catching an eyeful of my brother getting his cock stroked. It wouldn't kill you to close your curtains you know…though I suppose then I would have burst in there with my gun aimed and I might not have realised it was you until it was too late, so I guess I'll accept the mental scarring."

My heart stilled in my chest. I'd known we had to leave here, that our bubble was bursting and I couldn't remain hidden away from the world on the side of a mountain forever. But *fuck*, I hadn't expected my demons to catch up to me quite so quickly.

"It's alright," I murmured to Winter, trying to reassure her about the man who claimed to be my kin and who was waiting outside my broken door. I was at least eighty percent sure that was the truth too. The Romeros didn't want me dead. At least not anymore. The real question was what *did* they want from me. "Get dressed," I urged.

I took my own advice and grabbed a pair of jeans, tugging them on over the bandage I'd used to wrap my leg and cringing my teeth at the twinge of pain it caused. I let Tyson out of the bathroom, silencing him with a sharp whistle and stalking towards the front door.

I looked back to find Winter buttoning one of my plaid shirts over her chest, a pair of my jeans awkwardly belted around her waist. She gave me a fearful look, but I knew I wouldn't be able to get rid of this house guest without at least some kind of conversation.

I hoisted the rifle in my arms and threw the broken door open, looking out at the man who I shared blood with and wondering if that even meant anything after all the things that had passed between us.

"Don't call me Angelo," I growled, taking in his expensive ski jacket and perfectly styled black hair. He had a pretty face, too pretty for a gangster with blood on his hands and darkness in his soul. He was clean shaven and clean cut, a far cry from me in my frayed jeans and nothing else with hair trimmed by a savage girl and stubble coating my jaw.

"It's your name though," Frankie said with an easy smile. "At least one of them anyway."

I huffed out a breath which was neither confirmation or denial and lifted my rifle an inch to remind him he wasn't invited.

"Are you going to introduce me to your lady friend or did you wear her out?" he asked, his eyes twinkling with amusement as his gaze slid over my shoulder to take in Winter. I didn't like the flirtatious smile he tossed her way and I stepped out onto the porch before forcing the broken door shut behind me.

"What do you want?" I asked, not bothering to ask how he'd found me. The Romeros were like a pack of wolves, I'd always known I wouldn't escape their hunt forever.

Frankie's gaze softened as he looked at me, something in his eyes making me want to lay off on the angry tone I was using and find out more about who he was. I could even see something of myself in his features now that I knew to look for it. We had the same hazel coloured eyes, the same dark hair and even the shape of our jaws held similarities. *Fuck.*

"We just want our brother home," he said softly, speaking for the others who weren't here. Enzo whose reputation of fear and violence proceeded him and Rocco...the man who'd stolen my bride...

"You already have two brothers, are you really so keen for a third?" I asked, lowering my rifle and turning away from him. He didn't want me dead. I already would be if that was the case. He'd snuck up on me and Winter while we were...*busy*...so he'd had the opportunity already.

"You know it's not a numbers game," Frankie muttered. "This, us, all of us, we were always meant to be banded together. We've been missing you for a hell of a long time, please don't walk away from us now that we have the chance to reunite."

The raw emotion in his voice made the words in my throat fall still. I ran a hand down my face and dropped onto the swing seat, ignoring the bite of the cold air against my bare chest as I looked up at the man who shared my blood. My brother.

"And what about your father? How does he feel about his long lost boy being raised by Calabresis and then just sauntering back into the fold like I was never gone in the first place?"

Frankie winced just a little, but it was enough to let me know that Martello Romero wasn't exactly waiting with open arms for me back in Sinners Bay.

"Papa is...*cautious,*" Frankie hedged, offering me an apologetic smile. "He'd like a DNA test before he will really believe that you're...you."

I snorted a laugh. *I* didn't even know who I was so I doubted some swab would have the answers for me. But I guessed blood was blood.

"But me and the others, Rocco and Enzo, we know who you are. We feel it. And we aren't looking for anything at all from you except the chance to know you. For you to know us. We don't expect you to come and join the family business or start running Romero jobs, or even take our name back if you don't want it. We just want the opportunity to know our brother."

My heart twisted at his words and for a long moment I couldn't say anything at all. I wasn't sure if I'd ever had a family member want something so simple from me before, so pure. Even when I'd been posturing as the Calabresi heir I didn't feel wanted like that. Like I had value just for being myself and not for the things I could offer up to others. It hurt and it stung and it opened up this desperate kind of want in me that was hard to resist.

"That's all?" I asked, as if it could be so simple. "After everything we've all done to each other?"

"That was all in the past. It was Calabresi verses Romero. War. Hate. Whatever you want to call it. But this is more important than that. It's blood, family, love." Frankie took a step towards me like he wanted something else from me, but I didn't know what. And that last word he'd spoken opened up a chasm in me which I was afraid to look at too closely. I didn't think I'd ever been loved. At least not by anyone I could remember. It was why I'd fought so hard for Sloan. That promise of undying devotion, of someone to give your heart to and trust with the keeping of yours.

"I..." I shook my head, pushing myself to my feet again as I tried to find some other protest, some reason to deny his offer and tell him to leave me alone for good.

Frankie stepped forward and dragged me into his arms before I could utter a single word. His grip was tight and bruising, one hand clasping the back of my head as the other arm crushed me to his chest.

"I've missed you all my life, brother," he said roughly. "Come home with me. Please."

My arms slowly closed around him too and something I'd never even known I'd been missing seemed to click into place in my soul. It was bloody and carved with rough edges so that I didn't know how to handle it, but it was also really fucking good.

"Okay," I agreed, not really understanding why, but knowing that I needed this, needed him and maybe even the others too. "But I don't really know how to be a brother."

Frankie laughed and released me, gripping my face between his hands as he looked at me with his eyes shimmering with emotion. "Well, the first thing we do is clean up each other's messes."

"Oh yeah?" I asked, wondering what he meant by that.

"Yeah. Our aunt Clarissa just so happens to be the bitch whose marijuana crop you just destroyed, so we're going to need to make sure she thinks this mountain man is good and dead."

"Shit," I laughed, unable to help myself as I pulled out of Frankie's grip. "And there was me thinking I'd gotten away from Romeros and Calabresis up here."

"Not likely, fratello, you'd have to run a lot further than this to escape us."

I stilled at the casual use of that nickname for me. I'd never really had the strongest grasp of Italian but I'd been surrounded by people speaking it often enough that I knew basic words like that. Fratello - brother. Just like that, he accepted the bond between us. Could I do so too?

"How do you plan on covering this up then?" I asked, skimming over the nickname issue and focusing on what mattered most right now.

"Simple. I'll grab one of those fucked up corpses you left on the mountain and take some photos of it in your lovely little home here, then we set the whole thing alight and fuck off before she sends anyone else to check my story. They'll find a burned down shack with a bunch of bones in it and you come back to the city with me and hide out for a few weeks before I reveal to everyone that I found you. No one will ever link the mountain man to Angelo and we'll be home and dry." He grinned like an over confident asshole and despite my better judgement, I found myself liking him. *Christ.*

"Why do I get the impression you've covered up shit like this before?" I asked him.

"We got away with hiding the fact that Sloan killed our cousin, Clarissa's son, Guido. Clarissa is a dumb bitch who believes what's convenient. If she wasn't Papa's sister she'd barely be involved in the family affairs at all. As it is..." He shrugged. "She's a thorn in our side. If you stick around you'll figure that out for yourself. But at least when you have to suffer through her company you can console yourself by laughing your ass off over the fact that you burned down her entire cannabis farm."

He started laughing and I couldn't help but join in. There was something free and light about him, something just so easy to like. I didn't know if it was just the way he was or if it was because our blood recognised each other, but I found myself relaxing in his company already. *Well, shit.*

"So who's your girl?" Frankie asked. "Are you going to introduce us?"

I hesitated. If Duke and his gang had been employed by Clarissa Romero then that meant that they worked for Frankie's family. So there was a damn good chance that Clarissa or someone else in their organisation had arranged for Winter to be tortured. If I trusted him with her identity then I could be risking her safety. But he seemed like he had my back, and maybe he'd be able to help me figure out who the fuck had organised what had happened to her.

"We're a package deal," I said, that growl coming back to my voice. "If I tell you what I know about her then you're going to agree to either leave her alone or help her. If you do anything to put her in danger I'll fucking kill you."

"Back the fuck up, stronzo, I asked her name not for a turn with her," Frankie joked, holding his hands up innocently.

I huffed out a breath but there was nothing I could do aside from tell him. I couldn't risk bringing her to his home without knowing what he'd do when he discovered her identity. At least if it happened here I had the upper hand.

"She was being held up at that camp. Tortured for information she doesn't even remember. The poor girl doesn't even know what her name was before all of this, let alone what they want to know."

Frankie released a long whistle, glancing at the closed cabin door and then back to me. "You sure she's worth the trouble?" he asked, not cruelly, just curious.

"Yes," I growled.

"Alright. But if she was up there then Clarissa will be linked to it. I dunno if it was her job or one she was paid for, but I can maybe find out why they had her." The calm sincerity in his voice had me relaxing again. He didn't even flinch at this new problem. Just took it in his stride and tried to figure it out - he was a fixer, the kind of guy you called when something went wrong because he always came up with a plan. And the fact that he was willing to help me with this so easily got my heart racing.

"You'll help me protect her?" I confirmed, needing to hear him spell it out.

"If she's your family then she's my family," he confirmed with a firm nod. "Now, get your shit together, anything you can't bear to let burn, and get your girl ready to go. If we're not off of this mountain within a few hours then we aren't going to get away before Clarissa's stooges show up. I'll go get a body to use for our fake mountain man."

He strode away like that was the end of it and I watched him head out into the trees in his designer ski-wear with my eyebrows raised. Apparently I'd gone from being all alone in the world to suddenly having a family who would help me with no question at all. Winter, Frankie, maybe even Enzo and Rocco too. I didn't really know how to process all of that so I just shook my head and turned away, heading back towards the cabin to prepare Winter to leave.

This mountain had been my refuge when I needed it most. But it was time to return to the real world.

CHAPTER NINETEEN

T he long drive back to the city was a quiet one. Angelo or *Nicoli* as I guessed he still wanted to be called seemed to have retreated into himself and the girl he'd introduced as Winter hadn't said a single word to me. Not one. I wanted to ask, but the look Nicoli gave me closed the subject for discussion so I guessed my curiosity would have to wait.

I drove through the brightly lit streets of Sinners Bay with my stomach rumbling and music growling through my speakers as some dude rocked out so hard I lost sense of the words. But the beat was good and my fingers were drumming against the steering wheel, so I guessed it was all good.

Winter had curled up on the back seat with her arms around the huge dog my brother had insisted on giving a seat in my luxury SUV about an hour into the journey and I'd been having discussions on and off with Nicoli ever since then. We talked about our family, people he'd heard of and those he hadn't. He was most interested in hearing personal stories about things me, Rocco and Enzo had gotten up to together over the years, like maybe he was trying to imagine where he would have slotted into them if things had been different.

I cast glances his way when I told them as often as I could, trying to gauge how he felt about all of these stories of three brothers who should have been four. It had to suck pretty hard being invited to join a group which was clearly so close knit already, but we all wanted this more than I could express. Yes, we'd grown up without him and I'd been so young when he'd supposedly died that I had no memory of him or our mamma at all, but that didn't mean we hadn't missed him. We'd all felt that hole in our lives where he should have been, all suffered through our papa's grief and we were all aching to return him to his rightful place amongst us.

"Give it a few months and there will be plenty of stories involving the *four* of us to laugh about," I said, wondering if telling him all of this just made him feel worse about everything or what. He was certainly a cagey bastard.

"I'm not really...*fun,*" Nicoli said slowly. "Not like those stories. When I worked for...your opposition, we were encouraged to conduct business quickly and efficiently. We didn't do any of that shit you guys do like dress men up as clowns and make them walk the plank with bricks chained to their ankles-"

"I'll have you know we gave that guy the key to his chains before he jumped in the water. He only drowned because he was a dumb shit. He had a decent chance at saving his ass - even if we did make him wear massive rainbow clown pants at the time."

"Did it occur to you that those clown pants might have gotten in his way when he tried to unlock the chains?" Nicoli asked, but I swear the corner of his lips twitched as he did. I probably wouldn't have noticed the movement at all except it was the exact same almost-smirk that Enzo always got on his face when he was trying to pretend he was a straight up psychopath. I mean, sure, he was an occasional psychopath, but I'd call it a killing hobby. He enjoyed taking out garbage when the occasion called for it and yeah he might have dressed the killings up in the odd show of theatrics, but there was really something so much more to that than met the eye.

"Did it ever occur to *you* that when people read a story in the news

198

about six mobsters being executed in the back of some old warehouse they curl back their upper lip and mutter good riddance beneath their breath then promptly forget the whole thing," I said slowly, turning off of the road we were on and onto the side street where my apartment was located.

"What's your point?" Nicoli asked, not brashly, more like he actually gave a shit about where I was going with this.

"Then those same people read a story the next day. Some guy has been strung up by the marina where a bunch of crazy assholes shot fireworks at him until he went up in flames so bright every fucker in the city with a view of the sea could see him. They don't forget about that story, in fact, they go around to their little friends whispering about it, the name Romero passed from mouth to mouth like a curse they hardly dare to mention. No one wants to die like that. *Jesus Christ, don't piss of the Romeros or it could be you next...*"

Silence hung for a long moment and then Nicoli started chuckling. "So you mean to tell me that you kill less people but just do it with more fucking drama and somehow your reputation is the most terrifying?"

"I told you being one of us was fucking brilliant, fratello," I replied with a grin, turning into the underground parking lot beneath my building. I slowed the car before the gates, waiting for them to open as the guard on duty recognised me. "And to make it even better, those guys we kill are the worst of the worst, fuckers with no goddamn morality, no code, monsters who need putting down. We do this city a service," I said, a teasing tone to my voice which didn't lessen the ring of truth my words held.

I glanced in my rear view mirror at Winter sleeping on the back seats with the dog and the smile slid from my lips as I drove towards my personal parking space at the back of the lot.

"Those people who had her hurt her real bad then?" I asked, watching Nicoli from the corner of my eyes as his smile slid away too.

"Most of them have paid for that in death now," he growled. "One got away."

"Clean?" I asked.

"I stabbed him pretty good before he ran. Kidney shot. He might have bled out or passed out and died from exposure before he reached help. He might have made it all the way back to the city. I won't let it go until I see a corpse," he swore and I could feel the tension rolling off of him as he gritted his teeth in frustration, clearly fighting to contain the rage he felt over all of this.

"Has he got a name?" I asked. If he was on Clarissa's payroll then I'd be able to find him sooner or later. I had loyal men hidden amongst hers and if they couldn't track down what I needed then I'd be able to buy the information from Clarissa herself. Everything had a price after all and some kidnapper slash drug dealer who'd lost his girl and all of the product he'd been responsible for wouldn't be worth shit to her anyway. In fact, there was a good chance that she'd take him out herself when she found out how royally he'd fucked up if he did show his face back here again.

"Duke Polinsky," Nicoli growled, like the name itself was the most heinous of curses.

"Leave it with me," I said just as I parked up.

Nicoli gave me a look which said he wanted to question why I'd help him like that, but I'd already made my position clear. Family was everything to us. Me and my brothers most of all. And he belonged in our circle even if he'd been absent from it for far too long. We'd never let his place get too cold for him. If he wanted in then that was that. And I really hoped he wanted it.

As I cut the engine, Winter stirred, bolting upright suddenly and looking around in panic as she took in the underground parking lot beyond the windows. She lurched for the door handle and released a frightened sound when it wouldn't open for her.

"It's okay, baby doll," Nicoli promised, reaching for her as she fought the door handle and I hit the button to unlock it for her.

She spilled out with a gasp of relief and Nicoli was out in the same breath, pulling her into his arms before I even unbuckled my belt.

I got out and closed the door, drawing closer to them and apologising to

Winter for frightening her.

"We're family now," I promised her as she turned her wild gaze on me. "You don't need to worry about me."

"Shit, Tyson, not inside," Nicoli groaned and I followed his gaze to see the huge dog taking a piss up the side of a flashy Audi which belonged to my asshole neighbour.

"Take a shit on it too," I encouraged the dog as I barked a laugh. "That guy is a total prick."

Nicoli snorted a laugh as Tyson darted forward and licked my hand and I had to admit that he seemed like a pretty decent dog.

I pointed toward the private elevator for the penthouse and Nicoli scooped Winter up into his arms, carrying her over to it as I moved forward to press my thumb to the scanner.

"I'll get you on the system so you can use it too," I promised as I noticed his interest lingering on the security I had. "Papa insists we all have the best security in place on our properties in the city. Ever since Mamma was killed and you were stolen from us..." I trailed off. It wasn't like I needed to remind him of the events that had led to his entire life being ripped away from him anyway.

"That makes sense," Nicoli said roughly. "And I'll certainly feel happier knowing Winter is safe here."

"That you are, sweetheart," I assured her and she blinked those green eyes at me without a word but she didn't seem so afraid of me anymore, so that was something. "I can order in some new clothes for both of you," I offered. "I'll have them here by tomorrow and then you can both get settled in and we can figure out the rest of it as and when."

The elevator started ascending and Nicoli lowered Winter back to her feet. She'd shrugged out of the coat and kicked off the massive boots she'd been wearing when we'd descended the mountain in the car so now her feet were bare beneath a pair of men's jeans which had been rolled up multiple times and held in place with a belt. The green check shirt she wore over it matched the red one Nicoli was sporting. They honestly looked like they were about to shoot a low rent lumberjack porno or something. It hurt my fucking eyes. I let my gaze skim over the two of them with a critical eye as I assessed their sizes then sent out a message to some of my people telling them to get on the case ASAP. I wished I could snap a picture of the shit show which was their outfits to accentuate my point, but I guessed as they were lying low that wasn't the best idea.

The elevator arrived with a ding and the door slid open to reveal two over excited assholes who'd clearly gotten into my liquor.

"Surprise!" Enzo shouted as Rocco pulled the string on a party popper which spewed a pathetic amount of paper streamers in our vague direction as he grinned at us.

"You decided to stop sulking and come join your brothers at last then?" Rocco asked, arching an eyebrow at Nicoli in classic alpha male bullshit posturing.

"I had hoped the months apart might give you time to work on your personality," Nicoli replied calmly. "No such luck it would seem."

"Who's the hot piece of ass?" Enzo asked with a big smile for Winter and I swear Nicoli actually growled as he took a step forward, placing himself in front of her so that Enzo couldn't keep looking.

"Winter's with me," he said in a tone that promised bloodshed if anyone in this room even looked at her wrong, let alone touched her.

Enzo laughed darkly, raising his hands in submission as he backed away. I noticed Winter was looking kinda horrified to be surrounded by four big, Italian men. And I guessed after all she'd been through I could appreciate her hesitancy.

Tyson ran past my brothers through the open space of my apartment. We were on the eightieth floor and were high enough to see the bay from the wall of windows which covered the far side of the space. Everything was simply decorated in tones of grey and white, though I had a set of blue scatter cushions and a rug in the living area which Rocco's wife, Sloan, had insisted on buying me to break things up. There was a scented candle which had never been lit lurking somewhere around here too. She liked to try and help me out with my 'hopeless bachelor ways' whenever she could.

"I can show you guys where you can stay," I offered, taking in Winter's nerves and how dead tired the two of them looked. "You can clean up and when you're ready to socialise, I'll order us all a pizza. How does that sound?"

Rocco and Enzo looked mildly disappointed when Nicoli quickly agreed, but I could see that he was getting overwhelmed, not to mention Winter's discomfort.

"We can just chill out and take things from there." I pointed them down the corridor to their right and as Nicoli led Winter along it, I shot my other brothers a dark glare.

We'd be having words when I got back from settling them in about how to deal with this sensitively. I hadn't gone this far to find Angelo only to have him run from us again. This had to go right or it was all going to fall apart. We had our brother back. And I intended to make sure he stayed for good this time.

CHAPTER TWENTY

I lay by the wall on the floor of the huge bedroom Frankie had gifted me, the door open so I could see out into the hall and know that I wasn't locked in. The single blanket I'd taken from the bed was silken soft and hugged my skin. My bruises had turned a sour shade of yellow, but the cuts were healing well and the pain had eased so much that I barely noticed it now. And yet sleep still wouldn't come. The Romeros had left us here alone for the night and I had a feeling that was to do with me, because as much as I wanted to trust them, I couldn't relax in a house full of men I didn't know. And something told me they understood that. I just hoped I wasn't always going to remain this broken.

When my eyelids fluttered closed, I saw Duke leaning over me with a belt wrapped around his hand. I saw his sneer and even when I tried to picture him dead, I couldn't. Seeing no body meant I couldn't put my nightmares of him to rest. And maybe that meant he would always be with me. The final dagger in my heart, forever twisting and drawing blood. It was better than before though. The ghosts of the others were gone. I was at peace when it came to them at least...

The air-con stirred my hair and I shivered. I'd been unsure of how to turn the thing off and it seemed to be set to some sub-zero temperature colder than the mountain we'd left behind. I curled up tighter on the hard wood and searched for peace somewhere inside me, but it wouldn't come. My past was awake tonight, clawing its way through my mind and bringing me to the mercy of Duke again and again. I could almost feel him striking that belt, splitting skin. He never stopped until I screamed, but I always held out for as long as possible. He'd build up a sweat then peel off his coat and light a cigarette, the heavy scent making me cough. He'd chained my hands to the table once and struck them with a cane until my knuckles had bled and every inch of my pale skin had turned red raw.

"What's the code?"

"What's the code?"

"What's the motherfucking code!?"

I flinched as a hand pressed to my arm, then relaxed as I recognised Nicoli, turning my head and opening my eyes to look at him. He was shirtless, his breath minty and a deep V was etched between his eyes. "Will you do something for me, baby doll? One favour?"

I opened my mouth, but my voice had been buried even deeper than usual by Duke haunting me so I gave up and nodded.

"Sleep in with me, in my room. I want to watch over you. And if you can, please sleep in the bed."

My heart knotted at his words. They terrified me in a way that something so normal shouldn't have. But I knew what he was asking was only for my benefit. Sleeping on the floor was a chain that still bound me to The Five. The only way I'd felt any semblance of safe in my cell at night was being tucked against a wall. But a bed? Sleeping in a bed with Nicoli... I loved the sound of it, I really did. The reality wasn't so easy though.

"Just try," Nicoli implored. "And if you don't like it, then I'll sleep on the floor with you. I know you don't need me close, but I...well fuck if I haven't gotten used to you being close. I don't think I can sleep without you near now."

My heart lifted at his sweet words and I smiled genuinely at him, reaching out to cup his cheek. Maybe that was another reason why I couldn't sleep. Nicoli's presence alone could banish the ghosts lurking in my mind.

"Shit, you're freezing." He pulled me into his arms, marching me out of the room and kicking the door closed as he headed down the hall and into his room. It was smaller than mine, cosier, but there was still a newness about everything that gave this place the feel of a hotel over a home. Not that I could remember being in a hotel, but there was something oddly familiar about all these shiny walls and expensive things. With Nicoli close, anywhere felt good though. Safe.

Tyson was sleeping on a blanket on the floor and he lifted his head as we entered, his tongue lolling out of his mouth. With him and Nicoli present, I already felt miles less anxious than I had alone.

He placed me on my feet and moved to the bed, drawing the covers back in an offering. I glanced at the bandage on his thigh which covered the stitches his brother Rocco had given him last night, wondering if he'd end up with a scar to remember that fight by forevermore.

I crept forward, wanting to feel self-assured but all I actually felt were brambles winding around my lungs until I couldn't breathe.

Duke was still too close for my liking and his voice was ringing in my head. *"Sleep on the floor like the rat you are. One word of complaint and I'll cut your tongue out."*

I'd wanted to remind him that cutting it out would defeat the purpose of my interrogation. But I supposed so long as I could still hold a pen to paper, any of my body parts had always been fair game.

I stepped past Nicoli, drawing comfort from his presence as I climbed onto the bed and pushed my legs under the sheets. I sat stiffly as my heart began to pound, then looked up at Nicoli as I bit down on my thumb.

"Lay whatever way you find most comfortable," he urged and I took a steadying breath, turning my gaze to the pillows and the large black headboard that rose up behind me.

I twisted around, moving the pillows so they lay horizontally along the bed then curled up against the headboard and rested my head on one of the pillows. It was like a cloud, the cool material drawing a sigh from my lips. It was way warmer in here than the other room and the flannel shirt I wore was far too snug against my flesh. I pulled it off and writhed against the silken sheets as I felt it everywhere over my naked flesh.

Nicoli chuckled and I turned to look at him with a grin on my face. My voice loosened and my smile grew even wider as I took that power back into my grasp, feeling like I was reuniting with an old friend. "Are you going to join me, mountain man?"

He stepped closer, blotting out the light so he was just a dark shadow above me and I shivered deliciously as he brushed his fingers over my back. "Give me one more minute, savage girl, you have no idea how good the view is from up here."

I laughed and he took several more seconds before he switched off the light, his weight pressing the bed down as he slid in behind me. The bed was so large that he could lie sideways comfortably enough and he moved up behind me, drawing the covers over us as he slid his arms around my waist and pulled me back into his chest. I was about to complain that that wasn't how I slept best, when he squeezed me tight and my worries ran away like water down a drain.

"Oh," I sighed, my eyes falling closed. And no nightmares seized me, no demon with a belt in hand came to terrify me. Nicoli's breaths skated against the back of my neck then he laid a soft kiss behind my ear.

"Do you think you can sleep like this, baby doll?" he murmured and I reached down to find his hand on my stomach, threading my fingers between his.

"I could sleep like this forever," I whispered and he kissed that same spot again, making a deep tremor race down my spine. He was so warm and solid and utterly real that it made my heart want to weep. I never wanted him to leave and I was starting to hope that maybe I would be lucky enough for him to stay. He was the only solid thing in my world, without him, I'd be lost.

I yawned, peace encasing me as I relaxed in his arms. I'd never felt so tired, like a thousand restless nights were begging to be made up for right here and now. And if I really did sleep for an eternity in Nicoli's arms, that wouldn't be the worst fate that could befall me.

I woke to a bang and jolted in alarm, pushing at the arms holding me captive as panic washed over me like ice cold water. I gasped and became frantic as I couldn't escape, my mind dizzy as I started to claw and rip at my captor. A dog started barking and my heart bashed against my ribcage in fear.

"*Winter*," Nicoli growled, holding me tighter and pressing kisses to any space of flesh he could reach. "You're safe. You're with me."

I rolled towards him, needing to see him for myself, but the daylight that should have brightened the room was blotted out by thick blinds, so I breathed in his hazelnut scent instead and leaned forward to find his mouth for a kiss. It stole my breath and made my heart start to slow. *I'm safe. No one can find me here.*

My kiss was an apology I couldn't give in words in that second as I caressed the scratches on his arms with a noise of pain in my throat.

"It's alright, I've got you," he swore.

My heart rate started to settle but before I could feel totally calm again, he slid away, storming to the door and flicking the light on. Tyson was bouncing up and down at the door and as Nicoli opened it, the dog shot out ahead of him. Nicoli strode from the room in his boxers with his shoulders tense, muttering furiously under his breath. Whoever had made that sound had better run for their lives.

"Could you fucking knock?!" Nicoli snapped and I finally relaxed as

Frankie answered. The clear perpetrator. It was just the beautiful man with the darkness behind his eyes.

"It's my apartment, fratello," Frankie laughed and I noticed Tyson had stopped barking.

"She's been through the fires of hell, so don't storm into the place like you're a pissed off hillbilly, understood?" Nicoli demanded.

"Alright, alright," Frankie said lightly. "No door banging. I've got the memo, stronzo. Where is the little beauty anyway?"

I slipped out of bed, walking into the hall and through to the lounge. The second I did, Nicoli ran at me like his ass was on fire and my eyes widened as he wrapped his whole body around mine and half carried me back down the hall. It was only then that I remembered I was naked.

"Jesus fucking Christ," he growled. "Please put something on when other people are around, Winter."

A laugh escaped me and he tutted angrily as he guided me back into his room, grabbing one of his shirts and tugging it firmly over my head. He was still tight-lipped when I turned to him and I smiled teasingly.

Woops, I wrote on his chest and he shook his head at me.

"I think I got you before he saw anyway," he muttered.

"You didn't," Frankie's voice sailed from out in the hall. "Nice scars by the way, Winter. You're a fucking warrior."

I blushed a little at the compliment. It might have been strange to anyone else, but it meant the world to me. He saw my scars as a sign of strength, just like Nicoli did. And after spending so long being told I was weak, even starting to believe it myself, it felt amazing to have these two brothers see that in me.

"Erase that image from your memory," Nicoli snarled as he pushed the door open again and Frankie stood there with a smirk on his face, stroking Tyson's head where he sat beside him, staring up at him like he was his new favourite person. Frankie acted like he owned the whole world and everyone in it and I wondered how rich he really was. I also wondered if all Romeros had the gift of calming any wild creature they set their sights on. Maybe Tyson could sense a predator in him like he could in Nicoli.

"No can do," Frankie said. "But don't worry, I've got a whole cordoned off section in my mind for girls my brothers fuck. It's a neutral zone with absolutely zero memories uploaded to the spank-bank."

I laughed and Frankie's brows lifted, his grin growing wider.

Nicoli folded his arms. "You better had. She's had enough men leering at her in her lifetime."

"Firstly, I don't leer. I throw a glance and curl a single finger if I want a girl's interest and they come running. One girl even had an orgasm before she made it to my table in Paulo's club once. Caused quite a fucking scene when she collapsed to the floor I can tell you. So if I turned on the charm you would be royally fucked, fratello - no offence Winter, but I am devilishly charming and impossible to resist. Plus I'm clearly the best looking brother. It's a plain fact." He grinned in a way that meant I couldn't quite tell if he was joking or not.

I tip-toed up to whisper something to Nicoli, struggling to get my voice to work for Frankie.

Nicoli roared a laugh. "She says, are you sure the girl had an orgasm and didn't just fall over your ego or slip in a pile of the bullshit that was coming out of your mouth?"

Frankie chuckled. "Did she now?" His eyes wheeled onto me and I blushed a little as I taunted him. "Well, *fuck*, funny *and* beautiful, why did you agree to be my brother's girlfriend again?" he teased.

Heat flooded my cheeks and I didn't know where to look as Nicoli cleared his throat uncomfortably.

"Woops-a-fucking-daisy, haven't had that conversation then I suppose?" Frankie threw his head back with a laugh. "Well, I've gotta go on a job I can't get out of today, but as soon as I'm done, we're going to have some serious bonding time, fratello. Sports channels, beers, pool, whatever the fuck you're into. I just dropped by to let you know there'll be a delivery of clothes for you both soon and a doctor will be stopping by this afternoon to check you over.

211

I'll see you tonight."

Doctor?

"You couldn't have called with that information?" Nicoli asked as Frankie strode away.

"I don't have a landline here, Nicoli, I'm not a housewife in the nineties. But I will call in future. You both have new phones waiting for you in the lounge."

"I have a phone," Nicoli said.

"One that's at least two centuries old and which you never answer. So now you have a shiny new phone. Enjoy." Frankie smirked. "I'll take Tyson with me too, he can have a run and then I'll use him to scare the assholes I'm meeting with later."

I prodded Nicoli in the side when he didn't thank him and he grunted as he looked to me then sighed.

"Thank you," he called and Frankie laughed loudly again then whistled so Tyson bounded after him.

"Whipped!" he called back before the door sounded and when I glanced at Nicoli, there was a smile playing around his mouth.

He turned to me, sucking on his lower lip as his gaze dropped to my bare legs. "We need to talk, baby doll," he said in gravelly tone.

"About me being your girlfriend?" I asked playfully, my voice loosening with Frankie gone.

"No," he said seriously and my heart jolted. *Oh.* "Not that I don't want... I mean not that I - not that *you-*"

I laid a hand on his arm, giving him a look that said he didn't need to explain and he grabbed my hand, lifting it up and pressing a firm kiss to the back of it.

"What I'm trying to say is that the term girlfriend just sounds far too normal for you. If you agreed to taking a place at my side, I'd be fucking humbled beyond words. But I would want to claim you as something far better than a girlfriend. I'd want you to be my goddess, my queen, my savage girl."

"I will always be your savage girl, Nicoli," I said, breathless from his words as my heart ignited and happiness filled every space inside me. I had been shattered, altered, changed by everything I'd been through. I may never fit into normal society again, but it didn't matter with Nicoli. He accepted me as I was, no matter how many scars I had or how little I knew of my past. He wanted this version of me. And I wanted this version of him too. No matter what.

His eyes lit up and he turned away, towing me after him into the lounge and pulling me into his lap as he dropped onto the plush white couch. I curled against him, brushing my fingers into his hair.

I reached out to paint words on his chest out of habit more than the need to right now. *What's on your mind?*

"Hmm." His thumbs trailed up my thighs, making my shirt ride higher up my flesh and revealing a criss-cross of scars. He caressed each one of them with intent and my heart swelled as each searing memory was eased by this new one.

"We've got a problem," he said, looking up at me. "We didn't use contraception when we..."

Had sex? I wrote on his chest and he laughed.

"Yeah. So do you want me to get you the morning after pill? I can head out this morning? Or I could get the details of the doctor who's coming today and see if they can bring it? Only if you want to though, it's your body."

My stomach writhed at the mention of the doctor and I dropped his gaze, lifting my hand to my mouth and biting down on my thumb.

"What is it?" Nicoli asked, concern in his tone as he pulled me closer.

The only people who had ever tended to my wounds were The Five when they'd cut me too deep or come close to breaking bones. They'd splash alcohol on my wounds, stitching them roughly until I was screaming all over again. The idea of a doctor coming here terrified me.

I'm not hurt, I wrote, hating that I couldn't use my voice as the thought of this made my throat close up and my pulse hammer.

213

"I know, baby doll. They'll just check you over, that's all."

I shook my head, panic seizing me again as I moved to get off of him, but he grabbed hold of me, not letting me go. He caught my chin, making me look at him and a ragged breath left my lips as I met his gaze.

"No one is going to hurt you," he promised, the air electric with his powerful words. "I swear it on everything I am. I will never let anyone hurt you again. I can stay with you if you want me to, but you really have to see them, Winter, they're just going to make sure you're okay."

My chest heaved, but slowly my breaths evened out. I trusted him. And if he swore no one was going to hurt me, then I had to believe him.

Nicoli rubbed his nose against mine. "Wanna explore Frankie's apartment together?"

I nodded, laughing as I slid off of his lap, glad to have something to distract me.

The place seemed to have endless doors and we soon walked through another lounge which felt more like a boudoir with its black leather seats and monochrome paintings of naked women on the walls. Beyond that was more bedrooms and we found Frankie's, guessing it was his because it was massive, the entire back wall of windows looking out over Sinners Bay. There was a roll of cash sitting on the nightstand and a pair of handcuffs hanging from a metal ring in the bedpost which looked specially fitted.

"Kinky fucker," Nicoli muttered and I snorted as we headed out the door again.

A black door at the end of the corridor drew my attention and I padded toward it, twisting the handle and pushing it wide. I stopped breathing as I stepped into the room, my jaw actually dropping.

The walls were black and at the centre of the space was a long wooden table with a hole at the top of it that looked like it was meant to put your face into. Beyond that was a tall metal rack with chains hanging from it and to the side of that was a perfectly made bed contained within an iron cage. On the walls were hooks with all manner of things hanging from them, whips, paddles, belts, shackles, riding crops.

I backed up and my shoulder hit Nicoli's firm chest. He reached out, closing his hands around my eyes and pulling me backwards.

I laughed, swatting his arm. "Your brother isn't just kinky, he's an animal."

"You think you know a guy," Nicoli murmured in amusement as he looked around the room. "And then you realise he likes to be tied to a bed with a ball gag in his mouth and have his ass whipped while listening to The Macarena."

A surprised laugh spilled from my lips as I stared at all of the things in the room with more than a little shock. "You think he likes having this done to him? I'd have guessed the other way around."

"Probably. But that's not a conversation I wanna have with my brother."

Nicoli spun me around, pushing me up against the wall and dropping his hands so I could see him.

"Do you...like that stuff?" I raised a brow, my gut tugging at the thought. I didn't want to deprive Nicoli if he shared his brother's fetishes, but I didn't think I'd ever want to be chained and whipped for pleasure. Not when I'd experienced the real thing.

He shook his head, leaning in and pushing his knee between my thighs to pin me in place. "You're all I need. Fuck toys and games. I don't need any of that, I just need you and your voice and your scars, baby doll."

I smiled, relaxing as I wound my fingers around his neck and tip-toed up to graze my lips over his ear. "You can have them all."

The intercom buzzed and my back hit the wall, my heart jolting at the noise. He frowned, brushing his thumb along my jaw before kissing me sweetly to chase away my demons. We walked back to the front room and I moved to sit back on the couch as he headed to answer it.

I hated that I couldn't react normally to normal things. Nicoli was so patient with me, but all of this newness was hard. Up on the mountain, it had just been us, even if my enemies had been lurking close by. Down here in the

215

city, there were countless people I had to interact with, what if I never fit in right? What if Nicoli got used to being back in society and I never did? What if he got tired of waiting for me to adjust?

I dug my toes into the soft couch as I took steady breaths to push away my anxiety. It wasn't long before a woman strolled in wearing high heels then ushered someone in behind her. A porter carried two large suitcases and the woman tossed her raven hair as she looked to Nicoli.

"I'll have the closets arranged for you in no time, sir." She fluttered her lashes at him and my upper lip peeled back on a snarl as she strode through the room, her heels clicking across the floorboards. When she glanced my way, her perfectly shaped eyebrows jumped up, but she quickly turned back to face the direction she was headed in, increasing her pace as the porter hurried after her.

Nicoli pushed the door closed, running a hand over his hair. "You'll have your own clothes now," he said. "If you want them."

I nodded keenly, getting up and climbing over the back of the couch. I loved wearing Nicoli's shirts sometimes, but I really longed for some underwear and some pants that fit. I headed down the hall into the room Frankie had offered me, finding the guy unloading one of the suitcases and handing items into the woman who stood in the large closet.

"Don't crease it Raul!" she admonished as he passed her a white cami.

They worked efficiently and were already through half the bag as I moved silently onto the bed to watch them work, wanting to get a closer look at everything. When the woman was done, she ushered Raul away again with the second suitcase. "Take it to the next room along the hall."

He hurried to obey and the woman headed after him, but shrieked as she spotted me there on the bed. "Oh – my apologies." She bowed her head, her eyes roaming over Nicoli's shirt swamping my body then down to the scars on my legs. She give me an uncomfortable smile then hurried away and when she left, I looked to those same scars with my stomach twisting.

How am I ever going to blend in when I'm always going to have to wear these?

I pushed the thought away as I slipped off of the bed, hurrying into the closet and heading straight to the set of drawers at the back to find the underwear. I pulled open the top one and my breath hitched as I found the most lavish, delicate things waiting for me there. Thongs, G-strings, little frenchies - even a few that were crotchless. *Oh my god.*

My cheeks burned as I hunted for something more practical, but all I found were transparent bras or push-up ones, stockings, garters, more lace and silk and *sexiness*.

Well...guess I'm wearing these then.

I took a black bra made entirely of lace and a pair of frenchies to match then headed out of the closet and into the en-suite. Nicoli had shown me how to use the shower yesterday, but there were so many buttons and knobs in the huge unit that it took me a couple of goes until I got it right. I used the sweet smelling products to wash my hair and skin until I was clean and warmed through, enjoying the feel of the water on my flesh. My skin was pruney by the time I stepped out and used the fluffy grey towels to dry myself off. My hair hung in damp strands when I was done rubbing a towel through it and I moved to the underwear I'd laid out by the large marble sink. I pulled on the panties first and *oohed* as the silk kissed my skin. They fit perfectly and it felt so good to have them on. I put on the bra next and looked down at the beautiful material, surprised when it seemed like I had actual cleavage.

The bathroom mirror was fogged up so I headed back into my room and hurried to stand before the mirror on the wall. My body was an etch-a-sketch of scars, but I still looked kind of *hot*.

"Are you going to recognise me in...this," Nicoli halted in the doorway and I turned to him, taking in the crisp white dress shirt and smart black pants he wore. They clung to his broad frame in a way that made my heart pound. As I met his gaze, I realised he was staring at me too, his eyes travelling over my breasts then down to the little frenchies. I smiled shyly as he stalked toward me like a hungry bear out for its next meal.

"Fuck me, baby doll. You look edible." His smile was all darkness and I offered him one back as he reached me. He looked so different, but I liked this smart attire on him too. He could have worn anything and I would have drooled for him though.

I opened my mouth to reply then halted, glancing past him as I worried the clothes woman was still here.

"She's gone," he growled, capturing my attention again and I could have drowned in the heat in his eyes. "We're all alone."

My throat loosened and I backed up as I grinned. "What are we going to do to pass the time?"

He hounded forward as the backs of my legs hit the bed.

"I have a few ideas, most of which involve peeling off that lingerie with my teeth."

"But I just put it on," I teased, climbing up onto the bed and looking down at him.

"And now I'll take it off," he growled, lunging for me and I leapt away with a squeal, diving off the bed and racing for the door. He released a low laugh as he took chase and tore after me into the kitchen. There was nowhere else to run in the large, white tiled space and I laughed wildly as Nicoli grabbed me by the waist and lifted me into the air. He placed my ass down on the kitchen worktop, the cold surface making goosebumps spread across my skin as he stepped between my thighs. His hands skimmed over my hips and he hooked his thumbs into my panties as he smirked victoriously at me.

His mouth dropped to my jaw and I wrapped my legs around his waist as he started kissing his way down my throat, pleasure dancing over my flesh at his touch.

I reached out, running my palms over the soft dress shirt he wore, taking in the new feel of it as his muscles tensed under my fingers.

"Do you like it?" he growled into my collar bone as I ran my palms over his back and fisted the crisp material in my hands.

"I like the wild man underneath it," I panted as he made it to my breasts

218

and sucked one of my nipples through the lace. "*Nicoli,*" I gasped, leaning back on the worktop as he reared over me.

"When you say my name like that, it drives me fucking crazy." He yanked my hips forward so his crotch lined up with mine and his solid length ground against the centre of me.

I moaned his name again as his tongue swirled over my nipple then the intercom buzzing made us both fall still. It came again and Nicoli snarled in annoyance, lifting his head and helping me down off of the worktop.

"Go get dressed," he instructed and I laughed at his serious expression before heading across the room and down the hall.

The selection of clothes in my closet were so beautiful, it took me a while to settle on something. It was all made to enhance my figure and I had to wonder how Frankie had worked out my size just from looking at me. After Nicoli's reaction to the lingerie, I wondered what he'd think of the low-cut white dress I picked out which clung to my hips and accentuated what little curves I had.

I walked back to the lounge and found a dark skinned woman there with kind eyes and grey hair pulled up into a sleek bun. "Hello, my love, I'm Dr Greene, you must be Winter?" Her eyes dipped to the dress I wore then flicked to Nicoli in surprise. "Are you...heading out somewhere?"

"No," Nicoli grunted, a smile playing around the corner of his mouth as he took in my outfit with an appreciative look.

"Oh okay...well I'm afraid I'll need you to take that off in a moment dear so I can have a look at you. Shall we do this somewhere more private?"

"You can use my bedroom," Nicoli offered, pointing us down the hall then looking to me. "Shall I stay with you?"

"We might need to discuss some personal things," Dr Greene said quickly, giving me an encouraging smile. "I don't bite."

"*She* does though," Nicoli laughed and I bit my lip on a smile. "She also doesn't speak to strangers, so if you need her to answer questions she can do so through me or write them down."

"Oh my, okay," the doctor agreed and Nicoli led the way through to his bedroom.

Dr Greene entered last, pushing the door closed and placing her bag down on the bed. "If you can take the dress off then and hop up here Winter that would be great."

I looked to Nicoli who gave me a comforting smile and I pulled off the dress, moving to the bed to lie down.

Dr Greene took in my scars with professionalism, but there was an underlying sadness in her eyes as she moved closer to inspect them. "Is it okay to touch you? I'm going to check for any nerve damage or lasting injuries. Mr Romero has instructed me to be very thorough so this may take a little time. I'll just apply a small amount of pressure in places and you tell me how that feels, okay dear?"

I nodded, a ball rising in my throat as she laid her hands on my right foot, checking each of my toes and confirming I could feel them all before moving up to my ankle then my calf, working all the way up to my thigh. She moved onto my stomach next, pressing down in places and watching my reaction closely as she asked if I felt any pain. I shook my head, feeling none. The only place I hurt were where the bruises and cuts hadn't quite healed from my last encounter with The Five, but there was nothing that wasn't on its way to mending.

Once she'd checked over my front, she had me roll over and she tutted as she took in the scars there. "Goodness me, you have been through the wars my dear, haven't you?" She sighed sadly as she started at my feet again, working up each of my legs until she reached my back. As her fingers grazed along my spine and onto my shoulder blades, the sensation dulled until I could hardly feel anything there.

"Feel this?"

I shook my head.

"How about this?" she asked, but again I felt nothing. "There's a little bit of nerve damage here. If you could have someone massage this area twice a day it may bring back the feeling eventually, but there are no guarantees."

"I'll do it," Nicoli spoke immediately and I turned my head to look at him across the room, my heart squeezing at the way he was staring at me.

The doctor finished her examination then asked me to roll back over. "I think it would be best if you step out of the room for this next part, sir." She glanced at Nicoli and he looked to me for an answer. I nodded in agreement, finding I was comfortable enough with the woman now. She clearly wasn't going to hurt me.

"I'll be just down the hall if you need me," Nicoli said then strode from the room and the door clicked shut as he left.

Dr Greene chuckled. "He's quite the catch, and the way he looks at you..." She laughed again. "Right, panties off, my dear."

I took them off and drew my knees up as she instructed me to. The examination didn't last too long and she chatted all the while, making me relax enough that it wasn't wholly awful.

When she was done, she announced I was fit and well and pulled off a pair of latex gloves, tossing them in the trash before making a few notes on an iPad.

"Okay, I need to ask you a few personal questions," she said as I put my panties back on and sat up. "Just nod your head yes or no. Were you sexually assaulted during your time in captivity?" she asked gently and I shook my head no.

She smiled kindly, seeming relieved at that before going on. "Are you having regular sexual intercourse or planning to in the near future with a partner?"

I lifted my thumb to my mouth, biting down and nodding.

She made a note on the page then ran through more intimate questions until reaching into her bag and taking out a syringe. "Okay my dear, nearly done. I'm just going to take some blood to send off to the lab and make sure you're in good health. We'll have the results back to you in a couple days. As you're sexually active, I recommend you go on some form of contraception unless you're looking to get pregnant?" I shook my head and she ran through each type as she took some blood and I didn't even wince when she slid the needle in. I'd felt far worse pain than that and something about this doctor felt trustworthy.

My head was spinning with all the forms of contraception by the time she was done and I finally decided on the contraceptive pill. She happened to have some with her and I couldn't shift the feeling that Frankie must have asked her to bring it. Not that I was complaining, but it was still a little weird that he'd thought about that.

I caught her arm before she left, needing to ask her something but unable to speak it. She offered me her iPad and I wrote the question on the screen.

I had unprotected sex a couple of days ago, what should I do?

She read the words then nodded. "The blood work will tell us if you're pregnant, but if you don't want to wait a couple of days then I could prescribe you the morning after pill. How regular is your cycle?"

I wrote down what I knew and she concluded that my chances of being pregnant considering the time of the month were seriously low so I figured I'd wait for the blood results.

She finally left and I pulled on my dress just as Nicoli walked back into the room.

"Everything okay?" he asked.

I moved toward him, answering him with a kiss on the lips and he wrapped me in his arms. My voice rose just for him. It was becoming more and more easy to speak every day and I adored him for that. "Never better."

CHAPTER TWENTY ONE

I'd made us some lunch while the doctor finished up with Winter, laying it out on the table right beside the floor length windows that looked out over the city and all the way to the bay beyond. My gaze caught on the sea in the distance as I sat in my chair and waited for my savage girl to return from freshening up in the bathroom. Frankie had explained that the doctor needed to check her all over, make sure she really hadn't been sexually assaulted and clear her for physical injuries, but I'd denied his offer to get her a psychiatrist. I was sure she would benefit from seeing one at some point, but it was all too much at once right now. I didn't want her to feel like a science experiment.

My chest felt heavy with so many conflicting emotions at coming back to Sinners Bay. This city had been my home for as long as I could remember. But that man hadn't really been me at all.

I certainly never would have found myself sitting in a Romero property before now. But the expensive clothes, the luxurious apartment, the scent of hundred dollar aftershave clinging to my skin, all of those things could have belonged to the man I once was.

I ran a hand over my face and glanced at the doctor as she finished typing out her notes at the breakfast bar. She hadn't told me much aside from assuring me that she didn't think Winter would have too much major long term damage physically aside from the superficial scarring.

"I'm going to write her up a prescription for some ointment to help with the scarring, but she'd really need to see a plastic surgeon if she wants to try and remove some of them permanently," the doctor hedged. "I could offer her a mild sedative too, if she needs them for nightmares or anything like that. You should watch out for signs of PTSD or-"

"I will," I said, not needing her to read me a list. Winter was taking her time and I wondered if she was exploring her new wardrobe some more. I didn't really want the doctor hanging around much longer and I wondered how she'd take it if I just told her to do her paperwork back at her office.

"I actually need to gather a specimen from you while I'm here," she said before I could voice the words.

"Me?" I asked in confusion. "What for?"

Winter walked into the room before I got my answer and my eyes caught on her as I found her in that clingy white dress.

Now I really want this woman to leave.

"I assumed you were aware..." Dr Greene said hesitantly, drawing closer to me with a cotton swab on the end of a stick clutched in her hand. "Your father requested a DNA sample..." She trailed off as I gave her a dark look. Martello Romero wasn't my father. Even if I was willing to accept my brothers into my life, I couldn't imagine having a relationship with that man. But I guessed I wanted a definitive answer too. Clear cut confirmation of my real identity to...well, I guessed just to put any lingering doubts I still had to bed.

"Get it over with then," I muttered, parting my lips and allowing her to scrape two cheek swabs around my mouth before sealing them up in a plastic tube.

"I'll be in touch when the results come back," she said, gathering up the rest of her things and exchanging a few pleasantries with Winter before finally leaving us alone.

I watched hungrily as my girl came to sit with me, her gaze slipping between me and the food I'd prepared us like she couldn't decide which to devour first.

"Eat, baby doll," I commanded, despite the way my gaze clung to the movement of that white material over her thighs and the way my dick was swelling in my pants. "You'll need your stamina for what I have in mind anyway."

Winter giggled like I was joking and I gave her a heated look which promised I wasn't. I was seriously tempted to pounce on her then and there, but she was still the wrong side of too thin and she needed the calories more than she needed sex right now, no matter how much I wished she didn't.

We ate in silence, my gaze fixed to her mouth as she devoured the sandwiches I'd made her before starting on a packet of Doritos. I could tell she wasn't done so I headed to the freezer and dug around in Frankie's supplies until I found a tub of Ben and Jerry's ice cream lurking in the back.

Winter's eyes widened as I scooped a spoon into it and held it out for her to eat. She moaned lustily as she devoured it, her tongue drawing a line around her lips as she chased down every last bit of it before opening her mouth again and waiting for more.

I smiled at her as I offered up the spoon again and she closed her lips around it seductively, her gaze boring into mine with a wicked kind of dare in her eyes.

"Are you hungry for something else yet?" I asked her in a low voice, feeding her again as my pulse pounded and my desire for her grew.

As she took her next mouthful of ice cream, she nodded slowly, her gaze staying pinned on me like she wondered what I might do and couldn't wait to find out.

I got to my feet, abandoning the ice cream on the table and tossing the spoon down as she licked her lips again. I rounded the table slowly and caught her chair in my grip, tugging it out and turning her to face me in it. I gripped the wooden arms either side of the chair and lifted them, rocking the whole thing back onto two legs as I leaned down over her and she gasped in surprise.

She grabbed my forearms to steady herself and the skirt of her dress fell back to pool around her waist as I tipped her further, revealing those little lace panties she'd put on so casually. Like she didn't know I'd be aching to destroy them and rip them right back off again the moment I laid eyes on her in them.

"Nicoli," she gasped as I tipped her so far back that the chair was practically lying flat and the only thing stopping it from falling to the floor was my hold on the arms.

"Lean back, baby doll, look at the view," I murmured, watching her as she tipped her head back, scarlet hair spilling over the back of the chair and hanging down to brush the floor as she took in the view beyond the glass upside down. "There's a whole world out there waiting for you."

"The only thing I want is right here with me," she breathed and I was pretty sure I'd never get enough of the sound of her voice. It was low and sultry, effortlessly seductive and always sounded like she'd just woken up after a night spent naked and panting in my arms.

I leaned down and dropped my mouth to her neck, running my tongue down her bare skin until I found the neckline of her dress. She moaned in encouragement, releasing my arm for a moment so that she could tug her dress lower, freeing the mound of her breast and the perfect peak of her hardened nipple.

I growled with desire as I captured it between my lips, sucking and teasing, holding her there in the chair so close to falling while still safe in my arms.

Her hand fell back against my arm as she moaned again, scrawling her fingertip over my sleeve as she traced out a single word over and over.

More. More. More.

Fuck, I didn't think I'd ever get over the feeling of her writing that on my body. I hoped she never stopped, even when words came as easy as breathing to her, I hoped she'd still trace that word on my flesh whenever she was hungry for me.

I sucked her nipple harder, my dick swelling until it was rock hard and desperate to escape my fly. My teeth grazed her flesh and she cried out in pleasure, her grip on me tightening so that her fingernails dug in.

A loud knock came from the door behind us and I stilled for a moment as Winter sat up, looking at me with concern as I quickly decided to ignore whoever the fuck it was.

"They'll go away," I assured her, dipping my mouth to her breast once more just as the knocking came again.

I growled as I continued to ignore it, biting down on her nipple as they knocked again and causing her to cry out, though the way her thighs parted promised me it wasn't in pain.

I mentally started cursing whoever the fuck was here now, trying to ignore them as they continued to pound on the wood when all of a sudden, the elevator dinged to announce someone else arriving.

I straightened instantly, slamming Winter's chair legs back down on the carpet and yanking her dress back up to cover her breast as her eyes widened in alarm.

"Christ, Nicoli, aren't you going to answer that?" a woman's voice came from behind me and I fell deathly still as I recognised her.

Winter's eyes widened like she could sense the tension in me already and I swiped a hand over my face as I forced myself to turn and look at Sloan Calabresi as she carried a car seat into the apartment and placed it on the floor before hurrying to open the door for whoever the fuck was still out there knocking. No, not Calabresi, *Romero* now. I'd gotten the messages from Rocco asking me to come back for the wedding. And the one telling me they'd had a baby girl and named her River. *Shit.*

A blur of white fur rushed towards me and I grinned as I dropped to my knees and Sloan's little Pomeranian Coco leapt into my arms, licking my face like crazy the moment he could get close. I made a complete ass of myself as I made a fuss of him before setting him loose so that he could tear around the apartment and sniff everything, no doubt realising another dog had been here recently.

Who's that? Winter traced on the small of my back as she stood up and looked over at the new arrival too.

Sloan's black hair was long and styled into perfect curls which hung down her back over the pale grey dress she wore. She wasn't looking our way as she pulled the door open and gave the men beyond it enthusiastic greetings, apologising for them having to wait and ushering them inside as they carried silver cases into the apartment.

"My fiancé," I explained to Winter, momentarily transported back to the past and forgetting to apply the word *ex* to that statement. It wasn't out of any lingering feelings on my behalf, just an old habit that slipped out right in time to put my fucking foot in it. Sloan's father had told me I was going to be marrying her long before he'd given her the same news and I'd just gotten used to referring to her as that. "I mean, the girl who I was supposed to marry," I clarified, looking down at Winter as she scowled back at me. "We were never actually together. We only ever kissed once and even that was kind of...forced."

Winter clucked her tongue at me and I tried to school my features, not wanting her to get the wrong impression. It wasn't that I felt anything towards Sloan as I watched her hurry back over to the baby in the car seat, it was just that she was this piece of my past as Nicoli Vitoli, she'd known me before I found out any of this, we'd grown up together for a while...

"I'm just going to go put River in another room so she doesn't wake up," Sloan said, glancing our way with a slightly nervous smile before carrying the baby away towards the bedrooms.

I looked at Winter again and found her with her arms wrapped around her body as the two men set about opening their silver cases to reveal a bunch of hairdressing equipment and grabbing chairs as they got themselves set up to cut hair. They were clearly here for the two of us and I cursed Frankie for organising all of this shit and not even doing us the courtesy of warning us about it.

230

"Do you want me to tell them all to go, baby doll?" I asked, reaching out to uncoil her arms from her chest before lifting her fingertips to my mouth and kissing them one at a time. "The only person who I care about in this place is you."

The irritation slid from her eyes as she read the sincerity in mine and I turned her hand over to lay a kiss on her palm, her wrist, her forearm.

She giggled and batted me off playfully but I didn't release her, tugging her closer so that I could wrap her in my arms.

"Hey," Sloan's voice interrupted us again and I turned my gaze to her as she stood a few feet away from us, looking a little lost. "This is weird, isn't it? Rocco said it would be weird and I told him he was just a possessive asshole and he needed to get over himself, so we can't let him be right."

"I wouldn't dream of it," I agreed, smiling as I looked her over. She'd changed since I'd last seen her, and granted that hadn't exactly been the best look of her life, half drowned and trying to accept the fact that her father was a complete and utter piece of shit - as well as dead. But it was more than that, she looked happy, content, it was nice to see.

"This is Winter," I said, pressing a kiss to my savage girl's head and causing her to blush as she offered Sloan a tentative smile. "She's my girl," I said simply, because it was true. She was mine and I was hers.

"I heard..." Sloan smiled warmly, looking between us both for a long moment before throwing her arms around the two of us at once.

Winter stiffened and then relaxed and I laughed as I scruffed up Sloan's hair the way I used to do when we were kids just to make her mad. She cursed me and shoved me away, laughing as we broke apart.

"See, not weird at all," Sloan announced with a grin. "That means I won the bet. Rocco will be pissed."

"What do you win?" I asked her and she bit her lip on her smile, shaking her head.

"I'll tell Winter, but not you."

I raised an eyebrow as she grabbed Winter's hand and tugged her away

231

from me before cupping her hands around her mouth and whispering into her ear.

I tried to listen in but I couldn't hear what she said. I could only watch as Winter's eyebrows went up and her cheeks heated. She bit her lip as she looked me up and down then turned to Sloan, murmuring in a low voice that took me utterly by surprise.

"I want to try that."

I tried to cover my surprise as Sloan and Winter both started giggling, and Sloan tugged her away whispering something else as they headed over towards the men on the other side of the open space and she gestured wildly with her hands. That was the first time Winter had spoken to someone aside from me and it lit me up to know she felt comfortable opening up like that with Sloan so quickly. She needed a friend and I knew Sloan well enough to trust her. It was fucking perfect actually. So long as none of us lingered on the weird fact that for a while there me and Sloan had been engaged. But that didn't even feel like it had been my life anymore, everything had changed so drastically for me that remembering that time in my life felt like looking at a different man.

Sloan started telling Winter all about how the guy with the perfectly styled blonde hair was the best hairdresser in the whole of Sinners Bay and talking about so many products and potions and fuck knows what else that I quickly tuned it out. The other guy who introduced himself to me as Andre turned out to be a barber sent to fix me up. Apparently Winter's home stylings didn't meet Frankie's standards and as Andre gasped and cursed at the state of my of hair, I was given the distinct impression that they didn't meet his either.

I watched Winter as the hairdresser whose name was Roy began fussing with her hair, inspecting the ends, cooing about the colour and telling her how lucky she was to have the blood of royalty running in her veins which apparently was the reason for her scarlet colouring. He was laying it on a bit thick but she was smiling, listening to Sloan as she chatted about the family, offering out tips on how to wrap each of the Romero brothers around her little finger.

"How would you feel about something edgy?" Roy asked, fiddling with Winter's hair and murmuring ideas about shaving one side or cutting in bangs while I frowned. He kept touching her face as he made his suggestions, holding her hair at different lengths while Sloan held up a mirror so Winter could see.

"How about you keep your hands in her hair and off of the rest of her?" I muttered, but it came out kinda like a bark.

Roy stilled, dropping the lock of hair he'd been holding and raising his hands in surrender while Winter frowned at me like I was spoiling her fun. I rolled my eyes and agreed to whatever the fuck Andre was suggesting for my own hair.

"I say we just go all in with this great new conditioning treatment I got from Paris," Roy said as he realised I wasn't going to make any further comment, his hands resting lightly on Winter's scalp and staying away from her shoulders as requested. "It's got colour enhancing properties too which will make this red really pop. And then I'll just take off these split ends and style it for you. If you want to be more daring next time then we can build up to it."

Winter nodded her agreement and we were soon having our hair fixed while Sloan and I discussed the things I'd missed in my year away and Sloan filled Winter in on what she deemed to be vital gossip about the Romeros. I had to admit that I was listening to that quite keenly too, wanting to get more of a feel for the men who were my brothers.

Eventually, Winter headed off with Sloan and Roy to wash the conditioning stuff out of her hair and have it styled away from me so that I could be surprised. It sounded like he was basically washing her hair and trimming the ends a bit though so I wasn't exactly holding my breath to be blown away by the transformation.

Andre finished up with me and packed up his stuff while I headed for a shower to wash the cut hairs from my flesh. When I got out again and ran some of Frankie's product into the longer length at the top of my hair to style it, I almost didn't recognise myself. Or more like, I recognised a man who didn't feel like me anymore. My beard had been trimmed down to a thick covering of stubble, my hair shaved in close on the sides. Once I slipped into one of the perfectly fitting suits Frankie had bought me, I almost felt like I was stepping into an old skin.

But maybe this wasn't the flesh of the man I'd once been. Maybe I didn't have to be Nicoli Vitoli anymore. And maybe I didn't have to pretend to be Angelo Romero either. What if I was Nicoli Romero? A little of both men and a lot of something new too. I liked the idea of that better than trying to play dress up as someone I wasn't anymore, or maybe never had been at all.

It was impossible to miss the sound of the three Romero brothers arriving back at the apartment as Rocco howled like a wolf the moment I heard the elevator doors ding and the other two laughed raucously like they were all sharing some joke.

I headed out to meet them and was almost bowled over by Enzo throwing his arms around me. "Look at that handsome fucker!" he cooed, the scent of whiskey washing over my face as he seemed to be using me to hold himself upright for a moment. "Now I know you're related to us. We're the best looking bunch of brothers in the whole of Sinners Bay."

Tyson completely ignored me as Coco came tearing out of whatever nook he'd been hiding in and the two of them instantly started chasing around and playing together.

I laughed as I pushed Enzo back a step, eying the tattoos which crept over his fingers as he fiddled with his tie. He looked the least clean cut out of the three of them, ink on show at his collar and cuffs, his black hair tied in a topknot and shaved on the sides and there was something animalistic about him. Although I guessed that could be said of all of us. But if I had to put a name to each creature, the others would be easier. Rocco was the wolf, leader of the pack, Frankie was a crocodile, lurking beneath calm waters, waiting to snap. But Enzo...he was something way less predictable and utterly fearless,

234

like a tiger, beautiful but fucking deadly. I guessed I was something a lot less subtle like a bear snarling over its territory and ready to take on the damn world for what was mine, which wasn't the worst thing in the world.

"Where's my woman?" Rocco called as he headed across the room and hunted down the sound system, turning on some music as he started to dance to All Star by Smash Mouth and the others groaned as he began singing at the top of his lungs.

Frankie called out to offer me a drink and I followed him over to the kitchen as he poured out a healthy measure of scotch and slid it across the table to me.

"We've ordered pizzas," he said with a grin. "I thought we could have a family bonding night. If it's not too much for your girl?"

"She's taken on worse than a night surrounded by a bunch of mobster assholes," I replied as I took a long sip of my drink. "But if she gets overwhelmed by all of the testosterone in the air then I'll gladly tell you all to fuck off."

"Don't forget this is my home, fratello," Frankie said with a laugh. "You can't kick me out of shit."

"I'm bigger than you, so I'm pretty sure I can."

He glanced at me like he was deciding whether or not that was true. All four of us were over six foot, but I was bulkier than him. His muscle was all clean cut and defined, I was just pure brawn.

"I'm willing to bet I'm faster though," he said. "Which would even the odds."

I laughed darkly, wondering if we should put that to the test with a brawl sometime. That was the kind of things brothers did, right?

"There they are!" Rocco called, forgetting his dance as he turned towards the corridor where Sloan had just emerged with River cradled to her chest. "The loves of my life!"

He ran across the room and swept them into his arms, lifting Sloan from her feet so that she squealed about the baby in her arms until he placed her down again with a filthy kiss. As he broke away, he stole River from her and went back to his dance with the baby girl, peering about and cooing excitedly.

"Close your eyes, Nicoli," Sloan demanded, pointing at me dramatically. "It's time for the big makeover reveal."

"This isn't some nineties rom-com," I muttered but Enzo moved forward to shove me down onto one of the bar stools and Frankie slapped his hands over my eyes to make sure I really couldn't see.

There was a lot of laughing and then Enzo wolf-whistled, making me want to punch him in the dick and Frankie finally lifted his hands from my eyes.

Winter stood wearing an emerald green dress which hugged her figure in all the right ways and made her green eyes pop from right across the room. Her blood red hair gleamed and had been styled into perfect loose curls which hung around her face, just caressing the low-cut neckline of her dress. She was wearing lipstick the same shade as her hair and her shadowy eye makeup took that innocent edge off of her features. Sloan encouraged her to do a twirl and I swallowed thickly as I took in the backless rear half of the dress, the fact that she clearly wasn't wearing a bra and the perfect way it hugged her ass.

"Have you got her locked down or is she fair game?" Enzo asked in a voice which was definitely loud enough to carry and I punched him on reflex. Only in the arm, but still.

He cursed me as he started laughing and Frankie groaned dramatically.

"Bad move, fratello, you just gave away your weak spot. He'll never stop winding you up over her now."

I glanced at Frankie with a frown but I was already forgetting his comment as I moved towards Winter, wrapping my arms around her waist and backing her down the corridor again as my mouth found hers.

She gasped as I kissed her and I drove her back against the wall once we were out of sight, groaning into her mouth as I ground my dick against her. I'd been hard from the moment I'd opened my eyes and seen her made up like this, but that wouldn't do at all.

"Let's go back to your room," I breathed as she wrapped her arms around my neck, nodding her agreement.

I lifted her into my arms, ignoring the howls of excited laughter and cat-calling that followed us and carrying her back into her bedroom.

"Pick another dress, baby doll," I growled against her mouth, forcing myself to put her down and meeting her eyes as she frowned up at me.

"Why?" she asked in confusion. "Don't you like it?"

"*Fuck*, yes, I like it, Winter. I like it too damn much. None of those assholes out there can keep their eyes off of you. You need to take it off."

She stared at me for a long moment and then her eyes narrowed into slits. "No."

"No?" I asked in confusion, irritation prickling through my skin.

"Am I a free girl or am I just in a nicer cage?" she hissed, all out glaring at me now.

"It's not about that, baby doll," I promised, not liking the way she was looking at me one bit. "It's just you...that dress...you're, well, you're *everything*. It's too fucking much. I can't stay away from you, I don't want other men looking at you like this."

"Am I free, Nicoli?" she asked darkly.

"Of course you are, but-"

"Then I can choose my own clothes. And I like *this*." She turned away from me and sauntered out of the room in her red high heels and the bottom dropped out of my gut.

Rage clawed through me and an actual snarl left my lips as I stormed out behind her, wanting to call her name but knowing that I couldn't. If she didn't want to change then I couldn't force her to...could I? *Fuck*, no, no I definitely couldn't do that. *Gah*. I wanted to chase after her, grab hold of her and drag her back into her room and make her change, preferably fucking her senseless somewhere in the middle of that, but I couldn't. And by the time I caught up to her, she was back in the living room, dancing with Rocco, Sloan and Enzo and there was nothing more that I could even say about it.

My jaw ticked and Frankie smirked at me as he pushed a full tumbler of scotch my way.

"She's a wild one, fratello," he said, looking like he was trying not to laugh. "And I don't think she's the type to be tamed. You don't survive the sort of things she has and come out weak willed."

"I don't want her weak willed," I growled. "I just want her properly dressed."

"She looks hot," he said with a shrug. "And she's only got eyes for you, so isn't that a good thing?"

I huffed and downed my drink, having to agree with him and hating it and also knowing that I might have been a bit of a dick. But I couldn't help it. She was mine. And I'd lost everything else I'd ever had already once. I didn't intend to let her go the same way.

I let Frankie pour me another healthy measure of scotch and savoured the expensive taste of the liquor as it rolled down my throat. The sun was beginning to set over the bay beyond the huge windows and I gave my attention to the view to stop myself for staring/glaring at Winter too much.

I drummed my fingers along my glass, keeping to my spot on the stool as Frankie moved to join the others dancing. He called over for me to join them, but that had never really been my thing. Sure, I'd spent plenty of time in nightclubs orchestrating deals or enforcing rules for the Calabresis, but I'd never seen it as a social experience. I'd been restricted to VIP areas and back rooms, not dance floors, unless you counted waltzing the way I'd been taught in my fancy private school and this didn't seem like that kind of occasion.

I'd never really had time for anything like that. Never really cared to try it either. I'd been a man with a purpose, a goal, a future that mattered...until I wasn't anymore. And now I realised I hadn't really been anyone at all.

My gaze inevitably slid back to Winter and fixed there. The way her body moved in that little green dress was hypnotic and she clearly knew what she was doing. I guessed that once upon a time she'd been the kind of girl who liked to go out dancing. As I thought about that, I couldn't help but wonder yet again about whether or not she had people missing her. Was I being selfish by wanting to keep her here with me? Should I have been encouraging her to look into it? I kept telling myself that Duke might not be dead, that whoever had organised for her to be tortured could still be looking for her and that was why I didn't want her to investigate it. But that was all bullshit really, I just didn't want her to realise she had something better out there than me and leave me behind when she reclaimed it.

I released a slow breath, pushing those feelings aside. We'd made it plain enough how we felt about each other so there was no point in me letting my insecurities spiral. Just because I'd never been important enough to fight for by anyone else in my life before now didn't mean she would turn her back on me too. Especially not after everything we'd been through together.

Enzo caught Winter's hand and spun her in a circle as she let out a surprised and slightly nervous laugh. My jaw clenched hard enough to crack a tooth.

I sank another drink, welcoming the burn in my chest as it went down and got to my feet, slamming the glass down on the side a little harder than I'd intended.

I moved to join the others and caught Winter's arm, dragging her against my chest and forcing Enzo to release her as I placed a rough kiss to her lips. Her mouth was hard and angry against mine for a few seconds but then she thawed like the first rays of spring sunshine were falling down on us and her lips parted for my tongue.

I ran my hands down the bare skin of her back, equally loving and hating this tiny scrap of fabric which apparently counted for clothing and squeezing her ass between my hands as I reached it.

She was pressed flush to my body and no doubt she could feel how much I was enjoying this kiss but with a wrench of determination, I pulled back, turning her in my arms so that her back was to my chest and dancing with her to the sound of I'm a Believer by Smash Mouth as Rocco kept the album playing and I wondered if he always listened to old music or if he liked modern stuff too. There was so damn much I didn't know about the three men in this room, but I found I wanted to learn all of it despite the months of hiding from them.

Rocco made a show of uncovering River's eyes and muttered something about public displays of indecency while Enzo roared with laughter.

A knock came at the door and Frankie answered it, grabbing the huge stack of pizzas and calling out for us to follow him as he carried them away. The dogs reappeared at the scent of cheese, Coco weaving between Tyson's legs and nipping at his feet like he expected to get first dibs on any scraps. And despite the massive size difference between them, I was fairly convinced of his chances. That fluffy little thing had the heart of a warrior beating in his chest.

Frankie led us down a corridor to the other side of the apartment to the bedrooms and I began to appreciate the size of this fucking place. With so many people coming and going all day, I hadn't had the chance to look around much but it was clear the penthouse was enormous.

He pushed open a door and we followed him in to a huge dining room with a heavy oak table big enough to seat twelve and a view through more floor length windows to the rear of the building where we could see mountains in the distance beyond the city.

Winter bit her lip as she looked out at the view and I took her hand, squeezing her fingers. She squeezed mine back and I was glad that I wasn't the only one missing our little cabin in the woods. Not that I could fault Frankie's luxurious apartment or even the company of my...*family*. There had just been something special about that place, the two of us alone, pretending that nothing else in the world even existed.

We moved to take our seats at the table as Frankie tossed pizza boxes down haphazardly and grabbed a bunch of glasses from a liquor cabinet before setting down two more expensive bottles of scotch and a bottle of orange juice.

Enzo pulled a pack of cigarettes from his pocket and placed one between his lips, lifting a lighter half a second before Sloan snatched it out of his mouth and Rocco slapped him around the back of the head so hard he almost head butted the table.

"You're supposed to be quitting, stronzo," Rocco growled and Enzo cursed him before reaching out to brush his fingers through the curls on River's hair where she lay in Sloan's arms. I hadn't even noticed her starting to nurse the baby, but the content little noises coming from her said she was enjoying her milk.

"I'm sorry, bambina," Enzo said, actually looking sheepish. "I forgot my manners in my drunken state."

Sloan snorted a laugh, pointing out the fact that he had no manners drunken state or not and Frankie confiscated the rest of the packet of cigarettes with little protest from Enzo. It was strangely endearing to see the brutish man putting the needs of his tiny niece -who I guessed was *my* tiny niece too actually- before his own and I decided to forgive him for riling me up about Winter. Or at least I did until his gaze shifted across the table and most definitely dropped to take in her tits for a moment.

"You look cold, baby doll," I said to her, shrugging out of my jacket as she looked to me with a frown.

She shook her head in denial and I smirked at her as I wrapped the jacket around her anyway.

Winter's hand landed on my thigh and my dick leapt to attention as she started painting words there almost too fast for me to catch.

I'm not cold.

"You're practically shivering," I said, choosing to casually ignore her declaration as I buttoned up the jacket and effectively covered her up. She still didn't seem to be comfortable to speak in front of my brothers and I was shamelessly using that to my advantage.

With a growl of frustration, she pushed her arms through the sleeves and I gave her a smile before pressing a kiss to the top of her head.

In response, she reached out and stole my scotch, drinking it down in one hit, her angry gaze locked on mine and her throat bobbing with each swallow.

"You might wanna go easy there, baby doll," I said in a low voice. "You're a lot smaller than me and you're not used to drinking-"

She dropped the empty tumbler down before me and arched a single eyebrow which seemed to very clearly say *fuck you.*

Everyone else had started on the food but as I pulled a pizza box closer to us, her hand landed on my thigh again and I paused to interpret the words she was spelling out.

Don't tell me what to do.

I pushed my tongue into my cheek and bit back the response I wanted to give as she reached out and snagged a slice of pizza. She may have not felt comfortable enough to talk in front of my new brothers, but she seemed perfectly capable of moaning in appreciation over the taste of her food.

My body grew rigid as she kept it up, Frankie and Enzo both looking her way more than once while Rocco shot me a knowing grin like he'd had his share of dealing with an impossible woman too. Though the way he looked at Sloan said he definitely thought she was worth the effort.

I forced myself to eat my own food, giving enough of my attention to the conversation to pitch in here and there, but as I didn't know much about the ins and outs of their businesses I couldn't contribute much.

When Winter finished eating, she slowly sucked on each of her fingers to clean them off, running her tongue up the length of them and looking anywhere but at me as my dick strained against my fly.

"Looks like you really enjoyed that pizza, bella," Enzo said to her and the smile she offered him made me want to punch him again.

I looped an arm around her waist and scooped her into my lap, placing her down over the hard swell in my pants and letting it drive into her ass in that too small dress, causing her to gasp.

"Are you trying to torture me, baby doll?" I breathed in her ear, so low no one else would hear it and causing a shiver to run down her spine.

She turned to glance at me from beneath her lashes and gave the tiniest shrug which made a damn growl escape my throat as I tugged her even closer.

She tried to shift back off of my lap but I held on tight, needing to keep her near to me or I was dangerously close to losing it.

Winter huffed in frustration and started squirming in my lap instead, her ass grinding against my dick in a way that made my heart pound. She kept doing it, not obviously enough for anyone else to notice, but she'd lean forward to take a sip of her drink then do it again to place the glass back down. She'd laugh at something that was said and wriggle about way more than necessary or even turn to look at me, swivelling on my cock and making me groan with need as I tried to focus on the conversation going on around us.

Eventually I couldn't take any more of it and I cleared my throat loudly.

"This has been really great, but I'm falling asleep in my chair," I said, interrupting the conversation. Rocco and Sloan had been making half serious announcements that they were leaving soon for the last hour anyway and the sun had long since set over the bay. "I think we're going to head to bed."

Winter twisted around to glare at me for speaking for her and I just smirked like an asshole. We needed to talk and I couldn't take any more of these games. If I had to carry her back to my room over my shoulder, I was happy to do it.

"We should go anyway," Rocco announced, stifling a yawn of his own.

"Shit, being a papa made you so boring, fratello," Enzo teased as his brother swept River up into his arms and he and Sloan prepared to leave. "I plan on hitting a club. You in Frankie?"

"Sure thing," Frankie agreed with a mischievous grin on his face. "I'll crash at your place after anyway. Let these love birds have their space."

Winter snorted like that was some kind of joke before pushing to her feet and I was forced to release my hold on her.

"When will you be back?" I asked him as I remained in my seat and everyone else stood. But it was either that or show off my raging hard on to the entire room so I was going with seeming rude over that.

"Whenever I wake up tomorrow," Frankie replied. "Don't get up to too much mischief while I'm gone." He winked at me, grabbing his jacket from the back of his chair and heading for the door beside Enzo.

Winter hugged Sloan and I managed to rearrange my dick well enough to cover up most of my arousal before I followed them out to say goodbye.

Sloan and Rocco offered to take Tyson with them for a sleepover as he and Coco seemed to have made firm friends and they had a yard where he could stretch his legs and do his business so I reluctantly agreed. I didn't like being away from my loyal friend, but a penthouse in the centre of the city wasn't ideal for a dog used to freedom in the mountains.

When they'd all piled into the elevator and the doors slid closed, I turned to look at Winter with my jaw ticking.

"What the fuck was that about?" she demanded angrily and my hackles instantly rose to the challenge in her voice.

"I don't like other men looking at you like that," I said in a low voice which brokered no argument, but she didn't seem to give a shit about that.

"It's my body, not yours. I didn't trade one kind of cage for another, *Nicoli.*"

I bristled at her tone and stalked towards her. "I don't want to cage you," I snarled.

"Well you could have fooled me. You acted like a total ass tonight."

Anger rose in me like a wild and unpredictable thing but as my gaze caught on the scars on her legs I blew out harsh breath and turned away from her, stalking towards the windows which looked out over the bay.

"Don't you dare do that!" she shouted and my heart leapt in surprise at hearing her raise her voice that way a moment before a goddamn metal dog bowl smacked me in the back of the head and bounced off to land on the carpet.

"Do what?" I demanded, whirling back around again angrily, wondering what the fuck she was thinking to start throwing shit.

"Look at me like I'm just some victim. Hold back on your anger because you think I can't handle it. I'm not made of glass, Nicoli! I went through something, something really fucked up that I'll obviously never forget, but I refuse to be marked by it forever. If I can't even trust you to be yourself with me then how the hell am I supposed to move on from it?" She looked angry enough to spit, but I was pretty pissed myself.

"Fine," I snapped striding back over to her and forcing myself to do as she asked, to give her what she wanted, not to hold back. "I'm pissed at you for that dress and for dancing with Enzo and for grinding your ass into my dick and driving me insane with desire when you knew I was angry already."

"Well guess what, Nicoli, I'm pissed at you for treating me like a fucking possession and for using the fact that I couldn't speak around them to get your own way. That was really fucked up." Her palms slammed into my chest, but I just took the force of her rage without moving.

She growled with fury as I didn't even move beneath her assault and she shoved me again. And again. The fourth time she did it, I caught her wrists and glared down at her. "Stop," I warned in a dark tone before releasing her again.

"No, *you* stop," she demanded angrily, red lips pursed as she glared up at me. "Stop treating me like I'm some fragile little flower. If you're angry with me then do something about it."

She shoved me again and I snarled at her as I caught her waist and shoved her back against the breakfast bar, kissing her with all the heat of my fury and knocking a glass to the floor where it shattered loudly. She moaned into my mouth, her fingers curling against my biceps and digging in until her fingernails cut into me.

I kissed her brutally, savagely, devouring her with the full force of my rage and driving my dick against her with a desperate kind of need. She started unhooking my shirt buttons, biting into my lip as she kissed me back with just as much anger in her. We were both furious and worked up and fucking addicted to each other, but I couldn't let this happen.

I wrenched away from her with a groan of frustration, tasting blood where she'd bitten me and turning my back on her as I clawed my fingers into

245

my hair and tried to calm down.

"Coward," she snarled, lighting my blood with even more rage.

"I can't be with you like this," I replied, refusing to look at her or rise to the bait of her words. "I'm too fucking angry, I'll be too rough with you."

"Maybe I want you to be rough with me," she snapped. "Maybe I want to feel your rage in every piece of my flesh and drown in it. Maybe I don't want to be the broken girl who you have to be soft with all the damn time."

A cushion hit me on the back of the head then another. I whirled around in time to catch the third, tossing it aside and accidentally knocking a lamp over, but I didn't give a shit about that.

"Don't push me, Winter," I warned her, but the fire in her eyes wouldn't be put out that easily.

She strode towards the coffee table, snatched a glass of scotch from it, took a long sip as she approached me then threw the rest of it straight in my face.

I yelled something unintelligible at her and I grabbed her, throwing her down onto the couch and pinning her beneath me as my lips found hers, tasting the scotch between our mouths as it dripped out of my hair. I was pretty sure that glass broke as she dropped it too, but I couldn't concentrate on the sound of breaking glass when I was consumed with desire for the girl beneath me.

Winter moaned into my mouth as I kissed her hard enough to bruise, driving her down into the cushions and fighting with myself over whether or not I really believed she wanted this. If I hurt her or frightened her then I'd never forgive myself for it, but at the same time I was angry as hell and aching to claim her body as mine and give her every reason in the world to want it to stay that way.

Her hand pressed against my chest, pushing me back and I groaned as I sat up, but my frustration was short lived as she climbed into my lap and kissed me again, that green dress riding up over her thighs as her hands fisted in my hair.

I grabbed the lapels of the jacket I'd draped around her and yanked hard enough to pop the buttons open and rip some of them too as I shoved the thing off of her.

"This is why I don't want you wearing this dress, Winter," I growled as my hands ran down her bare back, caressing every inch of her scarred flesh and dragging her even closer to me. "Because it makes men want to do this to you."

"I don't care what anyone else wants to do with me," she hissed back. "I care about what it makes *you* want to do, and so far, I'm enjoying the effect."

She tugged at the front of my shirt as she kissed me again, yanking it out of my waistband before pushing it down my shoulders as she ground herself against my throbbing cock.

I ripped the thing off then stood suddenly, gripping her ass as I lifted her and carrying her in the vague direction of the bedroom. She crossed her ankles behind my back, her fingernails gouging lines into my shoulders as she held onto me, showing me how angry she still was and taking it out on my flesh.

A snarl escaped me at the bite of pain and I slammed her back against the closest wall before I could overthink it, knocking a framed picture from the wall with the vibrations and earning myself a lust-filled moan from her in response.

"You're impossible," I hissed as I used one hand to hold her there and hooked the other beneath her thigh, slipping her panties aside so that I could feel how wet she was for me with a groan of desire.

"You're a caveman," she bit back, trying to unhook my belt despite the fact that there wasn't so much as an inch of space between us.

"No. I'm a mountain man and I think you're just as savage as me, baby doll." I forced myself to place her on her feet then grabbed the hem of her dress and tore the whole thing over her head.

She stumbled back a step in her blood red heels and I just stared at her standing there with only her lacy black panties on and her long hair brushing her hard nipples.

"Prove it," she dared before darting away from me and pulling open the closest door.

I followed her into the dark, finding a switch on the wall and flicking it on. A dim light illuminated a games room with a snooker table in the centre of it with Winter sitting on the edge of it, her eyes full of heat and mischief.

She picked up a red ball and rolled it between her fingers before throwing it at me. I ducked aside and the glass door of a cabinet behind me smashed as it sailed by.

"What the fuck are you doing?" I demanded as she snatched the black ball next.

"Waiting for my apology," she said, parting her thighs as she watched me prowl closer. My gaze dipped to the sight of her wet panties and she smiled wickedly like she knew she had everything I wanted in the world in her possession.

"No chance, baby doll."

She threw that ball too and I ducked aside, a dull thump sounded it slamming into the wall. Before she got the chance to grab another one, I darted forward and caught her wrists in my grasp.

"I'm not going to say the words, Winter," I growled. "But I bet I can make you forget to be angry with me with actions."

"Then don't hold back," she breathed, dropping the ball she'd been holding and letting it roll away across the floor.

I kissed her again, this time letting myself believe her, she wanted this, the look in her eyes told me that clearly enough and I knew for a fact that I was going to go insane if I didn't get it too.

This time when she reached for my fly, I didn't stop her, growling with desire as she freed my cock and wrapped her hand around my thick shaft.

I caught the edge of her panties and tugged them down, leaving the red stilettos on as I kissed her again.

I forced myself to pull a condom from my pocket and roll it on before we went any further, growling with frustration at the moments it cost me while she watched with hungry eyes. The doctor had called to confirm she wasn't pregnant, and we didn't want to take any chances from now on.

I grabbed her legs behind her knees and tugged her to the very edge of the table. She moaned as the head of my cock teased her opening, sliding over the wetness that had gathered there as I looked into her green eyes.

She reached up to take hold of my neck and with a single thrust, I sheathed myself deep inside of her. Winter cried out as my cock filled her to bursting, taking up every inch of room inside her pussy and causing her to dig her nails into my neck again.

I didn't give her a moment to catch her breath, pulling back then driving into her even harder than before. The snooker balls on the table began to crash into each other as our movements made them roll about and I fucked her so hard that she could only scream with pleasure in time with each thrust.

My fingers dug into her ass hard enough to bruise as I guided her hips too, bringing us together harder and harder until her pussy clamped tight around me and she cried out so loudly that I was sure everyone in Sinners Bay must have heard.

I kissed her through her orgasm, slowing my rhythm just a little so that she could catch her breath.

"I want it off," she breathed between kisses and it took me a moment to understand she was referring to the condom.

"Your birth control won't be working yet, baby doll," I breathed, rocking my hips a little slower as I held her against me, kissing her long and deep and dirty as I gave her a moment to recover, because I wasn't even close to done with her yet.

"So improvise," she insisted. "I want to feel your naked flesh inside me."

I groaned at that demand, wanting that more than anything and wondering if she did too.

"Do you trust me, savage girl?" I breathed, sliding my cock out of her and pulling the condom off too.

She bit her lip as she nodded, her eyes glued to my dick like it was her favourite thing in the whole world.

I smiled darkly before lifting her off of the table and turning her around so her ass was to me. She bent forward eagerly and I groaned as I looked down at that perfect fucking view.

"I can't fuck you here without protection," I murmured, sliding the tip of my bare cock around the wetness of her pussy until it was coated in enough lubrication for what I had in mind. Winter moaned and panted as I teased her and I slowly slid my cock up to her ass, nudging her opening so she knew what I was suggesting. "But I could do it here."

She gasped, her hands fisting against the table as she lifted her ass a little higher and started nodding. "Yes. I want to feel you."

Fuck.

I growled with longing as I shifted my hips forward and pressed the tip of my cock against her ass, lowering my other hand so that I could tease her clit. She started panting even louder, rocking her hips back into me in a silent demand as I held her in suspense.

I kept circling her clit with my fingers as I slowly increased the pressure of my dick against her ass and I groaned as I began to slide inside.

"Christ, Nicoli, that's...*fuck*."

"You okay, baby doll?" I asked as I slid in deeper, the tightness of her ass even more intense than her pussy.

"Yes," she gasped. "More."

I groaned again as I pushed myself all the way in, holding her still there for a moment as I circled her clit a few more times and then I started moving. Slowly at first but getting faster and harder as her cries of pleasure spurred me on.

The snooker balls rolled and bounced all over the table and I pushed my hand lower, driving two fingers into her soaking pussy while still maintaining that circling motion on her clit with my thumb.

She was calling out my name and begging for more as I fucked her harder still, my dick aching with the need to come while I gritted my teeth, chasing her orgasm first.

She drove her ass back into me, meeting my thrusts hungrily as I filled her up, pounding into her relentlessly and bathing in the sound of her moaning for me.

When she came it was like the ocean crashing against the shore in a storm, every muscle in her body tightened too and I came hard inside of her the second it did, my dick throbbing and pulsing in the most delicious way as I groaned deep and low.

I collapsed over her, panting like I'd just run a marathon and pushing red hair out of her face so that I could kiss her perfect mouth.

"You might be free, my savage girl," I breathed. "But I'm never going to let you go."

"Good," she replied as she looked into my eyes with so much heated emotion in her gaze that I couldn't believe it was really me she was looking at. "Because I'm never letting you go either."

CHAPTER TWENTY TWO

I took the direct route to Clarissa's house, not bothering with any detours because this time, she wasn't even expecting me. Rocco and Enzo were meeting me there too for backup, not that I needed it exactly but if it came down to a vote, three against one always won and she couldn't make any threats about running to Papa to try and argue her side of things.

Besides, the three of us showing up together said we meant business. We weren't fucking around. And I needed to make it abundantly clear that we especially weren't fucking around where Winter was concerned.

I pulled up outside her house, barely flipping the guys at the gates a look and pulling my car up beside Rocco's dad-wagon.

"What the fuck is that monstrosity?" I asked as I got out, pulling a face at the soccer mom car he'd decided to drive today.

"I had River in the car this morning," he replied, shrugging unapologetically. "And I couldn't be fucked to swap over. Besides, I like the view of the road better in this."

"The view of the road? *Christ*, the world really is ending if Rocco Romero is going to swear off sports cars."

He rolled his eyes at me, leaning back against his admittedly damn expensive daddy day care car. "I'm not swearing off shit, but I'm also giving my bambina the best of everything. This is River's car, not mine, so stop being such an ass."

"River is only a few months old and she already owns a car. What next? A holiday home in the Bahamas?"

"Her holiday home is right next to Disney World, idiota, babies like princesses and super heroes, not sunbathing."

I snorted at him, looking up the steps to the house as our breath fogged between us and the same girl from the other day waited patiently at the open door for us to approach.

"You look cold, bella," I said to her, my gaze slipping over her black uniform with interest as I tried to figure out exactly what she had going on beneath it. "Do you want to come over here and let me keep you warm while we wait?"

A flush lined her cheeks as she looked up at me, raising her chin as she narrowed her eyes. "I'm a maid, not a whore, sir. You can warm yourself up just fine."

Rocco fell into a fit of laughter and my eyebrows rose as she officially piqued my interest. I licked my lips as I assessed her, that fire in her eyes begging for my full attention.

"Aww, don't be like that, carina, it was an innocent offer," I promised, laying a hand on my heart and giving her my winning smile. "Why don't you let me buy you dinner one night to make it up to you?"

"I'm busy," she replied dismissively, looking away like I hardly even held her interest and Rocco nearly fucking died of laughter.

"I didn't suggest a day yet." I tried not to let my irritation show, but I was pretty sure I was failing at that.

"I'm busy all day every day for you, sir. I'm afraid you're not my type." She casually rearranged her dark braids, giving me a look at the length of her slender neck and I punched Rocco in the bicep to shut him up.

"And what type am I?" I insisted, moving closer to her as my arrogance demanded I call her bluff.

"I don't believe it would be polite to say," she replied casually, not even looking at me.

"Please, bella," Rocco begged, his hands clasped together in prayer as he continued to chuckle away like an asshole. "I'll give you a thousand dollars to answer his question and guarantee he won't do anything to jeopardise your job too. I need to hear it."

"Back off, Rocco," I huffed, still trying to catch the pretty girl's eye but her gaze was firmly on him as the sound of Enzo's car pulling up behind us drew my attention for a moment.

"In cash. Up front," she said, holding out a hand and Rocco grinned like a stronzo before pulling a wedge of cash from his pocket and counting ten, crisp hundred dollar bills into her hand.

She tucked the money into her pocket and flipped her eyes to me with a deadly smile which said she'd have told me this without the cash incentive and my heart beat a little faster as I waited to hear it.

"You're the type of man who doesn't hear the word no often enough," she said to me with a curve of her full lips. "Because you're a big, scary mob boss with a beautiful face and a smile that melts panties. Well, sorry it doesn't melt mine. I like my men to come with a soul and my sex to come with some meaning attached. But don't worry, I'm sure there are plenty of willing virgin sacrifices waiting back at your lair to keep you busy tonight."

Rocco roared with laughter and Enzo's deep chuckle joined in too as he arrived just in time to hear me get shot down spectacularly. I couldn't even fight my own grin as I climbed the last few steps until I was standing before her, towering over her. I placed my hand on the door beside her head, leaning forward and boxing her in against it.

She raised her chin, holding my eye and I smirked at her as my heart pounded and I leaned close to speak into her ear. "Challenge accepted, love." My mouth just brushed her flesh and the slight shiver which raced along her skin gave me the answer I'd been hoping for. I'd win her over within the month.

I backed away suddenly, dropping the flirtatious attitude and ignoring my brothers as they continued to taunt me, letting the girl lead us through the house to find our not so beloved aunt.

She was sitting in the same conservatory as last time, sipping coffee in a move designed to look casual, but I could see the hasty way her hair had been styled and the slight flush to her complexion which said she'd been exerting herself. No doubt she'd been racing to get into this position to await our arrival from the moment she was informed of Rocco's car pulling up, and I couldn't help but grin at the fact that she already knew this was an ambush.

We greeted her with fake warmth, pressing kisses to her cheeks before taking seats around the table with her. It didn't escape her notice that the three of us all sat together on one side of the table either, a united front as always.

"What a fucking pickle you got yourself into with that mountain man, Aunt," I said casually and her face instantly darkened. "If I hadn't seen it with my own eyes I'd have had to worry that your story was bullshit, but it was a fucking massacre up there. I don't think I've ever heard of such a complete and utter disaster to take place on a Romero run enterprise."

"You said you killed him?" she asked irritably, clearly not needing the reminder about her destroyed cannabis farm, though I knew the shame of it would be haunting her forevermore. Even better than that, I'd heard that Papa had been over here ripping her a new asshole the moment he'd found out about it for bringing shame on the family name. It was definitely all working out in our favour.

"I did," I agreed. "I managed to sneak up on him while he was tending to his wounds in his cabin. It was too easy, all things considered."

Enzo barked a laugh, leaning back in his chair and draping himself all over it as he widened his legs.

I took my cellphone from my pocket and brought up the photos I'd taken of the body we'd used as our fake mountain man lying dead in the middle of Nicoli's cabin. She scrolled through them, glancing at them with little interest and only a slight sense of satisfaction at his death. She seemed a little more pleased as she scrolled over the shots of the cabin burning, but it still didn't warrant a smile apparently, much less any thanks.

"This whole thing is a total shit show," she growled eventually, sliding my phone back across the table to me with a huff of frustration. "Why the hell did some freak in the woods decide to attack a whole host of my men?" Though something about the way she said it had me wondering if she already knew the answer to that and was just lying about it.

"I actually have an answer to that," I said, the real reason for this visit hanging in the air between us.

She looked up at me sharply as she detected the irritation in my voice and Rocco leaned forward to drum his knuckles on the table.

"Have you been breaking any rules lately, dear aunt?" he asked in a low voice that promised violence.

"Is there anything you wanna say in your defence?" Enzo added, making it clear there was no point in her lying to us. We knew.

She pursed her lips, glancing between the two of them before settling her focus on me again. I was the one leading this little chat, so it only made sense.

"Perhaps you want to explain to me," I said in a dark voice, leaning back in my chair and fixing her with a stare. "Why it is that I found an innocent girl up there, covered in cuts, bruises and scars?"

Clarissa raised her chin but I didn't miss the flash of panic in her gaze before she stifled it. "The girl isn't innocent," she said firmly. "She stole something apparently. And she holds the information required to get it back. My client pays a lot of money for us to retrieve that information and never misses a payment, so-"

"So nothing," I barked, slamming my hand down on the table and making her coffee slosh over the rim of her cup. "That's not how we conduct our business and you know it. Cutting up girls for information that isn't even for us? Letting some stronzo pay you to do it like we're a bunch of common

257

street thugs for hire? What the fuck?"

"You bring shame on our family by doing this shit," Rocco snarled. "Not to mention how fucked up it is."

"I think I can decide what jobs are suitable for my men to-"

"Bullshit!" Enzo roared, standing up and flipping the table over so that her coffee went flying and the mug smashed on the tiled floor. Always the flamboyant asshole. Just had to steal the show.

The doors swung open at either end of the room and armed men rushed in, but the moment they realised who was causing the conflict, they lowered their guns and quickly backed out again. No fucker in our organisation was stupid enough to aim a weapon at Martello Romero's sons, much less fire one.

Enzo cackled with glee as Clarissa remained in her seat, chin raised, waiting.

"I want the heads of every man who was willing to break our rules and do that job for you," I said in a low, dangerous voice. "The mountain man did most of the clean up for me, but if any of the surviving rats come scurrying back here then you're going to hand them over. Got it?"

Her eyes flashed with some knowledge and I knew, just fucking *knew* that she'd already seen at least one of them. But she said nothing, only pursed her lips like enduring this conversation was wearing on her.

"Give them up, dear aunt," Rocco purred, leaning forward with his elbows on his knees. "If you're hiding some of those men-"

"Don't be absurd, Rocco," she muttered. "If any of them came back here, I'd kill them myself for their failure on that mountain. Do you have any idea of the money I'm going to lose without that crop? I'm going to have to try and source more replacement stock and sell it at a loss if I want to keep the sales flowing and-"

"We don't give a fuck about your fucking drug deals," I snarled. "That shit is so amateur it's embarrassing anyway. But I'm telling you now, that girl has our protection. All three of us. And I want the name of the client who paid you to torture her."

Clarissa sighed dramatically. "Unfortunately I can't give you that. It was all done anonymously. The payments are wired through various accounts each month and we return footage of the interrogations via a secure website. I have no way to trace the client directly, that was the way they wanted to do business. And like I said, the money was good enough not to bother questioning it for the sake of some *girl.*"

The way she sneered told me all I needed to know about any guilt she may have been feeling over what had happened to Winter and I bristled. I fucking hated having to work with her all the damn time. Infuriatingly, I believed her about the stronzo who'd organised the torture though. Which meant I was going to have to go back to Nicoli without the answers he sought. For now.

"Fine," I snapped, rising from my seat with Rocco beside me. Enzo had picked up a delicate looking pot plant and was tossing it between his hands. Clarissa's eyes followed the movement with barely concealed rage. She was particularly fond of her plants, always wasting time cultivating things which were damn near impossible to grow. "Papa will be hearing about all of this," I warned as I turned to leave.

"We'll see ourselves out," Enzo added, flipping the pot into the air and laughing as it smashed across the tiles.

Clarissa cursed as Rocco purposefully stepped on it and the three of us strode out of the room without bothering to say anything else.

She was in our shit books but she was still our aunt which luckily for her meant she was untouchable.

At least I could assure Nicoli that Winter's safety was guaranteed as far as the Romeros were concerned. But I still intended to figure out who Clarissa was protecting as well as track down the mystery client who'd paid for the girl to be tortured in the first place.

All in all, I imagined I had a few weeks of work on my hands. Luckily, this kind of hunt was my favourite hobby.

CHAPTER TWENTY THREE

A couple of weeks slipped by and I knew I was holding onto each day with all my might, trying not to let it get free. But it always did. I knew I couldn't continue to stay in this apartment forever. Now that some time had passed, Frankie had announced to everyone he knew that he'd found their lost brother, so there was no reason for us to hide anymore. Nicoli didn't push me to go anywhere, but sometimes I could see that question in his eyes. He was wondering the same thing I was wondering, how long were we going to stay up here hiding from the world?

I'd left him sleeping in bed and was curled up on the couch with a mug of peppermint tea sweetened with three sugars, watching a nature documentary about emperor penguins. They were huddled against a storm, using each other for warmth but those on the outside would surely freeze. I only relaxed when it was over and the footage changed to show the fathers with eggs resting on their feet and their partners returning after weeks at sea. They sought each other out amongst the masses, finding their mates and reuniting with beak rubs and nuzzles.

Nicoli suddenly dropped down into the space beside me in his boxers and I didn't even jump. His presence was so familiar now, I didn't live on the edge of my nerves anymore. But outside of these walls, who knew how I'd be?

He frowned as he looked at me, taking my mug and placing it on the table before dragging me closer. "Why are you crying? What's happened?"

"Am I?" I sniffed as he rubbed his rough thumbs over my cheeks to wipe the tears away, a deep crease in his brow.

"Yes, baby doll. Talk to me. You can tell me anything, you know that, right?"

I parted my lips, looking to the TV and I waved a hand at him as I realised what was up. "It's the penguins."

"The penguins?" he deadpanned, shooting a suspicious glance at the TV.

"They mate for life." I sniffed again and his frown deepened.

"I don't understand. Do you...not like penguins?"

"No, I love them," I gasped, horrified that he'd suggest such a thing.

He remained silent for a long moment. "Look, Winter, I really fucking hate seeing you cry, but I am so confused right now. Please explain."

I smiled through my tears, leaning into kiss him. "You're my penguin, that's all, silly."

"Oh...right. And how am I the silly one in this situation exactly?" He laughed as he wrapped his arms around me, laying back against the sofa so I was snuggled against his chest.

I grinned up at him, brushing my fingers over the stubble on his jaw. "You're always the silly one."

"I'm the least silly person in Sinners Bay," he disagreed and I sat up to straddle him, leaning down and tickling his sides.

No matter how much I tickled him, he didn't react at all, smirking up at me like an asshole.

"I'm not ticklish," he growled. "But you, on the other hand-" He grabbed my waist and I screamed through a laugh as he pushed up the shirt of his which I was wearing to tickle my bare flesh.

"Enough fucking, you have company again," Frankie's voice cut through the air and Nicoli yanked the shirt down to my thighs in an instant. I was kind of getting tired of being walked in on all the time. I knew it was Frankie's place and was so grateful to him for everything he'd done, but sometimes I really did long for our own space.

Frankie strolled over to an armchair with Tyson in tow; the dog was often coming and going between the different Romeros to ensure he had enough exercise.

He dropped down into the seat and looked to the TV as Tyson rushed over, licking my hand before jumping up on Nicoli. "Jesus, that's not my choice of porn but each to their own, I suppose."

Words snagged in my throat as I tried to reply to that. I was starting to get really fond of Nicoli's brothers, but I still couldn't talk to any of them. Sloan was the only one I felt comfortable around to speak with and it was extra frustrating when I naturally wanted to counter Frankie's sass.

Nicoli pushed me off of his lap, sitting up and tugging the blanket over my legs in a causal move that could have been mistaken for endearing if I hadn't known he was being a total jealous idiot.

I leaned close to him, whispering in his ear and he released a rumbling laugh as he looked to Frankie and relayed my words. "Winter asks if you prefer shark porn or is it the dolphins that do it for you?"

"Yeah, those blowholes get me real hard, bella." He smirked. "Speaking of blowholes, can you both stop blowing things and filling holes everywhere around my apartment? I don't even give a fuck about the cum, but can you stop breaking priceless heirlooms?"

I laughed into my blanket and Nicoli slung an arm over my shoulders.

"I suppose I can try," Nicoli snorted, looking to me. "What do you reckon, baby doll?"

I nodded, biting my thumb as my gaze was drawn to his mouth.

"Fuck me, if I ever look at a girl like you two look at each other please put a bullet between my eyes. No questions asked, just pull the trigger, capisce?"

"If you ever look at a girl like I look at Winter, you'll be a lucky man. And she will be an unfortunate girl," Nicoli taunted and Frankie laughed deeply.

"I have the most beautiful girls in the city on tap, fratello, if I don't look at any of them like a doe-eyed stronzo by now, then I think it's safe to say I will be a bachelor 'til death. And don't pity me because I'll have Enzo for company."

"Enzo won't warm your bed at night," Nicoli pointed out.

"He happens to run at approximately the temperature of lit rocket fuel, so I think he'll manage it just fine." Frankie grinned, leaning forward in his chair and resting his elbows on his knees. "So, I have an offer for you both. One you can decline if you would rather, but I told everyone I'd put it out there."

"Cut to the chase," Nicoli pushed.

"Dinner. At Bora Bora," Frankie announced. "Tonight," he added hopefully. "The whole city is buzzing with the news that Nicoli has re-joined his brothers and wondering whether we really are united now or not and I'd love to ram it down their throats."

I shared a look with Nicoli, my heart hammering and my stomach knotting. It wasn't nerves for once, it was excitement.

"A car will drive you there and back. No detours. What do you say?" Frankie asked and I nodded keenly.

"Are you sure?" Nicoli took my hand, winding his fingers between mine. I nodded again and his face lit with a smile. "Then we'll be there."

Sloan arrived with River just before seven o'clock and we slipped away into the room Frankie had given me, leaving Nicoli to head off to the shower.

I was already clean, wrapped in a robe, uncertain of what to wear and Sloan immediately started going through the closet.

"You have such a great figure, you have to show it off tonight," she said, bouncing on her toes as she looked through the rack of dresses. She'd kicked her heels off by the door and I admired the bronze dress she wore which had delicate off-the-shoulder sleeves and hugged her hourglass figure perfectly as she swayed her hips to a song in her head. Her dark hair tumbled down her back in soft curls and glinted in the light. She really was beautiful, the sort of pretty that usually came packaged with arrogance, but she wasn't like that. Sloan was sweet, kind. She cared about her family more than anything in the world, she loved baking and taking long walks by the ocean. She had a free spirit which was intoxicating and she spoke about everything with such passion that it glowed from the depths of her eyes.

While she was busy, I looked to River in her travel carrier on the bed beside me, her dark eyes rising to meet mine.

"You can hold her if you want," Sloan offered like she did every time she came over.

I was about to refuse like I normally did, but River cooed softly and my tummy squeezed. She was too damn cute. I didn't want to admit the real reason I hadn't cuddled her yet, but deep down, I knew it was because looking at her was confronting. As far as I knew, I had once been as innocent and as pure as her before I was taken by The Five. They'd had no reason to hurt and whip and beat me. My skin had once been as perfect as River's, my eyes had once held no pain in them just like hers. But then I'd been twisted into this imperfect creature I was now, riddled with scars and my innocence stripped away like green leaves turning brown and crisp, falling to the ground and left to rot. Looking at her made me ache, because I wanted to protect her like no one had protected me when I'd been snatched away by five devils.

I took her out of the carrier, closing my arms around her and hugging her against my chest. She blinked up at me and I wanted to apologise for what she saw. Just a girl whose path nobody would choose in life.

"Oh, she likes you," Sloan announced as she returned to the room with a beautiful red halter neck that would be skin tight on me.

"Do you think so?" I looked up hopefully and whatever she saw in my expression made her frown.

"Are you okay?"

"Yeah," I breathed, but my voice came out a little choked.

She moved to sit on the bed beside me, placing her hand on my knee. "You can talk to me. I'm good at keeping secrets, I promise."

I smiled at her, then looked back to River with a sigh. "I just wonder if... somewhere out there I have a mother who loves me like you love River. What if she's looking for me?"

"Then you will find each other," Sloan said gently. "There's not a force on earth that could keep me from finding River if she was stolen from me. And she would seek me out too. When you're ready to start looking, I'm sure you'll find your family."

"But what if I'm never ready?" I voiced my deepest fear. Part of me was desperately clinging to this new life I'd found and searching for a life I'd lost made me fear that this one would slip away through my fingers. I couldn't let that happen. I would never let go of Nicoli.

"Trust yourself," she urged, reaching out to tuck a lock of hair behind my ear. "There's no rush, Winter. You've been through so much. Just take your time."

"But what if I do find them and they don't want me anymore?" I whispered as I looked down at the scars on my arms. "I don't have any memories of them, and after everything The Five did, there's no way I'm the same girl they'd remember."

"If they truly love you, they will love you in any form, no matter what," she promised and I smiled at her, taking comfort in her words.

"I'm still not ready," I admitted.

"Then hold on a little longer. You have all the time in the world now."

I nodded, breathing a sigh of relief as her words helped ease the weight on my shoulders. I passed River to her, picking up the dress she'd chosen and realising it had a long slit up the centre which would partially expose my breasts. I snorted, looking to Sloan. "You know Nicoli's going to freak over this, don't you?"

She nodded, smiling conspiratorially. "Yep."

"Well, he really has to learn to stop being so jealous," I said, pushing my hair away from my shoulders as I undid my robe.

"He's never going to stop, all the Romeros are possessive. But that doesn't mean you have to stop wearing things you like. He just has to learn to deal with it." She laughed and I grinned.

"Exactly," I agreed. I was already in my chosen white thong for the night and I pulled on the dress without a bra, figuring it didn't require one. It fit like a glove, falling just above the knee and hugging my small frame. I moved to the mirror and eyed the gap between my breasts which drew attention to the swell of them and made them seem bigger than usual. I spent a little time doing my makeup and Sloan styled my hair in a delicate chignon bun, allowing a few locks of red to hang free around my neck.

I grinned at my reflection, turning to her for approval when she was done and she nodded keenly.

"Perfect," she announced, picking River up from the middle of the bed and putting her back in her carrier. "Ready to go?"

I grabbed a clutch bag and a black evening coat from the closet, pushing my feet into some heels and heading back out to join Sloan. She was back in her heels too, her arm hooked through the carrier as she walked out of the room. I did my coat up, a smile playing around my mouth as I strolled after her down the hall. By the time we got to the restaurant, it would be too late for Nicoli to even think about trying to make me change my outfit. Plus, I was kind of looking forward to the look on his face when I took my coat off in a public place. It was the ultimate test and one I was hoping he would pass. He'd been getting better at biting his tongue whenever I wore something he deemed inappropriate in front of his brothers. So maybe he'd finally accept I was never

267

going to dance to his tune.

Nicoli was waiting in the lounge, rubbing Tyson's head while the big dog seemed more interested in Coco who was curled up between his legs. They'd been inseparable since they'd first met, a ruthless little duo and Rocco and Sloan often kept Tyson overnight so he'd have somewhere outdoors to play with his new friend. It was kind of adorable.

Nicoli stood up and my breath hitched at the sight of him in the fine white button down and silken grey tie which hung from his throat. He pulled on his suit jacket and I just about melted as his muscles strained against the fabric. I wanted to run my hands all over this fine man and mess up his hair, rip open the buttons of his shirt and find my mountain man beneath it all. *Later*.

He held out his arm for me and I took it just as the door opened and Rocco strolled in looking like a dark god in his black suit and equally dark eyes. He smiled, rushing over to Sloan and taking the baby carrier from her before planting a lingering kiss on her mouth, his gaze trailing all over her before his eyes swung to us.

"Our ride is downstairs, Frankie and Enzo have gone ahead. And by the way, fuck me with a ten-incher, you really are getting that Romero shine on you Nicoli. No wonder Winter's fucking you, are you glad you shook off the dirty Calabresi name after all?"

"Rocco!" Sloan slapped him in the arm and he shot her a hungry smile.

"Come on, principessa, you know you're the only exceptional Calabresi. Nicoli Vitoli was nothing but a wet sock hanging out to dry on a mild Tuesday morning."

"Don't be rude," Sloan growled.

"Nah, he's got a point," Nicoli laughed, pulling me closer to him.

"See," Rocco said with a smirk, looking to his brother again. "Now he's got a dark brutality in his eyes which makes me fucking hungry. When are we going on a job together, fratello?"

Nicoli looked to me then shrugged. I took his palm and painted a word on it, giving him a stern look. *Go*.

He frowned and I knew he didn't want to leave me here alone, but I had managed far worse things on my own. I stared him down until he sighed.

"I'll think about it," he told Rocco and his brother smiled like a demon.

"I'll be checking in regularly on your deliberation," Rocco said, then headed to the door. "Now let's go. Frankie and Enzo are probably on their second bottle of scotch already and you can only get sense out of them before the third."

Nicoli kept me close as we headed out the door, taking the main elevator downstairs to the foyer. My breaths came a little heavily as we walked across the beautiful gold and white atrium, a doorman opening the door and bowing his head to us as we passed. There were two fancy black cars waiting for us outside and Rocco and Sloan moved to the rear one while Nicoli guided me to the one in front.

He ushered away the man who tried to open the door for me, doing it himself and I murmured a thanks as I slid inside, moving across the leather seats as he followed me into it.

As the door closed, my heart rate settled a little. I was anxious, but looking forward to this too. I needed to start taking hold of my life again. I didn't want to avoid the world, I wanted to take it all in, start really living. Even if I was frightened of what the world would think when it looked back at me.

The driver remained silent as he drove us downtown and Nicoli threaded his fingers through mine, shooting glances at me occasionally.

I'm alright, I wrote on his palm and he smiled like he was relieved.

"Just say the word if you want to go home at any point tonight," he said, his eyes on mine.

I nodded, giving him a grateful smile before turning to look out the window. The city was modern and full of life. There were lights glinting around the entrances to swanky bars, and restaurants were thronging with people as we sailed by them all. We soon arrived at a skyscraper with shining walls of glass, the car pulling up in front of it as a doorman rushed to let us out.

Nicoli kept my hand in his as he exited and I followed, looking up at the imposing building that stretched high above me toward the clear sky. My breath fogged out around me and a shiver rolled down my spine.

Rocco appeared with River in her carrier, his arm linked with Sloan's as they took the lead towards the entrance. We headed into an incredible space with water flowing down a clear wall behind a primped woman at her desk. She directed us to an elevator and we soon stood in the huge, gleaming metal box as it sailed upwards towards the fiftieth floor.

The doors slid open and I took in the room that spread out towards huge windows that looked over the entire city in every direction.

The place was thronging with people and leafy plants were positioned everywhere around the tables, giving it an exotic feel, especially with the tiki bar set up to my right and the waitresses in beautiful summer dresses and the waiters in smart chinos and loafers. Running water caught my ear as we moved further inside, my gaze drawn to a glass stairway to my left that ran up to a waterfall at the top, the cascade spilling down a flat plain of glass. It led to a huge balcony above the restaurant that contained a living rainforest within it.

I was so in awe of the place that I barely noticed the people staring at us. Mutters passed behind hands as we walked. Everyone was looking at Nicoli, the Calabresi turned Romero, but no one dared stare long enough to catch his gaze. We were led to a table at the far end of the restaurant, the space was cordoned off and my heart lifted as I realised it had the best view in the entire place. It looked down over the bay and the twinkling lights of the buildings that spread out around the water's edge in a crescent, moonlight gilding the water in silver.

"Can I take your coat, ma'am?" a waitress asked as her colleague took the men's, eyeing Nicoli with curiosity with the hint of a thrill in her eyes. I had the feeling she was going to go running back to the bar soon enough to tell everyone that Nicoli Romero had just made his first public appearance at their establishment.

I stripped out of my coat and the girl took in my scarred skin, her eyes widening for a moment before she ducked her head and moved to take Sloan's coat.

My eyes found Nicoli, his body rigid as his gaze travelled down my dress, pausing on my cleavage before falling all the way down to my toes.

"Where are Frankie and Enzo?" Sloan questioned as she placed River in an honest-to-god crib that had been set up beside the table.

"Holy fucking hot sauce on an octopus." Enzo slid an arm around my waist, his whiskey-tainted breath filling my nose as he placed a kiss on my cheek. His shirt sleeves were rolled up to reveal so much ink on his muscular arms, it would have taken me weeks to study it all. "You look ravishing, bella. Scars and all."

I blushed, waving a hand at him as Frankie pulled me into his arms next, cologne and whiskey tangling with the air, the scent of the two of them like a drug made specifically to weaken girls' knees. Not mine though. Mine would only ever weaken for Nicoli.

Enzo pulled out a chair for me and Nicoli all but leapt forward to snatch it from him as he offered it to me instead. Nicoli's eyes were on Enzo as I dropped into it so he missed the look I gave him that warned him to behave. He missed it again when he dropped into the seat beside me and Enzo lowered into the chair on my other side. Nicoli looked like a rabid dog about to start ripping into his brother at any second and I placed a hand on his knee to try and calm him down.

The others took their seats and I was glad that I'd gotten to face the view and not the people behind us who were no doubt wondering who the new girl amongst the Romeros was. Frankie and Sloan had been keeping us informed of all the gossip in town. I wasn't going to cause the biggest stir, it was Nicoli being seen out with his true brothers for the first time that would be the talk of the city. Trust me to fall for the only mountain man in the whole of America who also happened to be pretty damn famous.

"There's a strict no photography rule here," Frankie told Nicoli as he finally gave up glaring at Enzo, leaning back in his seat and settling his arm over the back of my chair to assert his dominance. "So you don't have to worry about your face hitting the papers tomorrow. Although, it wouldn't surprise me if a crowd is gathered out front when we leave...I'll arrange for us to take the back exit."

"Thanks," Nicoli said, his shoulders relaxing as a waitress arrived and took our drink orders. Sloan ordered me and her a whole selection of cocktails, non-alcoholic for her as she was breastfeeding, but I was more than happy to have some Dutch courage. I loved trying new things, discovering what I liked and what I didn't. It was like finding pieces of the puzzle to my old life and fitting things back together.

After a few taste tests, I worked out that passionfruit daiquiris were my new favourite thing, and I didn't like glacier cherries one bit. Which worked out well because apparently Nicoli loved them. He especially enjoyed me lifting them to his mouth and feeding them to him while I laughed.

"So, do you not remember anything at all about your old life, bella?" Enzo asked me as Frankie and Rocco ordered every starter off of the menu for us all to share. It was Polynesian food and I was so excited to find out if I liked it. Nicoli got up to go to the restroom, squeezing my shoulder as he left and shooting Enzo a final glare before walking away.

I shook my head in answer to Enzo's question.

He frowned. "Well, if you like, I can tell you a few things about yourself."

I rolled my eyes and he smirked.

"Indulge me," he pushed and I shrugged, waiting for him to elaborate.

"You were once the kind of girl who drew every eye in the room. Men bartered for your hand in marriage, would cross oceans in a fucking tin can just to see you."

I snorted and he barked a laugh.

"Alright, they wanted to fuck your brains out-"

"*Enzo*," Sloan scolded and my tongue itched with words I longed to say myself. After a few drinks, the idea didn't even seem so frightening.

272

"What? It's the truth. You think Rocco looked at you for the first time and thought 'oh what a lady, I shall marry her and treat her like a true principessa and worship her chastity belt twice a day'," he put on a girlish voice and Rocco threw bread roll at him that bounced off of his head. Enzo ignored him, continuing on, "No, he thought fuck me, I want to be on top of that, under that, inside every hole of that-"

"Enzo!" Sloan snarled. "River is right there."

Enzo roared a laugh and Frankie snorted into his whiskey while Rocco didn't say a word to the contrary.

Enzo grabbed the bread roll Rocco had thrown and took a vicious bite out of it. "When she can say a single word, I will then watch my tongue around her, sorella."

"It's not a negotiation," Sloan sang.

"She has a point," I said and the whole table fell quiet, looking to me in shock.

Nicoli arrived back at that very moment and I looked up at him, sucking on my lower lip.

"Her voice is fucking angelic, don't you agree?" he broke the tension and Sloan beamed at me while Rocco howled and Frankie pounded his fist on the table.

"Told you she wouldn't sound like Elmo," Frankie spoke to Enzo and Enzo smirked at me.

"I guess you're right, she could give Cecilia Bartoli a run for her money."

"Who?" I frowned, but before I got an answer, a sharp, feminine voice cut through my thoughts.

"Well, isn't this just bellissimo, our little family of Romeros all out together."

I turned in my seat, finding an Italian woman with raven hair and beautiful but blade-like features staring directly at Nicoli who was still on his feet.

Rocco leaned back in his chair, spreading himself out like the alpha he was and Frankie straightened his tie casually as he looked to her. Enzo pointedly ignored her, playing with the bread knife like he was deciding how best to slit her throat with it.

"Oh, except for me and your father of course," the woman snarled.

"Clarissa," Sloan said curtly. "How nice to see you." Her tone said it wasn't nice at all and Clarissa gave her a fleeting look that said she was little more than a fly buzzing around her ear.

"I must have missed the memo on Calabresi cretinos being invited out to dine with us now." Her eyes moved to Nicoli. "No matter how much of our blood is on their hands."

Nicoli stared coolly back at her, his eyes assessing. I hadn't missed the way he'd inched closer to me with that protective gleam in his eye like a bear protecting its cub.

"You look starved, Aunt, you must eat. Or did Dr Frederico just take too much off your hips the last time you visited him?" Rocco tossed a bread roll at her and it bounced off of her hiked up boobs, hitting the floor by her feet.

"Figlio di puttana," Clarissa hissed. "You're not too old for me to clap you round the ear, Rocco Romero."

"You never could catch me as I remember," Rocco laughed while his brothers smirked.

Clarissa rolled her eyes then her gaze fell on me and a frown tried to inch its way into her smooth brow. She took in my scars with some dawning comprehension on her face and she immediately looked to Frankie. "Please tell me this isn't the girl you found on the mountain."

"But if I told you that, it would be a lie," Frankie said coolly and the temperature plummeted ten degrees.

I noted that she wasn't even asking me directly, her gaze shifting between her nephews like me and Sloan were invisible.

"It's not good business for her to be here," Clarissa clipped and my heart thudded angrily in my chest.

"But it was good business when you took the money from an anonymous buyer to have me kidnapped and tortured?" I asked heatedly before the Romeros could answer, lifting my chin, surprised and delighted that my voice was staying firmly with me tonight.

"It wasn't personal, *ragazza*." Her eyes moved to my scars again, narrowing. My skin crawled under her inspection and as her upper lip peeled back I knew she was disgusted with me like I expected most people to be. But her relatives had never looked at me that way and now that she was, I found I didn't care for her scrutiny. Who was she to judge me?

"Her name is Winter, not *girl*," Nicoli growled, a note of warning in his tone. "You're lucky I haven't slit your throat for your part in what happened to her. You can thank your nephews for that."

I took his hand, partly to show solidarity and partly because I really thought he might use the nearest knife to fulfil his threat. And as much as I disliked this woman, she wasn't worth my mountain man going to prison for.

Clarissa scowled at him. "You really ought to watch your tone with me, Calabresi boy."

"I am not a Calabresi. Never was. Never will be," Nicoli snarled.

"If you raise a dog to kill its own kind in fights, it will never stop hungering for their blood. Even when it is cared for and taken from that life, it will never change. The kindest thing to do is put it down." Clarissa sneered and in a heartbeat, Rocco, Frankie and Enzo were on their feet, shoulders squared and eyes fierce. Enzo even still had the bread knife in his grip.

"We are getting to know our brother, he is one of us now," Rocco said firmly while the others nodded.

"Papa will accept him for who he is when he has the DNA results, and you will have to as well," Frankie said evenly, a smile on his face but his eyes were void of light.

"I suggest you welcome your nephew back into the fold, Aunt C," Enzo said, grazing the bread knife over the ink of his forearm. "Wouldn't wanna piss off our old man, would you?"

"He's is on *my* side in this," she said firmly.

"You know full well that if Papa was against this whole idea he'd have tried to kill Nicoli already. He's living in hope, waiting for proof and once the DNA results are back everything will change," Rocco growled. "Now, we're not going to discuss these private matters in public any further. Go back to your night, Aunt."

Clarissa ran her tongue over her teeth, looking between all of us then shrugging with a light laugh. "Of course. No harm meant. Enjoy your night miei cari ragazzi." Her eyes swept over me and Nicoli one last time, telling me she was nowhere close to accepting us into anything and she strutted off to meet a beefy man at the bar before the two of them promptly left.

"So, that's Clarissa," Frankie said to me, tossing a healthy measure of whiskey down his throat. "Total bitch if you hadn't noticed."

"I noticed," I said and everybody laughed, the tension shattering in the air and we'd soon long forgotten about her as we fell into idle talk.

I ate my way through three platefuls of food, trying bits of everything and enjoying the explosion of flavours in my mouth. None of the Romeros cared when I used my hands on occasion, even when the waitresses and some of the clientele gave me wide-eyed looks. They were so much fun to be around that the time flew by, all of us laughing at tales of the three boys getting up to mischief together as kids. Nicoli even chipped in with a few stories about him and Sloan winding up the kitchen staff which had everyone in stitches.

I found myself aching to have something to contribute, jealous of their pasts, their families. I had so few good memories to offer and all of them involved Nicoli, and most of them were either wildly inappropriate or totally violent. So I just listened, soaking it all in and loving that I was a part of it all even in some small way.

After another couple of drinks, I was almost sitting in Nicoli's lap with how close we'd gravitated towards each other. My hand rested on his thigh and his arm squeezed my shoulders as he kept me near. Every now and then he'd turn and place a kiss to my temple or my hair and I felt so adored that it made every inch of me tingle.

I ran my hand a little further up his thigh and he cleared his throat, glancing down at me as everyone else looked at Enzo who was up on his feet, acting out the time he'd strung up a guy by his ankles and danced for him to the tune of Wannabe by the Spice Girls in his own special form of torture.

Nicoli's eyes were as dark as two stormy seas and the world faded as I looked up at him under my lashes and inched my hand even higher up his leg.

"Baby doll," he growled a warning.

"Nicoli?" I arched a brow, sliding my hand even higher until my little finger grazed the bulge in his pants.

"Time to go home?" he asked, a note of hope in his voice.

"Hmm, but I'm having so much fun." I leaned in, kissing his cheek and getting to my feet.

"Where are you going?" he asked.

"The restroom," I laughed, tossing my napkin at him and he smirked, watching me go and I let my hips sway as I felt his eyes dropping to my ass.

I ignored the stares I got as I crossed the room, the buzz of alcohol in my veins and the happiness in my heart making me zone the world out. I used the facilities at the bottom of the huge staircase and when I exited, I was tempted up the stairs, wanting to see the jungle on the first floor. I headed up the glass steps to the waterfall at the top of it, rushing down the glass to a pool down below. This place was a man-made jungle and it got my pulse rising. I'd never been anywhere like it.

I pushed through a frosted door and a wave of humidity hit me as I stepped onto the balcony, finding myself in a maze of trees and exotic plants. Flowers bloomed from waxy stems and bird music was fed into the place, making it seem so real. Like walking into a dream.

I followed a winding path into the forest as heated droplets of water collected on my skin. I reached up to pull my hair free from the tight chignon it was tied in and kicked off my heels, abandoning them on the path, wanting to let loose. There was no one up here, but as I rounded through a stone archway

277

covered in vines, I arrived at the edge of the balcony, the huge glass box I was in overhanging the restaurant below.

My eyes found Nicoli magnetically where he sat by the far window with his family. He kept glancing towards the restrooms, not really listening as they all laughed and joked together. I could see his anxiety in the crease of his brow even from here and I shook my head at my mountain man. He would always worry about me, but I didn't want him preparing to start murdering people whenever I went to the restroom. It was no way to live. And as much as I could tell I was never going to be seen as normal by him or anyone else, I could be seen as capable.

I took my phone from my clutch, shooting him a text.

Winter:
Look up.

I watched eagerly as he took his phone out of his pocket so fast that he nearly elbowed Sloan in the face beside him.

I laughed as his eyes shot up, immediately finding me where I stood in the glass box. I hadn't yet drawn any attention from others in the restaurant, but anyone could glance my way at any given moment. A wild idea came to me which made my heart pound and as I held Nicoli's gaze, I leaned down, reaching under the short red dress and pulling my panties down. I knew it was reckless, but that was what we were. And I wanted to remind him I was still the savage girl from the mountain. That I still didn't play to the same rules that everyone else did. I would always be dancing to my own tune.

I slid them over my bare feet, standing and dangling them on one finger in an offering.

He rose from his seat in an instant, fury lining his features and my heart tripped over itself as he started marching away from the table without an explanation.

I bit my lip as I watched him make it to the stairs and out of sight then

I turned back to the maze of potted trees with adrenaline filling me up. He was coming for me. And I liked being hunted by him, but tonight, I wasn't the prey. He was.

I hung my panties on a branch just behind where I'd been standing then darted down another path, running deep into the heated jungle. The door sounded and heavy footfalls thumped inside.

"Winter!" Nicoli barked. "Come out here."

I laughed, my voice no doubt carrying to him as I slid behind a large palm tree and pressed my back to it.

"Someone could have seen you," he growled.

"Someone *did* see me," I called, taunting him. "And he's come to find me."

"You're in trouble."

"I like being bad, good is so boring. Do you really want me to be good?" I asked sweetly.

"I like you just as you are, baby doll. But you're trying to bait me and now I'm angry."

I laughed, my heart thumping against the base of my throat.

"Fuck," he snarled somewhere to my right and I had a feeling he'd just located my panties. "What if someone else had found these?"

"There's no one in here but us," I pointed out, my breathing coming heavier. "Don't you like them?"

"They're wet," he growled, a heat to his tone that got my thighs clenching together.

"For you," I said breathily. "Only you."

He groaned like that pleased him and a smile quirked up one corner of my mouth. His footsteps drew closer and I slipped away again, padding down another path and arriving beside a little rock pool before the glass wall of the balcony. A few trees and bushes gave cover from the restaurant, but I only had to lean past them to see back downstairs. I pressed my back to the widest tree in front of the window, hiding myself from view, but close enough to being visible that it got my skin flushing hot.

Nicoli stalked into the clearing the same moment I put my hand up my dress, dipping my fingers between my thighs and tipping my head back against the trunk.

His eyes darted to the restaurant behind me and back to me with his shoulders tense. "Stop," he demanded. "If someone sees you-"

"They won't see," I panted, circling my fingers over my clit in the same way Nicoli always did to me. "Come here."

He had my panties clutched in his grip and his eyes darkened as he watched me. As my gaze roamed down him, I realised he was already hard for me, his cock straining against his fly. I smiled at the sight, moving to step toward him, but he held up a hand.

"Don't you dare move," he warned and I laughed lightly. He was always so jealous, wanting to keep me as his, but he didn't understand that he never needed to worry about me straying from him. I didn't care if the whole world saw me naked, my flesh was his.

He walked toward me, loosening his tie like he couldn't breathe well with it knotted at his throat. The smile fell from my face, replaced with a look of longing as he made a slow and measured approach. I'd lured this predator into my trap, but now the tables were turning. He was setting me in his sights, ready to pounce like the animal he was. We brought out the most primal parts of our nature in each other and I loved that. I didn't ever want to stop being his savage girl and I didn't want him to stop being my savage man either. Everything away from the mountain was begging us to conform, but if we ever did, I knew I'd hate myself. I'd hate him. We weren't meant to be like the rest of the world. We knew pain and blood and because of that, we knew how to be free. Really, truly free.

His thumb rubbed over the centre of my little white panties in his hand, coating his skin in my desire as he came to a halt in front of me.

"You don't want to play this game with me, baby doll. You're going to regret it."

I pushed two fingers inside myself, arching my back so my breasts pushed out and my dress rode higher over my hips. I moaned at the thought of his hands on me, needing him to want this like I did.

"Are you afraid we'll get caught?" I asked through heavy breaths.

"I don't fear anything for myself. I fear for you though, savage girl." He stepped closer, the space between us spiking with a fierce energy. "I would murder anyone who laid eyes on your flesh without your permission."

"I only want *your* eyes on me," I swore, meaning it from the bottom of my soul. "Don't you like what you see, mountain man?"

He hummed low in his throat, moving closer until I was consumed by his shadow and the heat of his body reached to me. My cheeks were burning hot as he surveyed me, his head tipped down, his thumb still circling in my panties in the way I so desperately wished he'd do to me.

The humidity was making strands of my hair stick to my cheeks, but the heat was nothing to the fire blazing between my legs. I needed him. If he didn't touch me soon, I was going to lose my mind.

"Nicoli," I moaned as I pushed my fingers into my wetness, slowly in and out as he drank in the movement, licking his lips like I was making him salivate.

"Hands on my chest," he instructed and I was happy to comply, taking my hand from between my thighs and resting it on his body with my other. His heart pounded out a dark and merciless tune beneath my palm and I looked up at him under my lashes, my hips rocking side to side as I ached for him to claim me.

He reached down with my panties in his grip, his eyes on mine the whole time as he slid them between my thighs and rubbed them into my arousal.

A whimper escaped me as he teased my opening, soaking my panties through then taking them away again. He balled them in his hand then brought them to my mouth, rubbing them over my lips so I could taste myself.

"You really shouldn't lure monsters into dark places, savage girl," he warned, taking the panties away and pushing them into his pants' pocket.

"Maybe I like this kind of monster," I whispered, his eyes on my mouth where they no doubt glistened with my wetness.

He leaned in eagerly and licked my mouth clean with a hungry growl before driving his tongue between my lips. It tasted of me and him and everything we were and were yet to be. He kissed me long and hard and I fisted my hands in his shirt, tugging him closer with a firm yank, reminding him not to be gentle. He still needed a nudge from time to time.

His teeth sank into my lower lip and I moaned in pleasure as he chased the pain away, sucking it into his mouth before plunging his tongue between my lips again. The kiss was filthy and perfect and made me long for even more of his rough touches.

I didn't want sweet tonight, I wanted nasty and sinful. I wanted to lean into my darkest urges and forget that I was ever abused, tortured, captured. None of that defined me. It didn't mean I needed to be mollycoddled for the rest of my life. I was no longer empty; roots had been growing deeper in me for a long time and now shoots were started to spring from the earth of my core. I was growing into a person I actually liked, who had needs and wishes beyond the deaths of The Five. Who wanted this man like she had never wanted anything. And who would happily spend the rest of her days loving him and being loved in return.

I broke the kiss, leaning back to look into his deep brown eyes, my palms still pressed to his chest. I could see the monster in him, peering out at me from behind his eyes and I longed to fall at its mercy once more. I wanted his worst, his darkest self tonight. The one he liked to hide from me more often than not. But he'd claimed me brutishly before and it was time for him to do so again.

"You know what I want," I told him, my lips quivering a little. "Remind me that I can't shatter."

He unbuckled his pants, a heathen in his gaze. "Your soul is made of iron, your spirit of steel and your body is a diamond, uncut, as sharp as a dagger. You're unbreakable, baby doll. But I'll always want to protect you, because you're also *mine*."

He grabbed my hips, caging me in with his powerful body and making sure I couldn't be seen beyond the tree shielding us from the window. He ran his palm over my bare ass and hooked the back of my thigh, tugging it up and wrapping it around his hip. He rolled his zipper down, taking his thick length into his grip as he freed it from his boxers. We didn't need condoms anymore now my pill was working and I was glad because I craved his skin against mine more than anything right now.

"Eyes on me," he demanded and I looked up, biting into my lip as he guided himself to my entrance. He nudged my legs wider then pushed the head of his hard length into me, teasing me as he gripped the base of his dick, circling himself inside me until I moaned. Then he pushed a little deeper. My lips parted and my head fell back, but he released my leg and gripped the back of my head, making sure I kept my eyes on his. He eased in deeper still and a desperate groan escaped me as he claimed me tortuously slowly, his hips rolling as he did so to make me gasp and pant.

He clamped a hand to my mouth a second before he slammed his hips to mine, driving the rest of the way in and making me cry out. The sound came out muffled and he smirked as he gripped my thigh over his hip again, holding me in place as he started to claim me with merciless thrusts.

The more he pushed me, the more I wanted. This was the beast who'd murdered in cold blood just for me, the creature who'd found me in the dark and hunted my enemies with a callousness that frightened and excited me. He was ruthless and vengeful as much as he was protective and caring. Every spark of light in him was mirrored by a slice of darkness. He would always be as bad as he was good. And I ached for both sides of him, finding myself lost between the two halves of him which created a beautiful whole.

He kept his hand over my mouth, his forehead gleaming as he took control of me, claimed me with the full strength of his body and made me scream for more against his hand. All of him, every last scrap. I wanted it. No, I *needed* it.

He dropped his hand and swallowed my cries with a kiss that made me ache on the inside. It was over barely before my tongue met his and he pulled out of me, grabbing my hips and turning me around. I braced myself on the tree as he thrust himself inside me from behind, his hand covering my mouth again and I bit down on his fingers to hold back my screams. He laughed darkly, his other hand twisting into my hair and pulling me further upright so I was crushed between his body and the tree. The rough bark chafed any inch of bare flesh it could find, my cheek rubbing against it.

He swelled inside me and I tightened around him, my pulse jack-hammering at my throat as he gasped, plunging into me hard then spilling himself inside me with a long groan that tangled with my name.

He eased out of me, releasing me and my nails dug into the bark as my body shuddered with need. I was so close to release, my legs quivering, but maybe now he was done, that was it. Even as the thought crossed my mind, his hands ran down the back of my thighs and I felt his breath against my lower back.

"Don't move," he growled. "And don't make a sound."

One hand pushed up between my thighs, his fingers slipping over my soaking entrance before he slid them onto my clit. My hips bucked with urgency and he drew them back, making me bend at the waist. I was so exposed to him, but I didn't even care. I needed him too much. And he knew every piece of me, scars and all. We never hid from each other and I wasn't going to start now.

His tongue ran up the centre of me and I brought my fist to my mouth, biting down to stop myself from making a noise. He did it again and pinched my clit at the same time, making me shiver right down to my toes. The next time he did it, he pushed his tongue into me, his fingers rubbing and circling over my pulsing flesh as he took control of me, driving his tongue in and out of me as he devoured the evidence of what he'd just done.

My hips swayed and I started to grind against his mouth, so close to ecstasy that it was driving me to insanity. He laughed and the sound rumbled right through me, his tongue swirling and flicking as he rubbed my clit, his fingers slick with my desire.

"Come for me savage girl," he commanded, the vibrations of his deep voice sending me over the edge and I came on his tongue as he lapped at me all the way through my orgasm. I lost all strength in my body and he pulled me down into his lap, tucking us up close against the tree.

"-finished building it last year. Isn't it beautiful?" a girl's voice reached us as she stepped into the garden.

"Oh wow," another girl cooed. "It's so hot in here. Did you see that man that came up here too. He was like, other worldly hot. Do you think the Romeros are recruiting?"

"Idiot, don't you know who that is? It's Nicoli Vitoli. A.K.A Angelo Romero."

"Holy shit," her friend gasped.

Nicoli tugged my dress down, pulling me to my feet and dragged me away from the window into the jungle as he rearranged his pants and did up his belt.

"Do you think he's dating that redhead he was sitting with?" the first girl mused as Nicoli guided me along a winding path that led towards the back of the jungle.

"The one with all the scars? Looked like a charity case to me. You totally have a shot with him, Felicia."

"Do you think so? I mean, she did look a bit like a lawnmower had run over her." She giggled and my upper lip peeled back the same moment Nicoli's grip tightened dangerously on my hand.

He changed course suddenly, guiding me down a path towards them with purpose in his stride.

"What are you doing?" I whispered, but he just locked his jaw tight, tugging me on. As we rounded down the next path, I saw them. They were inspecting my abandoned high heels on the ground in confusion and as we approached, they looked up in surprise.

"Oh, hi Nicoli, I'm-" the blonde one – Felicia - started.

"You're nobody," Nicoli growled, his gaze moving to the pretty brunette beside her. "And if you don't get on your knees and tell my girl you're sorry right this second, I'll make sure you never step foot in this restaurant again. Possibly the whole of Sinners Bay too if your apology doesn't come up to par."

They gawped at him, lip-glossed mouths wide.

Nicoli took a step closer and they shrank like wilting flowers. "Normally, when I tell people to do things twice they've already pissed themselves and are missing a few limbs. I'd rather not make a mess of my clothes tonight though, so if we can move swiftly fucking on with the apology, that would be ideal."

The brunette looked like she wanted to run for the hills but the blonde fell to her knees, her shoulders trembling. It was clear they knew enough about Nicoli, that his words scared them on a real level and the brunette suddenly crashed to her knees too, obviously thinking it was the safer option.

"I'm sorry," they said at once, looking to Nicoli with desperation.

"To her!" he bellowed and they immediately turned to me, wide-eyed and fearful. Not even just of him. They were looking at me like I held all the power in the world, and I guessed with Nicoli Romero willing to go to bat for me, I did.

"I'm so sorry," Felicia begged, tears welling in her eyes.

"Really," her friend added, nodding ferociously as sweat beaded on her brow.

I pulled my hand free of Nicoli's, walking toward them and bending down to grab my shoes. Felicia caught them before I did, holding them in front of me to help me into them. Her friend leapt on the opportunity, grabbing one shoe from her so she could offer it to me too.

I glanced back at Nicoli in alarm and his shadowed eyes and folded arms told me to show them my strength. So I rested my hands on their heads for support and slipped my feet into the shoes. When they'd strapped them on, I walked between them, holding my head high as I made it to the door and stepped outside. Nicoli didn't appear for several more seconds and I had the feeling he was telling them something that would give them nightmares for the rest of their lives.

When he stepped through the door, he curled an arm around my waist and pressed a kiss to my temple. "You're a queen and the whole of Sinners Bay will know it soon enough, baby doll. I will silence anyone who says otherwise."

I smiled broadly and he grinned darkly right back.

"You have lipstick all over your mouth," I told him with a laugh.

"So do you," he teased and I shrugged.

He crowded me in against the wall, using his thumb to wipe away the smears at the corners of my mouth. "You bring out a wild side of me, savage girl. But I'd prefer if my brothers didn't know I just fucked you above the whole restaurant. I will never hear the end of it."

"That's the first time you called them that," I said, smirking and he smiled.

"Go clean up." He pulled me away from the wall, directing me down the stairs towards the restrooms.

"Bossy," I arched a brow.

"Guilty," he growled, stern.

I moved forward, reaching out to tighten up his tie. "They're going to be able to tell anyway."

"Bullshit."

I laughed and walked away, heading downstairs into the restroom as Nicoli slipped into the men's. By the time I'd touched up my makeup and pulled my hair back into a bun which wasn't nearly as neat as the one Sloan had done for me before dinner, I looked totally innocent. Apart from the missing panties, but it wasn't something anyone was going to notice and Nicoli apparently had no intention of giving them back. Still, the way the Romeros seemed to act so intuitively with one another, I just knew they weren't going to swallow a lie about us wandering through that garden for all that time together.

I stepped out of the restroom, finding Nicoli waiting for me, the lipstick washed from his mouth and his hair pushed back into place. He offered me his arm and I smiled as I took it.

"Bet you five dollars that they know," I whispered.

"You don't have five dollars to barter with," he murmured.

"I will have in a second."

He laughed as we approached their table and Enzo immediately stood up, starting to clap dramatically. "You dirty fuck!" he pointed at Nicoli and I held out my hand to Nicoli in a clear demand.

He sighed, taking out his wallet and planting ten dollars in my palm as Rocco howled like a wolf and Frankie slammed his hand on the table with a loud laugh, making the cutlery jump.

"You are such a fucking Romero," Rocco taunted Nicoli and Sloan jabbed him in the side.

"They are totally innocent," Sloan defended us.

"Yeah as innocent as you were, principessa, when you hung upside down off of that kitchen island and sucked my-"

"Rocco!" Sloan punched him in the arm and me and Nicoli burst out laughing.

Nicoli's family had seriously grown on me. And there was a part of me that really dared to hope that I could stay a part of it forever.

CHAPTER TWENTY FOUR

I sat in a chair by the floor length windows, looking out at the slowly brightening sky in the distance. My gaze hooked on the glimmering lights of street lamps and cars which lined the edge of the bay as I waited for the sun to crest the distant waves. After our run-in with Clarissa, Frankie had decided it was best to lay low again for a while. I trusted that bitch about as much as I trusted a snake in the grass. She would no doubt be more than happy to slide a knife into my back given the opportunity, so I had to trust my brothers to deal with her and to track down Duke for me too.

I sighed as I stared at the view. I wasn't even sure why a single text had woken me from my sleep, but I guessed even on a subconscious level I'd been waiting for it. The results of my DNA swabs. I'd sat and stared at the unread message for a long time before tapping on the little icon to open it. And the relief I'd felt at having real, undeniable proof of who I was had overwhelmed me. For a moment there, I'd feared the result, terrified that it would all turn out to be just some new lie designed to torture me. Because I couldn't bear that, after weeks spent getting to know my brothers, my niece and being made to feel like a part of a real family for the first time in my life, I didn't think I would have been able to cope with hearing that I wasn't really their flesh and blood.

So when I'd finally opened it and found that confirmation of my identity staring back at me, I'd been overcome with relief to find that it was all true. I was born Angelo Romero. Giuseppe Calabresi stole my life from me when I was four years old and I'd never even known my real father.

Which was the thing that had drawn me out of bed, leading me away from Winter to sit in this chair and wait for the sun to rise. Today, I'd be meeting Martello Romero. The man who I should have known my entire life. My biological father. And even after how well I'd managed to start forming bonds with my lost brothers, I still felt undeniably anxious about this meeting.

His reputation preceded him. He ruled his family with an iron fist and his word was the difference between life and death for countless people. I'd heard so many awful things about him over the years that I wasn't sure how I would be able to form a fresh opinion of him. Or if he even deserved any differing opinion than what I'd held before. He certainly hadn't felt the need to come and see me in the weeks that I'd spent living here in Frankie's apartment, though I knew my brothers were seeing him almost daily for work. He was in the city. Just a few blocks away apparently. And yet I hadn't been worth the visit without that shiny little print out confirming we were a biological match. How touching.

Soft footsteps made the hairs raise along the back of my neck and I frowned to myself as I realised my absence had woken her up. I'd left the peace of our bed so that she could rest while sleep refused me, not have to follow me out here to find me sitting in the dark like some kind of wraith.

"When we were on the mountain, you'd have played your guitar when you felt like this," Winter murmured as she came up behind me, wrapping her arms around my neck as she leaned over the back of my chair and held me close. "Do you want company out here, mountain man?"

"When that company is you? Always," I replied in a low tone.

She pressed a gentle kiss to my cheek before drawing away from me so that she could circle my armchair and come to stand before me. She was wearing a white silk nightdress which clung to her breasts and hips, skimming her mid-thigh and catching the light in the dark room so that my gaze was instantly locked to it.

"I had the confirmation about my DNA," I said in explanation for my late night wander and vacant mood.

"And you're worrying about meeting your father?" she asked though it wasn't really a question, more a statement of fact.

I reached up to take her hands, rubbing my thumb over her knuckles and sighing at the feeling of her flesh against mine. Even this small contact was like a balm to my soul, but I was greedy for more all the same.

"I was always so eager to impress Giuseppe," I admitted in a low voice. "So much so that I didn't question anything when I probably should have. But I was desperate for his approval, his love, aching to feel the pride of a father because I'd never had one. And now...I have one when I'm too old to need one. And I'm afraid that it's too late."

"He will love you," she breathed, saying the thing I hadn't. That gut-churning ache which I didn't want to admit. That I'd always craved the love of parents and now that I really had one, I was afraid that the time we'd spent apart, the things I'd done with my life up until now would make me lesser in his eyes than his other sons. That I'd never match up to them when it came to his love. "How could he not?"

I looked up at her for a long moment, the sun cresting the horizon through the windows behind her and gilding her in warm light which shone through her red hair and set it alight with colour.

"I think I'd still be lost on that mountain if I hadn't found you," I breathed, tightening my grip on her hand and tugging so that she would come and sit with me.

She lowered herself onto my lap, straddling my thighs and moving into my space, brushing her hand along my jaw and looking into my eyes until I couldn't hold her gaze anymore. Frankie was still hunting for information on Duke for me, but he'd managed to unearth enough hints to suggest the motherfucker had survived and the fact that he was still out there somewhere filled me with a darkness so black that I couldn't see through it whenever I gave it my attention. I'd promised her the heads of the men who'd hurt her and I hadn't delivered on that yet. It cut me up inside.

Winter either didn't notice the dark turn my thoughts had taken or she chose to ignore it, perching her ass on my knees as she brushed her hands over my body in a way that felt so good, I couldn't help but relax a little. I watched her as she looked at my chest, her fingertips caressing the scars that adorned my flesh, making my skin tingle with her gentle touch as she explored my skin with fervent adoration.

"None of them hurt like the one in here, did they?" she breathed, her fingers trailing over my chest as she painted patterns over my heart. "The one you were given when they killed your mother and took you from your family. The one you always felt but never understood..."

"I don't feel it so much when I'm with you," I admitted, my arms still laying on the arms of the chair we sat in, purposefully not touching her in some vague attempt to keep my darkness from infecting her. "But I'm not good company right now, baby doll."

"I don't have pain like yours in my heart," she said. "I didn't have anything at all in my heart before I met you...it was just *empty*."

My gut twisted uncomfortably at her words and I hated that there wasn't anything I could say to make that better.

"But now," she went on, leaning down to brush her lips over my pounding heart. "It's filling up."

I groaned as she moved her mouth to the scar which ran across my ribs, the mark left by a bullet on my shoulder, the one on my cheek too. My fingers curled around the armrests and dug in as she continued to hunt out my scars and kiss them all - not like she was trying to make them better, but like she adored each and every one of them.

She slid from my lap and onto her knees between my parted thighs, rolling down my sweatpants to reveal the thick length of my cock. When she kissed me there, I groaned, my eyes falling shut as I tipped my head back and focused every inch of my attention on what she was doing.

Her tongue ran in a smooth line from the base of my shaft right up to the head before she swirled it around the tip, moaning softly at the taste of me as she licked the bead of moisture into her mouth. Her lips closed around me and my fingers dug into the armrests as she took me all the way in, sucking long and hard on my cock like there was nothing in the world she'd rather be doing right now than worshiping it.

I groaned again as she took me in and out, her lips hot and her tongue devilish while the stifled moans escaping her damn near drove me to ruin.

I forced myself not to thrust my hips or grip her hair as I gave myself over to her control, letting her steal away my worries with the movements of her mouth.

"Come here, baby doll," I begged, needing to kiss her before my heart burst open and bled all over both of us.

I was so stuck on this girl, so obsessed with her that I knew it would never end. She was all I'd never even known I wanted and I couldn't even imagine a tomorrow without her by my side anymore.

Winter took my cock in and out of her mouth a few more times like she really didn't want to stop before getting up and climbing into my lap.

I kept my hands fisted on the armrests as she moved to straddle me again, wanting her to possess me, take me, own me in that moment. She was tending to my needs in a way that only she could, soothing an ache in me that was once raw without her. She wanted to take care of me and right now I just wanted to let her, relinquish control and let her have me however she wanted me.

She leaned forward to kiss me deep and slow, her tongue salty with the taste of my desire and her lips plump from their time wrapped around my cock. Her hand came between us and she took my shaft, guiding it towards her soaking wet core before she sank down onto me so slowly that it ached.

Her pussy was tight and so fucking ready for me and as she moved her hand away, she slid all the way down so that I was buried deep inside of her. Then she began to move, rocking her hips slowly at first and lifting her ass high with each roll of movement so that my dick shifted in and out of her over and over again.

She was moaning, sighing, her hands in my hair and all over my body as her mouth devoured mine and she rode me hard.

I groaned beneath her, bucking my hips into hers so that I drove into her harder, deeper, loving the gasped moans that came every time my dick hit that magic spot within her, but it wasn't enough.

I gave up on restraining myself, gripping her ass in a sudden move and holding on so tight that my fingers dug into the round flesh and I helped her to ride me even harder, slamming my hips against hers and staring at her as she writhed and cried out in pleasure on my lap.

"Lean back, baby doll, I've got you," I commanded and she did as I said, leaning so far back that her hair swung beneath her and I was gifted the perfect position to claim ownership of that most sensitive spot deep inside of her.

The first solid thrust of my hips stole her breath away and by the second she was screaming loud enough to wake the entire neighbourhood.

Her pussy tightened around me as I fucked her harder and she drew closer to the edge with every punishing thrust.

When her orgasm tore through her, her muscles clenched deliciously, gripping my dick in an iron fist which instantly had me coming hard and fast deep inside her, filling her with warmth as I pulled her back up onto my chest so that she could collapse against me and ride out the final waves of her pleasure.

We sat there panting for several minutes as I ran my hands over her back, caressing her and holding her against me, our bodies still joined as we just took a moment to bathe in each other's company.

"You gave my life meaning again when I had none," I breathed as my hand stroked through her red hair and her face remained buried in my neck.

"When I found you in the snow that day, you were the one who saved me, not the other way around."

"We saved each other," she breathed, leaning back so that she could look at me properly and I ran my hand down the side of her face, pulling her in for a gentle kiss for a moment before pushing her back again gently.

"I love you, Winter," I said roughly, meaning those words more than I'd ever meant anything in my life. "And I always want you to be mine."

Her eyes filled with moisture and her lips parted on an answer, but I didn't give her the chance to speak it, tugging her close so that I could kiss her again.

I groaned as her tongue slid over mine, my dick growing hard for her again already, swelling within her with hopes of a round two.

I didn't let her pull back when she tried to, not wanting her to say it back to me just because I'd declared my own feelings, but she wasn't going to let that stop her.

Her hand moved to my bare chest and she wrote a message across my flesh in strong strokes that couldn't be missed.

I love you.

My heart pounded with a wild kind of excitement at those words and as she began to move her hips slowly again, my dick grew ever harder inside her. She moaned into my mouth and I swallowed it whole as our bodies continued to move in that beautiful, rhythmic pattern and I lost myself to her as I fought the desire to grin like a damn fool.

I'd fallen in love with a savage girl, and somehow, I'd earned her heart too.

Breakfast was tense. Frankie tried to crack jokes to lighten the mood, a lot of them about how he'd woken up in the night to what was either someone watching really loud porn or a seriously horny poltergeist. I really needed to sort out getting a place for me and Winter of our own but as Frankie pointed out, he still hadn't figured out why Duke and the others had been torturing her or what Clarissa had to do with it. This apartment was a fortress that no one could get into and until we knew why someone had been trying to peel Winter's brain open for information on the mysterious code, we couldn't guarantee her safety anywhere else.

Winter kept yawning and I felt bad for being responsible for her lack of sleep at both ends of the night, though a little less so when I remembered how good it had felt to bury myself inside of her and make her scream.

"You wanna have a movie morning in the TV room while Papa's here, Winter?" Frankie asked her as he finished his toast and lifted his coffee to his lips.

He'd dressed himself in an expensive looking suit today and had warned me that Martello liked to see his sons looking their best at all times. But that left me in a dilemma because I didn't want to go to too much effort trying to impress him, but I also didn't want to end up disappointing him on first impression. In the end I'd opted for a charcoal suit with a crisp white shirt, but had left the tie off as a small act of rebellion against the idea of trying too damn hard. I wasn't even sure I wanted a relationship with this man yet, I certainly didn't want to go overboard on the sucking up.

"That sounds good," Winter agreed with a smile and I was glad he was giving her something to do while I met with Martello.

My biological father had insisted on a private meeting with me initially and Frankie had agreed without bothering to ask me about it. But as much as I didn't want to cut Winter out of anything, I could accept that this was a fairly private matter that we needed to work through alone. At least at first. After that, I guessed I'd just see how I felt about progressing the relationship or not. I was a grown ass man after all - I hardly needed my papa to look out for me anymore.

"What kind of movies are you into?" Frankie asked her.

"Action," Winter replied instantly then froze, dragging in a sharp breath as she looked at me in surprise. "I don't know how I know that, but I do," she said and I reached out to take her hand with a smile. I wanted her to get her memories back even if I was afraid that they might make her feel differently about me. She deserved to know who she was before all of the shit she'd been through.

"I've got you covered then, bella," Frankie assured her, not even noticing that she'd just remembered something, or maybe just not making a fuss in case she didn't want to. "I'll go and make sure I didn't leave any of my home movies in there and get some popcorn cooking."

"Home movies?" I asked him in confusion and the smirk he shot me was pure filth.

"All consensual and for my eyes only," he assured me with a wink and I couldn't help but think about that kinky ass room me and Winter had found the other week. I hadn't asked him about it but the weird and wonderful things he'd had hanging from the walls had left me pretty fucking curious.

Frankie paused for a moment, looking at me like he could read my mind and as Winter got up to take her plate over to the sink, he leaned low to speak to me. "Have you been exploring the back bedrooms, fratello?" he asked me with a dirty grin.

"Why?" I asked, careful to keep my face neutral. "What would I have found there if I had?"

"The very best kinds of fucked up shit," he assured me, laughing to himself before strolling away to go set up the movie for him and Winter.

I cleared my throat, wondering if I wanted more details on that or if I was better off left in the dark and settling on the latter. No one needed to hear about their sibling's sex life.

The elevator dinged and I pushed to my feet suddenly, my heart hammering inside my chest as the door slid open and Martello Romero stepped into the apartment.

Winter froze in her position by the kitchen sink and I seemed to have forgotten how to move my damn legs. It wasn't like this was the first time I'd ever met him, but it was certainly the first time he'd ever let his attention linger on me, or for me to see him without his eyes filling with hostility. He was a tall man, at least my height and despite the twenty five year age gap between us, he looked in good enough shape to give me a run for my money. His dark hair was streaked with subtle lines of silver and his navy suit was pristine to the point of immaculate.

"Angelo," he said, his voice rough and low like a soothing caress against my soul.

"Nicoli," I corrected quietly, feeling like an asshole at the pain that flashed in his dark eyes. "But...it looks like I'm a Romero instead of a Vitoli."

Martello smiled a little at that, his gaze flicking to Winter as he slowly tugged his leather gloves off and tucked them into a pocket of his woollen coat before slipping that off too.

"Winter's with me," I explained, though I guessed Frankie had probably already let him know that anyway.

"Of course," he agreed with a nod, moving to take Winter's hand and pressing a kiss to the back of it. "Ciao, bella," he said in that utterly soft voice of a gentleman which made it hard to believe he was one of the most ruthless monsters in the entire country, let alone Sinners Bay.

Winter bit her lip as words failed her and I hurried to explain before he thought she was rude or something, but before I'd even gotten the words out, Martello was talking again.

"My son explained your silence to me, bella," he said, "It takes great strength of character to survive all you have and come out so strong and beautiful on the other side of it. If you ever have words to speak to me then I will be honoured indeed."

Winter flushed red at the compliment just as Frankie strode back into the room with an excited greeting for his papa. He pulled him into an affectionate hug and they had a brief exchange in Italian which was spoken too quickly for me to understand, though I guessed that was the point.

A moment later, Frankie turned away, grabbed Winter's hand and whisked her out of the room, leaving me alone with the man who had contributed his DNA to my existence.

Martello cleared his throat and indicated the armchairs sitting by the floor length windows. I followed him over to them and he paused to grab two tumblers and a bottle of scotch from the liquor cabinet before taking the seat opposite me.

"This seems like a conversation that will go down easier with a stiff drink, even if Frankie's tastes are a little cheap for my liking," he muttered, filling the glasses to the top despite the fact that it wasn't even nine am yet.

"I'm pretty sure this stuff is over a hundred dollars a bottle," I commented, but the look he gave me said that that was cheap to him. *Fair enough.*

I only hesitated briefly before lifting the glass to my lips and drinking the whole lot. It burned on the way down and filled my belly with fire, but I didn't really give a shit. I just wanted to take the edge off.

"I'm sorry I didn't come and meet with you the moment you returned to the city," Martello began, looking at me over the rim of his glass as he took a sip. "I only have one excuse, but I hope you can understand it."

"Go on," I encouraged, waiting, wondering how much I cared or if I even wanted to admit to myself that it had stung that he'd left it so long.

Martello offered me a sad kind of smile and for a moment I could see a bit of myself in him. In the colour of his eyes and the set of his brow. It was so odd to be looking at a stranger and recognising them so instinctually.

"All those years ago, when Giuseppe Calabresi broke into my home and killed my wife and child...when I *thought* he'd killed my child, something broke in me. It's not something that can be explained by anyone who hasn't lived it. But I loved your mother fiercely, she remains to this day the only woman I ever loved or ever will love. I'm a shell of the man I was when I had her by my side. And my boy, my beautiful boy with the biggest brown eyes and the easiest laughter you've ever known..."

I held my breath as real tears shimmered in his eyes for a moment and he shifted to the edge of his seat, looking at me intently, studying my eyes as if he was searching for that child.

"I failed you, Angelo," he breathed and some of the hard walls I'd been building around my heart against this man began to break apart. "I failed you and I can never make that right. I can't imagine the life you've led and if that Calabresi scum were still alive today, I assure you I'd take great pleasure in ripping him apart piece by piece for what he's done, but I..." He looked up at me like he didn't have words and I found my resolve to keep this man out of my life breaking down too. I could see what losing his wife and child had done to him. More than that, I could see how much time he'd spent thinking about me and the life I should have lived. Probably at least as much as I'd spent wondering what I might have had with my real parents when I'd believed I was an orphan. It was why I'd hungered for Giuseppe's approval and affection so much. I'd just been looking for it in the wrong place.

"We can't do anything about the past," I said, the regrets I felt for that plain in my voice. "But the future belongs to us. We can do whatever we want with it."

Martello looked at me for the longest time before lifting his glass to his lips and draining the contents in one hit like I had. He pushed to his feet in the next move, closing the distance between us so that I stood too.

The moment his arms closed around me, I may as well have been that young boy he'd lost all those years ago. The scent of spice and cigars clung to him and I could have sworn that it was familiar to me, comforting and soothing. I felt at home there with him in a way I couldn't explain as anything less than love. He loved me, his child who he thought he'd lost and there was a deep kind of beauty in that, the likes of which I'd never known.

My throat thickened as we held each other tightly and I tried not to lose myself in regrets for the life I should have had. I could carve my own path from here on out. And that meant shedding the lie of my old name for good. I was a Romero born and bred. And I was finally home.

Two more days of hanging around the apartment with nothing to do but wait for news on Duke and Clarissa from Frankie was enough to make my feet itch. As enormous as this place was and as many wildly expensive and interesting things that Frankie had bought to entertain himself and us with while we were staying here, I needed fresh air. And so did Winter.

At first, Frankie had been against it, but in the end he had to agree. We couldn't stay locked up in here forever and I was confident that no one would get close enough to Winter to harm her in any way with me there. I was going to be carrying, of course, a sidearm concealed beneath my jacket and a flick knife in my pocket. But we were just going out for dinner by the marina. Me and my girl. It was a fancy ass restaurant and I'd booked a table up on the top floor with a view across the water so I wasn't too concerned about anything happening there. It was deep in the Romero part of town and Martello had already spread the word far and wide about my true heritage so I didn't have to fear an attack from any of them. The Calabresis had fallen apart after Giuseppe died and I disappeared anyway. In the last year, the Romeros had all but taken complete control of Sinners Bay.

I drove Winter in Frankie's Ferrari F8 right up to the valet waiting outside the restaurant. I cast a lingering look over her in the stunning black maxi dress she was wearing. It had a slit right up one leg and was low cut enough that I knew I'd want to gouge the eyes out of every man who looked her way tonight, but it was worth it for the fact that I got to see her like this too.

Sloan had come over to help her get ready and had styled her deep red hair into a knot of curls pinned to the back of her head, a few loose tendrils hanging down to tickle her neck and draw my eye. In fact, if this car wasn't so fucking small inside, I definitely would have pulled over in a quiet spot on the way here and dragged her into my lap to show her exactly what I thought of the way she looked tonight. But as it was too cold out for me to even bend her over the hood, I was going to have to wait until I got her back home before I could begin on the list of things I had planned for her body. And as that list was only getting longer every minute I spent in her company, I didn't imagine either of us would be getting much sleep tonight.

I got out of the car and rounded it quickly, tossing the key to the valet before opening the door for my savage girl who looked anything but wild tonight. She took my hand with a heated smile, letting me help her up in her towering stilettos and instantly curled my arm around her, gripping her hip and tugging her to my side as I led her towards the doors where a doorman opened them for us and ushered us inside.

I didn't even have to give my name to the girl waiting behind the desk, her eyes widening with recognition as she swept forward to greet us.

"Right this way, Mr Vit-Romero." She blushed so deeply that I couldn't even be bothered to mention her blunder. I still forgot I was a Romero myself more often than not so it was hardly a surprise that other people were taking a while to adjust. Fuck knew what they were all thinking. I'd been one of the biggest players on the Calabresi board a year ago and now here I was, firmly in the inner circle with the Romeros, declaring myself to be one of them. Not that it mattered, no one would ever dare question the law of Martello Romero. His word meant more than that of God himself in Sinners Bay.

We were led to a table on the top floor, sitting beside the wide glass window which looked out over the bay and afforded us the illusion of privacy so long as we didn't look to our other side where the rest of the diners were currently eating their meals.

I told the server to bring us a bottle of wine and she headed off before we'd even taken our seats.

I pulled Winter's chair out for her like a real gentleman before taking her napkin and laying it in her lap too, using the act to disguise the moment when I slid my hand inside the slit in her dress and onto her thigh.

I leaned down to kiss her and she moaned softly, just for me to hear as her lips parted for my tongue and her thighs parted for my fingers. I teased them beneath her panties for an all too brief moment, groaning in pleasure as I felt how wet she was and she moaned a little louder into my kiss.

I forced myself to pull back again and took my own chair, smirking at her as I slowly sucked the taste of her from my forefinger and she bit down on her lower lip to try and dampen the heat I'd awoken in her flesh.

"This place is beautiful," she murmured, glancing around at the other diners as her voice stayed low.

"It pales in comparison to you," I said, not giving a shit how cliché I sounded as I stared at my girl and tried to quiet the desire I was feeling for her before I ended up dragging her into the bathroom for a quickie. Not that that was a terrible idea...

"Sasha?" a woman's voice interrupted us and I looked up just as a blonde in towering heels and an unnecessary push-up bra which made her huge tits almost spill out of her dress came barrelling towards us. "It is you!" she screamed, running towards Winter as she broke into loud and obnoxious tears. "We've all been worried sick!" She threw herself onto Winter just as four more girls and a group of guys came running over too.

The world dropped out from under me.

My fingers curled around the edge of the table as I forced myself to remain in my seat, my heart pounding as reality sucker punched me when I was least expecting it. I'd been worried about all kinds of things when I'd decided to take her out tonight, her being recognised from her old life hadn't even occurred to me. *Holy fuck.*

The glimpses of Winter which I caught between the crush of sobbing bodies and people who kept calling her Sasha told me that she was terrified and I got to my feet in an instant.

"Back the fuck off and let her breathe!" I roared, moving forward to peel the girls away from her as one of the guys shouted something about calling the police.

Members of staff were rushing over to try and make sense of the confusion and I ended up knocking the blonde with the huge tits on her ass as I fought to pull Winter out of the pile up.

Her eyes were wild as I pulled her against me and I could see that her voice was locked away deep inside her once again as the group who claimed to know her refused to back off, shouting and crying and demanding to know where she'd been all this time while I pulled her against me and snarled at all of them.

The tell-tale flash of blue and red lights came from beyond the window and I cursed our luck for being in such an upscale part of town. The cops never turned up late to disturbances in places like this. They wouldn't want the obscenely wealthy clientele to have anything negative to say about their response times.

"Back the fuck up!" I shouted, keeping Winter close to me as I tried to push through the crowd and find a back exit.

Some of them started screaming about me kidnapping her again and I cursed as one of the guys took a swing at me. I ducked aside and punched him in return, realising that I really should have thought about holding back as he dropped like a sack of shit and the girls only started screaming louder.

Winter gripped me even tighter, burying her face against my shirt as she tried to block out the insanity surrounding us and I snapped as I felt a shiver of fear run through her body, whipping my gun from my holster and aiming it into the crowd to make sure they got out of our fucking way.

Of course that was the exact moment that the police made it to the top of the stairs and I cursed as they bellowed at me to freeze and drop my weapon, pointing their own guns at me as anyone who hadn't been screaming in this damn place decided to start.

I wasn't a fucking idiot so I tossed my gun to the floor, raising my hands in surrender as I tried to figure out how to explain this shit show and get my girl out of here.

"That's Sasha Hernandez!" Jumbo Tits cried before I got a chance. "She was kidnapped eighteen months ago and that man was trying to drag her out of here before you arrived! Arrest him!"

Winter gave me a fearful look as the cops called that information in and I cursed, realising we weren't getting out of this mess easily. These people knew the girl she used to be. They knew the life she used to live. And no matter how much I might have been enjoying this tiny bubble we'd created for ourselves to live in. It looked like reality had finally caught up to us.

CHAPTER TWENTY FIVE

The police surrounded Nicoli, handcuffing him and pulling me away from him like he was a threat to me. My voice wouldn't come out, but a scream of desperation left me as I tried to reach him.

"It's alright, love. Take a deep breath. You're safe now," the officer holding me said, his grip on me firm enough to suggest he wasn't going to let me go. "Let's get you down to the precinct."

Nicoli spat curses between his teeth as he was manhandled out of the restaurant and it took me a second to realise I was moving too. Every eye in the place was on me now that Nicoli was out of sight and my heart lurched and twisted as the group who'd grabbed me huddled together, their expressions pitiful as they took in my scars. The girl who'd spotted me first was sobbing into the shoulder of another girl as I was escorted past them and more officers kept them from following.

By the time I made it outside and I saw Nicoli being shoved into the back of a squad car, panic took hold of me.

"Nicoli!" I screamed, my voice tearing from my throat as I tried to fight my way free of the officer clinging to my arm.

"Calm down, ma'am," he said, his hold on me tightening.

Nicoli looked back at me through the window of the car, his expression fierce. The vehicle pulled away and I twisted towards the officer holding me, trying to force out the words I needed to tell him, but they got locked in my throat again.

Nicoli's innocent.

He helped me.

Saved me.

Please don't take him away from me.

But none of it came out and the man gave me a sad frown as he guided me into the back of another car.

The door closed and the world became muffled, silence pressing in on my ears so loudly that it hurt.

I wasn't aware of the car starting or of us sailing through the streets of Sinners Bay until we arrived outside the grey stone walls of the police precinct. The building dominated the whole road, every other house or store seeming to cower away from it. When the car door opened, the officer helped me out and snowflakes swirled around me in the air, the cold biting my flesh, awakening my wounds. My scars were prickling like they were suddenly still healing and the ones on my heart and soul split open altogether.

Inside, I was taken to a room with four blank walls, a single table and a mirror opposite. I was put in a chair, offered coffee, a blanket, a phone call. I shook my head in response to each and when I was left there alone I slid off the seat, moving to the wall and dropping down to curl against it on the cold floor. I'd left my cellphone back at the restaurant, so I didn't have Frankie's number to ring him even if I'd been able to speak right now.

Think, Winter. Think of a way out of this. Think of a way to save Nicoli.

I had to talk, but my throat was so tight and panic was crawling through my skin like ants. I curled up tighter, whispers filling my ears. The Five taunting me. All of them back to destroy me. *You'll never get away. You'll always be ours.*

I felt the whips, the cuts of a blade, I heard my own screams rattling inside my head. My heart was pounding too fast and my throat was too tight. *I can't breathe. I can't breathe!*

Hands gripped me and I shrieked, wheeling around and throwing punches and kicks as terror drowned me. The female officer gasped, trying to hush me and another ran forward, restraining me as I thrashed and snarled at them.

"Jesus Christ," the man holding me muttered and I realised he was the one who'd brought me here. "It's alright, love. I've got you."

"No one's going to hurt you," the woman vowed and I fixed my gaze on her, my heart rate starting to slow. She was middle aged with almond eyes which were warm enough to give me a little bit of hope. I opened and closed my mouth, trying to speak, to beg, to demand that they free Nicoli and return him to me. But my treacherous lungs wouldn't fight for him.

I shut my eyes, my teeth clenched, my body shaking violently.

Say it. Tell them. You have to do it for him.

"He's innocent," I forced out in a ragged breath, my voice strained and immediately closing up again.

The woman helped me to my feet and the guy backed off to give us some room. "Here, sit down. Tell us what you know."

I dropped into the seat, my hands still trembling as I rested them on the table and I tried to focus for Nicoli's sake. I couldn't let him down now. He needed me.

"I'm Sergeant Lovette," she said gently. I glanced over my shoulder at the man lurking behind me and she looked to him too. "Take a break, Havers, I'll call if I need you."

"Yes ma'am." He strode from the room and silence fell again.

"What's your name?" Lovette asked and I opened my mouth to give it, trying to squeeze it out.

I pointed to my throat then shook my head and she frowned, realising my struggle before heading out of the room and returning a moment later with a notepad and pen. She pushed it across the table and I took it, my fingers tightening on the pen as I steadied it above the page and wrote *Nicoli is innocent. He rescued me.*

"From who?" the officer asked as she read the words.

I was being kept by five men. Jax, Farley, Quentin, Orville and Duke. They tortured me. Nicoli found me. He saved me.

Her eyes widened as she read it then slowly nodded. "We need your name, miss."

I don't remember anything from before they took me. But I go by Winter now.

A knock came at the door and Lovette tutted. "I'm busy," she called.

"It's about the girl, miss. It's important."

Lovette apologised, standing and heading out of the room. The door shut behind her and I strained my ears, but whatever conversation they were having, they'd moved too far away for me to catch it.

I chewed on my thumb as I waited for her to return, rereading what I'd written and knowing it didn't encompass my story nearly well enough. I had to tell them everything, then they'd understand. They'd release Nicoli, they'd send out officers to hunt down Duke.

Lovette returned, her eyes swirling with some thought as she surveyed me. "Ma'am, there's someone here to see you. Officer Havers tells me you were recognised back at the restaurant and it seems word has travelled..."

I scribbled furiously on the pad. *The only person I want to see is Nicoli.*

She moved forward, slipping into her seat and I realised she had a phone in her hand. She read the words then nodded slowly. "Winter, I need you to be honest with me. When you say you remember nothing before your time with these men -" she tapped the page where I'd written their names "- are you entirely sure that is true?"

I nodded furiously, anger flaring up inside me. I hurriedly wrote down an answer when she didn't look convinced, my strokes growing bigger with my rage. *All I know is how I received every one of my scars. I was tortured for information I have no memory of. I managed to get free. Then Nicoli found me.*

I don't want to see anyone from the restaurant. I only want to see HIM.

"Okay, I believe you," she said gently. "But this person isn't from the restaurant." She placed the phone down, pushing it across the table so I could see an image on the screen.

I blinked hard in surprise as I recognised myself in a beautiful white gown and a veil, laughing as a man kissed my cheek. The officer flicked it onto the next photograph and I saw his face clearly. It was the same day, our *wedding* day, his arm wrapped around my waist as he held me close to his side. He was tall with eyes that shone with adoration, his head was shaved and his face was handsome and full of life. But I didn't know him. The girl in that photo was a stranger too. I wasn't someone's wife.

I'm not someone's wife.

"This is your husband, Winter. He's here waiting to see you. He says your name is Sasha Hernandez. You got married three years ago. He asked me to give you this." She reached into her pocket, placing down a simple gold band with the word *forever* engraved on the inside of it. "Do you recognise it?"

I shook my head, leaning away from it, rejecting it with every fibre of my being. Panic swelled in my chest and closed up my throat. I tried to rationalise what I was seeing, but it was there in plain sight. And worst of all, I couldn't deny the dull, ringing sensation in the back of my head that said I *did* recognise that ring. That if I picked it up and pushed it onto my finger, it would fit perfectly.

I continued shaking my head in refusal of this life. I couldn't be married. I was with Nicoli. Of all the time I'd spent picturing a mother, father, siblings or friends missing me, I'd never considered this. Because my heart belonged so wholly to Nicoli that it simply wasn't a possibility that I could be bound to someone else. If I was married, why hadn't I felt that hole in my chest, why hadn't I ached for my husband even if I'd lost my memories of him? But then I thought of the hollowness I'd felt with The Five, wondering if some of that could be related to this. Had my body known all along? Had my heart hollowed out because of him?

I forced those thoughts away, not allowing them to take up residence in my head. Because there was no way I'd ever felt this for someone other than Nicoli. He consumed my entire heart. He'd been the one to fill it up, to give me something to live for again, who took the emptiness away. There couldn't be anyone else for me but him.

"I understand this is a lot to take in," Lovette said with a frown. "But you need to be with your loved ones right now. Perhaps seeing your husband will help jog your memory?"

I pressed my lips tight together and started writing on the paper. *What about Nicoli? Are you going to free him?*

"He pointed a gun at innocent people in a public place," Lovette sighed.

He was trying to protect me. I underlined the words three times, shoving the notepad towards her.

"Be that as it may-" she started, but someone knocked on the door.

"Ma'am we have a problem. The Romeros are here." The same male voice called from beyond the door as before, his tone nervous.

I got to my feet the same second Lovette got up. My lips twitched with the need to speak because I could tell she was going to leave me here. I needed to get to Frankie, Rocco, Enzo. They'd help. They'd fix this. But she wasn't just going to let me walk out of here for them.

"Take me to my husband," I forced out, knowing it was my only chance to see them. To help Nicoli.

Lovette picked up the ring and the phone from the table, nodding and heading to the door. I followed her out and my heart beat wildly as she led me down a long hall then through a security door.

My gaze locked on the three Romero brothers who were leaning over the front desk and intimidating the man sitting there as they demanded to see their brother. They blocked my view to the waiting room beyond where I suspected my so-called husband was waiting, but I didn't care. I flew at them, my heart leaping into my throat as Frankie caught me in his arms, hugging me close and kissing my head. "It's okay, bella. We're going to be walking out of here with him in two minutes. Isn't that right Officer George?" he spoke harshly to the guy behind the desk.

"You cannot walk in here and order my officers about," Lovette clipped. "And you will unhand that girl this instant. She is under our protection."

"No, she's under *ours*," Enzo snarled as he and Rocco moved shoulder to shoulder with Frankie who held me firmly against him.

"Bring Nicoli out here this second or I'll shut down this whole fucking precinct," Rocco snarled.

"You don't have the authority-" Lovette began but the door opened and a tall man with a captain badge on his breast strode through the door behind her, guiding Nicoli along beside him.

"No harm done, eh friends?" he boomed, clapping Nicoli on the back and shooting Lovette an expression that told her to back down. My heart lifted as the captain released him. There were no cuffs on his wrists, he was free. They were letting him go.

I pulled out of Frankie's grip, racing toward Nicoli with a gasp of desperation and he caught me in his arms, lifting me off the floor and squeezing me tight against his chest. His heart pounded against me and I shut my eyes, drowning in the feeling of his arms around me.

"I want to go home," I whispered in his ear.

"We're going home. And I'll never leave you again," he swore, his words echoing through my soul.

"Get your hands off of my wife!" a harsh male voice made my heart lurch and I loosened my grip on Nicoli just enough so that I could turn and look at the huge man who'd stepped past the Romeros with four muscular bodyguards in tow. The man from the pictures -my husband - gazed at me with a desperation that said he really did know me. Love me. Had once promised to honour and protect me in front of family and friends I didn't even know. But that frightened me because I didn't love or adore him. I couldn't remember my vows, I wasn't the girl he'd watched walk up the aisle towards him. I was as

315

much a stranger to him as he was to me, he just didn't realise it.

"She's lost her memories," Lovette told him and his face twisted as he took in that news.

"She'll know me," he insisted, reaching out for me, but I shrank away.

Nicoli's posture stiffened and my fingers dug into his shoulder as I half climbed him to get away.

"What's going on?" the captain looked to Lovette who flushed a little like she was embarrassed at the chaos that had descended. She strode over to my husband and handed him the phone and the ring, looking to her boss while the Romeros lurked closer like stalking wolves.

"This is Ramon Hernandez," Lovette said. "He has proved he is this girl's husband. He's been searching for her for a long time and the case is still open."

"Darling, come here to me. You must be so frightened. Who is this man?" Ramon asked, his brows pulling together as he stared at Nicoli with a threat in his stance. "Unhand her this second."

More officers moved around us until we were all encircled by enough manpower and weapons to spill a lot of blood if things turned south.

"I said unhand her!" Ramon snapped, glaring at Nicoli in a way that terrified me.

I shook my head, clinging to my man as Ramon twisted his phone around to brandish the photograph of me and him on our wedding day together.

Nicoli's hold on me only firmed and I fisted my hand in the front of his shirt, sensing a deadly energy rolling off of him.

"I'm not that person anymore," I breathed to Nicoli, needing him to know I didn't want to be taken from his arms. Not for anything or anyone.

"I'm sure this can be resolved," Frankie stepped in calmly. "We'll have words with you Mr Hernandez, but let's do this somewhere more suitable, hm?" His tone was rational, but the looks on his brothers' faces said if we took this away from the police, it was only going to go one way.

"Don't patronise me," Ramon snarled at Frankie, then pointed a finger at Nicoli. "*He* could be the one who took her. I've been hunting for my wife for over a year, I will not walk out of this precinct without her!" he boomed and fear wrapped around my heart.

I shook my head in refusal as he held out a hand for me, but officers were starting to close in around me and Nicoli. I didn't like the threat in their stance or the glances exchanged between them.

"I'm sure Mr Vito- Romero - is not responsible for any such thing, but we will explore all avenues, of course Mr Hernandez," the captain assured the man and I had the sense that Ramon held nearly as much sway as the Romeros here. From the sweat on the captain's brow, I guessed he was caught between several powerful men and didn't want to upset any of them.

Ramon moved towards me, raising his hands in innocence. "Please, my darling, come with me. I only want to take you home."

I clutched onto Nicoli. *He* was my home, not this stranger. I didn't want to go anywhere with him.

"It's best you let go of her now, sir," the captain spoke to Nicoli. "It's only right she speaks with her husband. She must have a whole family missing her. I'm sure Mr Hernandez will ensure your friendship with her remains intact." He said the word friendship like he was begging Nicoli to agree with that label and let me go to another man's arms, but it wasn't going to happen.

"Sasha," Ramon begged. "It's me. Ramon. Please don't be frightened. I can help you remember everything. I'm sure Mr Romero wants what is best for you." He looked to Nicoli, his eyes imploring. "Perhaps you can come visit her soon?" he said seriously and Nicoli growled low in his throat.

"Winter has only had Nicoli to depend upon, he is all she knows," Frankie growled. "You won't separate them. He's what's best for her."

"I am her family!" Ramon wheeled towards Nicoli's brothers and his bodyguards flexed their muscles. "*I* am what's best for her. I have hunted for my wife, I have begged the stars and the moon to return her to me. I will not have a single man keep her from me a moment longer."

Frankie looked between us all, his eyes flickering with shadows as he tried to work out a solution here.

Lovette frowned at Nicoli. "Sir, you need to let her go."

"*No*," Nicoli hissed immediately, backing up and pulling me with him.

"You can visit her on our terms, if she agrees," Frankie told Ramon, but he just bared his teeth at him.

"She is my wife!" he yelled again. I could see the wind changing in his favour and my stomach churned at the thought of having to go with him.

I wanted to leave with the Romeros. I wanted to go back to Frankie's apartment in the sky and curl up in bed with Nicoli. If this was what getting my memories back would cost me, then the past could keep them.

"Come on now, sir. He has a right to see his wife," an officer moved towards Nicoli, reaching for me and Nicoli lunged at him, pushing me behind him and shoving the officer back a step. Another officer leapt forward to subdue him and Nicoli threw a fist into his face, sending him crashing to the ground. Havoc broke out as more men and women dove on Nicoli, forcing him to the floor and trying to hold him down as the captain took hold of my arm, guiding me towards Ramon.

I dug my heels in and the Romeros rushed forward to intercept, but Ramon's bodyguards formed a wall against them as I was handed to my husband. He wrapped his arm around my shoulders and I shoved him away, trying to run, but strong arms grabbed me and one of the bodyguards clutched me hard against his side as he dragged me out of the station.

"When she is well again, I will ensure she gives a statement about who took her and we will hunt them to the ends of the earth," Ramon growled, looking over to Nicoli with a sneer.

My throat was burning as I tried to get words out, kicking and pushing and tearing at the men who were taking me away from the only good thing I'd ever known.

"Nicoli!" I screamed, his name slicing its way out of my lungs as I was shoved into a car.

I turned frantically to look out of the window, finding Rocco, Frankie and Enzo racing toward the car with furious expressions. I yanked at the door handle, desperate to get out, but I was locked in. Trapped. We pulled away down the road and I slammed a palm to the glass, before thumping my fist on it and screaming from the depths of my lungs.

"It's alright, darling," Ramon promised, turning to face me from the passenger seat in the front of the car, his face a picture of worry as he ignored the way I was fighting to escape. "You're safe now."

CHAPTER TWENTY SIX

I wasn't in a good way. My cell mates were even worse off. Blood dripped from my knuckles and I'd thrown my jacket aside, my white shirt was bloodstained and torn and the cops were screaming instructions at me to back the fuck up, but I was beyond listening. My ears were ringing with the sound of Winter screaming my name. Every time I closed my eyes I could see her being dragged away from me.

The taser hit me in the side and I fell back against the bars of the holding cell they'd tossed me in as I was momentarily paralysed by the electricity slamming through my body.

Darkness curtained my vision and I almost fell to the floor, but I gripped the bars beside me with a snarl of rage. I couldn't manage anything more than that as the pain of the strike blinded me and I forced my breath in and out through my teeth.

By the time I could move and think again, the cell door was crashing shut and the three assholes I'd just beaten the living shit out of were being dragged over to a different cell. Someone really should have realised that putting me in a cell with other people was a bad idea.

I started pacing like a caged animal, glaring at the officers on duty beyond the bars while they eyed me warily. Which they should. No one got between me and my girl.

"I have an amazing memory for faces," I said in a deadly tone. "And names too," I added, looking pointedly at the name badges they were wearing as they shifted uncomfortably.

"We're just doing our jobs, Mr Vitoli," one of them said nervously. "I'm sure your lawyer will be here soon."

"Romero," I growled at him and he blanched, picking up the phone on his desk and dialling out to check on my lawyer.

Before he got an answer, Enzo's voice reached me from somewhere beyond the holding cells. "You're lucky our father is out of town tonight or you'd have a real problem to handle," he said loudly.

It wasn't the first time I'd heard one of them yelling something, but it was the first time it sounded that close.

Two of the officers headed away to see what was going on out there and I gave the last one a death glare as he squirmed in his chair.

My brothers appeared a moment later with a woman who I guessed was the lawyer, the police captain trailing along in their wake too.

"What has my client been charged with?" the middle aged blonde asked, her gaze sweeping over my bloodstained appearance for a lingering moment before she turned away again.

"Let's discuss this in an interview room," the captain replied, scraping his fingers through his beard as he gave me a rather more concerned look.

Frankie crossed the room to look through the bars at me. "We'll find her, fratello," he said to me in a low voice. "Just play nice so we can get you out of here, yeah? We'll figure it all out. You've just gotta trust us."

I grunted an answer. I'd sated enough of my rage on my cellmates to remain calm long enough for that. Hopefully.

Frankie nodded to the lawyer while Rocco crossed the room to peer in at the criminals I'd beaten up. They were all slumped against the walls, groaning in pain and covered in blood within their new cell, but it didn't make me feel much better.

"Any of you boys pressing charges against our brother?" he asked, the threat in his voice clear.

The three men hastily refused, claiming they'd started it, one of them even saying he'd fallen over and hit his face on the bars. The police officers who'd witnessed the whole thing frowned, but apparently they weren't dumb enough to add anything to the exchange.

"Let's get this over with then," the lawyer said, beckoning for me to follow her even though there was still a locked door separating us.

The captain nodded and one of the officers hurried to unlock my cage. He reached for the handcuffs at his belt and I snarled at him as the lawyer protested. None of the officers seemed happy about leaving me un-cuffed, but none of them seemed to want to be the one to try and get them on me either so they abandoned the attempt.

I followed the lawyer, the captain and my brothers away from the cells and down a long, grey corridor to an interview room where I dropped into the seat with my arms folded and my muscles twitching with the desire to get the fuck out of here and find my girl.

"We'll be looking into pursuing charges of police brutality against my client," the lawyer said as my brothers lined up against the back wall. I'd been in plenty of interview rooms like this in my life, but I couldn't say that I'd ever had this kind of support before. Giuseppe certainly never would have hauled his ass down to a police station to get me out, though the high priced lawyer would have shown up to fix whatever mess I was in.

"Mr Vitoli knocked out one of my officers," the captain growled, offering me a look which said he didn't appreciate that at all.

"Mr *Romero* no longer goes by that name. He has reclaimed his birth name as is his right and is fully legal. In fact, Nicoli Vitoli never existed at all and we may seek to press charges in relation to the bad police work done at the scene of his mother's murder too, seeing as you failed to notice a kidnapping had taken place," the lawyer said smoothly.

"I can't just click my fingers and make the charges against him go away," the captain snarled.

"You can if you don't want anyone looking into your personal finances too closely," Enzo purred from his spot against the wall and the captain glanced at the closed door anxiously.

"He pulled a gun on innocent people in a crowded place. He put one of my officers in the hospital, he-"

"My client was trying to protect a girl who had been through serious trauma from a raving mob who were causing her great distress. I have three witnesses who saw your officers attack him and manhandle him within this very building. Add to that the fact that he was clearly attacked by three other detainees in his holding cell and I have the beginnings of a strong case here."

The captain stared at my bloodstained knuckles for a long moment before sweeping his eyes over my brothers behind me and sighing.

"Right now, the best I can do is bail him and-"

"Perfect, I'll have the charges dropped at a more convenient time of day." The lawyer stood and I followed suit.

"Will you take cash for that bail now, sweet cheeks, and save me the walk to the desk?" Rocco purred, pulling a roll of dollar bills from his pocket and tossing it down on the interview table.

"I need some time to get the paperwork ready," the captain protested, but I was already walking out of the room with my brothers while Rocco told him to forge the signature and suck his dick.

I didn't bother questioning it as we headed back out into the corridor and the captain hurried to pass us by and let us out of this fucking building. He was clearly deep in the Romeros' pockets and I didn't even want to know why right now. The only thing I gave a shit about was finding Winter.

"Where is she?" I demanded as we stepped out into the freezing night air and the sounds of the city washed over us. Even in the dead of night, Sinners Bay didn't slow down. That was when the monsters came out after all and there was certainly a high population of them living here.

The silence that followed my question made me fall still and I turned back to look at my brothers as they looked between each other hopelessly.

"It happened so fucking fast, fratello," Frankie said in a low voice, looking all kinds of cut up over his answer. "There were so many people in there and we were trying to help you when the police started grabbing you, and-"

"I know he took her, I'm asking *where?*" I demanded in a low voice. If he seriously thought my gaze hadn't been pinned on her throughout that entire fucking exchange then he was deluded. I'd seen the way she'd been dragged out of the precinct and it had damn near ripped me apart.

I didn't give a shit if that motherfucker used to be her husband. She'd forgotten that entire part of her life and even if she hadn't, I knew she'd still be mine. Her heart beat for me just like mine beat for her. There wasn't a single thing in the world that would stop that from being the truth. Certainly not some long forgotten husband crawling up out of the past and hungering for something which wasn't his anymore.

"We've got people combing the streets and we managed to get our hands on some CCTV to get the registration from the car," Enzo said, rubbing a hand over the back of his neck. "But so far...nothing."

"Fuck that," I snapped. "She didn't just up and vanish. I'll find her myself if I have to. I'll rip down every fucking door in this city and then move on to the rest of the state. Nothing will stop me."

"We know, fratello," Rocco said, moving forward to clasp my shoulder. "We won't stop until she's safe in your arms again. None of us."

"Good," I growled. "Then let's start hunting.

CHAPTER TWENTY SEVEN

amon had given me my own room in the huge mansion he called home. The grounds were fortified with iron gates and the place felt more like a military base with the fleet of armed men he had patrolling the perimeter. He'd left me to calm down, ensuring I had more food and water than I could ever need and he'd brought me an iPad too, leaving it silently on the bed while he gave me a wistful look from my position on the floor in the corner of the room. He'd told me the iPad was full of photo albums of us and when I was ready to remember, I could look through it. And if I needed anything I only had to ask for it. Except Nicoli. He would doubtfully give me him.

I'd held out for a while before taking the iPad from the bed and preparing myself to face more of my past. The air was cool in the room, my dress still in place since I'd arrived back here, not wanting to change into the comfy sweats he'd had a maid bring me. I wanted to hold onto every single thing that bound me to Nicoli, but the contents of this iPad could rock the foundations of all of it. Still...I had to know. As much as I feared the truth, it was clear I couldn't hide from it anymore. And looking at it didn't mean I had to change. It just meant I'd finally have some of the answers I'd yearned for during my time in captivity.

I clicked on the icon for the photo albums and my breathing quickened as I located the one for our wedding day. I had so many questions as I scrolled through the pictures, hunting for anyone who resembled me. A mother, a father, a sister, a cousin. Someone. But if I was related to any of these people, I couldn't tell.

My mind tugged with familiarity as I took in the eight tiered wedding cake, then the two of us cutting it together. I was smiling, seemingly happy. And as I traced my fingers over my face, I could almost remember the taste of that cake. Vanilla with a strawberry filling. The next page made my heart knot as I found my arms wrapped around Ramon's broad shoulders, his mouth against mine. We looked like a typical couple, in love on their wedding day. No matter how hard I tried to pick holes in the perfect images, I couldn't find any at all. No frown in my brow when he wasn't looking, no hint of distress or upset. As horrible as it was to admit it, it looked like I had once been very much in love with Ramon Hernandez. Either that or I was a better actress than I realised.

A soft knock came at the door and I tossed the iPad back onto the bed, not wanting to admit I'd caved and started looking through the pictures.

"Darling, can I come in?" Ramon asked.

I said nothing, having no words for him like every time he'd come and he pushed the door open after a beat, leaning his head through. "Is that okay?"

I clenched my jaw then shrugged, turning my gaze to the wall beside me.

"I'd like to talk...to explain myself." He ran a hand over the smooth sheen of his head, perching on the bed as he gazed at me on the floor. "I know you think the Romeros are your friends..."

I glared at him furiously, daring him to finish that sentence.

"And perhaps they have looked after you," he immediately changed tack at my expression and some of the tension in my shoulders eased. "But you belong with me. I have never stopped searching for you, my love. I had every cop in Sinners Bay hunting for you, your face was all over the papers." He clutched at his chest like his heart hurt. "And now I've found you and you don't remember me," he said with an ache in his voice that chipped away at my barriers. He sighed, dropping his head into his hands. "And I see those scars on you and wonder...fuck, my darling, I can't stop imagining what it is you've faced all this time."

I remained silent, my eyes falling to a scar on my arm in a criss-crossing shape. I traced my finger across it, remembering the blade Quentin had twisted into me and the scream that had raked my throat raw. If I had lost Nicoli and found him again months later, cut up and hurt, with no memory of me, wanting no memory of me...how terrible a fate that would be.

I looked to Ramon with my heart weighing down in my chest as he lifted his head from his hands.

"Is there anything I can do to get you to speak with me? Are you truly so angry with me, darling?" he begged, his voice rough with grief.

Tears burned the backs of my eyes. I hated being someone to this man. I hated that I was hurting him and that he'd suffered all this time while I'd known nothing of him. But I also couldn't give him what he needed to heal. The person who had worn his wedding band, who'd smiled mischievously at him on his wedding day, who'd licked vanilla frosting from her fingers...was gone. She was the caterpillar and I was the butterfly. At our cores we were the same being, yet we were nothing alike. To look at each of them, you wouldn't know they were related at all.

"That man...Nicoli, did he...hurt you?" he growled.

I shook my head fiercely and he nodded, seeming to accept that.

"You seem very attached to him," he said, his voice breaking a little and I nodded, my eyes filling up with tears. Tears for Ramon, for me, for everything lost between us that I could never know again. My throat eased and I was grateful when words came to my tongue.

"I'm sorry," I whispered and his eyes widened as he slid off the bed, lowering down to his knees before me in his fine suit trousers.

"You have nothing to be sorry for. I'm sorry I didn't find you, I'm sorry you were taken...do you remember that night my darling?"

I shook my head, my interest piqued as he inched a little closer, but not close enough that he could touch me.

"They came into the house and stole you away from me. Five men," he growled, hatred in his voice. "That was back before I upped security on my home - *our* home," he corrected quickly. "They beat me bloody and stole you from my arms."

My breath caught and suddenly an image flashed through my mind. Ramon yelling the name Sasha, desperation in his voice. There were hands on me, digging in, bruising. I blinked hard, drawing my knees to my chest and burying my face against them. I tried to hold onto the memory, although it made my heart pound and my palms sweat. I could taste cigarette smoke in my mouth. *Duke*.

"This was the day they took you."

I lifted my head, finding Ramon with the iPad, showing a picture on it of me in a white dress with little red flowers peppering it. I wasn't looking at the camera, I was lying on the grass, gazing up at the sky with a book resting against my chest.

"Do you remember anything about this day?" he asked, hope in his voice. "You baked bread in the morning and we ate it out on the lawn in the sunshine."

The scent of hot dough seemed to drift under nose as I pictured it, but I couldn't quite grasp anything more about the memory than that.

"You went to the bank that afternoon," he said. "You said you were going to withdraw some money for a surprise for my birthday. We were in my office. I told you you looked like a summer rose. Red with-"

"With skin like petals as soft as velvet," I finished for him, those words winding through my mind. A flicker of Ramon sitting in a wing-backed chair in a fine suit and a seductive smile on his face flashed through my mind. But it was gone before I could fill in any more of the details. My heart thrashed, hungry for more now that these channels of my past were opening. But I feared that remembering would mean losing a piece of my new self. I didn't want to straddle two worlds, I only wanted to be a savage girl. One who was held in the arms of her mountain man day in and day out. The girl he loved...

My stomach clenched. As much as I didn't want to be the girl in those photographs, I knew I couldn't deny that part of me forever.

"See, I know you'll come back to me, darling." Ramon's eyes glowed with hope and he rose to his feet with a sigh of relief. "You'll remember it all soon."

He turned, walking to the door. "Get some rest," he said as he paused. "A doctor will be here to see you in the morning."

I opened my mouth to say I'd already been checked over by a doctor, but by the time I got the words to my lips, he was gone.

I lay down on the floor again, my back to the iPad as I resisted looking through more of my past. I ached for Nicoli. And nothing I ever was before I'd met him would sate that need.

In the morning, I finally took off my dress, my limbs aching from my night on the floor and I realised how much I missed sleeping in a bed. But without my mountain man, I didn't want it. I fell back on my coping mechanisms instinctively, but I was trying hard not to disappear. I needed to hold onto my voice so I could stand up for myself. I needed to ask for what I wanted. Demand it. And I wasn't going to take no for an answer today.

I headed into the en-suite and showered before returning to the bedroom and dressing in the sweatpants and shirt that had been left for me. Then I moved to the door, turning the handle and cursing as colourfully as Nicoli often did when I found it locked. That bastard.

I started hammering my fist on the wood and it wasn't long before footsteps hurried my way and the door opened. Ramon stood there in a pair of cream chinos and a white dress shirt which hugged his muscular physique.

Speak, I told myself, my tongue wrapping around the words I needed to say, but not releasing them.

"Are you alright, my darling?" Ramon reached out as if to touch me and I jerked backwards, baring my teeth. "Forgive me." He dropped his hand to his side, sadness in his eyes.

"You locked me in," I growled, finally getting the sentence out.

"Only to protect you," he said earnestly. "I won't do so again."

I pressed my lips together as he stepped back, opening an arm in an offering for me to come out.

"I want to see Nicoli," I told him, staring him dead in the eye.

"My love..."

"I want to see him. Now," I insisted, my heart jack-hammering in my chest.

"Am I not owed a little time with you first?" he all but begged and a weight of guilt pulled at my chest at his broken expression.

I chewed on my lip. "Why can't he come here? I'll look at the albums, I'll face my past, but I want him here while I do it."

"You're asking an awful lot of the man who once got down on one knee for you. Who offered you a life at his side. I did not expect another man to enter that arrangement when you agreed to be mine always and forever," he said, firm enough that I could tell he was hurting.

"I don't remember that agreement," I breathed, heat carving a line up the back of my neck. "I'm sorry if this is upsetting-"

"Upsetting?" he balked, his eyes flaring with emotion. "It breaks my fucking heart."

I swallowed thickly as I stepped out into the hall, my fingers curling up into my palms and my nails biting into the skin. "I don't want to hurt you-"

"You *are* hurting me, you're crushing me, Sasha."

"Winter," I corrected and his face screwed up.

"No," he growled. "You're my Sasha. After the months of suffering, thinking the worst, fearing you were dead and now...now I finally find you again and I see your body marred by all those scars and you won't even let me hold you and it breaks me, darling, it *breaks* me."

"I..." I shook my head, my heart twisting at his words as I struggled for what to say.

"*Please*," he implored, reaching for my hand. He took it and I fought the urge to drag it out of his grip as he stared at me like the world began and ended with me. "Give me a day or two, aren't I owed that much?"

"Ramon..." I glanced away from him, gently tugging my hand free. "I will explore my old life with you, but my heart isn't yours anymore. I'm sorry."

"*No*," he hissed. "That's not fair. You will love me when you remember. You will, Sasha."

"That's not my name," I said, my heart beginning to hit a wilder tune. "I know this is hard to hear but I have to be honest with you."

"You don't know yourself," he insisted, loosening a button at his throat as his muscles bunched. "I deserve a chance. I spent years loving and caring for you, I can win your heart again."

"I know who I am," I said passionately, but even I heard the doubt in my tone. There were still so many unanswered questions. How could I ever be a whole person when I didn't even know what kind of childhood I'd had, who my parents were, if I'd been to college, or had a job?

"You know who you are *now*, darling, but you don't know who you *were*. And that is just as important. So please give me the opportunity to show you. I will have the best therapist in the world come and help you get your memories back," he pushed and I felt my resolve cracking.

"I don't need that. I'll stay here for a day," I offered him.

"A week," he countered and I started shaking my head. He sighed. "Come downstairs, you must be famished, you didn't touch any of your food last night. The maid will prepare whatever breakfast you like."

My stomach did feel painfully empty, but I wasn't done with this conversation yet. It seemed Ramon had other ideas though as he left me in a vast kitchen with dark red accents and a mahogany breakfast bar. The maid made me eggs on toast and I sat alone while I ate, the huge house seeming to echo with a thousand memories I couldn't grasp. It made me feel lonelier than ever.

When I was done eating, I expected Ramon to show up again, but he didn't. So I explored the cavernous house, moving from room to room and taking in the pictures on the walls of us. Mostly of our wedding day, but some on vacation. We'd been to Rome, Venice, Paris, London. It was so strange to see myself standing in front of landmarks I recognised, yet couldn't remember my time spent there. As I drifted through the huge entrance hall and gazed up at the curving oak stairway that led to the first floor, my mind flashed with some vision as I recalled stumbling down those very stairs, a man's hands locked around me, heavy breaths in my ear. Cigarettes. *Duke*. And my husband yelling *Sasha!* in desperation.

I shuddered at the fear that crept into me as the memory slipped away again. The door opened behind me and I leapt in alarm as I turned and backed up, finding Ramon strolling through the door with a wiry man with a buzz cut and a doctor's bag under his arm.

"This is Dr Eckhart," Ramon explained. "He will check you over in your room."

I tried to speak in front of the stranger and my voice finally came out constricted. "I saw a doctor at the Romeros'."

"Indulge me, darling, I wish to see that you're okay for myself," Ramon said with no room for negotiation, directing us upstairs and I gritted my teeth as I headed that way.

When I made it to my room, Ramon left me with Eckhart and my skin prickled as he looked me up and down like an animal about to be slaughtered. My voice drifted down into my belly and I lost my hold on it completely.

"Take your clothes off and lay on the bed," Eckhart clipped and I turned my back on him as I did as he asked, stripping down to my underwear before lowering myself onto the bed. He checked over my scars with cold hands and grunted a couple of words to say I was fine. Then he took a syringe from his bag and my tongue felt heavy as he moved toward me with it. I flinched away as he approached me again and he sighed.

"It's just a vitamin shot. You are no doubt deficient in Vitamin D amongst other vital nutrients."

I swallowed thickly then nodded, allowing him to get closer and he gripped my arm, pushing the needle into the top of it. It sank in roughly and I bit down on a yelp as he injected the vitamin solution then pulled it free.

"Good. Now take your panties off and draw your knees up." He pulled out a pair of latex gloves from his bag, gazing down at me with impatience in his eyes and I shook my head. "I need to check that you haven't been violated."

My pulse skipped with anger and I sat up, hugging my knees to my chest and shaking my head.

"It is important," he pressed, stepping forward and reaching for my panties. I gasped in horror, lunging for him and I sank my teeth into his arm. My jaw locked as he yelled and I dug my teeth in deeper, rage coursing through me. *Don't you dare lay a hand on me, you asshole!*

He shoved me off of him, backing up and snatching his bag. "Crazy bitch." He strode from the room, slamming the door shut behind him and I was left with the lasting taste of blood in my mouth and hatred in my soul.

I grabbed my clothes, pulling them on and hurrying to the window, opening the shutters and rattling the handles, but I needed a key I didn't have.

I was trapped in this house and I didn't want to indulge my so-called husband in his need for me to remember him. I wanted to run until I couldn't run anymore. Find my way back to my mountain man and bind myself to him heart, body and soul. No matter what it took.

CHAPTER TWENTY EIGHT

Night turned into day and back into night again and still I hadn't found her. Hadn't come fucking close to finding her.

Frankie had been doing everything he could to try and track down her husband but he was nothing, no one, a fucking ghost so hard to find that the only thing that we could know for sure about him was that he was most definitely *someone*. You didn't end up that far off of the radar without some serious muscle behind you. The kind of muscle only seriously dark motherfuckers had. Like us.

That in itself helped a little. There were only so many organisations that could pull that kind of sway, especially around here.

Rocco and Enzo had managed to track down the so-called friends who had recognised Winter in the restaurant, but they hadn't been much use. They were socialites, who had attended all kinds of parties and social events with Ramon and 'Sasha', but despite their claims of being such good friends of hers, none of them had ever gone to their main house. Only to an apartment on the east side of town that he apparently owned too. Except when we'd gone there we'd found what amounted to little more than a show home which seemed to be set up entirely for the point of hosting parties. Worse than that, it was owned by a shell company with offshore accounts that were practically untraceable. A dead end. And the more of those I came up against, the more my gut tightened with unease.

Whoever this man was, he was dangerous. Even if that was only by association. I needed to find my savage girl and get her the fuck away from him, but every minute that passed me by only made that seem more and more impossible.

I felt like I was re-living a nightmare, only this time it was somehow so much worse than it had been when I'd been hunting for Sloan after Rocco kidnapped her from our wedding. I was still plagued by that crippling fear for her safety and beating myself up over my failure in finding and protecting her like I'd promised. But unlike with Sloan, this time my heart felt like it was ripping apart too. The way I felt about Winter cut me right to my core. She'd found her way into the deepest, darkest depths of my soul and I couldn't bear to even consider the idea of a future without her in it.

"Eat," Enzo snarled, shoving a paper bag with a burger and fries in it into my hand. "Your lost girl won't be found if you drop dead of hunger and exhaustion in your hunt."

I cursed, leaning back against the brick wall of the night club we'd come to check out. We'd managed to figure out that it was owned by the same shell company which owned that apartment so we were hoping it was the beginning of a lead. So far, it seemed like a low rent club with hookers working long shifts outside and little to no attempt being made to conceal the copious amounts of recreational drugs being consumed, but it was all we had to go on.

It was late and the place was heaving, the clientele spilling outside to smoke and even fuck in the alleyway close by. There was the distinct scent of piss in the air which did nothing at all for my appetite, but I did as commanded anyway, waiting for him to go on as I tore into my food like a beast.

"The owner isn't in tonight," Enzo said in a low voice, dragging his thumb along the side of his jaw thoughtfully as I narrowed my eyes. "Sounded like he's never really in if I'm honest. But I'm pretty sure the girl running the bar had his number, she just didn't wanna offer it out."

"I'll convince her otherwise," I growled, taking a step towards the door of the club just as a guy stumbled out of it and began puking. Fucking great.

Enzo's hand landed on my shoulder to hold me back and I scowled at him as he stopped me from going after her.

"Relax, fratello, don't have so little faith in me. Eat your burger, I have a plan."

"And what's that?" I asked, eyeing him in his ripped jeans and leather jacket as he kept his heavily tattooed hand on my shoulder to hold me still. He looked more like an MC douchebag than a mobster half the damn time.

"The girl is hot and her break is in ten minutes." He raised his eyebrows suggestively.

"So?" I asked, wondering why the fuck he thought I'd have any interest in that.

"So, I invited her out here to fool around with me. I'll distract her, lift her cellphone, pass it to you and then you've just gotta get it to Frankie who will be waiting in his car at the end of the block so that he can clone it. Then you get it back to me before I blow her mind and I slip it back to her without her ever knowing it's gone. Simple."

"And why do I give a shit if she knows we took it?" I asked, finishing my burger and starting on the fries.

"Because if her boss goes to this kind of trouble to make himself untraceable then you can bet your ass he'll change his number and everything associated with it the moment he gets a whiff of it being compromised. We aren't taking any chances with your girl, fratello. And if I have to take one for the team to get her back safe and sound, then I'm willing to make that sacrifice." He grinned wickedly and I was struck with the desire to smack him and hug him in equal measures.

"I missed you, brother," I said to him in a low tone, not knowing why it felt like I should say it now even with everything else going on. Perhaps this was just making me realise how fleeting our lives could be and I didn't wanna let moments pass me by anymore. "Even though I never knew what I was missing."

"Aw, shit, stronzo, you're gonna make me weep like a newborn babe if you keep that crap up for long," Enzo replied like he was brushing me off, but he caught my head between his hands and pulled my forehead against his for a moment, the gesture echoing powerfully through my core. "Ti amo, Angelo."

My heart leapt painfully and I gripped the back of his neck with my free hand as I held him close too, closing my eyes and bathing in that feeling of love between us until it made me ache. This was what I'd been missing my whole life. My brothers, my father, *family*.

"I love you, too, Enzo."

He held me for another moment before releasing a heavy breath and shoving me off. "Finish your fries, stronzo, my girl is gonna come looking for me in a minute and I'm gonna have trouble getting hard for her with your meaty hands all over me."

I snorted what might have been a laugh if I hadn't been hurting too much over losing Winter to feel anything close to amusement.

I finished up my meal and tossed the empty wrappers into a dumpster on the far side of the alley before heading into the shadows further along it to let Enzo wait for his waitress.

There were used condoms and even a few needles tossed all over the place and my lip curled back as I rounded the building, hating the way the breeze kicked up that piss stench yet again. We were about as far from our usual part of the city as you could get and I was getting an up close and personal reminder about just how grim Sinners Bay could be in the shadows.

"Looking for some fun, big boy?" a woman's voice drew my attention and I looked up at her as she approached me wearing booty shorts, high heels and a red bikini top despite how fucking freezing it was tonight.

I could see the goosebumps peppering her skin and I looked beyond her to the other four girls who were huddled together in a blanket in an attempt to keep warm between clients. I guessed they were taking turns to hawk for work tonight rather than fighting it out.

I was about to tell her to fuck off when my gaze caught on the blood red colour of her hair and I hesitated. These girls were just desperate souls in need of money more than anything, and I had no way to know what had driven them to this life. But the subtle reminder of my broken savage girl had guilt twisting in my gut.

"How much do you and your friends need to earn tonight before you can turn in out of the cold?" I asked her and her eyebrows rose.

"All of us?" she questioned, looking over her shoulder to the other girls. "You wanna have a party?" she asked, a little hope mixed with a little fear in her voice that let me know men who asked for that weren't always kind about what they wanted from these girls.

"How much?" I insisted.

"Two hundred each and we'll do anything," she said, a little fearful again like she knew how depraved that might get, but was willing to do whatever she had to if it meant that much money.

I sighed and pulled my wallet from my back pocket. The Romeros had been quick to give me access to my share of their wealth, though I hadn't touched it until I'd begun this hunt. I was carrying cash in case I needed to pay someone for information, but I could just as easily beat answers out of them anyway, and in my current state I'd likely prefer that.

I beckoned the other girls over and they hastily slid the blanket off of their bodies to show me as much skin as possible, but I didn't bother looking below their faces. My savage girl was the only girl I wanted and I couldn't imagine that ever changing now.

"A thousand each," I said, counting out the money as they salivated over it, though the first girl looked more terrified than ever and I could only guess what horrors she'd endured for that kind of money before. "All I want you to do is go home and get warm. That's it."

I offered them the cash but they all recoiled.

"Nobody just hands out money like that for nothing," one of them said angrily.

"I ain't a fucking charity," another growled.

The third licked her lips and looked inclined to snatch the lot and run. I sighed heavily, hearing footsteps approaching around the corner and Enzo's unmistakable dirty laugh. I needed them gone and fast.

"Fine," I grunted, wondering why I'd even bothered trying to be nice in the first place. "Do any of you know who I am?"

They all narrowed their eyes suspiciously then the first girl gasped as the ball dropped. Gangsters were pretty much celebrities in Sinners Bay, though it was our infamy that kept our faces known, not that most people seemed to care. They knew that we were all bad people, killers even and yet their fascination with us only seemed to grow because of it.

"You're Nicoli Romero," she murmured.

"Good. Then I'll tell you what you can do to earn this money. You can keep your ears out for any and all information on Ramon Hernandez. And Duke Polinsky for that matter too. I wanna know anything and everything about those two men - particularly where I can find them. You can take this as a down payment and there will be more of it if you give me any solid leads."

Their attitudes instantly changed and they quickly snatched their money from me, programming my number into their cheap cellphones and grinning like they'd just won the lottery before turning away. I guessed that was how life made sense to them. Everything was a transaction. Sinners Bay wasn't always the city of dreams.

As the girls hurried away, shooting me appreciative grins and even a half-hearted offer of a blowjob on the house, I turned my attention back to the alley.

A woman was moaning in pleasure and I caught the sound of Enzo saying something about wanting her on her knees in a minute.

I gritted my teeth against my irritation at his unprofessional methods and kept my steps silent as I slipped back around the corner and found them there in the shadows. Enzo had the bartender pulled against him as he leaned back against the wall, one hand beneath her leather skirt as and the other fisted in her short hair as he forced her to look up at the sky overhead. She was panting and moaning at whatever he was doing to her and as I moved closer, his gaze flicked up from admiring her to meet my eye. He smirked at me like a total asshole then yanked her head towards him as he kissed her, releasing her hair and running his hand down her side.

She moaned into his mouth as he kept moving his hand beneath her skirt and he hooked her cellphone from her jacket pocket without her even noticing. He tossed it to me and I caught it silently, leaving them to it as I hurried away to find Frankie.

It wasn't hard to spot his car even though he had tried to go for something less conspicuous tonight. But the black SUV was still worth more than every other car on the block combined.

The back door slid open and I found another guy sitting in there, holding out his hand for the phone.

"This is Fabio," Frankie explained. "Our second cousin and tech support. Rocco had to head home for a bit - River likes sleeping on his chest and isn't settling without him tonight. He promised he will only be five hours - long enough for them both to get some sleep and then he'll be back on the hunt fresh in the morning with us. Assuming we haven't found her by then."

I nodded, eyeing Fabio as he took the phone from me and plugged it into his laptop. I didn't want to address the idea that we still might not have found Winter in five hours. Five minutes was too fucking long for me to go on without her.

"The only security she's got on this is a passcode," Fabio muttered with a snort of laughter. "I could do this in my sleep."

I tried to take comfort from that, but I knew the only real comfort I'd be able to take from anyone would be in the form of Winter's arms wrapped around my body. Until then, I'd remain in this hypersensitive state of desperation and rage.

"We'll get her back," Frankie murmured, not for the first time. I just nodded, snatching the phone from Fabio again as he confirmed he'd cloned the information on it and left him to start deciphering it as I jogged back towards the alleyway.

The girl's moans had stopped now and for a moment I worried I'd taken too long but as I rounded the corner, I found her on her knees with her lips firmly wrapped around Enzo's cock instead.

His tattooed hand was fisted in her hair again as he fucked her mouth with hard thrusts of his hips and she moaned like it was a fucking ecstasy flavoured popsicle.

He cracked his eyes open, grunting as he spotted me and holding his free hand out for the cellphone. I wasn't risking getting closer to that shit show though so I just tossed it at him, averting my eyes before I was scarred for life. Luckily, he caught it and I was out of there before I had to witness him getting it back into her pocket somehow.

I hurried back to the car and climbed into the front beside Frankie, swiping a hand over my face to banish the image of my brother getting his dick sucked from my memories. This sibling stuff was layered with issues I'd never even considered before and that was one thing I could go without.

"I swear, at least sixty percent of Enzo's cunning plans involve him getting laid," Frankie grunted, clearly reading my disgust and correctly judging the source of it.

"I feel like I need to scrub my eyes clean somehow," I muttered.

"Coming from the man who kept me up all hours of the night while screwing his girl in every possible room of my fucking apartment," Frankie scoffed and I winced a little at the reminder. Not that I'd take it back, but I couldn't wait to get a place for me and Winter all of our own. Somewhere we could just be us, away from the world and free to be ourselves whenever we wanted to be.

The back door slid open and Enzo leapt in, grinning like an asshole and sprawling across the back seat beside Fabio just as he finished typing something on his laptop.

"I've got a cellphone number for 'boss'," he said proudly, looking around at all of us. "I'll get a trace set up on it then all we have to do is wait for him to take a call and I should be able to lock down his location."

"Good," Frankie said. "Let's go grab showers and a change of clothes, maybe a few hours of sleep. The minute we get that location we need to be ready to move. We'll have your girl back before you know it, fratello."

I grunted my agreement because I had no choice. I hadn't slept in over forty eight hours and something was going to give. But the moment we got that location I'd be there, charging in and saving my girl from whatever the fuck she was enduring now. Because I didn't care if she was his wife, I didn't care if she'd sworn some vow to him once upon a time or if he really did love her. That was before she became my savage girl, my goddess, my queen, and there was no way in hell I was letting him keep her from me.

CHAPTER TWENTY NINE

The longer I spent in this house, the more caged I felt. Every time I tried to go outside, I'd find locked doors or armed guards telling me to stay inside for my own safety. I was more suspicious than ever about who my husband actually was. Because if he needed this many people stationed around his home, he must have had a lot of enemies.

I sat in the lounge as Dr Ramsey tried to hypnotise me for the third day in a row. I didn't want a therapist. I just wanted to leave this damn house.

"You really must focus today," she pushed as I lay on the couch with my eyes closed. Her heavy perfume assaulted my sense and I held my breath as she tried to get me to relax enough to open my mind. But I didn't trust this woman and I refused to breathe a word to her about anything I may or may not have remembered. Mostly, she dragged up memories of The Five and that made me dislike her on principle, but sometimes there were glimmers of something else. Some life before all of that. I saw myself in pretty dresses, I caught the sound of birds in the trees, a woman with hair as red as mine…

But as soon as I tried to hold onto any of it, it slipped away again. Dr Ramsey finally gave up on our session for the day when I continued to give her the silent treatment after two hours. I had to hand it to her, she was tenacious. Although I imagined that had more to do with what Ramon was paying her than her desire to see me improve.

When she left, it was past six and I headed deeper into the house in search of Ramon. I hadn't seen him all day because he had business to attend to, but I hoped he was still in his office right now. I'd seen him walk in there just before Ramsey had arrived and heard him speaking in harsh Spanish tones on the phone to someone. Apparently I wasn't able to understand the language which was just infuriating.

I walked up to the door when silence fell beyond it and knocked, straightening my spine as I prepared to make some demands. Not that he ever seemed to listen to what I wanted.

"Enter," he growled and I pushed the door open.

He sat in the wing-back chair behind his huge cherry wood desk, the space wide and sparse, his aura dominating the room. The harsh expression on his face fell away as he realised who had come looking for him and he smiled warmly.

"My darling, what a surprise. I've missed you." He gestured for me to take a seat opposite him, but I remained on my feet, folding my arms.

"I want to go out. I want to be free to come and go as I please. I'm starting to feel like a prisoner here and I've been a prisoner for too long in my life."

His eyebrows jumped up and he took a moment to form his response. "I...can't let you go anywhere alone, my love. It's not safe."

"Why?" I hissed.

"You were kidnapped, darling, and the perpetrator has not been captured. I have my men hunting for them, but until they're caught, I must protect you."

I narrowed my gaze on him, sensing a note of insincerity in his voice that made the back of my neck prickle. "I didn't ask you to do that. It's my life, and if I want to risk it-"

He slammed his hand down on the desk. "No," he barked and my blood chilled. "I am your husband, I swore an oath to protect you and I will do it

Sasha."

I practically growled at the use of that name. "*Winter*."

"Stop that," he tsked. "I'm growing tired of your refusal to even try and fit back into our life."

"That's because I don't want to fit back into it," I clipped. "I want to go home."

"Home?" He rose from his seat, his cheeks turning blotchy with anger. "You are home!"

My voice cracked like an eggshell in my throat. It wanted to hide and disappear at his tone, but I wouldn't let it, holding onto it with sharp fingernails.

"I don't feel safe here," I admitted, my tone slightly strained. "I felt safe with Nicoli and the other Romeros."

"That's ridiculous," he spat. "I have a hundred armed men out there who would die keeping you safe."

"Keeping me chained," I countered angrily. "I don't want to live a life where I can't do what I please. I've lived in a cell for ninety percent of what I remember of my existence. I won't stay here inside another one, no matter how big and shiny it is."

Ramon dropped back into his seat, running a hand over his face as silence pooled between us and filled the air with so much tension that my ears started to ring.

"Look, I didn't want to tell you this, but I've been doing some digging into the Romeros. And..." He rubbed his brow like he was concerned.

"What?" I pushed, my heart skipping.

"It seems Clarissa Romero may be linked to the men who took you. They worked for her...and as upsetting as this may be to hear, I believe she and perhaps even the rest of the Romeros had a hand in your kidnapping."

"I already knew Clarissa was involved," I said, my cheeks flushing hot. "Nicoli knew it, so did his brothers, they were investigating-"

"Then they were most likely lying to you," he cut me off, his expression imploring. "Think about it my darling, they were trying to cover their tracks."

"Nicoli found me up on that mountain after I escaped. He had nothing to do with kidnapping me. He protected me. He hunted down my torturers and made them bleed for what they did to me." My shoulders heaved with my frantic breathing, my skin burning with rage at his insinuation. Whether he was trying to protect me or not, I wasn't going to let him drag their names through the dirt.

He considered that, running his index finger over his lips. "I just don't think I can take the risk of you seeing them until I am sure of their innocence."

"Since when did a wife have to ask permission of her husband to do anything in the twenty first century? Married or not, I don't belong to you," I growled, my fingers curling into fists.

"You need to take a breath," he encouraged and I noted that he hadn't responded to what I'd said. "I'm not trying to cage you."

"Then why can't I go out?!" I shouted, surprised by the ferocity in my voice, but liking it too. I sounded strong.

He pursed his lips, surveying me with a calculating look in his gaze. "Fine," he said eventually. "We'll go out. You and me. Tonight."

My lips parted in surprise. That hadn't been quite what I'd meant, but now he'd suggested it, it sounded like the perfect opportunity to run. I could slip away from him, find Nicoli, return to where my heart longed to be.

"You mean it?" I pushed.

"Yes, darling. Now I need to work for a few more hours. Go and eat some dinner."

I nodded obediently, figuring I needed to play along to make sure he didn't suspect that I would try to run. I gave him a sugary smile too and he wet his lips, undeniable heat filling his gaze. *Shit, too far.*

I hurried out of the door, shutting it firmly behind me and heading off down the hall towards the kitchen. I was going to fill my belly so I had the energy to run a hundred miles tonight. And before dawn tomorrow, I'd be back in the arms of my warrior, and I'd never part from him again.

CHAPTER THIRTY

I couldn't help but keep glancing at my phone as I sat in the passenger seat of Frankie's car, Mr. Sandman by SYML playing on the radio and mirroring my mood.

"You're sure you want to do this alone?" he asked for the hundredth time, but my answer wasn't changing.

"The message said to come alone," I reminded him.

We'd been getting ready to head back out on our hunt this morning while Fabio tried to explain exactly why his idea to track Hernandez's cellphone hadn't worked out. The asshole had a masking device on it which encrypted the signal, sending it pinging off of multiple towers and making it impossible to lock onto the real location because the man never let a call go on for longer than two minutes. It was infuriating and even more concerning. The kind of people who went to those lengths to avoid being found were not the kind you wanted to meet in a darkened alleyway at night. Certainly not the kind I wanted anywhere near my girl.

But while I'd been in the middle of losing my shit and trashing Frankie's dining room, my own phone had gotten a text. One single message which might have been exactly what I'd been hunting for dropping straight into my lap.

Unknown:

We need to talk about Sasha Hernandez. Club Vitro, ten pm. Come alone or you won't hear from her again.

It could easily be a trap. It was also my only lead so far. So I'd sent a one word answer. *Okay.*

"Stay close, I'll text you every few minutes," I assured Frankie. "But you can't come in."

"One of ours works the bar here anyway," he muttered. "I made sure she was on shift tonight and she'll keep an extra eye on you. The three of us are right here, we won't be more than a block away at any time."

"Just stay away unless I say otherwise," I growled as he pulled up at the curb. "I can handle myself. I spent years doing far worse things than this alone."

"You'll never do anything alone again, fratello," Enzo grunted from the back seat.

"So get used to it," Rocco added, the tension in his posture clear. But he got it. If it was Sloan on the line, he'd risk this or far worse too. And I doubted I was walking into an ambush set up inside a heaving night club. There were far less conspicuous places available to try and kill a man.

"Thank you," I grunted, opening the car door and stepping out.

They lingered as I strode past the long crowd, levelling a flat look at the bouncers that had them stepping aside to admit me, not even conducting a search. Which was extra helpful as I was carrying a gun and two knives. I may have been walking into this place alone, but I wasn't dumb enough to do it unarmed.

The club was a pretty exclusive venue and I glanced around at the black and silver theme which ran through the place. The lights were low but the music was loud. I'd done my homework on this club before coming here. The

DJ currently playing music from her podium was pretty famous and the dance floor which was thick with writhing bodies said she was pretty good too. The bar stood to the right of the space, lit in sapphire blue with the staff putting on a show of mixing cocktails flamboyantly.

The VIP area was to my left, booths with supple navy seating laid out with a view over the dance floor filled with assholes who had more time on their hands than sense for what to do with their money. I'd studied the layout before coming here; there were two exits out the back plus a store room beyond the kitchens with windows I could smash if I really got desperate. I always liked to have an escape plan or two up my sleeve.

"Mr Romero?" A leggy blonde hostess in a dress short enough to flash her panties as she approached me and I raised my chin as I held her eye. "Your VIP table is waiting for you. If you'd like to follow me?"

I scanned the room slowly, taking note of a few assholes who were looking my way, but I was well enough known in this town that I wasn't surprised by their attention. And they definitely weren't anyone I needed to be worried about. But there was bound to be someone watching me arrive.

I motioned with my hand for the hostess to lead the way and she gave me a broad smile as she took the lead towards the VIP area, shaking her ass in a way designed to lure attention as her cheeks hung out beneath the skirt. I could practically see what she'd eaten for dinner and I couldn't say it was doing anything for me.

She led me up a short set of stairs to a table that was marked with a reserved sign and laid a hand on my arm, leaning close to ask me what I'd like to drink.

I shook her hand off of me before I answered, giving her a flat look which didn't seem to put her off nearly as much as it should have as she just licked her lips seductively instead.

"I'll take a scotch," I told her, mostly to get rid of her. "The best you've got."

"Coming right up," she said, flashing me a smile and letting her eyes run over my body appreciatively before strutting away. She was giving me some serious hooker vibes, or maybe she was just desperate, but either way, the only thing I was interested in tonight was meeting whoever the fuck had information on my savage girl.

I glanced at my cellphone irritably, shooting Frankie a quick text to tell him I was inside but no one else was here yet before sending another to the unknown number, letting them know I was waiting.

I didn't take my seat in the designated VIP area, instead standing beside the railing which divided this slightly raised level from the masses below and leaning my elbows on the silver bar as I scanned the crowd again.

The DJ was good, even I could appreciate that with my small experience of clubs like this, and the dance floor was packed with people moving and grinding against each other to the beat.

A pretty bartender caught my eye as she mixed drinks for a pair of preppy douchebags and she inclined her head respectfully, just enough for me to see and to let me know that she was our insider here tonight. I didn't react, moving my gaze on, knowing full well that my position standing by the railing like this meant I was far easier to scrutinise than most people here. There were probably eyes on me already, checking that I kept to my word and had come alone. I just needed to spot them and assess my odds. In a place like this, it was unlikely to come down to guns and even knives would only be saved for desperate measures. No, if I needed to fight my way out of here, I'd most likely do it with my fists.

It didn't take long for me to pick out the lurker in the shadows by the speaker and another lingering on a stool at the far end of the bar, nursing a drink with the ice almost entirely melted inside it. The dickheads in the VIP booth three along from mine were laughing in a way that seemed fake to me and as I turned to look at them in a sharp motion, I found two of them looking right at me before they could cover their asses.

I strode straight towards them and the four men dropped the act sharpish, giving me resigned looks as I stood over them.

"Am I that terrifying?" I asked. "Your boss is too afraid to come alone too?"

They exchanged looks before the biggest guy spoke up. "We were just ensuring that you're alone. We'll leave you to your meeting now. He'll be with you shortly."

With that, the four of them stood and filed away and I let them go with a sneer before heading back to stand at the railing before my booth once more.

"Here's your drink, Mr Romero," the hostess announced as she reappeared, a tumbler with a triple shot on the rocks held out to me in the centre of a small, black tray.

I grunted out a thanks as I took it, bringing the glass to my lips and drinking as I looked out over the crowd.

"Can I get you anything else?" she purred, laying a hand on my arm and leaning close to speak to me like she was using the volume of the music as her fucking wingman or something.

"No," I said, not really caring that I was being rude. This chick needed to get the fucking hint.

I took another long sip of my drink and kept my eyes on the crowd, but she wasn't done there. Her hand landed on my chest over my spotless dress shirt and she leaned in again to speak as she trailed it down my body.

"I wasn't just offering drinks," she said, biting her lip and looking up at me with lust in her gaze.

I caught her wrist as her fingers brushed against my belt and I practically snarled at her as I yanked her close to hear me clearly. "I said, *no*. Are you deaf or just plain stupid? I have no interest in your herpes infested pussy or how much you like to choke on dick as a hobby. So tuck your camel toe away, stop embarrassing yourself, and fuck off."

I tossed her hand out of my grip with disgust and knocked back the rest of my drink before thrusting the empty glass at her. Her eyes widened with rage and embarrassment, but she said nothing, just took the glass and scurried away.

I might have been a little harsh, but my mind was full of worry for my savage girl and I didn't need some high end hooker trying her luck with me while I needed to concentrate.

My tongue felt thick in my mouth as I looked out over the club again and for a moment my vision blurred, causing me to press my fingers to my eyes and release a slow breath. I was spreading myself too thin, burning myself out with the desperation of my hunt but unable to stop myself all the same. I couldn't slow down and I'd never give up. Winter belonged with me. There was no doubt in my mind about that and I refused to even consider relaxing the pace of my search.

I opened my eyes again and looked back out over the dancers as my ears began to ring. My gaze slipped in and out of focus and the colours of the flashing lights seemed to pulse more vibrantly than before.

My heart felt like it was falling into time with the thrashing rhythm of the music and I couldn't decide if that felt right or not.

A wave of dizziness passed over me again and I blinked as my vision blurred around the edges and the ringing in my ears grew louder.

A smile was tugging at the corner of my mouth and I was struck with the urge to laugh even though I didn't know what was funny.

I gripped the railing in front of me as the floor beneath my feet started to sway like a boat rocking on the tide and I shook my head again as the colours of the room made me want to dive into them and bathe in all of that orange...

"Are you alright there, handsome?" a voice came from near and far away at once and I turned to find the hostess there again, all blonde hair and tiny dress, tugging on my arm like she wanted me to go somewhere.

"Ge-offa-me," I mumbled, trying to shake her off but doing it too hard so that she was knocked on her ass instead.

I shook my head as I tried to focus on what I was supposed to be doing. My savage girl with blood red hair and eyes the colour of emeralds, with scars that mirrored the strength inside her and a soul so pure and fierce it took my breath away.

Something was wrong.

I slipped my hand into my pocket, feeling the smooth, silken shell of my cellphone and remembering the three men who could help me. My blood, my kin, my brothers.

I fumbled the phone from my pocket and tried to call them, but the world was spinning and the music was creeping into my head and filling my brain with this constant drone of white noise which I couldn't think through.

My cellphone slipped from my fingers as it was taken away and a soft hand replaced it.

My feet stumbled over themselves as she tugged me along and I fell into the padded seat which lined the VIP booth, groaning at the softness of the cushions as they hugged me like a cloud.

"Are you sure you don't wanna have fun with me, handsome?" the hostess asked as I found myself looking up at her, my head swimming, heart pounding, arms two leaden weights at my sides.

She looked funny, or at least she must have because I was laughing and I wasn't sure why else I would have been.

She placed my cellphone down on the table before me and I could only stare at it. So close and yet so fucking far away.

The colours of the room were pulsing between bright and dim, my lips were tingling and I sucked in a sudden breath as I realised I'd forgotten to take one for a while.

The hostess climbed onto my lap, straddling me as she brushed her hands along the sides of my face.

"I would have given you a ride for free, gorgeous. But the cash is a nice bonus all the same," she purred, her lips brushing my ear as my head fell back against the seat and I tried to remember why I was here.

My savage girl, with the soul of a warrior, owner of my heart...

CHAPTER THIRTY ONE

We left the house in a black Rolls Royce with a group of Ramon's men and I noticed that even the driver was packing heat. Not to mention the guards in the other two cars, one driving in front and one behind.

I wore a champagne coloured dress that had a high neck and went down to the knee. There hadn't been anything in my closet which suggested I'd once liked the sexier sort of clothes Frankie had provided me with. But I didn't see why my taste would have changed so drastically, kidnapped or not. I definitely preferred Frankie's clothes, but I wasn't exactly upset that I didn't have to wear anything more attractive in front of Ramon.

My husband was in a black dress shirt, navy slacks and a blazer which I suspected concealed a gun of his own. All of the weapons surrounding me made me feel uneasy even though I was used to the Romeros carrying them.

"What is it you do again?" I asked lightly. He'd told me he was a businessman which was about as clear of an explanation as telling me he was a red blooded human being.

"I work in the oil industry," he said smoothly, the lie almost sounding true.

"You need this much protection because of that?" I frowned and he waved a hand dismissively, not looking me in the eye.

"There are plenty of activists in Sinners Bay, not to mention I am on high alert since you were stolen from me, my darling."

I turned my gaze out the window, figuring there was no point pushing the subject. As soon as I got the chance tonight, I'd be making my escape anyway. I'd even picked out the lowest pair of heels in my closet to make running that much easier. And I could always kick them off if things got really hairy.

We arrived downtown and drove alongside the glossy exterior of a high end club. The cars didn't stop there though, instead turning a corner and driving down an alley where a man was waiting beside a side entrance. He hurried forward to open Ramon's door and my husband took my hand, pulling me after him as we stepped onto the concrete.

The cold air made me shiver as Ramon led me to the door and we were allowed inside with six men flanking us without so much as a pat down. My heart tripled its pace as I glanced back at the wall of muscle following behind us. I was going to have to give them the slip somehow. Maybe if there was a restroom with a window, I could climb out of it and disappear into the night…

The heavy pounding of a bass sounded above us and we were soon heading up a sleek black staircase and arrived in a club that was thronging with people. The crowd were dancing in a sea of swinging blue and white spotlights, crying out to the DJ and singing along to the fast song. The noise and the amount of people made my chest tighten. This didn't feel like my kind of scene, but I just had to suck it up and seek out the exits. Even at the thought of being so close to freedom, adrenaline was surging into my blood.

A hostess appeared with shiny brunette hair and a pearly smile. Her breasts were pushed up in a glitzy silver crop top and Ramon's eyes dropped down to her ass as she turned and started leading us past the crowd to a group of booths on the other side of the dance floor.

The music changed to something pulsing with an incessant duf duf duf sound at the core of it that made my ears bleed. We climbed up a few steps and were let past a cordon to a circular booth that overlooked the rest of the club. Ramon's guards stayed beyond it, fanning out and trying to blend in, but with their steely expressions and black attire, they blended in as well as foxes amongst chickens.

The hostess brought us some drinks without our input and placed down a vodka and soda for me and a port for Ramon.

"This used to be one of our favourite places together, does it jog your memory?" Ramon asked and I looked around the space, shaking my head. I must have been a very different person once if this had been my kind of place.

My nose wrinkled as I sipped the soda and vodka. *Bleugh*. Why would I ever have chosen to drink something so gross?

Ramon chuckled as we sat down and he shifted up close beside me, his thigh against mine. "You were always watching your figure." He gestured to the drink. "It was your favourite choice."

"That doesn't sound like me," I said as my upper lip peeled back and he shrugged.

"No doubt you'll fall back into place amongst our friends soon enough. You and your girlfriends were always counting calories and competing to look the finest. You of course, always outshone them." His hand dropped onto my knee and he circled his finger around a scar there with a frown. "I know a fantastic plastic surgeon who can ensure all of these are removed. You won't even be able to tell you ever had them."

I pushed his hand off of me with my heart lurching. "I like my scars."

"What?" he balked, looking up at me with incredulity. "But they're hideous." His upper lip curled and I glared at him. "Not that I love you any less because of them," he backtracked quickly, but the damage was done.

"They're a sign of my strength," I said, rising to my feet in irritation. "I need a moment. Where's the restroom?" My plan hadn't been to run off immediately, but I couldn't stand staying in the company of this man a second longer.

"I didn't mean to offend you, darling." He reached for my hand and I fought the urge to smack him as he took it, placing a kiss on the back of it. "I just want you to be happy."

I feigned a smile and let my shoulders drop. *Then don't suggest taking my scars again, you asshole. I bit my tongue on those words and moved to the edge of the booth. "The restroom?"*

"Carlos," Ramon called, snapping his fingers and the biggest one of his bodyguards turned my way. "Take her to the ladies'."

"Sure thing, boss." He beckoned me out of the booth and immediately took hold of my arm.

I shook him off, shooting him a scowl and he thankfully didn't touch me again.

"This way," he growled and I headed after him. We walked along the row of booths and I gazed in at the wealthy people dancing and chatting within them, looking like they were having the time of their lives. As we reached the last one, I fell still, the noise in the place dulling to a droning in my skull. My heart hit a frantic beat as I tried to refuse the sight unfolding before my eyes.

There was a man in there with a beautiful blonde woman in a slinky dress. She ground herself against him in his lap and he had his fingers knotted in her hair. As she smirked down at him, he laughed, his head falling back against the couch. And I saw his face clearly, though I'd sensed it was him from the moment I'd seen them. Nicoli lifted his other hand and grabbed her hips, his fingers digging in and she moaned like she liked that, dropping low to grind her crotch against his.

He stared up at her with a fire in his eyes, starting to mouth something, but I couldn't watch a second longer. My heart was turning to ash in my chest, crumbling away into blackened flakes and disintegrating to nothing. A gaping wound was left in its place, the kind that made everywhere hurt.

Carlos turned to me, a question in his eyes but I was already running, taking the steps off of the raised platform and shoving through bodies, trying to escape as I forced my way through the crowd. I needed air. I needed to get outside. I had to score that image from my mind. I needed to take back the last minute of my existence and crush it to nothing.

I heard grunts and shouts of protest behind me as Carlos followed and I moved faster, shoving and pushing until I made it to the main exit and ran in a full sprint out into the freezing air.

Even then I kept running, suffocated by what I'd seen and the need to be as far away from that club and the people in it as possible.

The world around me was a blur of streetlights and headlights on cars. A vehicle honked loudly as I ran across the road without looking. I needed to find a dark, dark space and crawl into it, bury myself and disappear. He'd broken his promise to me. He hadn't been aching for me like I had for him. The moment we'd been parted, he'd looked elsewhere for a woman to satisfy him.

I kept running until I was sure I'd left the club far behind, doubling over and clutching my side as a stitch ripped through me. As soon as I could, I started jogging again, moving along as quickly as I could as the freezing wind enveloped me.

A car drew up beside me in my periphery and someone slammed into me from behind in the same moment. I screamed as they pushed me into the car, glancing back as I threw my elbow into their gut. It was Carlos and his muscles were folding around me like iron, forcing me to his will. He placed me in the car, firmly shutting the door and a click sounded as it locked.

"Sasha!"

I turned as Ramon pulled me into his arms, hugging me tight.

"What happened?" he growled in my ear. "You frightened the life out of me."

I was shaking my head, pulling away, pushing him back and he thankfully let me go. My head was spinning and I clawed at my hair, drawing my legs to my chest as I tucked myself into the space beside the window.

"Darling, please talk to me," Ramon pushed.

I said nothing, refusing to give him the satisfaction of letting him know how much seeing Nicoli with another girl had shattered my heart.

How could he do this to me? How could he forget me so easily?

I curled up tighter into myself and Ramon rested a hand on my back, rubbing in soft circles. I wanted to tell him to stop, but my voice was long gone, trapped in my chest, maybe forever.

"Perhaps we went out too soon. I'll keep you safe, my darling, I won't take any risks with you again. You need to do as I say. I know what's best for you," he said and I cried harder because now I knew I'd blown my only chance at escaping as well. I'd lost Nicoli the same moment I'd lost my chance at freedom. And with it, I was vanishing too.

CHAPTER THIRTY TWO

T he steady *bleep, bleep, bleep* of a heart monitor machine drew me from the pitch black darkness of my mind and I groaned as I slowly became aware of the things surrounding me.

I was lying in a bed, sheets covering my body and warm light pushing against my eyelids with an insistent kind of urgency to it. My tongue was thick and my throat parched and I took a deep breath as I peeled my eyes open.

"You really know how to scare the shit out of us, don't you, stronzo?" Rocco growled, leaning over me and blotting out the glare from the light above me as he cupped my cheek in his hand and looked at me intently.

"Why am I in hospital?" I asked, my voice coming out rough and brittle as my memories rippled like a pool disturbed by a falling stone.

"Here." Enzo leaned over me too, holding out a cup of water with a straw in it and placing it between my lips. His usual cocky smirk was replaced by a concerned frown and I couldn't help but stare at these two men I'd once thought of as monsters, falling apart at the thought of something happening to me.

I drank it, ignoring the babying as I just let my body come back to life in its own time and Rocco explained. The last thing I could remember was being in that club, that hooker tugging me towards the VIP booth...then it was just a blur and darkness.

"That whore drugged you, fratello. Then climbed up into your lap and tried to fuck you in front of the whole goddamn club," Rocco said with a sneer.

"Why?" I gritted out around the straw before going back to drinking. She might have been gagging for it, but that seemed a bit extreme for a girl who needed a pay day. It wasn't like she'd have had trouble finding a dick to ride for cash in that place.

My brothers exchanged a look and I could tell they didn't want to tell me.

"We didn't know it until after we'd gotten you to hospital and Frankie went back to get his hands on the club's CCTV, but that piece of shit Hernandez turned up with your girl in tow," Enzo explained slowly. "He let her see you with the hooker in your lap and she ran out of there, crying her heart out-"

"What?" I yelled, lurching upright, my heart leaping as I found my hands strapped to the bed either side of me. "Why the fuck am I tied up?" I bellowed and the door flew open as a doctor strode in, his eyes dark with concern and two nurses on his tail.

"Calm down, fratello," Rocco commanded. "It was just to stop you from hurting yourself while you were fitting. They can take them off now, can't you doc?"

"Yes, of course, if you're feeling recovered, Nicoli?" he asked me, hesitating to approach as I thrashed like a bear in a trap for a moment before forcing myself to fall still.

"Get them off," I snapped. "And take that needle out while you're at it," I added, bobbing my chin at the IV stuck in my arm.

"I'd prefer if you kept that in until you've emptied it. Then I need to go over your stats and-"

"I'm not staying here," I snarled, ignoring his request.

"With respect, Mr Romero, I'm not sure your legs will carry you far. You've been out of it for two days. You had a very bad reaction to the overdose,

I really wouldn't recommend-"

"Two days?" I bellowed, staring between my brothers in horror as I realised my savage girl was still out there somewhere, stuck with some psychopath who'd set me up to look like I'd been cheating on her, like I didn't give a shit about her.

"Leave him tied up and check whatever you need to, doc," Rocco said, backing up and exchanging a look with Enzo that made me want to fuck him up.

"Let me go!" I roared but they just frowned at me as I struggled against the restraints and Rocco gave a small shake of his head.

"Not until they've done what they need to," he said. "We nearly lost you the other night, fratello. We aren't going to let you out of here until we're sure you're okay. Our family can't grieve you for a second time and you'll be no good to your girl if you drop dead while trying to find her either."

I glared at him as his words slowly sank beneath my skin and made their way to my heart. I could see the concern in their eyes, the fear. They weren't going to let me out of here without making sure I was alright and he was making a frustrating amount of sense.

"Tell me all of it," I growled as I fell back against my pillows and the doctor warily approached to check me over.

"Our insider, Cherry, who was working the bar saw you getting unsteady on your feet," Enzo said in a low voice, moving to stand at the foot of the bed so the doctor and nurses had room to work while I ignored the way they poked and prodded me, murmuring responses to their questions when I had to but mostly pretending they weren't there. "She took a walk past you and saw you were barely conscious beneath that hooker." Enzo paused as he glanced at the doctor, clearly being careful not to say anything incriminating. "She called us right away and it can't have been ten minutes between that and us arriving to help you. But by the time we got there, the hooker was gone and you were out of it, twitching and vomiting and...*fuck*, Nicoli we thought we were losing you all over again."

I could see the way thinking about that was haunting him and I cleared my throat, realising how close I must have been to death for it to have affected them like this.

"It'd take more than a spiked glass of scotch to kill me," I joked, though the way my body was aching said that had been dangerously close to a lie. Neither of them replied and the doctor muttered something which sounded like 'lucky son of a bitch'.

"What happened to the hooker?" I asked, anger rising in me at the thought of that bitch doing this. She'd clearly been paid off, but she'd also had no issue with it either.

Rocco glanced at the doctor and nurses to make sure they weren't looking his way then ran a finger over his throat.

"Papa questioned her," he said slowly. "But she didn't know anything about the people who had paid her to do it. Just that they'd given her five grand and she'd never seen them before that night. She's a dead end."

"The police want to question you," the doctor said as he finished checking me over. "I can tell them you're fit now, if you're ready? I'd prefer it if you would stay in another night, but I'm guessing you want to be discharged right away?"

"You guessed right," I said, trying to stop myself from snarling at the guy who'd saved my damn life. But I really wanted to get the fuck out of here and start up the hunt for Winter again.

"We've still been looking for your girl," Enzo said, seeming to guess where my mind had gone. "Frankie is following up on a lead right now. Otherwise he'd be here too. And Papa's been sleeping here, he only left an hour ago because we insisted."

My throat tightened as he said that but I just nodded, not having words to express what that meant to me. I really did have a family, didn't I?

The doctor hesitantly took the restraints from my wrists and I shook my hands out, rearranging myself so I was sitting up in the bed. A wave of dizziness and nausea passed through me and I grimaced at the movement.

"I'll get your discharge papers organised while you speak to the police," the doctor said and I called out a thanks to him as he headed out of the room. He had stopped me from dying after all, so I didn't have to be a complete asshole.

"We'll go find you some breakfast," Rocco added as the two officers walked through the door before it had even closed. "Don't try to get out of that bed until we get back."

I clucked my tongue at him for fussing, but I had to admit it felt good to have someone who gave a shit about me like that. A whole family of someones actually.

"I'm Officer Hoskins and this is Officer Barlow. How are you feeling, Mr Romero?" the first cop asked. She was petite with her dark hair braided down her back and if it wasn't for the savage look in her eyes I'd have totally underestimated her. But on closer inspection I'd prefer her odds in a fight over the giant guy looming behind her.

"Like I got fucked in the ass by a dinosaur and he didn't even buy me flowers after. What difference does it make to you?"

Hoskins laughed before she could help herself and Barlow raised his eyebrows in surprise.

"And you're familiar with that feeling, are you?" she asked, biting on her lip like she was picturing it.

I shrugged. "I'll try anything once. But that doesn't help me with understanding why you're here."

"We heard that you were in the hospital and the doctors said that no one knew what you'd taken. We've got no record or even rumours of you being a recreational drug taker and there's a tale going around that someone tried to assassinate you," Hoskins said, clearly fishing without any bait on her hook.

"You heard wrong. I like to party like that. I just took too much is all," I said with a shrug. This issue wasn't going to be a police matter. It had already been handled anyway.

"We also wanted to ask if you know Maria Pembroke?" Barlow asked, pulling out an iPad and showing me a photograph of the hooker who'd fucked me over.

"Can't say I do."

"We have footage of her with you the night you overdosed," he pushed.

"I can't remember shit from that night."

They exchanged a look then Barlow flipped the image onto a crime scene photograph of Maria hanging upside down by her ankles from a bridge, quite clearly dead. I guessed my father didn't take kindly to people trying to kill his children.

"She was found like this last night," Barlow prompted when I said nothing.

"Like I said, I don't know the girl. Plus, if you're looking to pin that on me, I've got a pretty tight alibi." I indicated the hospital bed and Hoskins sighed.

"We were wondering more about the possibility that she had something to do with your overdose. If that was the case, I can imagine you have a family member or two who might be a little angry about that. Maybe they'd be out for revenge?" Hoskins pressed.

I barked a laugh right in her face. "My family are businessmen, not criminals," I said, completely deadpan. "But we have had issues with police harassment before. So perhaps it's time you fuck off before I have to call the family lawyers on you."

"You used to be aligned with the Calabresis," Hoskins pushed. "How can you go from hating the Romeros to undying loyalty to them?"

"Blood will out," I said in a deathly tone. "You need to leave now."

They did as I asked and as I waited for the doctor to come and discharge me, I realised how true that statement had been. I was at home with my family now, no matter how many years had passed with us away from each other, my blood sang in their presence. There was something so right about being one of them. My family meant more to me than I ever could have imagined. And Winter was my family too. I was going to get her back. And I was going to rain

374

down death on anyone who stood in my way.

CHAPTER THIRTY THREE

The days slipped by and I swung between being distraught and feeling nothing. But as I faced another day in my room where I tried to shut the world out and refused to speak to Ramon or any maid who brought me food, I was starting to feel something else. Fear.

Fear that I had made a mistake. That I'd too quickly thrown away everything between Nicoli and myself because of what I'd seen. *What if I'm missing something?*

Despite what I'd seen as clear as day, I couldn't shake the feeling that Nicoli wouldn't have moved on so quickly after everything we'd been through. As I thought over each moment we'd spent together, I just couldn't marry that man with what I'd witnessed. But then what did it mean?

I'd had to rely on my gut feelings for a long time, having no past memories to defer to instead, and I had to have faith in them again this time. So I needed to speak with Nicoli and confirm what had happened, be sure he wanted nothing more to do with me before I could bear to let go of him.

I rubbed my eyes, getting up from the floor and dressing in some yoga pants and a sweater. Then I walked over to the door, turning the handle and sighing in relief as I found it unlocked. I slipped out into the quiet hall, heading to the stairs and padding down and along the empty halls towards Ramon's office.

I knocked and he grunted a response and as I pushed the door open, he lifted his head and gave me that warm smile he always reserved for me. He barely looked at the maids and only spoke in clipped tones to his guards. But when it came to me, I had his full attention. And maybe that was something I'd liked about him once.

"I'm so glad to see you out of your room," he said brightly. "Perhaps we can have lunch together today?"

I hadn't spoken since it had happened, but I had to now. I had to claw my voice out of the box it was hiding in.

Several beats of silence passed and he drummed his fingers on the desk impatiently as I opened and closed my mouth, but no sound came out.

Finally, I managed it. "I need to speak to Nicoli," I said firmly, my voice croaky from lack of use.

His eyes flashed and he stood abruptly from his desk. "Excuse me?"

I cleared my throat, speaking louder this time. "I said-"

"I heard what you said!" he barked and my heart lurched in alarm. His face screwed up with anger and suddenly he swept everything from his desk, his laptop crashing into the wall and papers scattering everywhere.

I backed up in fear, but he came at me fast, and I was still in shock from his outburst, too slow to remember to run. He caught me by the throat, slamming me against the nearest wall and my head cracked against it. I gasped, fear clinging to me as I grabbed his hand and tried to pull it from my neck as he squeezed.

He got up close in my face, leaning down as his upper lip peeled back.

"I'm done," he snarled. "I've been patient, I have given you time, I have been a good husband, but I've had enough of this."

I started to shake, clawing at his hand as he increased the pressure on my throat and I struggled for air. Memories flashed through my eyes of his hand smacking against my cheek, his dark shadow looming over me, of me hiding in my closet when his rage got out of control. I remembered him shouting, cursing my name. I remembered my fear of him and it returned to me now, burrowing deep into my heart.

"You are *mine*," he hissed, his teeth bared. "My wife. My Sasha. You will not speak that man's name inside my household again, do you understand?"

I choked, fighting him with everything I had, but he wouldn't let go. My heart was beating too hard, my pulse pounding against my temples.

He sneered, releasing me and I slumped down the wall, coughing and spluttering as I dragged in air. Bile hit my tongue and I heaved, trying to swallow past it to get in more oxygen. I could already feel the bruise forming on my throat and was reminded of Farley, of my cell. And now I found myself at the feet of another monster.

"Go back to your room," he growled. "I will expect an apology when I come and see you later."

He stepped aside and I half crawled to the door before managing to scramble to my feet and run out of it. I clutched my throat as I fled, quickening my pace to put as much distance between me and him as possible. I didn't go upstairs as he asked, I started moving methodically around the house, checking every window, hunting for a way out.

I couldn't stay here. I couldn't be kept by that bastard. But it wasn't long before I had to once again accept that I was trapped in this place.

I returned to my room, shutting the door and sinking down to press my back to it. My breathing was ragged and I tried not to fall into the dark, numb space inside me. I had to stay present, I had to think of a way out.

I have to get out.

No matter how beautiful this bedroom was, how soft the carpet, or how far apart the walls, it looked just like my old cell to me in that moment. And I knew I was back in hell.

He came for his apology and I moved away from the door, standing with my fists raised in a threat. If he attacked me again, I'd at least try and fight him off.

He laughed throatily as he stepped into the room. "Don't be ridiculous, my darling. You are not going to fight me."

I lifted my chin, telling him that he was very wrong about that with my eyes.

He pushed the door shut, running a finger across his mouth as he moved toward me. "You always understood my rage. It's a part of me which I'm not proud of, but you embraced it, Sasha. You know how I can be. You can learn again."

He moved closer and I backed up, baring my teeth at him as I fell back on my feral ways. He tutted at me, his gaze skimming over my face, then down to the scars peeking out from under the neck of my sweater.

"I'll let you off of the apology this once as you're still adjusting back into your old life. But I need you to start making more effort, darling. I need you to drop this wild girl pretence and be the girl I married."

I shook my head in refusal and his eyes darkened to burning coal. "It isn't a request, Sasha."

A growl rolled through my throat at that name.

His jaw started pulsing. "There are questions I need answered before things can return to normal. I will call Dr Eckhart back here in a couple of days. If you refuse to let him examine you again, you will not like the consequences. But perhaps I can save you the discomfort of the worst of it if you are truthful with me now..." He stepped closer, his imposing height casting a shadow over me. "Did you fuck Nicoli Romero?"

Ice dripped down my spine and I swallowed hard as I battled the urge to back up. I didn't want him to see my fear, but he was a cruel hunter, seeking it in my eyes with a frightening intensity. I wasn't foolish enough to give him the truth, but that meant convincing him to believe me. And I didn't know if I was a good enough actress for that.

I shook my head, my eyes on his as I tried to keep my expression neutral. He caught hold of my chin and I threw my palms into his chest to try and keep him back, but he was an immovable force, glaring down at me.

"Say it with words," he hissed and the scent of cigars tingled my nose. I caught a glimpse of the past, a moment much like the one I'd had this morning. The first time he'd laid a hand on me. I'd been shocked, terrified, the mark of his palm stinging my cheek. I'd wanted to call my mother, but he'd refused. He hadn't let me speak with her since the wedding and for half a millisecond, I caught a vision of her, her long red hair flowing around her, her cheeks dotted with freckles, tears in her eyes as she stood on the porch of a large white house. That was the last time I'd seen her, I was sure of it. But who was she?

"Speak," he snapped and my heart jolted. I needed to give him this, I could see how important it was. If I didn't do it, I was going to fall prey to more of his rage. I had to cover up the truth about me and Nicoli. I had to ensure this dangerous bastard had no reason to turn his hatred on my mountain man.

It felt like tearing my voice through sharp nails and broken glass, but I managed to get it free. "We were just friends. He helped me," I rasped.

He surveyed me suspiciously then slowly nodded, drawing me close and wrapping his arms around me. "My sweet girl, you are such an innocent and fragile creature. I will always protect you."

I wasn't either of those things, but I bit my tongue on a retort until I tasted blood, remaining in his arms as I hoped to placate him long enough to form a plan. Because I wasn't staying here. I would find a way out even if I had to burn this house to the ground.

His hands roamed over my back, pulling me closer and pressing his mouth to my temple, seeking out more skin as he tried to find my mouth. I turned my head sharply in refusal and his fingers dug into my back. He made an angry noise in his throat and moved his mouth to my ear. "As soon as I've had the surgeon remove those scars, you will start sleeping in our marital bed again, Sasha. Get used to the idea."

He released me, leaving the room and I glared after him with my breaths coming out raggedly. Seething, blinding hatred filled me to the brim. I would die before I gave my body to him. And I was never going to give up my scars.

I am savage and strong, and I will make you regret trying to cage me.

"I need you to come to the bank with me this morning," Ramon said as he strolled into my room and pulled the blind up so I winced from the sunlight. "I want you washed and dressed in fifteen minutes." He pointed to the en-suite and I got up from the floor, scowling at him before heading into the bathroom. "And sleep in your bed, you're not a damn animal," he called after me and I slammed the door.

I scrubbed my skin angrily as I washed and soon strode back into the room with a towel wrapped around me.

Ramon had left an ugly pair of pants and a cream button down on the bed for me. It looked like something a secretary would wear. And as I pulled it on over some simple white underwear, I felt like I was pulling on a mask – a hideous mask. One that made me look like Ramon's ideal version of his wife who was obedient and boring.

I moved to the mirror, brushing my hair and putting on a little makeup, sure he would demand it of me anyway. I noticed the clothes covered most of my scars and I left a few buttons open at my neck in defiance, showing off a crescent shaped scar on my collarbone.

I headed out the door and Ramon did up his suit jacket as he swept his *gaze over me analytically. He moved forward, instantly buttoning the top of my shirt before cupping my cheek and smiling.*

"Beautiful." He took my arm and guided me down the hall, the heels he'd picked out for me pinching my toes. "This trip will be quick. There and back. If you cause a scene or try to run, I will not take you out of the house again and you will be punished. Understood?"

I nodded, not looking at him, my jaw tightening. If I had a chance to run today, he better believe I was gonna take it.

He led me into his Rolls Royce out on the drive and an entourage of guards followed in more cars as we exited the property, sailing into Sinners Bay.

"Dr Ramsey says you're not making any progress," Ramon commented after a while. "You must try harder. Then things can go back to normal."

I kept my gaze on the window, pointedly ignoring him.

"You must remember some things," he muttered angrily. "Like the day I proposed. I took you to the La Petite Fleur, got down on one knee in front of the whole restaurant. You smiled so bright...I'll never forget it, my darling."

I pressed my lips together and shrugged, my mind blank on that memory and I was glad of it.

"For fuck's sake," he growled.

We made it to the centre of town and I gazed out at the busy streets, wondering what would happen if I started screaming for help. But my voice was locked up tight today and I wasn't sure I could force it to work enough to speak to strangers.

Carlos opened Ramon's door to let him out and my husband pulled me after him, keeping me close. I looked to the people on the street, trying to catch someone's eye but everyone was in commute mode, heading to work, their eyes on their phones or directed straight ahead. As a man half jogged past us, I opened my mouth but only a hoarse noise came out.

"You can't even speak to me, of course you cannot speak to anyone else," Ramon said in a low growl as he pulled me along.

Carlos hounded me so closely that he was practically breathing down my neck and I shot him a glare over my shoulder. One he returned, his beady brown eyes becoming even beadier.

Ramon led me up the steps through a rotating glass door into the bank and a flicker of some memory passed through my mind. I'd been here before, I was sure of it.

He led me to the front desk, but before we got there, a Chinese man with wispy hair came rushing towards us. "Good morning, Mr Hernandez. We have everything organised, follow me this way."

We were led upstairs into a fancy office with leather chairs and abstract paintings on the wall. Ramon kept my hand in his as we dropped down into two seats opposite the man and Carlos stood right behind me like a dragon guarding its treasure.

"Can I just say, we here at Squire's Bank are so, so pleased to see your wife has been found safe and sound," he said, bowing his head to Ramon then me.

"Thank you, Lin," Ramon said politely. "Now, onto business?"

"Yes of course." Lin took some papers from his drawer and pushed them towards Ramon. "I just need your signature, here and here." He pointed with his pen. "Then the funds will be released for you."

"I want half in small bills," Ramon growled.

"Yes, we have prepared it for you as requested." Lin bowed his head again.

Ramon signed his name then pushed the papers back towards him.

"Wonderful, and you would also like to empty a couple of safety deposit boxes today, yes?" Lin asked.

"That's right," Ramon said. "I'll empty box eighty eight and box three fifteen."

"No problem." Lin started tapping something on his iPad. "I'll get the code for box eighty eight first."

He slid the iPad over to Ramon who typed some numbers in then passed *it back to Lin.*

"And...oh, box three fifteen is in your wife's name, sir." Lin looked to me and Ramon squeezed my hand.

"Yes, I thought maybe you might remember darling? Not to worry if not, we can access it another day. The most important item is in box eighty eight." He smiled at me like he had a secret and I frowned. What important item?

Lin tapped something on his iPad again then passed it to me. "Please just enter the numbers and we can proceed."

I stared down at the screen, dumbstruck and then an awful sequence of memories ran through my mind from my time with The Five. What's the code? What's the fucking code?!

The numbers came back to me in a blazing trail of fire through my brain. Three – nine – eight – four – four - seven.

My heart went haywire, but I kept my features neutral as Ramon and Lin waited patiently. I could type those numbers in. Maybe they were to do with this, maybe they weren't. Either way, this little white box on the screen had triggered them at long last. The code The Five had tried to beat and batter from me. And that made it the most precious thing in the world. The reason for my scars.

I didn't know what this meant. But Ramon must have had enemies everywhere in Sinners Bay. Men who would have gladly tortured his wife for this number. Was this the code they'd been trying to pull from my lips all along? And if it was, did Ramon know that? Did he want to move whatever was in that box and hide it from the men who sought to steal it from him? But how could he know?

"Darling?" Ramon pushed, his brows arched.

I shook my head, feigning ignorance. I wasn't going to give this vile man the numbers which I'd bled for. There was only one person in the world worthy of those if he asked for it. And Nicoli wasn't here anymore.

Ramon looked to Lin, pushing the iPad back towards him. "Her memory is foggy at the moment. Perhaps next time."

"Okay, follow me to box eighty eight." Lin stood up and Ramon went with him, leaving me with Carlos who was as silent as a covert fart, but just as impossible to ignore.

I glanced over my shoulder at the guy who was built like a basketball player on steroids and raised my middle finger at him. He grunted in irritation.

"Ramon will hear of this," he growled in his heavy Spanish accent and I rolled my eyes before offering him my back again.

My husband finally returned and Lin clapped excitedly as Ramon held out his hands, showing me a choker necklace which was an inch tall with a ruby at the centre of it.

"For you, my darling." He moved up behind me in the chair and clipped it around my throat without permission.

I instantly despised it. It was heavy and felt like a dog collar rather than a necklace. But maybe that was what he wanted me to feel. Like I was owned. And as he trailed his fingers down over my shoulder, I started to fear that if I didn't get away from him soon, he would try to possess me in other ways too.

CHAPTER THIRTY FOUR

I lay awake in my bed, staring through the window at the moon with my fists bunching and goosebumps lining my skin. But it wasn't the temperature that had me cold. It was the dull ache in my heart that wouldn't quit. It was the place beside me where my savage girl should have been. It was the way I had nothing and no one to hold close and the way I was failing her so completely.

Three weeks since I was drugged in that bar. Three weeks of fuck knows what happening to her fuck knows where. I'd even tried to follow up with the police, thinking they'd have had to interview her over her abduction, but their investigations were stalled too. That motherfucker Hernandez had gotten his lawyer to block their attempts to contact her for her official statement, claiming she wasn't of sound mind to give it. Who knew how long it would be before he allowed her to speak to them about what had happened to her up on that mountain? And it certainly didn't seem like they had any intentions of following it up.

I knocked my head back against the pillow and tried to remember how it had felt to hold her in my arms. I thought I'd had each of her scars memorised, but I wasn't sure anymore. I wanted to taste them on my tongue, trace them with my fingers, replicate them on my own flesh, just to feel closer to her.

My phone started ringing and for a moment I almost let it go to voicemail, not caring who was calling me or why. But then my brain kicked into gear and I remembered it was the middle of the night and very few people even had this damn number.

I checked the ID and my frown deepened at the unknown caller. The last time I'd been contacted from an unknown number it had been Hernandez setting me up in that fucking nightclub. If it was him again, I'd be sure not to fall into any traps this time.

I answered the call, pushing myself to sit up in the bed and swivelling so my feet landed on the floor.

"What?" I barked. It was four am after all and I could have been asleep.

"Erm...Is this Nicoli Romero?" a hesitant female voice came down the line and my frown deepened.

"Who's asking?"

"My name is Elsa...we kinda met a few weeks ago outside a bar in the lower east side? The Satin Press?"

I scoured my brain for a moment then realised that was the name of the bar where I'd had to see Enzo getting his dick sucked. I was still sporting the mental scarring, but I had been trying to block that night from my mind forever.

"Me and a few other girls were working that night and you gave us a pay-out. Asked us to call you if we found any information on a guy called Duke Polinsky...?"

My pulse quickened at the sound of that scumbag's name. I'd had to forget my hunt for him while my savage girl was still missing, but I abso-fucking-lutely wanted to know where that motherfucker was if she had the information.

"You know where he is?" I demanded, not caring that I was close to shouting and probably freaking her the fuck out.

"You still paying for that info?" she asked in reply, a slight shake to her voice but a dollop of determination too.

"How much?" I asked.

There was a long pause where I guessed she was trying to figure out how much she could get away with. But whatever she said, I'd happily pay it twice to get my hands on that son of a bitch. He was the last man left alive who had put his fucking hands on my girl and I'd be damned if I wasn't going to squeeze the life out of him just as soon as I could.

"A thousand," she said, almost making it a question as her fear for me coloured her words.

"If you can lead me to him then it's yours," I agreed and I almost felt bad as she actually squealed with excitement.

"I'll text you my address and you can come give me the money. I'll tell you everything then," she said and I could tell she was afraid of making demands on me like that, but it would have been a dumb move on her part to give up the information I needed before the cash was in her hands.

"I'll be there within the hour." I hung up with my heart pounding excitedly. Finally, there was something I could do for Winter even if I still wasn't any closer to finding her.

I pushed myself upright and tugged open the top drawer of my desk, grabbing a thousand dollars in cash and hesitating as I looked at the rest of the money in there before grabbing that too. It was over ten K but I didn't care. If Elsa pulled through on this for me and I got my hands on Duke Polinsky then she'd be getting a ten thousand dollar tip when I was done and she'd have Romero protection for life as a bonus.

The text with her address came through and I wasn't surprised to see that it was out in the lower east part of town, some old apartment block which had a reputation for the clientele being up for sale.

I pulled on a shirt and a pair of jeans, grabbing the nine millimetre glock from my nightstand, followed by the hunting knife which I strapped to my belt before kicking on a pair of solid boots. I didn't care about looking the part of the sophisticated mobster tonight or dressing in my best Romero style, designer label suit. If Frankie hadn't stolen all of my plaid shirts and gotten rid of them then I would have worn one of them. I wanted Duke to know who I was the moment he saw me. I wanted him to realise that I'd come down from my mountain to hunt and destroy him.

I marched through the apartment and banged my knuckles against Frankie's door before tossing it open.

He was bleary eyed and scowling, aiming a gun at my face while he still tried to blink the sleep from his system and took me in with a frown.

"What is it?" he asked, lowering the gun as he recognised me and pushing himself out of bed like he'd already figured out that we had somewhere to be.

"I've got a lead on Duke Polinsky," I explained. "I need you to come with me."

"You know I've always got your back, fratello," he said, getting up and heading to his closet butt naked.

"I don't need you to have my back," I assured him because I wanted no help at all in tearing Duke limb from limb. "I just need a cameraman. Winter will want to see this when I find her."

Frankie snorted a laugh and I turned away from the view of his toned ass, leaning against the doorframe as he got himself dressed.

"Whatever turns you guys on is fine with me," he muttered. "So long as you're not breaking any more of my shit."

I almost smiled at the memory of us trashing Frankie's apartment with our passion, but without my savage girl at my side, it was hard to find joy in anything. Even memories of the two of us together, her safe in my arms, her flesh hot and aching against mine.

I shook my head to clear it and strode away to the kitchen to make coffee. I hadn't slept and I needed the caffeine to help me stay sharp. Duke Polinsky stood no fucking chance against me, but I'd be a fool to underestimate him all the same.

I made myself and Frankie a mug of steaming black coffee each and it burnt my mouth as I drank it down in one long go, settling in my stomach with a heat almost as keen as that of my rage.

Frankie soon appeared, dressed in a sharp suit as usual and accepting the mug of coffee I'd made him with a word of thanks before grabbing a set of keys and leading the way to the elevator which led down to the private parking lot beneath the building.

"Is this lead solid?" Frankie asked, his expression hopeful as bloodlust danced through the air between us.

"Hopefully," I replied, fighting against the urge to get too excited. I needed to contain myself in case this led to nothing like our leads did time and again at the moment.

Frankie just nodded, shooting a text to Enzo and Rocco to keep them in the loop as we descended in the brightly lit box.

When we reached the lot, Frankie led the way to an inconspicuous black Ford at the back of the cold space, with a set of fake plates already in place on it just in case the cops happened to get a lead on it.

I hopped into the passenger seat, loading up the satnav with Elsa's address as he peeled out of the lot and started heading east.

We were silent for the drive, both of us slipping into that dark place within us which allowed us to execute jobs thoroughly and efficiently without letting ourselves get killed. He was like me in that sense, preferring a moment of silence to the brash bragging and fist pumping shit that Rocco and Enzo went in for.

We were soon making our way out of the expensive part of the city, the apartment blocks getting smaller and packed closer together as the streets got narrower and the darkness in the alleyways began to look more ominous.

Elsa's apartment was in a rough neighbourhood and when we pulled up outside her building, the shadows moved with gangs of kids just starting out on their criminal careers, eyeing up the expensive car with interest.

We got out and Frankie looked right at the gang of kids, ignoring the menacing look in their eyes or the way more than a few of them had pulled knives free from pockets and seemed eager for a kill.

"Any of you stronzos know who we are?" he barked at them, moving forward a few steps towards the building and allowing the orange glow of a street lamp to wash down over his face.

Looks were exchanged, mumbles pouring from the lips of the kids lower down the pecking order as their leaders assessed us hungrily.

"Fuck," one of them grunted, his gaze slipping between Frankie and me as the penny dropped. "They're Romeros."

The fight instantly went out of them and Frankie smirked like a self-important douchebag. "Good. You won't mind keeping an eye on my car for me then, will you?" he said, not waiting for an answer as we strode towards the door again.

There was a buzzer, but the door was also broken and hanging open so we headed straight inside and started climbing the dimly lit stairwell.

On the second floor, we walked down a darkened corridor with stained carpets until we came to the right door where I knocked softly so as not to draw too much attention. It was pulled open almost instantly and the dark haired girl we found there blinked up at us nervously before stepping back to allow us to enter. She was vaguely familiar to me, but I couldn't say I'd paid a lot of attention to her when we'd met before. Her gaze snagged on Frankie and I guessed she was trying to get a read on this Romero. I'd already proven myself to be better than a total asshole in her eyes, but he was untested.

"Do you have the cash?" she asked, raising her chin defiantly as I looked around at the little apartment. We'd made it into the living room and there were three doors leading off of it, all closed. It was small but clean and I could tell she took pride in the place. My gaze snagged on a box of baby toys in the corner of the room and she cleared her throat as she moved to stand before it like she didn't want me to see that.

I pulled a roll of hundred dollar bills from my pocket and waved it at her, admiring the fact that she had the balls to demand it even with two of the most dangerous men in the city standing in her home.

She licked her lips but had the good sense not to try and snatch it, adjusting her dark hair over her shoulder as she nodded.

The room was only lit by a lamp and her features were cast in shadows so I reached out to flick on the overhead light, wanting to see the truth clearly in her eyes. She flinched as it came on and my eyes narrowed as I took in the bruises around her throat which marked a perfect hand print against her skin. She had a busted lip and a black eye too and I was willing to bet that hadn't been a part of the deal she'd signed up for from whoever had done it to her.

"This afternoon I got picked up over on Bay Street," she said, not commenting on the bruises and just cutting to the point of this visit. "The guy wanted me for four hours and agreed to my rates but when he took me back to his hotel, it turned out I wasn't there for him. He dropped me off with another guy. Tall, kinda wiry but strong enough to pack a punch when he wanted to and with this stupid ass moustache that made him look like a total dickhead."

I nodded, her description matching up to my mark and anticipation building in me as I waited to hear the rest.

"He...had that look in his eyes when he saw me, the type that girls who have done this job for long enough know to look out for. I would have refused the job if he'd been the one to try and pick me up but once I was there..." Her tongue darted out to lick her busted lip and a growl escaped me as she moved on beyond what he'd done to her, though it had clearly left more of a mark than just the ones I could see on her flesh. "Anyway, his men called him Duke and when I was trying to put myself together afterwards, I saw an envelope on the side with Mr Polinsky on it, so I thought he was probably your-"

The sound of a baby crying from within one of the closed rooms cut her off and she gasped, shooting me and Frankie a fearful look before another door opened and a second girl hurried out. She darted into the room with the crying baby, only sparing us a terrified glance as she ran to hush the child. In her haste she didn't pull the door closed properly and it bounced open again, revealing two cribs inside and a toddler sleeping on a mattress on the floor in the corner. The girl picked up the crying babe and hurried back to close the door between us again with a murmured apology and fear in her eyes.

I frowned deeply, looking back to Elsa as she wrung her hands together.

"I have the name of the hotel and his room number. There was enough of his shit around the place to let me know he wasn't going anywhere today at least," she said hastily, handing over a piece of paper with the information on it.

I took it slowly, exchanging a look with my brother. "Did he do that to you?" I asked her, indicating her bruises and she exhaled slowly before nodding once.

"Some men are that way," she said with a shrug, eyeing us like she was deciding whether or not we were those kinds of men before seeming to decide we weren't and relaxing a little.

My muscles bunched with the desire to punch something and a furious noise left my throat.

"I'm going to kill him," I said in a low voice, not giving a shit that it wasn't a great idea to admit that to some random girl, but I wanted her to know he wouldn't be getting away with this shit. "For hurting the girl I love and for hurting you too. He'll beg for death before I'm done with him."

Her eyes widened but it wasn't with fear, just surprise and gratitude as she realised I meant it. And that it was the reason for me wanting him dead. I purely wanted to remove the piece of shit predator from the face of the earth and make sure that he couldn't hurt a single soul ever again.

"You live here with that other girl?" Frankie asked, drawing my attention to him and away from the rage burning inside of me.

"She's my sister," Elsa muttered. "We take it in turns to watch the kids and work the streets.

My gaze slid to the closed door where the baby had stopped crying and the low sound of her sister singing just made it to us.

"You're attractive," Frankie commented, assessing her with a clinical kind of gaze. "You could fetch a higher price with a better standard of clientele. What are you working with?"

She glanced between the two of us for a moment then tugged her hoodie off, standing before us in her bra with a shrug. Frankie bobbed his chin at her sweatpants and she dropped them too, turning around as he twisted a finger so that he could inspect her ass as well. But he wasn't looking at her like he wanted to fuck her. More like he was assessing her the way he would something he had an interest in from a business perspective.

"You can get dressed again," he said, picking up a pen and a piece of paper from the kitchen worktop and scribbling a phone number on it. "This is the number for a woman called Christy. If you and your sister want to start working with clients who pay better and don't treat women the way you were treated tonight unless they want to take a beating themselves then call her. She'll set you up with an apartment in the centre of the city and approve all of your clients. It means attending dinners and parties and shit like that with them too, but the money is a shit ton better than you get here. She'll set you both up with suitable child care when you're working as well and she'll teach you how to play the role of a socialite so that you can fool everyone into believing it. It's still whoring but it's a lot better than this."

He held out the piece of paper with the number and Elsa gaped at him, like she thought this was some kind of prank.

"Unless you were hoping to leave the sex trade altogether?" he asked curiously, like they were discussing her leaving an office job.

She shook her head, her gaze darting to me for a moment before she snatched the piece of paper from him. "Whoring pays better than anything else we can do for money. But I'm already working for someone and I don't know how I'm supposed to get out of that-"

"Christy will sort all of that for you," Frankie said dismissively. "You just tell her the offer came from me."

Elsa nodded mutely like she didn't even have words for what that offer meant to her and I placed the entire roll of hundred dollar bills down on her kitchen side before the two of us strode from the apartment and closed the door behind us.

"Sometimes I forget that this place is its own slice of hell," Frankie muttered as we headed back downstairs and outside to find our car exactly where we'd left it, the gang members keeping a respectful distance from it while still casting looks its way like they wished they didn't have to leave it alone.

We got in and Frankie set a course straight to the hotel where Duke was staying while I seethed, my muscles flexing and bunching with the desire to finish this thing. I was about to annihilate the last member of the five men to have abused my girl. I'd make him scream and bleed for her and I'd bathe in his blood until I fucking drowned in it.

Before long we were pulling up in the shadows of the hotel parking lot and Frankie turned to look at me. "I say we snatch him and take him somewhere where he can scream as loud as he likes and not a single soul will care," he suggested.

"Sounds good to me," I agreed heavily. I wanted to make this last as long as I could. He owed Winter eighteen months of suffering and I was willing to pay him back for every injury over a course of the night or more.

It didn't take much for us to get inside the hotel unseen. Someone had left the rear door wedged open and we snuck inside, passing by the kitchens and slipping past a cleaner as he set his cart up with supplies from a large closet. I swiped his master keycard from the top of his cart and flashed it at Frankie with a triumphant grin.

We made it to the central stairs and paused, keeping an ear out for the signs of anyone awake, but the place was quiet. It was a nice enough hotel though not exactly high end, but I was willing to bet it wasn't the kind of place where people regularly went missing or ended up with their blood splattered over the walls.

We made it upstairs, moving silently towards Duke's room as we went.

I exchanged a loaded smile with Frankie as I used the keycard to open the door, my heart thundering in anticipation at the idea of waking this motherfucker up and seeing the look in his eyes as he realised his death had come for him.

Frankie took his cellphone from his pocket, smirking at me as he started recording, the light from it illuminating the dim room as I closed in on the bed where my prey lay snoring softly.

Duke turned with a murmur as if he sensed something was wrong and I got a clear look at his face, victory sailing through me as I confirmed it was him.

He was shirtless, the sheets tangled around his waist and spotted with blood which I was willing to bet belonged to Elsa.

He grunted again, shifting on the bed and I didn't waste another moment. My hands wrapped around his throat and I slammed my knee down on his chest as I squeezed tight, making sure not a single sound could escape him as I cut off his oxygen supply and his eyes flew open in alarm.

I smiled down at him as recognition and terror filled his gaze and he bucked and thrashed beneath me, his fists knocking against my sides pathetically before he grabbed my wrists and tried to force me off of him.

But he was no match for me even before I'd gotten the jump on him and his eyes just bugged out wider as he desperately fought for a breath he couldn't take.

"Winter sends her regards," I purred as the strength left his limbs and the fear in his eyes was like a pure adrenaline shot to my heart as he lost consciousness.

I kept my grip on his neck tight until I was sure he was out of it, but released him before he could up and die on me. Oh no, Duke Polinsky wasn't going to get away with a quick, easy, pain-free death like that. He was coming on a little trip with us to a nice, quiet, secluded spot where I was going to take my time making him suffer.

I'd paint myself red in his blood before the night was out and I'd make him beg and plead for forgiveness from my girl. He'd apologise and cry and scream, and when I'd had enough of listening to it, I'd make sure he never laid his hands on anyone else ever again. Especially not my savage girl.

CHAPTER THIRTY FIVE

I was corralled around the house since I'd tried to break a window in the middle of the night and alerted the guards. I cursed myself for not being strong enough, and I was furious for not leaving more marks on the men who'd dragged me back to my room. But none of that came close to the hate I felt towards Ramon Hernandez. Who'd beaten me for trying to escape, who kept me in this house like a wild animal in captivity.

Now, my door was locked between eight pm and eight am the next day and a guard was posted beneath my window during those hours. I was escorted to breakfast by Carlos or one of the other meatheads who Ramon employed. I was watched at all times, never left long enough to hide a knife up my sleeve from the kitchen or sneak around the house to check for weaknesses in his defences.

I had to eat dinner with Ramon daily but apart from that, I rarely saw him. He worked all hours and I had to be thankful for that at least. But I knew I was running out of time before he sent me to some surgeon to remove my scars. And if he got his way, I'd be back in his bed not long after that. I shuddered at the thought as I sat with my back to the wall in my room, waiting to be summoned for dinner. I was glad my scars repulsed him, because they were the only thing keeping his hands off of me. I didn't think Ramon was the type of man who would accept me saying no to his advances. But for now at least, I was safe from that.

As usual, I was coming up with escape ideas to pass the time. Every plan I came up with met a dead end before I could even try and work out the details. Even if I could have gotten beyond the house, the gates were heavily guarded and I doubted I could easily get through one of the fences. But no matter how hopeless it seemed, I refused to accept this fate. I was going to free myself from this trap if it was the last thing I did.

A knock came at the door and I stilled as Ramon stepped into my room in a tuxedo with the scent of cologne hanging around him. My heart lifted at the thought of him going out. I could skip a torturous hour of dinner with him and have more time to think up a plan. Maybe he'd take enough of his lackeys with him to give me more of a chance to get free.

"I have to attend a gala in the city. The mayor will be there with his family, so I need to present a good front. You will accompany me. It is important that I'm seen as a family man and besides that, our friends will be curious about why you haven't been seen out in public yet."

My lips parted in surprise, my heart racing at the idea of getting out of here, of getting another chance to run.

He stepped toward me, his face darkened by shadow. "My men will be guarding every exit and Carlos is going to be personally assigned to watch over you. You will not test me this evening."

Fear crept under my skin at the warning in his tone and I bowed my head as if submitting, but I wasn't. Inside, I was a raging inferno ready to be set free. I didn't care what he did if he caught me, there had to be an opportunity to escape tonight. And the moment I got it, I wasn't going to waste it.

"You will wear this."

I looked up, finding him carrying a navy gown from the closet with long lace sleeves and a high neck. The trailing skirt would mean every one of my scars would be covered and I knew that was no coincidence. My upper lip peeled back as I stood, taking it from him and turning to head into the en-suite.

He caught the crook of my elbow, yanking me back to face him. "Change here. I want to see the extent of your scars," he growled and my throat thickened, but I wasn't going to blink.

I glared at him as I tossed the dress on the bed and pulled off my sweats to reveal my simple black panties and bra. His eyes roamed down my body, taking in the scars with a grimace.

"Turn around," he commanded and though I didn't want to turn my back on this monster, I did, not showing a flicker of fear as I let him see the damage Duke and his men had done to my skin.

His finger pressed to my spine, running down the length of it and my flesh prickled from his touch. "This will all be fixed soon, my darling. You won't have to hide away after that."

I said nothing. I hadn't spoken a word to him since he'd started hitting me and I knew that infuriated him at times, but I wouldn't give in. I was seasoned in this. My silence was a rebellion I could hold firm with and feel that I was at least striking back at him in some small way.

He watched as I did my makeup and hair and I was soon dressed in the gown which covered me up, wearing a pair of silver heels beneath it which were higher than I'd have liked, but I could run on stilts if it meant escaping this bastard before midnight.

He took the huge choker necklace from the vanity unit, winding it around my throat and fastening it in place. "If you try to run off tonight, I will not be pleased. And when I catch you, I may just have to add to your collection of scars, my darling. They are being removed by the surgeon tomorrow anyway." He smiled kindly like he'd just told me he loved me, turning his back on me and leaving my body frozen in a pool of terror. But it didn't deter me from trying to escape. Because I had faced nearly every kind of pain known to mankind and survived. I could risk facing a little more. And it was in his underestimation of me where I found my greatest strength. He would soon learn I didn't break, I never bowed, and he would *not* take my scars.

I followed Ramon from the room and steeled myself as he offered me his arm and I took it. He smiled at me approvingly as he led me downstairs and out the front door where our entourage were waiting. There were four cars total and I knew Ramon hadn't been joking when he said every exit would be covered at the venue. I was just going to have to work my ass off to distract Carlos and find a gap in Ramon's defences.

Ramon guided me into the back of his Rolls Royce and the cars all pulled away, heading down the long drive and through the tall iron gates at the end of it. I gazed out at the snowy countryside as we took winding roads into the heart of Sinners Bay and my pulse leapt and thrashed the whole time. By the time this night was over, I would no longer be in his possession. I vowed that on everything I was.

Ramon spent the journey tapping out emails on his phone and ignoring my existence which was fine by me. But when we arrived on main street and pulled up in front of a huge old theatre, he took my hand and squeezed firmly. "Here." He reached into his jacket and took out two masks, one with navy feathers which matched my dress and another which was plain black. "It's a masked ball," he explained, circling his finger to motion for me to turn around.

I did so, letting him slide the mask over my eyes and secure it in place. When I faced him again, he had his own half-mask in place, making him look like a villain about to rain down chaos.

"Smile, darling," Ramon instructed as Carlos opened the car door in a plain black mask of his own and I was led out of it.

I faked a smile as his grip on my hand became painful as he led me up the stairs. I was swept inside into a glitzy entrance hall and we were guided upstairs to a vast ballroom with chandeliers hanging over tables laid out with silverware and champagne glasses. Ramon led me to one of them and a bunch of people I didn't know jumped up, embracing us and complimenting my dress. I responded with simple nods and smiles, my voice not loosening an inch for them.

"Sasha is still adjusting back into normal life. She only feels comfortable enough to speak with me at the moment," Ramon explained for me and they all cooed and awwed like I was some puppy who'd just gotten home from the vet.

I sat through a meal, picking at the tiny portions of food and zoning out of the boring conversation everyone was having about the stock market, some celebrity who'd put on weight and the new mall opening up a few blocks away.

Carlos stood against the closest wall behind me and I felt his presence like a lurking ghost. One I needed to exorcise pronto.

After our meals, we were led through to another room with a mahogany dance floor and a crescent bar at the end of it. A string quartet were playing music which should have been impossible to dance to but some of the pretentious idiots were managing it, swaying along like their souls thrived on it.

"Carlos, take Sasha to get a drink, I'm going to speak with the mayor," Ramon directed, his gaze on a man with ashy hair and an overly tanned face across the room.

The moment Carlos stepped to my side, Ramon headed away and I glowered at my beefy companion before he pointed me to the bar. The guy had the personality of a turnip and the head of a potato, so at least he wouldn't bother trying to strike up a conversation with me.

We sat side by side at the bar and I remained silent as Carlos ordered me a vodka soda and himself a Jack on the rocks. When our drinks arrived, I snatched his, tossing it down my throat and pushing the vodka soda at him with a raised eyebrow, challenging him to defy me. It burned all the way down and I smiled satisfactorily at the scowl on his face.

He ordered another and the barman glanced between us curiously as he placed it down in front of Carlos. I reached for it again, but Carlos pushed the glass down the bar so it was out of reach, his brows pulling together. He nudged my vodka soda toward me and I tsked.

"Would you like something else, miss?" the barman asked, glancing at my muscular companion curiously.

I nodded, grabbing up a menu and flipping to the shots section. I pointed at the one I wanted with a smirk and the barman chuckled.

"One Redheaded Slut coming up," he said, setting to work making it for me.

When he placed down the little glass full of red liquid in front of me, Carlos tried to swipe it away, but I grabbed it before he could.

"If you get drunk, Ramon will be unhappy," he growled, his voice a deep baritone.

I raised my middle finger as I held the shot, lifting it to my lips so I was flipping him off as I drank it down, the sweet cranberry juice sharpened by the schnapps.

He muttered under his breath in Spanish and I distinctly heard the words *la puta* which I was pretty sure meant he was calling me a bitch, but I didn't give a damn what he thought of me.

I turned my gaze to the room, seeking out the exits and finding each of them manned by one of Ramon's men as promised. I'd have to scout out the restroom soon, but before I did that, I really needed to lose the vegetable following me around.

CHAPTER THIRTY SIX

I strolled through the party with a beautiful girl on my arm and a smile on my lips beneath my elaborate black and gold mask as I took a turn around the room, making sure to take note of every bodyguard and henchman I spotted. It was impossible to say for sure who each of them worked for of course, but it was simple enough to guess that those with a clear eye line to Winter where she sat at the bar were probably working for Hernandez.

I pulled the girl I'd brought with me into my arms. Donna was my second cousin Edwardo's girl and had been for years. The only reason she wasn't officially a Romero yet was because the lazy fucker still hadn't popped the question. But I'd promised her that I'd put the pressure on him for a big fat summer wedding with all the family if she helped me out tonight, so here we were.

She wrapped her arms around my neck and laughed loudly as we began to dance and I subtly sent messages to Rocco and Enzo, pointing out the positions of the men I'd spotted so that they knew where to direct our people. Groups of excitable partiers soon appeared as if randomly, some of them sporting masks with huge plumes of feathers which concealed the bodyguards' views of our target as they stopped in the perfect position to block their sight of her.

It really had been nice of Duke to start squealing before he died. He'd told us all about Winter's identity before he'd kidnapped her and how he'd been paid to get a code from her which led to something important. He'd even been good enough to explain how her husband was one of the higher-ups in the Dominguez Cartel and how their family was supposed to be untouchable.

My own contacts within the Santiago Cartel had already informed me of the war taking place between all of them, though most of it wasn't conducted on American soil. But it turned out that there were a few things they knew about their rivals and Hernandez was on their radar. They'd been only too happy to relay information to me about him, hoping that we might just kill him for them and save them some effort in the matter. Turned out he was working on a major import scheme which he wanted to run through the Sinners Bay docks. To do that though he really needed to have some political sway around here and it just so happened the mayor was looking for donors tonight at this big charity event.

Couple that with the fact that I knew full well that Mayor Hythe was up for sale because he was well and truly in our pockets already and it hadn't been hard to assume that Hernandez would show his face. To make it even better, the mayor was big on family this year after his opposition was caught fucking a hooker on camera and cheating on his wife, so he'd made this whole thing a family event and put a heavy emphasis on spouses coming to support the cause with their wealthy husbands. We'd hoped that our guesses would pay off and the moment I'd set eyes on Winter, I'd known that they had.

My friendly Santiago Cartel buddies had also kindly given me a run down of the way Hernandez's security detail operated, so I was pretty confident that we could work around them assuming this all came together. It wasn't like we could just come in here guns blazing and take her back by force with half of the state's police in attendance and the press taking photographs at every opportunity either, so we had to be smart about his.

Donna excused herself to the ladies room with a knowing smile and I made my way to the bar, stumbling a little as if I was drunk and taking a spot right beside the big stronzo who was babysitting Winter.

Nicoli's girl wasn't looking my way, her gaze skimming over the people at the far end of the bar instead as she seemed to be focusing on anything other than the guy sat beside her. But that was for the best, because the last thing we needed was her recognising me and him realising it before I'd had the chance to take him out of action.

The moment my ass hit the bar stool, a seriously hot brunette appeared at my side, leaning in close and whispering into my ear suggestively, being loud enough to be overheard by the henchman who cast a curious look our way as she begged for a taste of my cock.

Natalia had spent a week fucking me last year and she was one of the best I'd had, so it was almost tempting to really take her up on that offer, but then I remembered the way she'd started to push for more than just sex from me and I easily dismissed the idea again. I didn't need that drama in my life. This shit with Nicoli and Winter was only proving it. Falling in love with a girl while I was in my line of work meant putting her at risk. And I had no intentions of ever quitting the family business, so why do it to her or to myself? It wasn't something I felt I was missing in my life and if I could go without that kind of love then I was happy to do so. I preferred to be the man with nothing to lose.

"How much for a night with me and my wife?" I asked, loud enough to keep the meathead's attention on us.

"For you pretty boy? Five grand," Natalia said, wrapping her arms around my neck and leaning in to kiss me.

She moaned into my mouth as I fisted my hand into her hair and I dragged her against me. Natalia responded, kissing me in a way that was way too dirty for a swanky party like this and I grabbed her ass, pulling her between my legs where I still sat on the stool so that I could grind her against my swelling cock. I hadn't gotten laid since all this stuff with Winter had happened as I'd been dedicating myself to helping my brother with his hunt, but I was getting a serious case of blue balls and I couldn't help but take advantage of this little game we were playing to take just a sliver of relief from the dry spell.

"What the fuck, Harrison?" Donna yelled as she reappeared from her supposed restroom break and I hastily pushed Natalia out of my lap as I made some shitty excuses to my fake wife and we drew a shit ton of attention.

She swore at me in Italian and I had to fight a smile at the creativity of her cursing as I put on a show of begging forgiveness and swearing she was my one and only before letting my gaze fall on Natalia's ass as she walked away from us.

Donna took a swing at me and I cursed as her knuckles cracked into my jaw, my gaze heating with real anger for a moment as I tasted blood and her eyes flared with that damn Italian temper. I'd been really fucking clear when I'd told her she could slap me and made it abundantly clear I didn't want her punching me in the face. But I should have fucking known she'd do it. Last year I'd tossed her in the pool at our second cousin Luigi's birthday party right after she'd gotten her hair done and she'd sworn she'd get revenge. Crazy lupa.

"You can come by the house for your crap in the morning!" Donna yelled dramatically, reaching out to snatch the big-ass bodyguard's drink from the bar beside me before tossing it straight in my face and storming off into the crowd.

I cursed her as I turned back to the bar, leaning close to the bodyguard and apologising profusely, making sure I slurred my words and ordering him a replacement drink from the bartender.

Winter's eyes were on me now too and as I spared her a glance I could tell she was frowning, trying to figure out if she really did recognise me beneath this mask or not.

The bartender placed two glasses of Jack Daniels down before me and I reached out to grab the one intended for the bodyguard, placing my hand flat over the top of it as I dropped the little pill inside and slid the drink over to my new best friend.

"To crazy bitches," I said, raising my glass at him as he seemed caught between finding me amusing and annoying and he half-heartedly lifted his glass too.

"To crazy bitches," he echoed, glancing at Winter pointedly before tossing his drink back and swallowing the lot.

It was so nice of his boss to give me the idea of drugging him like that. Little bitch moves weren't my usual go-to, but I had to admit that I experienced a fucked up sense of satisfaction as I watched the motherfucker seal his own fate with one big gulp just like they'd done to my brother.

I bid him goodnight and pushed away from the bar, stumbling off like the drunk he believed me to be and falling back against the bar just as I passed Winter.

I dropped the cellphone I'd had hidden up my sleeve into her lap and leaned in close to her for a moment, just long enough to breathe a message into her ear.

"Your mountain man says hi."

She turned to look at me sharply but I was slurring another apology and stumbling away already as the jumbo sized henchman got to his feet like he intended to rearrange my face for getting close to her.

I risked a single look back before the crowd swallowed me and grinned at the look of shock on her face beneath the delicate mask she was wearing.

My part had gone down perfectly. Now I had to hope that the others could be so flawless for their parts of the plan.

CHAPTER THIRTY SEVEN

I gazed after Frankie with my heart in my throat, hope ripping through my soul like a tsunami. Was he here to rescue me like some sort of drunk hero who'd go to hell and back for their kin? Or was he here just to give me this phone?

It was now tucked up my sleeve and I needed to get away to look at it as soon as possible. But as I turned my gaze to Carlos to tell him I wanted to go to the restroom, he face-planted the bar with a gut-wrenching crack. I gasped in alarm and looked over to the barman, but luckily he was serving someone else and no one had noticed this ten ton wildebeest passing out. The crowd jostled around us with drinks in hand, laughing merrily, too wrapped up in their social bubbles to have realised what had happened.

I looked around as if hunting for an answer to what had just happened. Then it all came together. Frankie had bought Carlos that drink. He must have drugged him. I swallowed a laugh of excitement as I got up, not wasting a second of the gift Frankie had bought me as I slipped away into the crowd, crossing the room in the direction of the restrooms. I slipped away from the throng of bodies and into a short corridor that led to two doors. I pushed into the ladies room, moving across the cream tiles and past the golden sinks before pushing into a cubicle. I locked the door, my breaths coming heavily and life rushing into my veins like ecstasy. I couldn't stop smiling as I put the toilet seat down, perching on it and inspecting the phone Frankie had given me.

I checked the messages first but there was nothing there, then the numbers, but the contact list was empty. I frowned, moving to the only other possibility as I opened the photo albums and I found one video waiting for me. I pressed play and my heart stammered at the sight of Nicoli standing in front of the camera. His face was flecked with blood and there was a darkness in his eyes which I'd missed on a base level. I bit my lip as he stared directly into the lens, my heart beating wildly as desire flooded me.

"This is for you, baby doll." He stepped aside and I got a view of Duke strapped to a chair in what looked like an abandoned warehouse, his crotch stained with urine and his face beaten bloody. It was him, my demon, my tormentor. *Oh my god, Nicoli found him.*

Hatred made my upper lip peel back and I watched, barely blinking as I refused to miss a single second of this. Because if Nicoli had gotten to him, that could only mean one thing. Duke was dead.

Nicoli took a hunting knife from his hip and I watched as he cut Duke apart piece by piece, my bloodlust rising, practically salivating as I devoured his demise. I had to turn the volume down so as not to draw attention to myself if anyone came into the restroom, but I made sure I heard his screams all the same, each one breaking an invisible chain on my soul and releasing me from The Five at long last. Nicoli was merciless, cold and driven with the ferocity I'd seen up on that mountain. Back when it had just been us and revenge, when our lives had been simple in a way I missed so goddamn much.

I starved for him as I watched every muscle in his body turn against my enemy. When it was nearly done, whoever was recording brought the camera close to Duke's face, his body now on the floor and his blood glistening around him in an ever-growing pool.

"Apologise," Nicoli snarled, pressing his foot down on Duke's chest.

Duke could barely speak through the swelling of his face, but his lips parted and he grunted out the word *sorry* pathetically.

"Say it to her!" Nicoli pointed at the camera and Duke's brown eyes fixed on the lens. On me.

"Sorry red," he rasped. "Just business."

Duke started haemorrhaging, choking and turning blue as he jerked on the ground.

One sharp kick from Nicoli broke his neck with a finality that made me drag down a lungful of air. I was sure I'd never breathed so deeply or so easily. Duke was dead. The last of my nightmares would shatter with him. I was free. And yet...I wasn't. I was still held by Ramon, but not for long. *I have to get out of here.*

I stood, lifting my dress and tucking the phone into the top of my suspenders to hide it then dropped my skirt and turned to look up at the wall above me. No window.

I growled under my breath, pushing out of the stall and thankfully finding the room empty as I checked every cubicle for a window, but there was none.

Shit.

The door flew open and Ramon strode in with his eyes like pitch. I acted fast, dropping my hands into the nearest sink as I washed them, my heart crashing into my ribcage.

"Where is Carlos?" he hissed, glancing at the stalls like his eight foot guard might appear out of a toilet.

I shrugged, not giving him my voice as I glared coolly at him. He strode forward, gripping my arm and staring down his nose at me.

"Drop the attitude, Sasha."

I bared my teeth at him, hissing like a wildcat and he shook me in fury. The door opened and a couple of women walked in, gasping as they spotted Ramon there.

Ramon looped his arm around my waist, planting his mouth on mine and I winced as I tried to draw away, but he gripped the back of my head so I couldn't.

"Forgive us," he told the women as he broke the kiss. "I can't keep my hands off of her since my wife was returned to me."

"Aww," one of the woman cooed and the other smiled at me with jealousy in her eyes. But if she wanted Ramon she could have him, his house, his army of assholes and she could have my ugly ass dress too.

He guided me out of the room and we strode along the corridor back to the party.

"You'd better not be up to anything, my darling," Ramon spoke into my ear, pressing a kiss to my temple and my gut churned.

"Ramon! Come speak with Sergio Vladisk," the mayor called as he spotted us, beckoning him over.

Ramon nodded keenly then guided me over to another one of his guards who I was fairly sure was called Juan and placed me in his arms. "Dance with my girl, keep her occupied."

"Sure thing, boss," he said and Ramon kissed my cheek, leaving my flesh pulsing like I'd been stung there by a bee as he hurried away to join the mayor.

Juan couldn't dance, but apparently I could, the waltz now playing awakening some muscle memory in me as I guided him around the room instead of the other way around. Despite my dance skills, I purposefully stepped on Juan's feet time and again, batting my lashes at him as he cursed under his breath and tried to keep up with me.

A man suddenly cut into the dance in a black mask, with eyes that looked directly into my soul. My heart stopped beating, my breath caught and my whole world tipped on its axis. He shouldered Juan out the way who grunted before stepping off of the dance floor and watching me from there instead, seeming glad of the excuse to stop dancing with me.

Nicoli's hands wrapped around me, tugging me close as we spun around the room in perfect sync with one another.

"Hey baby doll," he breathed in my ear and I clutched him tighter, my hand sliding up the back of his neck as I just drank in his hazelnut scent and my face grazed against the stubble on his jaw.

"You came for me," I whispered.

"I'd face every force of nature on this earth to free you, Winter," he growled low and deep, sending a shiver through me that made me pant.

I looked into his dark eyes and drank in every golden fleck in them, my soul seeming to connect with his. But there was one thing I still needed to confirm. "That girl I saw you with-"

"I was set up," he cut me off instantly. "Drugged." He didn't elaborate, but his eyes moved to Ramon across the room and if hatred could sear flesh then my husband would have been barbecued by now. It didn't surprise me that that bastard was responsible, but it awoke a fresh kind of rage in me that longed to be sated. "I would never touch another woman, you're my one and only, Winter. The one I'd seek out in every crowd in every part of the world, who I'd know in any form."

"I'm your penguin," I breathed and he chuckled.

"Nah, baby doll. You're no penguin. You're a snowflake. Unique in every fucking way. I found you in a snowstorm, I'd recognise you anywhere. There will never be another like you."

Tears pricked my eyes and my chest swam with love. "I knew you wouldn't betray me," I said, my heart lifting at knowing I'd been right. That Nicoli Romero was mine and I was his. No one or nothing could change that.

"Did you watch the video?" he asked, that darkness twisting in his eyes again and lighting up my soul with pleasure. I fisted my hand in his suit jacket, biting down on my lip as I nodded.

He smiled like a psycho and I loved that. I loved that he would kill and butcher for me. I loved that he wasn't a good man and that he would fight bloody battles and tear through the black hearts of my enemies to reach me. Always. And I would do the same for him.

"Thank you," I breathed, longing to seal those words with a kiss.

"I'm getting you out of here, savage girl," he swore and I believed him with every fibre of my being.

I'd spent so long in the dark, countless days in pain, screaming while no one could hear. I'd once believed that I wasn't worth saving, that there was no knight in shining armour coming to save this damsel in distress. But I'd forgotten one thing. I'd never been a damsel, so a knight could never save me. I was a savage girl with a heart of steel. My saviour was a bare-chested villain who would set the world on fire to keep me in his arms. And the intensity in his eyes said he was about to strike the first match.

CHAPTER THIRTY EIGHT

One thing I couldn't curse Giuseppe Calabresi for was the classical education he'd extended to me. The elitist private school he'd enrolled me in had taught me everything from foreign languages to playing the guitar to countless sports including swordsmanship and boxing, and had even ensured that I could dance at an event like this with the ease of someone who'd been doing it for years. And as I led Winter around the ballroom in my arms, her heavy skirt swinging around her, I could at least be grateful to him for that one thing.

My gaze kept roaming over her features like I might be able to tell everything about what had been happening to her during these weeks we'd been parted just from looking at her.

As we swept around the floor again, my gaze caught on the bodyguard I'd snatched her from just as Frankie appeared beside him and I spotted the syringe in his hand a moment before he stabbed it into the man's thigh. There was no way to be subtle with that particular attack, but Frankie had already thrown an arm around his neck, his hand slapping over the guy's mouth when he started to shout out and a group of Romero employed girls crowded close around them for a moment as the drug took effect.

By the time the girls moved aside, Frankie had made it to a shadowy corner where he was settling the guy down in a chair and positioning him to look like he'd merely passed out from over indulging.

No one seemed to notice the exchange and I grinned down at my savage girl as I felt her eyes on my face.

"What's your plan?" she breathed, her green eyes taking me captive and the desperate need to kiss her almost overwhelming me. But I couldn't afford to be distracted. Her husband was still talking to the mayor, but his attention would turn this way again soon enough.

Frankie had managed to work a small miracle and with a considerable donation from Martello, he'd acquired twenty invitations for tonight's ball which had been dished out to people he trusted for the various roles our night of scheming would require.

"Just follow our lead, baby doll," I murmured. "We'll get you free of him before you know it."

She opened her lips to ask how again, but there wasn't time for me to tell her.

As we made it to the darkened corner of the dance floor, my grip on Winter's waist tightened briefly, wanting to keep her in my arms more than anything despite understanding how the plan required her to leave me again now.

I twirled her under my arm and as she spun away from me, Rocco caught her other hand from the edge of the crowd. Her green gaze caught mine in surprise and a little fear for a moment, but I gave her a firm nod as I released her.

Another hand quickly replaced hers in mine and I tugged my new partner close as Sloan twisted into my arms and I moved her around the dance floor as if nothing at all had happened.

"We have her now," she breathed, her hand resting lightly on my shoulder as her gaze found mine. "Before you know it we'll be clear of this place."

I offered her a tight smile as I led her around the room, her silver mask catching the light as the music wove a spell over this whole place.

"I won't relax until I have her home again, safe in my arms and away from this party and that man," I growled, my grip tightening on Sloan's waist as I imagined choking the asshole out.

"God save the man who tries to come between a Romero and his woman," she said teasingly, offering me a warm smile as her fingers squeezed mine where I held her hand for the dance. "I'm pleased for you, Nicoli," she added in a low tone. "So pleased you found Winter and happiness with her after everything that happened between us and the wedding-"

I looked down into her dark eyes and offered a mocking smile. "One of the first things I came to terms with alone on that mountain was the fact that you had never been meant for me," I assured her. "I don't mean it to sound harsh, but I didn't miss you or pine for you like I have for Winter since she was taken from me. I care about you and I want you to be safe, but knowing you were with a man who loved you was enough for me to make peace with it."

"And there was me thinking I'd broken your heart," she teased and I scoffed.

"Bullshit. You're just surprised to find I had one after all."

Her laughter was loud and uninhibited, not like the preening socialites who surrounded us and I smirked as I whirled her back around the room to the place where I'd left Winter. The music came to an end and we stepped off of the dance floor, exchanging a conspiratorial look as we headed for the staircase which led up to the mezzanine level above us.

Enzo strode down the steps towards us with a girl on each arm and a whole entourage of girls at his back. He'd chosen to wear a black batman mask despite how prestigious this event was supposed to be and he grinned around the room as he drew more than a few shocked looks. Add to that the fact that the eight girls surrounding him really weren't doing the best job of covering up their usual occupations as high end call girls with their plunging necklines and constant sexual jokes and he was causing quite a scene. Of course, that was exactly what we'd wanted him to do, so it worked for our plan but the look he was giving me said he had intentions to move this party back to his place once our work here was done.

We strode straight towards him and his entourage and the girls quickly surrounded us on the stairs, giving me the chance to strip off my black mask and tie a plain red one to my face instead, giving me a different look to the man seen dancing with Winter a few moments ago.

"He's looking for her," Enzo said, leaning close to speak to me as the girls all made a lot of noise, giggling and preening around us and hiding us from close inspection by anyone who might be looking. "His men are on the prowl, but so far he's not panicking."

"We'd better hurry up then," I said, clapping a hand on his shoulder and continuing up the stairs with Sloan on my arm.

She gave me a reassuring smile as Enzo's group split apart around us and continued down the stairs while we climbed again.

At the top of the sweeping staircase, we turned left onto the mezzanine and I had to fight to keep my pace measured. Frankie was leaning over the railing which surrounded the upper level, looking down at the dancers below and he subtly pointed to his left with a twitch of his thumb. I followed the direction he'd indicated with my eyes and saw the man there who was pushing between the crowd, hurrying along and giving off the distinct impression that he was looking for something.

A waiter passed by with flutes of champagne and Sloan and I took one as we stopped walking and waited for the all clear. The henchman kept going through the crowd, pushing his way through the doors which led out to the balcony which fronted the building and leaving us free to move again.

I left my champagne on an empty table and Sloan followed suit as we slipped away between the press of bodies, heading for the darkened corridor leading away from the corner of the room.

I cast a glance over my shoulder before stepping into it and Sloan bit her lip as we hurried along the carpeted floors.

We rounded a corner and I caught her arm, making her wait as I paused to make sure that no one had followed us.

Sloan nervously chewed on her lip as we maintained the silence and I waited with nothing but the heavy beat of my heart to hear above the noise of the party we'd just left.

Once I was sure no one was following us, we hurried on, slipping along the corridor and jogging down a back staircase so that we could head towards the party once more from downstairs.

Before we could reach the ballroom again, we fell still beside a small restroom with an out of order sign hanging from the door.

I checked the corridor once more then pushed the door open, coming face to face with Rocco who looked ready to murder anyone who tried to come in here.

His face split into a wide grin as he recognised us and we moved into the small space quickly.

There were only two toilet stalls and one large vanity unit with a sink set into the marble top, but they'd spent a lot of money making it luxurious. I'd never really understood the need for such lavish surroundings for a place where people just came to take a shit, but I guessed it was better than walking into some piss-stinking, green tiled monstrosity.

Winter leapt at me the moment the door swung closed behind me, her arms curling around my neck as she crushed me against her and held me like she never wanted to let go again. I wanted to lift her into my arms but as I gripped her ass to pick her up, the tightness of her full skirt stopped her from wrapping her legs around me and I just ended up holding her against my chest, her feet several inches from the ground as she half laughed and half sobbed into my neck.

"I just got done telling your girl about the way her husband almost killed you by spiking your drink and then made that hooker climb you like a pole to put on a show for her," Rocco explained and I wrenched myself away from Winter with some difficulty, setting her back on her feet so that I could

427

look at her.

"I've got you, baby doll," I promised her, twisting a finger through one of her red curls as I drank in the sight of her.

There was still a sense of hesitancy between us, like we both needed to know exactly what the other had been doing in the weeks we'd been parted, but we had no time to ask the questions which sat on our tongues.

"Time for the strip show," Rocco joked and Sloan moved to put her back to him so that he could unzip her dress.

"What are you doing?" Winter breathed, frowning as Sloan dropped the dress to her feet and carefully stepped out of it.

"I'm going to be the decoy," Sloan explained with a mischievous grin as she stood there in her underwear and opened her purse to take out the red wig she had hidden in there inside a vacuum sealed bag.

As she took it out and started work on fixing it over her black bun, I gently turned Winter around and began unbuttoning her dress for her.

"You look edible no matter what you're wearing, savage girl," I breathed as my fingers skimmed down her spine and a shiver followed in response to my touch. "But this dress is fucking hideous."

Instead of the laugh I expected, she turned her head so that she could look at me over her shoulder.

"Not as hideous as my scars apparently," she explained and I could see the flash of hurt and hatred in her eyes at admitting the reason for her wearing this heap of fabric.

"Fuck anyone who thinks that," I snarled, anger coursing through me at the reason for her wearing this thing. "Your scars only enhance your beauty, my savage girl. Don't ever let anyone tell you otherwise."

She nodded firmly then reached up and unhooked the heavy choker necklace from her throat, tossing it to the floor and stamping her heel on it.

I ached to lean forward and kiss her, but with Hernandez already on the hunt, we didn't have time to waste. Sloan and Rocco needed to get the fuck out of here as fast as possible.

I finally undid enough of the dress to be able to pull it off of her and I groaned with longing as I took her in, standing there in her underwear.

"Let us get out of here first, stronzo," Rocco barked. "Then you'll have twenty minutes to kill however the fuck you like."

I cursed him half-heartedly as I offered Winter's dress to Sloan, not looking at her as my gaze stayed fixed on my girl. Sloan switched the dresses over and I offered her green satin piece to Winter instead. She took it, holding it to her chest just as Sloan started cursing.

"What in the hell is this fugly thing?" she said as a Rocco began buttoning her into it and I couldn't help but laugh as I glanced over at her in the swathes of navy material which looked more suited to being worn by a great grandmother at a funeral than a beautiful woman at an elaborate ball.

"I'll rip it off of you with my teeth when we get home and show you how sexy it can be, principessa," Rocco promised her and she laughed as she adjusted her red wig, casting glances at Winter's hair so that she could style it as similarly as possible.

"You're going to make him follow you?" Winter gasped as she fully grasped what was going on and Sloan offered her a reassuring smile.

"Yeah, but don't worry about me, I've got a flick knife ready to go and the most aggressive guard dog in the city holding my hand." She smiled at Rocco as he finished buttoning her dress and pressed a kiss to her lips hungrily.

"Damn straight you do, wife," he said to her. "And I think I'll let you keep that wig on when we get home too, I can pretend to be shocked that it's not your natural colour when I get between your thighs."

Sloan smacked him as she feigned acting outraged and he nipped at her ear with a possessive growl that said he was only half joking. Sloan took Winter's mask from her, leaving her own beside the sink as she completed her transformation and I was left looking at every perfect inch of my savage girl's beautiful face at last.

"Time to go," I said firmly, grabbing my brother by the shoulder and shoving him towards the door.

"Okay, okay," Rocco agreed, holding his arm out for Sloan and wrapping it around her waist as she stepped into him. "I'll text you once we make it outside with them tailing us. Fabio has the getaway car warmed up across the street. We'll meet you back at Frankie's when it's done."

"Good luck," I said seriously, looking between the two of them as they headed out of the restroom again and the door slowly swung closed behind them.

Silence hung thick and heavy in their wake and I slowly turned to look back at my savage girl.

It had been so long since we'd seen each other, too long since we'd been alone and every single moment that I'd spent hunting for her, aching for her, just seemed to lead me to this. And now I didn't know what to say or do first to show her just how much she meant to me.

Neither of us said a word and the air in the small room seemed to grow heavy with expectation as we just looked at each other, drinking one another in and tasting the desire that was building between us.

Winter still gripped Sloan's dress to her chest, but her fingers slowly loosened on the fabric until she dropped it and it slipped down over the curves of her body like a spill of water so that she was left before me in her matching black bra and thong. She swore a set of suspenders with a garter belt securing them over her panties and the sky-high heels she wore made her legs look longer than ever. The cellphone Frankie had given her was tucked in the top of one of them and I smirked at it.

"I missed you more than words can say, baby doll," I breathed, my throat thick and my words rough with lust.

"Show me how much," she replied, her voice catching as her chest rose and fell heavily.

My gaze roamed over her and I took a step closer, then another, until there was nothing but an inch dividing our bodies and that space was filled with the heavy pants of our needy breaths.

"I feel like a poor man standing before his queen when I look at you,"

I said to her. "Like I'm staring at something so much purer and better than me and that I'm sullying you just by being in your presence. Like I'm making you dirty just by thinking about all the ways I want to worship you."

"Then make me dirty, mountain man," she begged breathily, still not touching me. "Make me feel the weight of the crown you'd place upon my head."

I kept my eyes on hers before slowly dropping my mouth to her collar bone where a crescent shaped scar marked her flesh and I ran my tongue along the length of it.

She gasped as I kissed it and I groaned at that sound escaping her, my dick swelling in my pants as I ached for more of her. All of her.

My mask bumped against her skin as my mouth moved over her flesh but when I lifted a hand to pull it off, she stopped me with a hungry groan. Like she wanted me to keep it on, a devil in a red mask painting her body in sin.

I knew I should have been paying attention to the door behind me, but we had to stay in here for the plan to work and we had time to kill. I'd waited so long to have her with me again that I was helpless to ignore this need in me or that in her too. We could be quick. And we both needed this too much to deny it.

My mouth moved to the next scar on her flesh and I kissed that too, moving my mouth over it slowly, tasting her skin and kissing every little bit of proof of just how strong she was. I hated and loved those scars in equal measure. I hated how they reminded me of all she'd suffered and yet I loved the strength each one of them had taken to survive. I loved the way she wore them like a warrior, proud of the fire in her belly and the strength of her soul and I needed her to know how much I appreciated each of them, how I saw them for exactly what they symbolised and how they only made her more beautiful in my eyes.

I moved lower, finding each mark on her flesh by memory alone and she pressed her hands to the wall behind her as she fought off the desire to touch me in response, bathing in the way I was worshiping her instead and allowing me to take my time in getting reacquainted with every single inch of her body.

When I got low enough, I dropped to my knees before her and tipped my head back to look up at her as she panted above me.

"Tell me you still want me like you used to, savage girl," I begged her, my hands curling around her thighs as my whole body began to tremble with anticipation.

My dick was hard as iron in my pants and I was aching for her in a way I knew couldn't possibly be sated by us coming together once, but I was sure as hell going to try if she wanted me to.

"Don't be gentle with me, Nicoli," she warned. "I don't want the refined man the world sees when they look at you. I want the brutal beast who killed for me. I want the man covered in the blood of my enemies and I want to forget that my name was ever Sasha and to just be your savage girl."

My gaze darkened at her words and my heart pounded to a wild beat as I stood again suddenly, sliding my grip to the backs of her thighs and hoisting her off of her feet. I kicked open the door to the toilet stall beside us and carried her inside, locking the door with a flick of my fingers before slamming her back into the wall. My lips met hers in a fervent, desperate, dirty kiss that was all tongue and teeth and need.

Her legs curled tight behind my back and I gripped her ass with one hand to hold her up before moving the other between us and groaning as I found her panties soaked for me.

I shoved the drenched material aside, meeting with the hot, wet, heat of her pussy and driving two fingers deep inside her, causing her to cry out.

I hushed her with another kiss, tasting blood as she bit down on my bottom lip and I drove my fingers in and out of her mercilessly, my thumb riding her clit as her thighs tightened around me and her nails dug into my back.

On the fourth deep thrust of my fingers, her pussy clamped tight around me and she screamed into my mouth, only the ferocity of my kiss stopping her voice from echoing all around the restroom.

"Shit baby, when was the last time you had an orgasm?" I accused, speaking against her lips as I unbuckled my pants and gave her a moment to recover. Because if she thought that had been intense then she had no idea what I wanted from her.

"I thought about it all the time," she breathed. "I even tried touching myself while I was thinking of you and remembering the two of us together. But that house he held me in felt like a prison, like I was locked up just as I had been with The Five and I just couldn't let go for long enough to find my release."

"Looks like I've got some making up to do then," I growled, freeing my cock from my pants and guiding it to her core.

She moaned as I rubbed it against her opening, coating the head in the evidence of her desire and looking into her green eyes as she squirmed in my arms, begging me to do it.

"Tell me baby doll," I growled, holding myself back through pure force of will as my dick ached for the feeling of just how tight I knew she'd be once I made it inside of her. "Are you going to be able to keep quiet?"

Her eyes widened as she thought about it and she slowly shook her head, disappointment filling her gaze like she thought that might equal the end of it.

I smirked at her as I released my cock, leaving the head pressed to her opening and flexing my hips just a little so that it flirted with the line of being inside her and not. I tugged my tie loose and pulled it free of my collar, balling it in my fist and pushing it into her mouth as her eyes widened with excitement.

The moment her mouth was full, I slammed into her, my fingers biting into her ass and her scream was muffled around my tie.

I didn't give her a moment to adjust as I used one hand to grip the top of the toilet stall and the other to hold her up, pounding my hips forward again and again until her screams were so loud even around the gag that I was almost certain we'd be heard.

I grunted as her pussy gripped my shaft, milking me and urging me on, the bite of her fingernails in my back begging for more and more no matter how hard I slammed into her.

She cried out again as another orgasm ripped through her and I groaned as her muscles gripped my cock in an iron hold, begging me to follow her into oblivion, but I wasn't done yet. I needed more than this, more of her.

I dropped her feet to the floor as I pulled out of her, spinning her around as I flattened her against the wall and parted her legs, driving myself into her again. I slipped a hand around her, running my fingers over her clit as I started up a merciless pace and slapping my other hand over her mouth on top of the gag as she started screaming again.

I was fairly certain no one would come in here with the sign on the door, but if Ramon was searching for her we couldn't risk him hearing her in here. I probably should have stopped, but I needed her so fucking much that I couldn't even if I'd had the slightest inclination to.

Her hips flexed into the movement of mine, her ass grinding against my body as I drove myself into her as hard as I could. But I wanted to see her, to watch her eyes as I brought her to ruin and know that I really did own every piece of her as I did it.

But there wasn't the room in here to have her the way I ached to and I needed more.

I cursed as I pulled my cock out of her again, flicking the lock on the door and dragging her out with me before bending her over the sink so that I could see her in the mirror. As my gaze fell on our reflection, I realised I still had the damn mask on but the moment I reached for it, Winter shook her head, tugging the tie from her mouth so that she could speak.

"Leave it," she breathed, biting her lip as her gaze locked with mine in the reflection and she pushed her ass back against my dick with a hungry moan.

I laughed darkly as I left the mask where it was, gripping my shaft and guiding my dick to the centre of her, waiting as she pushed the tie back into her mouth and gripped the sink tightly in anticipation.

"Ready, baby doll?" I asked her as she looked back at me, her eyes two emerald pools of lust and her teeth clamping down on the red tie.

I kept my gaze fixed on hers as I took hold of her hips and drove into her again, the new position allowing me to get even deeper as she pushed her ass back into me, feeling every inch with a hungry moan which had my dick getting even harder.

My hands tightened around her hips and I knew I was going to bruise her with this, but the marks I was going to leave were those of a devout servant worshiping his queen.

I pulled back and slammed into her again, groaning at how tight she was, how perfect she felt and the look in her eyes as she took every inch of me almost had me coming already. I started moving faster and faster, my pace punishing and brutal as I gripped her hips and she let me control every moment of it.

Winter gripped the edge of the sink so hard her knuckles turned white and her moans around the gag were the most seductive kind of music I'd ever heard.

As she tightened around me again, my dick pulsed and thickened and as she screamed through another orgasm, a deep, guttural groan left me too and I spilled myself deep inside her.

I fell forward over her, reaching out to tug the gag from her lips as I pulled her around for an awkward kiss.

"I love you so much, Winter," I murmured against her mouth.

"I love you, Nicoli," she replied. "I never want to be away from you again."

I slowly eased my dick out of her and she moaned softly as she remained where she was for a moment, panting over the sink. I finally tugged the mask from my face, passing her some tissues to clean up and she did so with a coy grin before slipping on the green dress Sloan had left for her and making some attempt to fix her hair and makeup. But I'd done a pretty good job of fucking it up and with her lips swollen and puffy and her pupils full blown with desire, I didn't think she'd be fooling anyone into thinking she was innocent any time soon.

I buckled my belt, some of the tension in my body relaxing after what we'd just done, but I couldn't really relax. Not until I'd gotten her out of here.

I checked the time on my phone and frowned as I realised it had been more than twenty minutes already. Rocco should have confirmed that they'd led Ramon's men away by now. I was sure they wouldn't have wasted any time hanging around.

I was about to send him a message myself when the sound of raised voices came from beyond the door and I quickly grabbed Winter's hand, tugging her behind me.

If it came down to it, I'd fight our way out of here with my fists alone. There was no fucking way I'd let him take her from me again.

"Stay behind me," I breathed as the voices got closer and she did as I asked, taking shelter in my shadow just as the door was thrown open and everything went to shit.

CHAPTER THIRTY NINE

Ramon stepped into the restroom with six guys at his back and a deadly expression on his face, all of their masks now removed. Nicoli took my hand in an act of solidarity, squeezing in a promise that said we were walking out of here together no matter what. With him by my side, my voice was free, my spirit was wild and I felt like the girl I was supposed to be. But my heart still pounded with a fearful energy.

Ramon's gaze moved from my reddened mouth to my ruffled hair with a sneer that made my spine prickle.

"How did you find us?" Nicoli snarled.

"We followed your decoy for half a mile before I checked Sasha's tracker," Ramon said with a smug expression.

"Tracker?" Nicoli hissed as my throat constricted.

"Dr Eckhart gave it to you," he said to me and I shuddered with rage as I recalled the so-called vitamin shot that asshole had given me. "I'm never going to lose track of you again, my love."

"Winter is coming home with me," Nicoli growled in a warning. "Step. Aside."

Ramon's eyes flashed and he jerked his head in some signal. In half a second, all six men had rushed at Nicoli and I lunged in front of him with a yell of fear before they could get near him. Nicoli dragged me back, trying to push me behind him, but I wouldn't go easy.

"Let go of her, Mr Romero," Ramon hissed. "Or she will be punished."

A low growl rumbled through Nicoli's chest, his hand still firmly around mine, his eyes aflame with fury. The six men made a wall in front of us, flexing their muscles as they waited on their boss's orders.

"Nicoli," I whispered in warning, catching his gaze and his brows pinched in agony before he let go of my hand.

Ramon caught my wrist, dragging me away from him and the second he had me, his six men swarmed past him.

"Get him on his knees!" Ramon barked as I clawed at his arm, shoving and pushing him.

Nicoli roared a challenge as they came at him, throwing one guy's face into a sink before the other five fell on top of him. He fought with the fury of a titan, throwing punches, but he couldn't land as many as he took. The four of them forced him down to the floor and held him in place while the meatiest one of them all pulled off his tie and wrapped it around Nicoli's throat until he started choking.

"No please - no!" I screamed as panic overwhelmed me and Ramon twisted toward me, smacking me so hard that my head wheeled sideways and my lip split open. He didn't stop there, throwing me against the wall and locking his hand around my chin, his fingers digging hard into my cheeks.

"I smell him on you, little whore," he spat, spittle peppering my cheeks. "Is this how you treat your husband? You spread your legs for Romero *scum*?"

Nicoli managed to get an arm free and yanked on the tie to loosen it from his neck.

"Get your hands off of her!" he bellowed, trying to get up, but several of the bastards forced him down again and the knot was tightened around his throat once more.

"You try to get up one more time and I'll have Antonio finish you,"

Ramon warned and fear made my body numb, my head spinning as I tried to work out what to do.

"Why are you doing this?" I begged of Ramon, drawing his gaze from Nicoli back to me, needing to keep his rage directed away from him.

"You know why!" Ramon gripped my face tighter, cracking my head against the wall as his upper lip peeled back. Memories shot through my brain like fireworks. The night Duke and his men had come for me in our home. Of being taken forcibly from our bed. Of Ramon crying out for help. But no guards had come. Why had no one come?

My life with Ramon came back in a flood. I'd met him at a party on the east side of town. He'd seemed charming, kind, protective. I'd been swept away by him in a whirlwind romance, but after we were married things changed. The last time I'd seen my mother, she'd cried saying Ramon wouldn't let her visit the house. I'd denied it, sure Ramon wouldn't do that. But when I got home and confronted him, he hit me for the first time. My world got smaller, escorts following me everywhere. And whenever Ramon's business didn't go in his favour, he turned his rage on me.

Eventually I started spying on him, trying to find out when he would be out so I could try and make a run for it. That was when I discovered he was cartel. A drug lord. And then....then-

"Oh my god," I breathed as Ramon glared at me.

His grip on me loosened, his eyes searching mine. "You remember," he growled, seeing that knowledge in my eyes and I hurriedly shook my head. "Don't lie to me!" He threw me to the floor and Nicoli roared curses as Ramon slammed his shiny shoe into my gut. "Tell me the code!"

The code. What's the code?

It burst into my head again like a lightning strike. The code for the safety deposit box at the bank. And now I remembered exactly what was inside. But if Ramon wanted the code, that could only mean one thing.

"You sent me to them," I coughed. "You bastard!" I pushed myself up, lunging at him and throwing a punch into his jaw. He grabbed my hair, yanking my head back until I screamed then gazed down his nose at me. I snarled at him like an animal, my nails digging into his arms. "I'll die before I tell you it."

He pulled me upright, his forehead resting to mine. "You stole from me. Now you give yourself to another man. You owe me *everything*. Sasha. The code, every drop of blood in your body, every scream you have to give. They're all mine. Each cut those men placed on you was put there because *I* asked it of them. And still you defy me?!"

"*I'll destroy you,*" Nicoli choked out as Ramon's men fought to hold him in place. I looked to him with desperation and Ramon wheeled around, tugging me in front of him and forcing me to look at Nicoli by pinching my chin.

"You won't tell me? Fine." Ramon gestured to the man gripping the tie around Nicoli's throat. "Kill him."

"No, wait!" I screamed and Ramon raised his hand to hold Antonio off.

Panic clawed at my insides as I stared down at the man I loved with every part of my soul. A soul he'd healed piece by piece, fitting me back together until I was something new, something strong, something I was proud to be. I wouldn't let Ramon hurt him even if it cost me every bit of myself all over again.

Nicoli was panting as Antonio loosened off the tie a little, his eyes pinned on Ramon with murder in his gaze. He hadn't even flinched in the face of death. He was lost to the bloodlust, ready to stop every man's heart from beating in this room given the chance.

Ramon curled a hand around my waist, tugging me against him as I stared at Nicoli with fear pressing in on all sides. His mouth moved to my ear and I cringed away from him as he whispered to me. "The code for his life. That's the price."

My ears rang with those words.

"Okay," I said heavily. "But you have to let him go."

"I'll let him go when I have what you stole from me," Ramon snarled, turning and dragging me through the door. I heard a struggle and glanced over my shoulder as the six men heaved Nicoli to his feet and pushed him along behind us.

He looked at me like I was the last sunset he'd ever see, but this wouldn't be it. Ramon could have the code if this was the price. I didn't care. I just needed Nicoli to be safe.

Ramon led the way out a back door into an alley where our entourage were waiting, the five gleaming cars ready to go.

"Hold him still," Ramon instructed his men, pushing me into the arms of one of the six men surrounding Nicoli. The other four shoved Nicoli towards my husband, keeping a tight grip on him, his hands pulled behind his back and the tie still locked around his neck like a leash.

Ramon was shorter by an inch, but he had enough muscle to be a threat. He threw his fist into Nicoli's gut, forcing him to buckle forward. I screamed, begging him to stop, but he threw three more punches, one to the gut and two to the head.

Nicoli's shoulders shuddered and it took me a second to realise he was laughing as he stood upright again, his mouth dripping blood.

"I'm going to cut out every one of your organs and feed them to a pack of street dogs while you watch," Nicoli snarled as Ramon shook out his hand.

"After tonight, we will never see you again, Mr Romero," Ramon hissed. "So I highly doubt that."

He turned to me, pointing me into the Rolls Royce and I looked to Nicoli in alarm.

"Wait! You can't take him, you said-"

"I never said he would stay with us, Sasha," Ramon spat. "He will be freed once I have my diamonds. Now get in the fucking car." He pulled me from his guard's arms, shoving me towards the vehicle, but I fought him like a tiger, ripping and tearing as I reached for Nicoli.

He was being hauled away from me toward another car and I cried out as Ramon's hand slammed over my mouth and he forced me into the back of the Rolls Royce. He followed me inside and the doors locked the moment his ass hit the seat. But I wasn't done fighting. I leapt at him, slapping him around the face and he snarled, capturing my wrists and forcing me down onto the seat beneath him. He weighed a ton and I couldn't breathe as he crushed me into the leather, the scent of port on his breath making my stomach writhe. It was a smell that made my mind spark with memories I'd rather forget.

He caught hold of the seatbelt behind me, binding my hands with it so they were pulled above me.

"You don't win this fight, my darling. You belong to me. And it's time you remembered that." He planted his mouth against mine and I wriggled wildly beneath him as he forced his tongue between my lips. But that was his mistake as I bit down and he reared backwards with a yell of fury.

He pressed his shirt sleeve to his tongue and it came away red, making his eyes darken to nightshade.

"You will pay for making me bleed later," he said in a deadly voice, then took out his phone, ignoring me as I yanked at my binds, my arms twisted awkwardly behind my head.

"After all I've done for you," he muttered. "You know it was me who told Duke and his men not to rape you?"

"How fucking grateful I should be," I spat. "I suppose you'll be running for the husband of the year award."

"I'll never let another man touch you like that and live, so maybe you should be a little more grateful. You're mine Sasha."

I glared at him and he tutted, tapping out some messages and I cursed him colourfully as he fought to block me out.

The driver headed deeper into the city and I gazed out the window as we sailed down thirteenth avenue and slowed in front of Squire's Bank. The lights were off inside and I knew it was past business hours, but with my memories seeping back to me, I recalled that Ramon had the bank owner, Lin, in his pocket.

The car engine idled as we waited for him and my mind rippled with memories, each of them giving me more and more clarity. My breath caught as I remembered the last time I was here in this very place. The day I'd been taken by The Five.

It was all fragmented, but slowly I could remember it. The week I'd decided to run from Ramon for good. I'd seen the pouch of diamonds he'd been counting in his office when I'd walked in one day. They were my freedom, the answer I'd been waiting for. I could find my way back to Mom and we'd disappear forever. He never let me withdraw more than five hundred dollars in cash from the bank, not nearly enough to help us vanish. And the credit cards could all be traced.

So I waited until he was out for drinks with his friends later that week, broke into his office and took the diamonds. His obsession with me meant he'd encoded his safe with my birth date. A date I now remembered as clear as day. The fifth of April.

I left the pouch in the safe, filling it with pebbles I'd collected from outside in case he opened the safe before I could get away. Then I hid the diamonds in a sock in my closet and the next day I went to him, telling him I was going to buy a gift for his birthday so I'd be withdrawing a little money from our joint bank account. I remembered how scared I'd been, how my hands had shook. And I'd had to act for my life when he laid me on the desk and kissed me until I couldn't breathe. I remembered his body moving inside mine with a frantic urgency that had made me shut my eyes and wait for it to be over. He was a selfish lover, but at least it never lasted long.

Carlos had guarded me at all times whenever I went out, and he had irritated me as much then as he did now. He'd taken me to the bank the next day, but thankfully waited outside while I'd headed in, withdrawing my stipend before asking to open a safety deposit box in my name. If Ramon discovered it, he would only be able to access it if he knew the passcode. If he found out before I could escape, I'd bargain with him for my freedom. Those diamonds had to be worth millions.

I went home that night and spent the next few weeks waiting for him to go away on one of his business trips so I'd have time to run. I'd have Carlos take me to the mall then give him the slip. There was a back exit in the changing rooms of Bloomingdales, I'd already sussed it out. I'd bought eight dresses there since I'd hidden the diamonds and knew every worker by name. If it came to it, they might even cover for me.

But that day never came. Ramon came home one night and took me to bed early. He couldn't get enough of my flesh, but his grip was bruising and the scent of port on him had told me he'd been drinking long and hard. When he finally passed out, I heard a window shattering downstairs. He wouldn't wake when I prodded him, he stirred too late when the men burst into our room and grabbed me. He fought with them as Duke dragged me downstairs. I'd struggled will all my strength, kicking him between the legs and managing to run. But we were halfway down the stairs and he knocked me over. I fell, hitting my head on a step. My memories faded away faster than I could hold onto them. Before I passed out, I smelled blood, I heard Duke grunt and slide his hands around me, cursing me. And when I woke, I was reborn in hell.

My breathing was frantic as I stared out at the bank, the street bathed in moonlight. Lin came hurrying up it and Ramon looked to me.

"The code," he demanded.

"I want to see that Nicoli's okay," I said in a sharp tone.

He huffed in irritation, but lifted his phone and made a video call to one of his lackeys.

The man answered promptly and the camera immediately swung onto Nicoli who was chained up in some dingy place, his arms yanked above his head. It looked like they'd been using him as a human punching bag and a choked sob escaped me at the sight of him so hurt. But at least he was alive, his eyes gleaming with a promise of death that would befall everyone in his line of sight if he got free.

"There. Satisfied?" Ramon cut the call and desperation filled me as I was caught in his trap.

"How do I know you'll stick to your word?" I asked, my lower lip quivering with rage.

He rested his hand on my thigh, his mouth twisting down at the corners. "You either tell me now, or I'll have him killed and beat it from your pretty lips instead, my darling. You will have to trust that I'm a man of my word. So what will it be?"

I took a slow breath, knowing I had no choice. I was backed into a corner, and I couldn't risk Nicoli's life.

"Three, nine, eight, four, four, seven," I said, bitterness lacing my tone.

He sighed happily, squeezing my thigh. "You could have saved yourself a lot of pain if you'd just given it up sooner, my darling. I only expected you to last a week or two with Duke and his men, you know? But you lost your memories and things got...complicated."

"You left me there to rot," I hissed.

"No...I had a plan in place to bring you home. When you escaped, you went and fucked that up. But when this is all over, I'm going to make it up to you. All of it. We'll start fresh."

I lifted my legs, kicking him hard with my heels and he swore as he tried to catch my ankles. "I will never want you," I growled, practically spitting poison as he opened the car door and hurried out.

He ducked his head down to look at me, pointing a finger. "You will," he warned, then shut the door with a sharp snap. The partition was up between me and the driver so I fought hard to get free of my binds while no one was watching. But Ramon had tied the knot so tight it was cutting off my blood supply. There was no way I could undo it.

My heart thudded out a furious, desperate tune in my chest as I thrashed and struggled, but it was no good. When Ramon returned, I would still be his captive, still bound to him like I always had been ever since I'd said I do. And the only small comfort I could take from it all was that at least I'd been a girl who'd fought back, who'd tried to escape. I didn't have to fear my past self anymore, even though we'd never be quite the same person. I'd grown claws and sharp teeth and I wasn't afraid to be wild. I wanted to be.

Ramon came striding out of the bank like he'd just been promoted to king of the world and dropped back into the car with a wide smile. I glowered at him as he took the white sock from his pocket, pouring the diamonds into his palm and smirking down at them. He placed them back inside it then tucked them into his jacket pocket.

I stilled as he took out his phone, making another video call, needing this to all be over.

Nicoli was even more bloody than before as the camera wheeled onto him and I cried out his name as I saw him. He lifted his head like he heard me, a dark smile on his lips.

"I'm coming, baby doll," he swore and I smiled through tears in my eyes, not knowing if he could see me, but hoping he could.

"I've got the diamonds," Ramon announced, ignoring us as the camera twisted around to face a guy with a goatee who legitimately looked like Satan's uglier, brawnier cousin. "We're heading home, but I'll be at the dock in an hour. Meet me at La Belleza Rosa." He paused, looking to me with hunger and vengeance in his gaze. "And make sure Nicoli Romero's head is waiting there for me when I arrive."

"No!" I screamed, kicking out at him, but he was ready this time, catching my feet and ripping my heels off so I couldn't do any damage.

He cut the call as I wailed and tried to fight with everything I had left. But a shadow was swallowing me up, dragging me down into the most desperate, terrifying despair of my life. One I would never, ever come out of if my mountain man was taken from me.

CHAPTER FORTY

Winter's panicked screams cut off abruptly as the asshole in front of me ended the call. He placed his gun back in his belt though, smirking at me as he pulled out a knife instead.

I smiled right back, rolling my shoulders against the pull of the chains which suspended me from the wooden beam overhead. The thing had been creaking ominously since the moment they'd hung me from it by my wrists and I was just hoping that it was close enough to breaking for me to get free.

There were six men surrounding me, testosterone rolling off of them in anticipation of the kill as they all waited for the strike to fall and my blood to spill. But the problem with them trying to have a dick measuring contest with me was that we all knew I had more inches in my pants than the lot of them combined. But if they were dumb enough to try and off me up close and personal, then I was willing to prove to them exactly what I had hanging between my thighs.

They'd made the rookie mistake of leaving my toes touching the ground too, so as the goateed asshole advanced on me, I backed up, smiling all the time as I stretched out, moving as far back as I could manage while he laughed like he thought I was a coward.

The moment he stepped close enough, I kicked off of the dirty concrete beneath my toes and swung myself at him, hanging my full weight from the chain and bellowing a challenge as I slammed into him.

He yelled out and tried to duck aside but I was too quick and I sent him crashing to the ground, the knife skittering away across the floor of the old abandoned warehouse and disappearing into a darkened corner.

The wooden beam above me creaked again and the hollow splintering of wood reached me as I swung back on the chains and kicked out at another one of the motherfuckers who were hoping for my death. But I refused to fucking die. Not while that piece of shit had my girl in his grasp. There was no way in hell I'd stop until I had her safely out of his arms and his head caved in at my feet.

As I swung wildly on the chain again, I managed to catch hold of a handful of it and heaved myself upwards. Hand over hand, I climbed the chain, swinging back and forth all the while and flinching as someone took a shot at me.

I got about halfway as the huge groan of breaking wood ripped through the air and suddenly, the beam above me shattered, a chunk snapping right out of the centre of it where the chain was secured so that I fell straight back down towards the ground.

My back slammed into the concrete and my breath whooshed out of my lungs as pain ricocheted through me and a sickening crunch sounded from somewhere to my right as hot liquid splattered over my arm.

I looked around in a panic, finding one of the guys already dead beside me, the lump of broken wood having smashed in his skull barely a meter to my right. His blood was plastered over my torn white shirt and I found myself with one less opponent already.

A savage grin twisted my lips and I looked up at the other men who had scattered at the sound of the beam breaking apart.

The fastest guy to recover lifted his gun and I threw myself aside as he fired, wrenching the meter long length of wood into my arms and running straight for him.

He fired again but his bullets sank into the wooden beam as I used it to shield myself and suddenly I was on him, swinging the beam with all of my strength and a feral cry. I slammed it into his skull, killing him with one furious blow that sent shockwaves rippling through my muscles.

I dropped my grip on the wood and snatched his gun from the filthy floor, aiming it just as two more of the men aimed their own weapons at me.

I caught one of them with a bullet right between the eyes before he even got a shot off, but the blinding pain of fire tearing through my bicep let me know the other guy had hit his target. Not well enough though.

The only thing that can stop me is death itself.

I put two in his chest and he dropped like a sack of shit as I used up the last of the ammunition in my stolen gun, leaving me with two more motherfuckers to finish and no weapon to hand. Not that I needed one. I was a weapon given flesh, especially when my savage girl needed me.

I turned and ran for the rusted old machinery that lined the side of the warehouse, ducking low to avoid their gunfire and dragging the broken beam behind me by the chains still tied to my wrists.

It clattered and thumped across the floor, slowing me down massively and yet somehow I managed to make it behind the rusting machinery without getting hit again.

I gritted my teeth against the pain in my left arm as I glanced at the bullet hole which had been punched into it. It was bleeding steadily but not in a way that made me fear for my life, so I quickly dismissed it as I reeled the wooden beam in and the sound of heavy footsteps drew closer.

The chain had been wrapped around the beam several times and as soon as I reeled it in, I uncoiled it so that the broken wood fell to the ground with a solid thump and I could wrap the chain between my hands instead.

I could hear the two assholes moving closer to me, one coming from each side of the machine, no doubt with guns drawn ready to shoot me down the moment I showed myself.

I took a deep breath, closing my eyes as I listened to their approaching footsteps before throwing myself around the left side of the machine and whipping the chain out as hard as I could. The thick steel links smacked the man there in the chest, knocking his gun from his hands and sending him crashing to the ground with a curse.

I whipped back around just as the other guy rounded the corner, somehow managing to dodge another bullet as he swung his gun around too fast in alarm and misjudged his shot. Before he could take another, I swung the chains at him with every inch of strength in my limbs, my grip on them tightening as I whipped them down on him again and again, blood flying until his screams of pain cut off sharply.

I turned back again, bellowing a challenge as I raced towards the last guy who was crawling towards his gun, his fingers reaching out to grab it half a second before I wrapped the thick chains around his neck from behind and pulled them as tight as I could.

He scrambled and flailed beneath me as I drove my knee into his spine to keep him still, firing the gun wildly as the position I held him in made it impossible for him to aim accurately. After the third bullet, the chamber rang empty and he was left twitching and gasping beneath me as he tried to fight off the grip of the chains with ever weakening muscles.

I grunted in pain as I held him there until he stopped moving, my arm burning from the bullet lodged into it and blood coating my tongue from all my other injuries.

When I was sure he was dead, I unravelled the chains and stalked back to the leader whose head had been caved in by the falling beam, the rattle of the metal chains snaking across the concrete behind me the only sound in the wake of all that death.

I dropped down and checked his pockets until I found the key to the cuffs around my wrists and his cellphone. I made quick work of removing the chains from my arms then used his thumb to unlock the phone.

I keyed in Frankie's number from memory, catching my breath as it started to ring.

"This had better be good news," Frankie barked as he answered and I sighed my relief at hearing his voice.

"That bastard Hernandez took Winter and tried to kill me. Is everyone else alright?" I demanded, not wasting time on giving him the full version of events.

"Nicoli! Thank fuck for that, we've been going out of our minds. Everyone else made it back just fine but his guys weren't fooled by Sloan's disguise for long. We figured he'd come back for you but by the time we got back there you were gone and we were all beginning to fear the worst."

"Like I said, he tried to kill me. But he also made the mistake of letting me know where he's heading. He's getting on his boat, La Belleza Rosa. You think Fabio can track that down?" I walked towards the metal doors as I spoke, nudging them open and taking in the view beyond. The tang of salt caught on my tongue as I inhaled and I recognised the huge cargo ships that docked at the far west of the city, outside of the picturesque centre of the bay. It wasn't the kind of place that I would have visited by choice but at least I knew where I was.

"He will if he doesn't want his ass kicking," Frankie said, barking orders at Fabio who must have been there with him.

"Good. Then I need you to come get me. I'm down at the marina, I'll text you the location from this number when I hang up. Bring a hacksaw, a cooler and something to get a bullet out of my arm and patch it back up again. I'll take a shot of morphine for the pain too. And guns. Lots of fucking guns."

"Just call me the cavalry, fratello. I'm on my way." Frankie cut the call and I looked down at the motherfucker beneath me.

His face had been fucked up by the wooden beam caving it in, but his hair was similar enough to mine that the ruse would probably work.

I texted Frankie the location from the GPS on the cellphone and spat a wad of blood from my mouth before ripping the tattered, bloody remains of my white shirt off and tossing it to the ground.

It was cold in Sinners Bay tonight. And that just happened to be perfect for raining down hellfire on everyone who stood between me and my savage girl to heat them right up.

CHAPTER FORTY ONE

I was left in the car while Ramon headed into his mansion and had his maids gather up several suitcases and pack them into another vehicle. My arms were aching from being tied so awkwardly for so long and I could hardly feel my fingers. But I didn't care about the pain. It was nothing to the bloody wound in my heart as I prayed to god Nicoli wasn't dead. But he'd been chained up, outnumbered…

A wave of grief made tears run down my cheeks and I choked them back as Ramon slid into the car once more. He'd grown tired of my thrashing and had had one of his men zip-tie my ankles together and bound them to the seat in front of me. I was immobilised and I couldn't bear to look at him as he directed the driver to take us to the docks.

I shut my eyes, trying to block out the world as grief bit into every inch of me. I couldn't live without Nicoli. We were bound by blood and revenge and love and destruction. No man could stand in his place. No one in this world mirrored my soul like his did.

"I suppose he will have been decapitated by now, my darling," Ramon mused and I opened my eyes, fixing him in my gaze. "I wonder what the last expression on his face will be."

Abhorrence curled under my skin like a flame, igniting every scrap of strength I had left and turning all of it against him. This man. This vile thing built of flesh and bone. He wasn't human. He was all monster. There'd been five demons who'd taken me, but the devil himself had been pulling the strings all along, puppeteering each strike they laid against my body. My scars seemed to writhe against my skin like angry vipers, each one hungering for blood in penance for the blood that had been spilled from me and Nicoli.

I will make you pay.

Ramon glanced at me, his brow pinching as he took in my expression. "You will forget him."

I said nothing, my jaw tight, my voice gone. I would only speak to him again when he lay dying at my feet, begging for mercy. Then I'd send him into hell with Nicoli's name on my lips. *Just give me something sharp and I'll make him bleed until my body is coloured as red as my hair.*

"Stop looking at me like that," he snarled. "You brought this on yourself."

I didn't stop glaring, a coldness washing through me as I sank into the darkest part of myself and let it take over like a murderous spirit inhabiting my body.

If he thought he was going to sail away into the sunset with his obedient wife, he was wrong. He was taking his own death with him. I would be at his side, waiting for the moment he let his guard down, the moment a weapon came into my possession. No matter how long it took, I would one day make him beg for mercy and offer him none.

We arrived at the dock, the sky clear and pricked with a million glittering stars. La Bellaza Rosa stood proud amongst a row of fine yachts, but none were so large as Ramon's. It had an outdoor deck on each level and the windows gave a glimpse in to luxurious interiors.

Ramon exited the car and directed Antonio to untether me. I didn't fight as the huge man released me from my binds and drew me from the car. I let him guide me towards the yacht at Ramon's side, my feet bare against the damp boardwalk. We headed down the pier and onto the yacht and I froze, my heart turning to a lump of ice as I saw the cooler box sitting on the deck before us with bloody handprints pressed to it. Sickness invaded me and I didn't know if I was screaming inside my head or if the noise was tearing from my lungs.

Ramon laughed darkly, striding forward and I pressed back against Antonio, too afraid to see the truth awaiting me within that box. He flipped the lid open and all I saw was blood and dark, dark hair.

"Want a closer look, my darling? He's not so pretty now that there's hardly anything left of his face."

I trembled all over, my mind trying to refuse it, but the evidence was clear. A switch flipped in my head and I ran at Ramon with a shriek, slamming into him before anyone could get near to me and gouging scratches across his face as I went for every bare piece of skin I could find. I uprooted him and he hit the deck with a yell beneath me. I grabbed hold of his head, pushing my thumbs against his eyes as hard as I could. I was shaking and full of hate and despair. I didn't care if his death equalled mine. I'd pay the price.

Before I could do nearly enough damage, Antonio dragged me off of him and I kicked and thrashed.

He swore as he fought to hold me still and more men came to his aid, two of them catching my legs as I battled them with every ounce of strength in my body.

"You fucking whore!" Ramon roared as he got to his feet. "Take her up to my cabin. I've had enough of this." He strode after us as the three men hauled me upstairs and I managed to leave marks on all of them by the time they carried me through a fancy lounge then into a large room beyond it with shiny wooden walls and a king sized bed at the heart of it. White satin sheets adorned it and the scent in the air was as crisp as newly printed dollar bills.

"Tie her hands in front of her," Ramon instructed and Antonio yanked my wrists together and slid a zip-tie around them, apparently always prepared for every fucking occasion.

"Leave us," Ramon growled.

"Okay boss," Antonio said as I continued to fight him like a feral cat.

"And don't disturb us until we're in Mexico," Ramon added.

They shoved me onto the bed, bowing their heads obediently and walked out the door. Ramon moved to lock it with a key which he promptly tucked into his pants' pocket.

He reached for his belt, unbuckling it and pulling it from the loops and I hurried to get up off the bed. "I'm done playing nice." He strode toward me and I lifted my chin defiantly.

He caught my hair, shoving me down onto the mattress again face first and I fought hard as I tried to get up, but his hand pressed firmly down on my spine. He ripped the back of my dress open, tearing through the zip and his legs clamped around mine to keep me in place as I tried to kick him. I growled into the sheets, tugging hard at the zip-tie around my wrists as I tried to snap it, my pulse thundering in my skull.

Ramon suddenly whipped his belt across my shoulder blades and my skin flared with fire. I didn't give him the satisfaction of screaming. Even when he did it again and again. I bit down on the comforter and took every whip as my skin burned under each strike. But it didn't matter. He could flay me alive and I'd still come for him. I'd still be his death.

Ramon was panting when he stopped, leaning down and resting his mouth against my ear, the slick sweat on his face making his skin stick to mine. His hand roamed down over my hips to grip my ass as he groped me. "I will break you, Sasha. You will learn to be an obedient wife again. If pain doesn't do it, there are other ways..."

CHAPTER FORTY TWO

We sat in the dark engine room of the enormous yacht, waiting for the thing to pull away from the shore with the blood of our enemies staining our skin. We'd only had to kill two guards to get onboard and with a boat this big and a crew this large, we were fairly confident that their absence would go unnoticed for a while.

Besides, it wasn't like there were any bodies to be found. We'd tied them to a couple of heavy crates that had been left out on the deck and dropped them overboard for the sharks to enjoy. A tasty snack of stupid motherfucker to eat before bed. I was a damn sealife hero, providing food for hungry creatures and saving them from the trials of having to hunt it down themselves.

I was dressed in a clean black sweater and a pair of jeans that Frankie had brought for me to change into. Rocco had pulled the bullet from my arm and stitched it up and Enzo had stuck me with a healthy dose of morphine which stole away the pain and left me floating on a cloud of happiness where I could focus on my intense desire to cut Ramon Hernandez's heart out and lay it at Winter's feet.

I looked between my three brothers in the darkened space as the engine growled and the boat bobbed on the water before moving away from the dock.

Rocco was humming low beneath his breath, it sounded like Hickory Dickory Dock and I raised an eyebrow at him in question.

"Rocco always associates murder with nursery rhymes," Enzo supplied with a roll of his eyes as he twisted a mean looking flick knife between his tattooed fingers.

"Maybe it's because our mamma was murdered when I was most attuned to hearing them," Rocco replied with an arched eyebrow before glancing at me.

We hadn't spoken about our dead mamma really. But sometimes I felt like he wanted to ask me about her, like he wondered if I remembered her too. Enzo and Frankie probably didn't. They'd been too young when she was killed. But if I strained my memory back as far as it would go, I was fairly sure I could remember some things. The touch of her hand on my cheek, the way she laughed when she danced with us, the songs she sang when putting us to bed at night...

That was a conversation that could wait though. Right now, I had a member of the Dominguez Cartel to execute. More than a member actually. There weren't many people who the Romeros were cautious about mixing with, but the drug cartels were one of them. They were big enough and brutal enough to cause real problems in Sinners Bay if they had a mind to. Just as the Romeros could cause them a serious headache in return if they decided to try and interfere with them too much. As such, there was a weighted peace between the two crime organisations. The mobs and the cartels didn't mix unless they had to and then deals were carefully struck to avoid blood loss. There wasn't going to be anything careful about what we were doing tonight though.

What we were about to do could quite easily start a war. Which was why we couldn't leave any witnesses alive on this boat. It was also why we were waiting until we were far out at sea to strike where no one else could possibly see us. The Santiago Cartel would happily take credit for this hit anyway. Besides, they'd struck at us first by trying to kill me. And as terrifying as the Dominguez Cartel might be. No one struck at the Romeros and lived to talk about it.

Frankie fiddled with the silencer on his pistol, seeming to be lost in thought as he adjusted it unnecessarily.

"In all of my wildest dreams, I never could have imagined ending up on a job like this with all *three* of my brothers," he said in a low voice, glancing up at me with a smile. "Do you think it was fate that brought us back together or just dumb luck?"

I grunted, shrugging but no, I didn't believe in fate. If it was fate for me to find my brothers again and to find Winter lost in the snow that day then it was also fate for me to have been stolen in the first place, for my mother to die, for my savage girl to have been tortured for months on end. I didn't believe in any form of destiny or in any deity that could choose such cruel things to happen to people.

"I think fucked up things just happen," Enzo said. "Especially to fucked up people like us."

"I'll drink to that," Rocco muttered.

My fingers were itching with the desire to wrap them around Ramon's throat and as the engine noise grew louder and the tug in my gut said the boat had picked up speed, I pushed to my feet.

"Time to go," I said. Not asking, telling. I didn't care if they thought we were far enough from shore or not yet, my savage girl was on this boat somewhere with that monster and I refused to leave her with him for another moment.

My brothers seemed to realise this and they stood too, each of us drawing our pistols and checking the silencers were in place. We were outnumbered here, but we also had the element of surprise and were on a seriously big yacht. This thing was so fucking huge that we had a good shot of moving around it unnoticed so long as we were careful. And by the time we made it to Ramon, I wanted him to know that there wasn't a single soul left to help him. That he was all alone out here and that death had tracked him down.

We moved to stand by the door and I peered out of the small, round window set into it to see if there was anyone out there for us to deal with first.

"Into the fires of hell we go," Enzo purred with a grin and I couldn't help but smile too.

We're coming, savage girl, god have mercy on anyone who tries to stop us.

I opened the door and headed out with my brothers on my heels. We jogged up a short flight of stairs and Frankie and Rocco turned left as Enzo and I headed right. We were going to work our way from the stern to the bow, one level at a time and move up as a group. Every man we found needed to die and they needed to go quietly so that no one sounded an alarm. There were three levels to the yacht and we were hoping that Ramon would have locked Winter away somewhere for us to find to keep her away from the bullets. But whatever way this played out, I was going to get my savage girl back tonight and I'd make a widow out of her too.

My heart pounded and adrenaline sang in my veins as we began to move along the ship.

A man stepped out of a door ahead of us and I fired the moment it closed behind him, catching him in the back of the head with the bullet and sending him crashing over the railing and into the sea below where he was quickly left behind by the speed of the boat.

Enzo clapped a hand on my shoulder before moving to stand beside a door and pull it open. I peeked around the corner, finding a staff kitchen which was clearly empty before we moved on.

Our feet moved silently across the deck and we stalked the yacht like death given flesh. Each man we found met with their end, more than one of them falling into the sea and the mercy of the sharks.

Though we used our guns most often, I was already ending up with a coating of blood on my flesh and I was sure I'd be dressed in red by the time this night was through, but I'd happily do that and more for my girl. I'd make the decks of this place run with rivers of blood if that was what it took to save her.

The cold wind whipped around us and I tasted salt on my lips as we prowled through the shadows and closed in on our target. Ramon Hernandez's minutes were numbered and each tick of the clock counted down to his last breath.

Look out for me, savage girl, the wolves are hunting tonight.

CHAPTER FORTY THREE

Ramon leaned over me, his hand in his pants as he fisted his dick, panting in my ear. I threw my head back as hard as I possibly could and he roared as his nose cracked loudly, his weight leaving me in an instant. My heart leapt as I scrambled off of the bed, rushing to the nightstand drawer and tugging it open. With my memories stirring, I recalled some of Ramon's habits and as I'd hoped, there was a knife waiting for me inside. I grabbed it quickly, twisting it between my fingers and slicing through the zip-tie.

I swung around, but Ramon leapt upon me in a rage. I screamed as I hit the nightstand and my back hit the wall behind it. I slashed at him with the knife with a yell of determination and it sliced along his bicep, making him grunt in pain. He grabbed my wrist, wrestling the knife from my hand and it fell to the floor with a thump that made fear clutch my chest. I tried to wriggle my way free, but he grabbed my throat and pinned me back against the wall with his teeth bared.

Blood was streaming down from his shattered nose and he sneered at me in abject rage as he forced my legs apart, my ass resting on the nightstand as he battled to hold me still. I dug my nails into his arms and shoulders, trying to push him back as he stepped between my thighs and pushing down his pants. I choked as his grip tightened, stars bursting in front of my eyes as I fought him, desperate to make him stop.

I could see the swell in his boxers and knew if he managed to get inside me, that was it. My fight would be over.

I reached around me for anything I could use against him and my hand slid onto the bulb of the lamp. I twisted it free just as he got his dick out, smashing it against the wall behind me then wheeling it towards his face. The jagged shards slammed into his skin and he reared backwards as I shoved off of the nightstand, punching it into his chest, his arms, his stomach. The wounds were shallow but bloody and he yelled in agony before throwing himself at me again. He tackled me to the floor, the full weight of his body making me cough out a breath as he crushed me into the carpet.

He caught my hand, slamming it against the floor to make me release the remains of the bulb and I grinned up at him as I felt the heat of his blood against my skin.

"You're fucking crazy." He slapped me and my thoughts spun, but I only laughed, the sound filling up the room. "Shut up!"

He knelt up, flipping me over beneath him and I managed to get on my knees as he gripped my hair. I spotted the knife on the floor and snatched it as he ground his hard dick against my ass.

I twisted around fast, aiming for his crotch with the knife but he jerked aside at the last second and the blade sank into his thigh instead. He released my hair with a yell, falling back onto his ass so I lost my grip on the knife and I leapt onto him, grabbing a pillow from the bed and shoving it down over his face. He threw heavy punches into my sides, shoving me off of him and I scrambled up onto the bed as he lunged for me. I made it to the other side of the room and stared at him as he ripped the knife out of his thigh with a growl of pain.

"Fuck you," he spat, pointing the bloody blade at me. "You want out of this marriage, then fine. You can leave it in a body bag, my darling."

He leapt onto the bed as he came at me and with no weapon, I knew I had no choice but to run. I dove into the en-suite, slamming the door shut and locking it just as his weight collided with the wood from the other side.

The space I found myself in had gleaming marble tiles and golden bath taps but nothing I could immediately see to use as a weapon. I retreated from the door, hunting for a way out. But there was none.

Terror rolled down my spine and I sought out my strength, thinking of Nicoli and my heart split into sharp pieces. I'd avenge him, cut out Ramon's heart and send his demonic soul into the hands of the devil. But even then, I knew nothing would heal the pain of losing my warrior.

I hurried to the vanity unit and started searching for anything I could use against the monster trying to get in.

Ramon kicked the door with a shout of anger and the wood splintered up the middle.

It wasn't going to hold.

I was going to have to fight for vengeance for my mountain man.

And I would win.

Frankie

CHAPTER FORTY FOUR

Rocco grunted as he kept his arm locked around the neck of the guy he was fighting, restraining him in a choke hold as I made sure the others were dead. The guy's feet were scrambling against the plush carpet in the games room we'd found him and his friends in as he fought to get free and Rocco grunted a laugh, knowing he'd already won.

A flash of moonlight catching on the blade was the only warning I got as the asshole yanked it from his belt and I yelled out to Rocco as the stronzo swung it back at him.

Rocco cursed violently as the small blade slammed into his thigh, shoving the guy out of his arms and crashing down onto the floor. He ripped the knife from his leg and pounced on his prey, but the fucker managed to yell for help before Rocco drove the blade home in his chest. He stabbed him again and again to make sure he was dead then shoved himself to his feet with a curse as blood poured down his leg from the wound he'd gained.

"Motherfucker," he snarled, pressing a hand to the injury as I hurried to his side.

Rocco raised his pistol and aimed it at the door as I ripped his jeans open to get a better look at what we were dealing with.

"Do you think anyone heard that stronzo?" Rocco hissed, scowling at the doorway as he kept his gun aimed at it. Knowing him he was probably more pissed about the fact that the game might be up than the hole that had just been punched into his flesh.

"This isn't too bad," I announced, tugging my belt off and wrapping it around his thigh above the wound, cinching it tight to stem the blood loss.

"The guy got off easy for stabbing me like that," he muttered irritably.

There was no sound from beyond the door which led back outside and no sign of anyone coming to investigate the shout, so it was looking like we'd gotten away with that. We'd have to be more careful as we moved onto the upper deck though.

Rocco lowered his gun as I stood and took aim at the door with my own then pulled a syringe from his pocket. He tugged the cap off of the needle with his teeth then stabbed it into his arm with a wild grin at me as he spat the cap back out again.

"Was that the morphine you brought for Nicoli?" I asked with a frown.

"I brought extras, stronzo," he replied rolling his eyes. "I'm not dumb enough to think we could take on a boat full of cartel assholes and come out unscathed. The only pain I wanna be feeling tonight is that of my enemies."

I snorted a laugh to dispel any lingering concerns for him which might distract me and took the lead as we headed to the door and back out onto the narrow strip of deck that ringed the boat. The night was dark but the sky clear so that a scattering of stars and a crescent moon brightened the sky overhead and gilded the waves with silver caps.

My breath rose before me as I held my pistol ready and inched towards the corner ahead of us at the bow where the stairs led up to the top deck. Hernandez was waiting for us somewhere up there, even though he hadn't figured it out yet.

I was willing to bet this was where our luck ran out though. At the top of the stairs we were about to climb was a huge area of open deck and I was guessing there would be too many men up there for us to take out quietly. But we'd done damn well to get this far without raising the alarm of everyone onboard so I was ready to face the rush of a full on shoot out if that was what it took to get this done.

I peeked around the corner cautiously and let out a breath of relief as I spotted Enzo rounding the corner from his side of the vessel.

"All clear?" I asked him, glancing at the blood which drenched his right arm and wondering if he was injured too.

"Don't worry about that, it's not mine," he said with a dark grin just as Nicoli followed him around the corner and Rocco moved to stand at my side. The Romero brothers united as we should be.

"You're hit," Enzo growled, pointing at the blood which still oozed from Rocco's wounded leg and he grunted dismissively.

"This little scratch? *Please*, I've given myself worse from shaving my balls." Rocco smirked like a cocky asshole and I explained for him because we all knew he wouldn't admit it if he was half dead anyway.

"It's not that bad," I reassured the others, glancing up at the curving staircase before us. "He'll be fine once we can kill the rest of these stronzos and patch him up."

"Good. So what's the plan?" Enzo asked and we all looked at Nicoli.

"Kill them all," he grunted. "And clear a path for me to get to my girl."

We all nodded, exchanging looks with each other just in case this was the last moment that we all spent together. It wasn't something we ever put into words, but on jobs like this we all knew the risks. It was part and parcel of being who we were. What we were. Romeros fought their own battles and looked their enemies in the eye when they tore them down. That came with plenty of risk though.

"Let's end this then, fratello. And remind the cartel exactly who rules Sinners Bay," I said and with that we all mounted the stairs with one goal in mind. To protect our family and bring Nicoli's girl home.

CHAPTER FORTY FIVE

I gave up hunting the cupboards in the bathroom as Ramon threw his weight against the door again with a cry of rage. The hinges rattled, the wood was splitting. I was down to my final seconds and as my gaze fell on my reflection in the oval mirror above the sink, my breath hitched. I saw a predator gazing back at me, her cheeks flecked with blood, her eyes burning with the fires of hell. And she knew what to do.

I grabbed a towel, wrapping it around my hand and punching the centre of the glass. It shattered in a cascade of jagged shards and I jumped back before picking up a long triangular piece, keeping the towel around my palm as I gripped it. Then I hurried to switch the light off and stand back against the wall opposite the door.

My breathing came heavily and I urged it to slow, falling into a calm and deadly place in my mind as I gazed at that door. My fate awaited me beyond it. No force in this world could change it now. I would face my final demon, but god only knew if I would win.

Time seemed to slow as I waited, the seconds stretching into little pockets of eternity as Ramon kicked the door hard enough to crush a man's skull and the lock shot off of it, the gold fixing skittering across the tiles with a tinkling noise.

I held my breath and readied my weapon as Ramon stood in the doorway. Darkness greeted him and he squinted into the gloom, buying me the precious moment I needed.

I ran at him, barefoot and wild and launched myself at his chest with the shard poised to kill. He jerked aside and I missed my target as he reacted, the glass sinking deep into his shoulder instead. He fell back with a cry of pain, stumbling as he caught my waist and tried to shove me away. But we were already falling. His back hit the bed and I straddled him, yanking the glass free from his shoulder with a grunt, about to drive it into him again as energy coursed through my veins like jet fuel. His fist snapped out, catching me in the jaw and my skull rang as I fell off of him and he rolled over on top of me.

He hit me again and hope snuffed out like a flame in my chest. My head spun and pain burst through my skull. I barely held onto my consciousness as the weapon slipped from my fingers and Ramon's hot hands curled around my throat.

"Look at me," he demanded. "Stay awake."

My eyes cracked open enough to see him glaring down at me, sweat beading along his brow and his gaze full of rage. His face was red and veiny, his handsome looks distorted by his fury.

"Beg me to stop," he growled. "And maybe I'll be merciful."

His grip on my throat eased enough that I could access my voice if I wanted to. But he wasn't going to get my words. And he certainly wasn't going to get me to beg.

"Beg me!" he roared, spittle flying from his mouth as his grip tightened once more and I choked as he held me down.

My fingers grasped for my weapon, but it wasn't there and I couldn't turn my head to search for it.

I was forced to look up into the cold eyes of my husband. The man who had destroyed my life. Who had taken everything from me. Who'd had Nicoli killed, the man who'd been every good thing I'd ever dreamed of, and now he'd been stolen away from me by this fucking asshole.

"You asked for this," Ramon hissed, leaning lower so all I could see were those dark eyes which held an abyss in them where I was about to be trapped for the rest of time.

My heart pounded so hard, I could feel it in every inch of my flesh. It was drumming out its final beats, fighting harder than ever to keep going, but no more oxygen was making it into my blood. I was running out of time to fulfil the vow I'd made for Nicoli, to destroy this monster for taking him from me.

I fisted my hands in the sheets, clawing and tugging at them and Ramon's eyes lit up hungrily as he watched me beginning to lose this fight. Somewhere in the distance was a rattling of gunfire, but I couldn't focus on it to wonder what it meant.

"Look at me," he purred again. "Look at the man who owns you."

My ears popped and darkness was shading my vision. My lungs burned for air and my body was getting heavy. I couldn't die without taking Ramon with me. If an afterlife existed, he needed to burn in it for the rest of eternity. And if it didn't, then I had to ensure he suffered, he had to pay for what he'd done to Nicoli. But my hope of that was failing by the second and my heart shattered all over again and as the strength in my body gave way. I'd dreamed of a life with my mountain man beside me, dared to hope that happiness could belong to us both, that I could know a world where no enemies lurked in the shadows, no one sought to own me, no one wished to see me bleed. Where it was just me and him and a sea of possibilities. But he was gone. And now I couldn't even give him the revenge he so deeply deserved.

Tears slipped from my eyes over my loss of him, of everything we could have had, of Ramon winning, evil prevailing. All I could hope for was that Nicoli was waiting for me beyond this cruel and brutal world. That there might be a place for me yet where peace was waiting for us.

My fingers grazed the fluffy edge of a towel and in the darkening haze of my mind, I managed to force myself to pull on it, reeling it closer, feeling the soft material pass beneath my palm. Then something sharp and cold touched my fingertips and a final ray of hope found me in the endless dark.

I tugged the towel once more and the shard of glass slid into my palm. I wrapped my fingers around it as my eyes fluttered closed and Ramon breathed heavily over my face.

His grip eased as he presumed I was dead and the animal in me coiled.

I heaved down a breath the same moment as I flung my hand toward his side and the shard slid into soft flesh, making him wail as he reared back. I lunged upwards with a gasp of hope, yanking it free and stabbing again. And again. And again. Blood spattered me as he crumpled backwards onto the bed and I scrambled up and over him.

He was still fighting, throwing punches as he tried to get me off, but I latched my thighs around his waist and screamed as I stabbed and stabbed, falling into the bloodlust as I took my revenge, destroying my final demon and freeing myself in the same moment.

"Please no - please!" Ramon begged as I buried the glass in him once more, my own hand bleeding where I gripped it so tightly. I couldn't even feel the pain as I drove it into him without mercy. He had offered Nicoli none and I would give him the same courtesy.

He should have known this day would come. There was only one possible fate for men who chained monsters. Sooner or later, they'd fall prey to their claws and teeth.

CHAPTER FORTY SIX

The upper deck was a chaos of carnage and bloodshed as shots were fired from all sides and men lay dead or dying across the gleaming floor and cream leather seats that filled the open space at the top of the stairs we were using for cover.

But despite the sound of the returning fire from the cartel making my head ring and my own pulse pounding violently in my ears, above all of it I heard one sound which tore me in two. Winter's screams were full of fear and rage and pain and fury and my muscles bunched with tension as my gaze fixed on the door to the rear of the yacht where they originated from.

"Cover me," I barked at my brothers, preparing myself to dash through the eye of the storm to get to my savage girl. Whatever the fuck was happening behind that door, it couldn't wait and I wouldn't leave her to suffer without me for even another moment.

Enzo grabbed my shoulder as he yanked me back down out of the way. He was breathing heavily, blood smeared across his cheek which I was pretty confident didn't belong to him and a look in his eyes that said he lived for this.

"Are you crazy, stronzo?" he snapped at me. "If you go up there before we take them all out then you'll die."

"I'm going with your approval or not," I snarled fiercely, wrenching my arm out of his grip as I prepared to run. "Some things in life are worth risking death for."

Two more hands grabbed me as Frankie and Rocco pulled me back too, leaving the deck quiet for a moment as the remaining members of the cartel waited to see what was happening.

"I told you it would come to this," Enzo said, his words for the others as his eyes lit with excitement and he shoved a hand into his pocket.

"Crazy motherfucker," Frankie growled, shaking his head before peeking up over the top of the staircase again and firing off a few more shots. The returning gunfire was loud enough to make my brain rattle and he quickly ducked back down. "Although at this point I'm unsure what other choice we have. Aim to the left of the deck, there's more of them there."

"Maybe you should let me do it, fratello," Rocco said with a wild look in his eyes that I was learning only ever spelled trouble, his grip on me remaining tight enough to stop me from leaping up onto the deck like I aimed to.

"Do what?" I snarled, yanking my arm out of his grip just as Enzo waved a grenade in front of my eyes.

"Have faith, fratello, I'm more than just a pretty face," he said as he pulled the pin.

My lips parted on a protest but he'd already thrown it, a moment of aching silence following as the gunfire ceased once more and Frankie yanked me down forcefully.

We ducked into the cover offered by the staircase, huddling together and covering our ears just as a cry of alarm came from one of the cartel followed by a deafening boom which rocked the entire yacht.

My stomach swooped at the violent motion of the vessel on the water but I ignored it, pushing myself upright and racing up the stairs to the top deck with my brothers at my side.

To the left of the deck, a huge hole had been blasted into the luxurious boat and blood speckled every surface that hadn't been destroyed. Debris was still falling from the sky, chunks of wood and metal railings crashing into the sea while pieces of the hand-stitched upholstery from the seating areas fluttered down more slowly behind them.

My gaze didn't linger there as I focused on the space to my right where the last of Hernandez's men were huddled behind whatever they could find to take cover.

I ran forward, taking aim at the first man to stick his head out of his hiding place and putting a bullet between his eyes as my brothers charged into the fight with cries of challenge and excitement. Rocco howled like a wolf as he opened fire on the cartel and I left them to it as I raced on towards the covered space at the back of the deck and the door which led into the master suite.

Winter was screaming again, but she sounded more furious than terrified now and my heart swelled at the sound of my savage girl fighting her own fight.

I threw the door open and raced through an opulent living area to the door beyond which I had to kick open to get through.

There was so much blood painting the room red that for a moment my heart leapt and tightened with fear. But then I saw them, fighting on the bed like a pitbull and a wildcat which should have been a fight that could only go one way. But my little wildcat had the heart of a lion and the fury of a woman made to bleed for no crime.

She hadn't even slowed her attack at the sound of me kicking the door open and with her back to me, she had no way of knowing it was me who'd come for her and not one of Ramon's men. She wasn't even going to try and fight anyone else off. This was personal and she wanted to make sure she ended that motherfucker, even if it cost her her life in the process.

Hernandez was bucking and thrashing beneath her, but the lack of strength to his movements told me she'd already done enough damage to seal his fate.

I stepped forward, catching her around the waist and yanking her back into my arms.

She shrieked like a banshee, whirling on me with a shard of bloody glass in her raised hand, her eyes widening a moment before it crashed into my bicep, cutting into the flesh with a twist of pain that somehow felt like a kiss instead.

"Nicoli?" she gasped in surprise which quickly flickered to relief and then horror as she realised she'd stabbed me. "Oh, fuck," she hissed, yanking the glass back out of my arm and trying to apologise as she dropped it to the floor. She started shaking, staring at me in utter shock as she traced her fingers over my face in disbelief, like she couldn't believe I was really here. I guessed she'd seen the head we'd left on the deck and my gut twisted at causing her so much pain.

"A scar from you is like a gift from a goddess, baby doll," I promised her, placing her on her feet at my side as I turned my attention to the dying man who lay on the bed watching us with venom in his gaze. He'd scrambled backwards and was rifling through the drawer beside him like he hoped to find something that he could use to save his miserable life with, but there was nothing there.

"You bought your death with this act, Romero," Ramon hissed, pressing at the worst wound on his stomach as he saw his death reflected in my eyes. "The Dominguez Cartel will destroy you and every single member of your family for it. They'll kill you all slowly, agonisingly, make you watch as they take your whore and every other woman any of you love and do everything and anything they want with them right before your eyes before killing them too. You've started a war. By the time they're done with you, the name Romero will be nothing more than a whispered memory and a warning against anyone who crosses us."

"And you know what you'll be when all of that is happening?" I replied darkly as I moved to stand over him where he lay on the bed, handing my pistol to Winter so that my hands were left free. "Nothing."

I lunged at him and he cried out half a second before my hands closed around his throat and I pressed him down into the luxurious bed with all the strength I possessed.

He kicked and thrashed, his fingernails gouging marks into the backs of my hands as he tried to fight me off. But I held the fury of a man whose girl had been battered, bruised and tortured and there wasn't even the slightest bit of mercy in me for him or anyone else who had hurt her. Because she *was* hurt and damaged and scarred by everything that had happened to her. But she wasn't broken. She had the spirit of a warrior and the strength of a thousand men. My savage girl was small and fragile and wounded. But she would never break.

My grip tightened as his attempts to fight me off weakened and soft fingers slipped into my hair as Winter came to stand beside me. Ramon's gaze found hers as he looked over my shoulder, his fingers twitching and his limbs falling still as he fell into death and I was glad she was the last thing he saw. My savage girl, sending him into death and delivering him to hell for the devil to torture forevermore.

CHAPTER FORTY SEVEN

Everything had changed in no time at all. I was staring at my mountain man, back from the dead. Or at least, that was how it seemed to me.

I didn't care to look at Ramon any longer, my gaze focused on the blood soaking into Nicoli sweater, the scratches lining his neck and cheeks, but most of the blood wasn't his. The cut I'd left on him was one of the worst wounds he had, but a few stitches would fix him up. He'd come for me despite the odds, torn into Hades like Orpheus coming for his wife Eurydice, refusing to give up on me even when all seemed lost.

He turned to face me as he left my husband's mangled body on the bed, standing upright so he towered over me. He reached out to score his thumb along my cheek, painting it red with Ramon's blood. He did the same to my other cheek then leaned down and caught hold of my chin. I realised I was shaking, relief making my knees nearly buckle.

"My warrior," he breathed, then he moved, circling me, keeping his hands off of my skin no matter how much I craved more of his touch. He growled when he saw the reddened belt marks on my back and as he returned to stand in front of me, his eyes were full of despair. "I broke my promise to you. I swore no one would ever hurt you again."

"You can't control life," I breathed and he shook his head in refusal of that, reaching up to hold my chin in the gentlest of grips. "There will always be times when it hurts."

"Then I promise you this," he growled, stepping closer until I was intoxicated by the scent of blood and man on him. "I will spend every day for as long as I have in this world making you smile and moan and sigh with pleasure. And when life hurts you, I'll be there to soothe the ache, to fight your demons, to follow you into the fires of hell and burn there to ensure you live to smile again. I promise that your sunrise will always come, no matter how dark the night gets."

I forgot to breathe as I leaned into him, placing my hand on his muscular chest and feeling the familiar thrum of his heartbeat beneath my palm. Then I pulled his sweater up a little and painted the words *I love you* on his skin and his eyelids half closed as he gazed at me, leaning towards me, slow and cautious.

"I'm not made of glass," I whispered, a smile pulling up the corners of my mouth. It seemed impossible to be smiling again, to be back in the arms of my mountain man with the world opening up before us to do whatever we wanted with.

Nicoli gripped my waist, growling as he tugged me close, but before I could fall into the kiss I so desperately craved, the door flew open and the rest of the Romeros poured into the room.

"Woah, sorry to interrupt this bloodfest of a kiss, but we need to fucking go," Frankie said as he took in Ramon's butchered body. He was the least covered in blood of all of them and somehow still had his hair perfectly in place and his dress shirt tucked neatly into his pants.

"I dunno, I think it's *Ramon*-tic," Enzo said, laughing like a hyena as he looked to my dead husband.

I snorted a laugh and Nicoli chuckled darkly.

"Come on, let's get back to shore. Everyone onboard is either dead or twitching into the afterlife as we speak," Rocco said with a wild glint in his gaze.

Nicoli took my hand as they turned away and I yelped as I realised he'd taken the one cut open by the shard of glass. He released it instantly, looking down at the jagged slice in my palm, cursing before heading away to Ramon's closet. He ripped a shirt in two then moved to bind my hand before grabbing Ramon's suit jacket which he'd worn at the masked ball and holding it out for me to put on. It swamped me but I was grateful for it as we headed outside and the freezing air whipped around us.

The deck was wet with blood and my bare feet slipped in it a few times as we followed Nicoli's brothers to the speed boat hanging on a crane at the back of the yacht. Frankie got the controls working, lowering it into the water while Enzo and Rocco disappeared off down a stairwell together.

"That's not good," Nicoli muttered.

"What isn't?" I asked as he wrapped an arm around my shoulders.

"Those two heading off together," he said with a smirk.

We waited for them to return and I took in the carnage around us, my heart lighting up at everything the Romeros had done to reach me.

"Thank you," I said to Frankie and he gave me a lopsided grin.

"You're family, Winter. And a Romero will do anything for family," he said intensely.

"Go go fucking go, power rangers!" Enzo bellowed as he and Rocco came tearing back up the stairs, laughing their heads off.

My heart juddered and none of us paused to ask why as Nicoli pushed me to the edge of the railing where a ladder led down to the water. I swung my leg over, looking up at the four men as they watched me go, all of them haloed by the moon, their faces cast in shadow so that I couldn't tell one from the other. They were four pieces of the same whole and there was something achingly beautiful in that.

As I made it down a few rungs, they followed and I hurried down into the boat, dropping onto its deck.

The four of them joined me a moment later and Nicoli tugged me down into his lap on a seat at the back, hugging me tight to his chest. He was warm despite the freezing air and I huddled against him with the happiest of smiles on my face.

Rocco started the engine while Enzo banged his fists against his chest, staring back at the yacht in anticipation.

"Get us going, stronzo," Frankie growled at Rocco, seeming anxious as he looked at the yacht too.

Rocco pushed the throttle and the boat tore away through the water at high speed.

I turned my head to look back at the yacht bobbing on the dark sea just as an explosion tore through it that made me gasp, the windows exploding and debris shooting out in every direction.

Nicoli held me tight while his brothers whooped and we were soon joining them, cheering for our victory as we watched the beautiful yacht begin to sink into the waves, the fire climbing high towards the sky.

Enzo and Rocco started telling us excitedly about how they'd cut the fuel lines in the engine room and used a line of rope doused in gas to create a fuse. I stopped listening as I turned to Nicoli though, his eyes tugging me in and claiming me with nothing more than a single look. My heart pounded out a wild, new tune that I loved the feel of. When we were together, everything just seemed *right*.

"Stop here, Rocco, let's watch it go down," Enzo said eagerly and Rocco killed the engine so the boat slowed and rocked gently in the water.

I nestled closer to Nicoli and felt a lump pressing into my side. I reached into the pocket of Ramon's jacket, laughing as I found my sock filled with diamonds. A symbol of the life I'd hoped to buy myself one day. But I'd found my way to an even better one without them in the end.

I showed Nicoli what lay inside and his eyes glittered as the moonlight made them light up like a sky full of stars.

"Holy fuck," he laughed too, closing my hand around them. "You're rich, baby doll."

"These are the price of my scars," I said darkly, my fingers tightening on them.

"If you go Titanic on those diamonds, bella, I will dive in after them like a fucking horny dolphin," Enzo taunted and I glanced over my shoulder at him with a smirk.

I turned back to Nicoli and he smiled serenely at me. "Do what you gotta do, my savage girl."

I looked out into the dark water for a long moment then pushed the diamonds back into my pocket as I made my decision. "I'll make them pay for something good. Something worthwhile. They're no good to anyone at the bottom of the ocean."

Nicoli's arms slid under my jacket, his fingers gripping the bare skin of my hips. My red hair whipped around me in the wind and he watched me like he was hypnotised. "When we get home, I'm going to tend your wounds, wash every fleck of blood from your flesh and brand you as mine all night long."

"I'm already yours," I teased, my heart squeezing with bliss.

"We both need a reminder." He smirked as we turned to face the fire, the heat of it reaching us as the red and gold light danced across our bodies.

I could feel the last of my chains falling from my soul as the yacht sank into the waves, allowing me to offer up myself to Nicoli fully. I was his in every way, in every lifetime, in every universe.

And as I leaned in and kissed him, our souls connected like two lonely stars who'd always been on a collision course in the sky, hurtling towards one another, never knowing that the other was coming. But now we were together and fire was bursting from every inch of our beings, fuelled by each other's strength. It was strange that I'd never realised he was headed my way when I'd been alone in the dark all those months. But now he was here, I realised we were bound so deeply that I didn't have to fear ever losing him again. Where his soul went, mine would follow. And into eternity, we would be together, just two savage creatures who could never be caged.

CHAPTER FORTY EIGHT

6 MONTHS LATER…

I carried Winter in my arms and she laughed as she tucked her head against my neck, asking for the hundredth time where I was taking her. It had been a long drive and she'd stoically played my game, keeping the silk blindfold tied around her eyes since before I'd come to collect her this morning so she hadn't even laid her eyes on me yet. She'd sat patiently in the car as we talked about all the things we'd missed about each other with her eyes covered and even when I'd parked up and let Tyson out, she'd still resisted the urge to peek, letting me carry her from the car so that I could pull off the surprise exactly the way I wanted to.

Two weeks was too long for us to be apart, but I'd had to help Frankie consolidate our ties with the Santiago Cartel in Mexico and there was no way I was going to bring Winter somewhere so dangerous. Not while they were at war. And despite her healthy cursing and demands for me to stop treating her like a lady and let her be an animal with me, I'd managed to get her to stay behind. Of course she'd instantly taken on a job with Enzo the moment I was out of the country which could arguably have been considered more dangerous than what I was doing anyway.

Despite my constant protests, Winter was well and truly a part of the family business now. Papa had christened her the Red Widow when threatening our enemies with her and the name had stuck, circulating around the city and whispered behind hands with fear. The beautiful girl with the blood red hair who was covered in scars and could kill a man three times her size in less than thirty seconds. Not that she'd actually been doing any work as a hit woman for us around the city, but her scars had given root to countless rumours and tales about their origins. The most popular of all was that she had a scar for every man she'd killed, which had sent the Sinners Bay gossips into overdrive when photos of the two of us at the beach got leaked online over the summer.

It went against all of my instincts to let her keep putting herself in danger by working for the family, but of course that fell on deaf ears and if I tried to stop her, she just went around me anyway. It was fucking infuriating and I was sure it was an argument we'd be having for the rest of our lives because we were both too stubborn to back down about it. But I had to admit that she could more than hold her own even with my crazy family surrounding her, so maybe I was worrying for nothing. Not that I could help it. It was in my blood to protect her at all costs. Though at least for the next few weeks, I was pretty confident I didn't have to. Aside from fully immersing herself into the Romero lifestyle, she'd also spent time sorting through all of the memories that had come back to her and we'd managed to track down her mom too. Winter was slowly figuring out who she used to be alongside who she was now and blending the two pieces of her soul together as she healed and grew more certain of who she was and what she wanted every day. She now had plans to set up women's refuges across the state with the diamonds she'd taken from Ramon, creating safe havens for those in need like she had once been.

There was a damn good reason for me fearing for her safety still though. One week after we'd sunk Ramon and his fancy yacht to the bottom of the sea, a letter had arrived with my name on it. Inside was a single line, handwritten especially for me.

Julio Dominguez sends his regards to the Romeros, we look forward to discussing our missing diamonds with you soon.

So our attempt to hide our involvement in the deaths of so many Dominguez Cartel men hadn't worked. Someone knew it was us and that someone had told the head of one of the most dangerous cartels in Mexico that we had something belonging to him too.

Hence our ever strengthening bond with the Santiago Cartel. We were fairly confident in our own abilities to defend ourselves against the Dominguez Cartel in our home city, but like the old saying went, the enemy of my enemy is my friend. And if there was a war coming to Sinners Bay then we wanted to face it head on with our allies at our sides.

I let out a long breath as I banished my concerns about the Dominguez Cartel in favour of focusing on the beautiful creature I had in my arms. We had two entire weeks to ourselves starting right now and I intended to start it off with a bang.

"I was hoping this blindfold would equal something kinky, orso," Winter said to me, using the fucking nickname that my brothers had given me again, though I had to admit in her seductive tones I didn't mind it quite so much.

Orso, or *bear* in Italian was their way of not so subtly pointing out when I was being overprotective. It was a warning which I was begrudgingly learning to heed because the last time they'd decided I'd gone too far in trying to keep Winter for myself, Sloan had taken her for a night out at a fucking strip club and had sent me pictures of the two of them swinging around a pole like it was a Christmas tree and they were Santa's little elves. Luckily they'd decided that doing it while fully dressed got their message across clearly enough, but it had made their damn point. Though I swear the two of them still made a special effort to drive me insane with Winter's choice of clothes every single time we went out.

"I guess it depends on what your idea of kinky is, baby doll," I replied, smirking to myself as I set her down on her feet and moved to stand behind her.

"After two weeks all by myself in that big house, you'd better believe I want kinky," she purred, folding her arms over the beautiful navy satin dress she wore against the chill of the breeze as she waited for the big reveal.

I laughed in a way that let her know I fully intended to see to her needs as soon as possible, then tugged at the knot in the silk to remove the blindfold from her eyes.

Winter sucked in a sharp breath, her hands covering her mouth as she stared at the log cabin which I'd had built especially for her. It had enough elements of the one where we'd once lived on the side of that mountain to be familiar, but I'd gone for more than a few upgrades as well.

There was a long porch with a swing sweat and chiminea already crackling with flames beside it, a thick grey blanket and even a guitar awaiting us as I'd requested. The wooden structure was built with a similar design but on a larger scale to the original. Inside, all of the furniture was new and I'd selected things with enough resemblance to those we'd once had that I knew it would draw up all of those memories. A king sized bed still dominated the central room with a roaring fire blazing in the stone fireplace and a couch a thousand times more comfortable than the one I'd spent nights sleeping on. It was the same but different. A whole new place to call our own while keeping the memories of our first few weeks together alive in its design.

In addition to that, I'd made sure this place had all the modern fixtures alongside a generator more than capable of running everything so that we could be comfortable out here whenever we wanted to escape the world. There was a huge claw foot bathtub awaiting us in the bathroom and I'd had the fridge stocked with as much food as we could eat, including an extra block of cheese in case she wanted to play savage for me again.

"Nicoli..." Winter breathed, her voice raw with emotion as she just stared at the cabin, not noticing as I backed away from her and dropped to one knee.

I pulled a blue velvet box from the pocket of the plaid shirt I'd bought for the occasion, much to Frankie's disgust, but I wanted to do this right. It wasn't about all of the money we had or the luxury I could offer her. This was about me and her. The savage girl who a mountain man had found shivering in the snow one day. I'd even let my hair grow long in the last few months, ignoring Winter and my brothers when they reminded me it needed cutting again. And while I'd been in Mexico, I'd let my beard grow in too.

Tyson bounded back and forth, barking excitedly like he understood what was going on and I cleared my throat to remind her that I was still here.

"Did you have this place built to look like-" Winter's breath caught again as she looked around at me, her eyes widening as she found me on one knee on the green grass which filled the clearing around the cabin. I'd wanted to do this in the snow like when we'd met, but I couldn't wait that fucking long. So grass it was.

"Winter," I said in a low voice, looking up at this perfect creature who had bound herself to me in love, blood and heartache. "Every day I spend with you, my heart feels whole in a way I never believed possible. Every day we spend apart I ache for you in all the ways a man can ache for his woman. I've killed for you, I'd die for you, but more importantly than any of that, I want to live for you too. I want to wake up every single day for the rest of my life with my savage girl by my side. I want to own and devour you, worship and consume you, I want to breathe you in and never exhale again. I'm already yours in every way that counts, but I want you to say the words. I want to hear you promise it in front of everyone we love and scream it for the whole world to hear with that beautiful voice of yours which was caged for too long. I want to carve your name into my heart and wear the scar as proudly as you wear all of yours. I want to own you, Winter. You and no other for the rest of time. I want you to be mine and only mine. So what do you say?"

Her eyes filled with tears as she stared down at the box in my hand, the platinum ring which I'd had made especially for her. It had leaves inlaid with emeralds the colour of her eyes moulded into the sides of the ring itself and the ruby at the heart of it was fitted in place to look like a rose, the deep colour matching her hair. We had a sock full of priceless diamonds I could have used to make it, but I didn't care about that, this ring was her, it was life and beauty and freedom and as she extended her trembling left hand towards me and let me slide it onto her finger, my heart pounded with happiness so great I felt like I could drown in it.

I pulled her hand to my lips and kissed her skin, growling with desire and pleasure as she ran her other hand through my hair before sliding it under my chin.

I looked up at her again as she tugged, her pupils dilated and her expression fierce as she demanded I get to my feet.

I stood up, as silent as she was, watching her as she stared at the ring on her finger for a long moment before slowly reaching out to unbutton the top of my shirt.

The moment she had access to the bare skin beneath, her finger pressed to my flesh and she looked deep into my eyes as she slowly traced three perfect letters over my heart.

Yes.

Before I could say anything to express the explosion of happiness that spilled through my veins at her answer, her mouth met with mine and I fell into her kiss like she really was a goddess and I was nothing but a slave to her. And a slave I would happily be, with no desire to ever break free of my chains.

Our lips moved against each other with the desperation of two stars destined to collide and consume one another, while knowing that we'd enjoy burning out together for as long as we possibly could before that final blast of power destroyed us.

I wrapped my arms around her and pulled her against my chest as I carried her towards our new cabin. Just a mountain man and his savage girl. Two lost souls who could only be found in each other's embrace. Filled with the knowledge that we'd never be alone again.

ALSO BY
CAROLINE PECKHAM
&
SUSANNE VALENTI

Brutal Boys of Everlake Prep

(Complete Reverse Harem Bully Romance Contemporary Series)

Kings of Quarantine

Kings of Lockdown

Kings of Anarchy

Queen of Quarantine

**

Dead Men Walking

(Reverse Harem Dark Romance Contemporary Series)

The Death Club

Society of Psychos

**

The Harlequin Crew

(Reverse Harem Mafia Romance Contemporary Series)

Sinners Playground

Dead Man's Isle

Carnival Hill

Paradise Lagoon

Gallows Bridge

Harlequinn Crew Novellas

Devil's Pass

**

Dark Empire

(Dark Mafia Contemporary Standalones)

Beautiful Carnage

Beautiful Savage

**

Forget Me Not Bombshell

(Dark Mafia Reverse Harem Contemporary Standalone)

**

The Ruthless Boys of the Zodiac

(Reverse Harem Paranormal Romance Series - Set in the world of Solaria)

Dark Fae

Savage Fae

Vicious Fae

Broken Fae

Warrior Fae

Zodiac Academy

(M/F Bully Romance Series- Set in the world of Solaria, five years after Dark Fae)

The Awakening

Ruthless Fae

The Reckoning

Shadow Princess

Cursed Fates

Fated Thrones

Heartless Sky

The Awakening - As told by the Boys

Zodiac Academy Novellas

Origins of an Academy Bully

Darkmore Penitentiary

(Reverse Harem Paranormal Romance Series - Set in the world of Solaria,
ten years after Dark Fae)

Caged Wolf

Alpha Wolf

Feral Wolf

**

The Age of Vampires

(Complete M/F Paranormal Romance/Dystopian Series)

Eternal Reign

Eternal Shade

Eternal Curse

Eternal Vow

Eternal Night

Eternal Love

**

Cage of Lies

(M/F Dystopian Series)

Rebel Rising

**

Tainted Earth

(M/F Dystopian Series)

Afflicted

Altered

Adapted

Advanced

**

The Vampire Games

(Complete M/F Paranormal Romance Trilogy)

V Games

V Games: Fresh From The Grave

V Games: Dead Before Dawn

*

The Vampire Games: Season Two

(Complete M/F Paranormal Romance Trilogy)

Wolf Games

Wolf Games: Island of Shade

Wolf Games: Severed Fates

*

The Vampire Games: Season Three

Hunter Trials

*

The Vampire Games Novellas

A Game of Vampires

**

The Rise of Issac

(Complete YA Fantasy Series)

Creeping Shadow

Bleeding Snow

Turning Tide

Weeping Sky

Failing Light

Made in the USA
Monee, IL
05 August 2024

63306979R00298